CW01083672

I KNOW WHERE YOU BURIED YOUR HUSBAND

www.penguin.co.uk

I KNOW WHERE YOU BURIED YOUR HUSBAND

Marie O'Hare

bantam

TRANSWORLD PUBLISHERS
Penguin Random House, One Embassy Gardens,
8 Viaduct Gardens, London SW11 7BW
www.penguin.co.uk

Transworld is part of the Penguin Random House group of companies
whose addresses can be found at global.penguinrandomhouse.com

Penguin
Random House
UK

First published in Great Britain in 2025 by Bantam
an imprint of Transworld Publishers

A CIP catalogue record for this book
is available from the British Library.

ISBNs
9780857506740 hb
9780857506757 tpb

Typeset in 11.5/16 pt Sabon by Falcon Oast Graphic Art Ltd
Printed and bound in Great Britain by Clays Ltd, Elcograf S.p.A.

The authorized representative in the EEA is Penguin Random House Ireland,
Morrison Chambers, 32 Nassau Street, Dublin D02 YH68.

To Katie. Every friendship in this book is based on my friendship with you. You are so rainbow rhythms and I love you.

And to all the students I've ever taught. Thanks for keeping me on my toes. I owe every one of you.

She is the storm. She is the sea. Innate. Intangible. Variable. A circle. Buttons within buttons. Loops within loops.

2016

'WE WERE TOLD that being sexually attractive to men was an achievement. That having men lust after us was some sort of honour. We were told to strive to be fit because it was tantamount to value. We were told that having lots of men' – Ajola held up a long, manicured finger – 'want to fuck you meant you were a successful woman. The truth is – and this is what they won't tell you . . .' she paused, '. . . men will fuck anything. They will fuck people they don't find physically attractive. They will fuck raw chicken breasts. They will fuck sandwiches. They will fuck tomato ketchup bottles. They will tie a pot of jelly to a mop handle and fuck it like a sex doll. My point – my point, my point,' she said, her voice getting louder above the calls of dissent, 'is that having a man want to fuck you doesn't make you special. Our achievements don't lie in the validation of men. I mean, have you seen a man's pants? Have you seen a man's back? That's who's judging us?'

'You're just upset that you've never been with a proper adult man,' Caoimhe said. 'You've just gone out with little boys.

3

Whoever heard of a proper man putting his dick in a tomato sauce bottle?'

Safa pulled her BMW 3 Series into the narrow layby opposite the house and killed the engine.

'It's all over the internet,' Ajola said. 'The depravity of men.'

'The internet is depraved,' Caoimhe said. 'That's its point. It's an outlet. People go over all kinds of fantasies on the internet. It doesn't exist in real life. Or – or, or,' she said, raising her own finger as Ajola tried to talk over her, 'it does, but it's a fraction of a per cent.' She nodded her head at the door. 'Get out. I'm squashed as hell here.'

Ajola opened the door and stepped out on to the quiet lane. Somewhere behind the hedgerow, a vixen shrieked. The leaves hissed. Above them, the moon was bright and full, illuminating Ajola's hands. The doors to the car slammed shut and the others grouped together, looking about the dark, isolated road.

'Must cost an armandaleg to live out here,' Caoimhe said.

'Armandaleg,' Sophia said, pulling out her keys and leading the others across the road. 'But it's private. Peaceful.'

'That's a Michael Morpurgo book,' Ella said, putting a fresh piece of gum in her mouth.

'Look at Ella,' Caoimhe said. She tapped her temple. 'Intelligent. Confident. Self-possessed. She isn't going to date a man who is putting his dick in sandwiches. Her men have that dignity,' – she raised her eyebrows – 'that majesty. You've seen that' – she grasped two handfuls of something invisible – 'masculinity. So don't come at us with nonsense.'

'I'm not saying good men don't exist,' Ajola said as Sophia put her key in the front door. The metal lock glistened in the moonlight. 'I'm saying, we let these men judge us. And they're scumbags.'

'Not all men. And for every scumbag man, I can give you the name of a scumbag woman,' Caoimhe said. Sophia pushed the door open. 'Try me. Remember Catriana from Year Ten business studies? Scumbag. Remember that girl – oh . . .' She looked at Ajola as they filed into Sophia's house. '. . . the one from our bus, what was her name? She used to always have a go at me in PE.'

'I remember her.'

'Fiona Green,' Ella said, offering the gum packet to Caoimhe.

'Yeah. Scumbag.'

Sophia came to a dead stop on the doormat. It had 'Welcome' written on it in a large, loopy, green font. The other four crowded round her and looked into the small living room. It was immaculate. The laminate floorboards were freshly swept, the ornaments on the shelves were dusted and turned to the correct angles so that they sparkled from the overhead lights. The envelopes on the coffee table were in a neat pile, perpendicular to the edge of the table. Chris, Sophia's husband of five years, was lying by the table, his face turned to the side so that his cheek was pressed against the floor and his glassy eyes stared at their feet. He had fallen awkwardly, his hands by his sides, palms up, his back arced in the air and his knees splayed. A huge pool of thick, black blood had spread around him like a dark lake, impenetrable and abject.

Sophia

AT THE START, Sophia had resolved to kill herself. It was the only way out. She had debated making it look like an accident. Just jump in front of a lorry as it came down the main road. Throw herself in front of a train. Everyone would swear she had slipped because why would she kill herself?

As the months wore on, she decided she wouldn't hide it. An overdose of painkillers, a carrier bag tied to her head, the hose in the garage that she had seen on television shows. Make it obvious what she had done so that no one could doubt how awful Chris was. How much she suffered. It really would be better for everyone if she was dead. No more stress, no more tension. Leave them all to sort it out between them. Fuck it. She'd be dead.

One morning, it must have been a Saturday or a Sunday, at about ten thirty, she came up the stairs and saw Chris lying in bed, flat on his back, the duvet tucked up to his chin, face tilted serenely towards the ceiling. He had already got up, spent ninety minutes on the toilet, snapped at her for not emptying the bathroom bin, got dressed and then gone back to bed. Isla was in the front room. She could hear the chatter of the television and Isla's excited responses. Chris had a slight smile on his face and Sophia could tell from the way his chest was rising and falling that he wasn't really asleep. He was lying there, awake, knowing she was watching him, knowing that she knew he wasn't asleep, daring her to say something. It was in this moment that Sophia realized she was living the life Jill Caister had always imagined for her.

And that's when Sophia decided the best option would be if Chris was dead, not her.

It was such an obvious solution. Why on earth would she arrange to kill herself when she could just arrange to kill him? She was the better caregiver for Isla. Chris didn't notice when she needed a nappy change. Chris left her without being fed for hours. Chris resented the time he had to look after her, as if being a parent was the same as babysitting. With Chris gone, Sophia could be an even more compassionate mother. She wouldn't be constantly cowed or walking on eggshells. She would be relieved of that unknowable guilt. Of the resentment. She could do the things she loved again. Her whole life flipped with Chris dead. She would be so happy. Again. So happy again.

She emptied the bathroom bin feeling lighter than she had in years.

'Wasn't hard, was it?' he called from the bed, eyes still shut.

Not hard at all.

Sophia hadn't really found her personality until she was twelve and had escaped the oppressive clutches of Jill. With Jill, she had always been so meek and unsure of herself. Without

Jill, she was fun and lively, an essential component in the quintet that was her, Caoimhe, Ajola, Safa and Ella. She flourished with them, always hoping, imagining, manifesting a situation where Jill could see her with her real friends.

See. This is me.

But, it turned out, that outgoing personality clashed with Chris's on a Tuesday evening at 7 p.m. when someone had to cook the dinner and someone had to bath Isla, and that someone was always her. Over time, it was easier to become quieter and quieter, meeker and meeker, her identity eroded away by the realities of life to the point where that personality didn't exist any more. She was introverted once more. Timid. Lacking any and all conversation. She didn't know why Ajola, Caoimhe, Ella and Safa still included her. Perhaps it was pity.

Since school, she had been a dedicated writer, constantly creating short stories, novellas, full novels, now sitting in dusty and unopened files on her computer. She was always sure she was going to write the great novel of their generation. She was going to be a somebody. To prove her worth, finally, to Jill. But, by the age of twenty-six, she had never had anything published, not even a short story in her university magazine. Her potential simply eluded her. One day, she presumed, Jill Caister would do it and finally win. For years, she ruminated on it, trying different methods to write better. It was only recently, about the time she started seriously considering killing herself, that she realized she just wasn't that good. That was it. That was the answer. That was life. Couldn't write, couldn't publish, couldn't marry someone who was kind. Not everyone could be accomplished. Not everyone could win the Man Booker Prize. Not everyone could be happy.

It would be better if Chris hit her. The needling jabs were too nuanced. If he physically abused her in some way, she could just leave. It would give her an excuse as to why she had never met her potential.

'*I was in an abusive relationship.*'

'*Ah, OK.*'

But he never hit her. He never pinched her. He never pulled her hair or roughly pushed her aside. He never laid hands on her and if she was to leave him, the pressure to get back with him would be immense.

'*That's just what some men do.*'

'*You have to work on this for Isla's sake.*'

'*People these days are so quick to quit when relationships get hard.*'

'*This is what marriage is.*'

Being unkind, being antagonistic: it wasn't enough of a reason. It would be so much better if he just hit her. That would be that. No questions asked. End of story.

'The thing about it is,' she told Ajola one night during their weekly phone calls. Chris was working late and Isla was asleep. The house was silent around her. A deep, thrumming silence that settled her core and made her feel safe. 'Chris is great. He works, he pays the bills, he cuts the grass.' She had never told her friends the truth. She wasn't sure why. Because Chris *was* great? Everyone really liked him. He was funny, sociable. He gave great advice about mortgages for free. People would think she was psychotic if she said, yes, but he expects me to always change the sheets. Yes, but he does this thing when he knows I'm calling for him but pretends he can't hear me. Yes, but whenever I raise a concern about his behaviour, I always end up apologizing for overreacting. 'I just feel . . .' She searched for the words with Ajola. A way of illustrating her discontent without badmouthing Chris.

'Speak from your soul,' Ajola said. 'No judgements.'

'I feel like I am the ideal wife for Chris,' Sophia said. 'If he programmed a computer with all his ideal characteristics of a woman, the computer would print me out. Exactly me. I'm smart, I'm attractive, I cook the dinners, I'm a good mum, I work. He can take me out to restaurants and be proud, he can introduce me to his family and feel successful. I'm it, you know.'

'I know,' Ajola said sagely. 'You are high value.'

'Right. That's it.' Sophia put her socked feet up on the hand-crafted Eichholtz coffee table, for once not having to be anxious that Chris would come in and tut at her. The socks were fleece and extra thick against her calloused feet. A gift from Chris. What was she even complaining about. 'I just feel there's something transactional about it.'

Sophia had met Chris when they had been at university together and she had been blown away by how handsome, how smart, how charismatic he was. This was a man. A real man. She had been almost giddy when he returned her interest. She was ready to settle down with him right then after their first date, desperate to prove something to Jill, to win that invisible duel, blind to any of Chris's shortcomings.

'Transactional?' Ajola breathed. 'Such a deep word.'

'I feel he picked me because I was the right spec. Ultra-limited-edition figurine. And he'll provide for us as long as I remain the exact model that he picked. But if I were to change in any way – say I was ageing terribly, or say I said, you know what, you can cook dinner tonight, or you can sort out the dentist's appointments, or actually' – she felt her voice straining – 'saying that I fail at everything I attempt *is* unkind, no matter how you try to defend it – I feel, I feel like he wouldn't want to provide any more. He'd feel short-changed. Like, this isn't the model I picked. Where's my ultra-limited-edition figurine? That's a very real threat. It's not *me,* you know, that attracts him. It's what I represent, I guess? It's my worth insofar as it extends to himself.' She picked a thread in one of the cushions. 'When I'm with him, I get such a strong sense of my physical self being separate from my mental self. Like my physical self is a slab of meaty flesh that isn't me.'

'Women have been commodified by men for centuries,' Ajola said. 'In King Henry VIII's court, Thomas Cromwell traded in women for the King's favour. It's natural to feel the way you do. Your issue shouldn't be with Chris, but with the patriarchy.'

'OK. Thanks.'

Sophia knew that if she had to stay in this marriage for the next fifty years, she would kill herself. A constant erosion to the point where she ceased to be. Her options were kill herself later, or kill Chris now.

She wasn't bothered how he died. She just had to make sure she didn't end up in prison. Perhaps she could try and cause a car crash whilst he was driving. Or push him down the stairs. She made notes in an old notebook that she hid between the mattress and the bed frame, knowing he'd never find it there because he never changed the sheets.

As the plan slowly took form, she found a greater sense of purpose, of identity. Her bubbling self began to make more appearances during her meet-ups with the others. She was happier. And when she smiled at Chris, it was with utter contempt. When she put his dirty crockery in the dishwasher, she did it with malicious relish. When he complained about dinner and she apologized, she did it with the calm voice that was completely devoid of abject loathing. When he snapped at her about hoovering the stairs, she bit her tongue and bowed her head, indulging in faraway fantasies about tightening the carrier bag around his neck and yanking it until the plastic was sucked into his gaping mouth.

Caoimhe

FOR AS LONG as Caoimhe could remember, she had been not like the other girls. She was always quicker, more dynamic, more confident of her own independence. She obviously excelled at sports, representing their secondary school in rounders, netball and cross-country running. The girls she met in these tournaments were always so ugly in their competitiveness that she knew she wasn't like them either. Caoimhe was poised, modest, a being possessed of an ineffable tenacity that meant she didn't have to huff and grunt and elbow her way through. She just naturally flowed. Of course, the other girls hated her for it. They resorted to making fun of her hair, her legs, her baggy sports clothes. They didn't get it. The boys did, though. The boys understood what a weighted talent she had. At the county rounders final, she had caught a low-flying shot one-handed, completely outstretched, diving through the air like a peregrine falcon. The girls on the supporters' line had barely reacted. The boys had erupted into roars of amazement and triumph. Caoimhe had stood there, ball still clasped in the one hand, grinning, and feeling as if there was no truer version of herself than the one listening to those cheers at that moment. She belonged with the boys. She was a step up from woman.

Her mum hated her for it. Whenever Caoimhe won a race or a match, her mum always rolled her eyes as though Caoimhe was being snarky. Whenever Caoimhe came away from an event disheartened, her mother would harrumph and clasp her hands together as if she was disappointed in her.

'You just need to try harder,' she once said in the car on the way home. 'If the other girls can do it, you can.'

Caoimhe refused to respond to that.

'Will you do your hair like the other girls?' she asked, glancing at her. 'Or a touch of mascara? Eyeliner? Some girls wear make-up whilst they compete. I've seen them.'

'Not me,' Caoimhe growled.

'When I heard I was having a little girl, I was excited, thinking about dresses' – her mum twirled her hand, singing the words – 'and hair, and pretty bows, and instead you came out' – she looked across at her again – '. . . not like that at all.'

With other girls, Caoimhe found it hard to relate and struggled to form friendships with her teammates. She was quicker, sharper, funnier. It was boring always talking to people who couldn't keep up. Sophia, Safa, Ajola and Ella were the exceptions. Caoimhe didn't mind spending time with them. They weren't the same, but they understood Caoimhe. They got her. She was Anakin Skywalker on Planet Earth. After university, she moved to a small town in Surrey and worked freelance as a graphic designer. Here, she dropped all her team sports and focused instead on long-distance running, where all the training and races were mixed.

She found a great sense of validation at the local running club. She was the only woman in the top group and she felt immensely powerful running alongside tall, toned, intelligent men who were full of nothing but praise for her. Sometimes, running by the canal, or up on the heath, their figures backlit by the cerulean evening sky, she felt that they should be photographed and put on the front of a magazine or *National Geographic*. The Fellowship of the Run. Running for Glory. Or something like that.

One evening, a great chubby man, Dean, joined and totally ruined the aesthetic. He was about her age but his hair was wilting and uncombed, his eyes dark and sunken in his head. He ran with Dre Beats on and a purple shell suit from Primark, the sleeves rolled up to reveal an obnoxious tattoo of Aristotle pontificating on his forearm. On the first 800 metres, he sprinted off as if he was in the 100-metre Olympic finals and ended up walking at the back by the end of the session, great, dark sweat patches bleeding through the thick, polyester weave.

'What's the club record over five K?' he asked at the end of that first session. Caoimhe had scoffed and rolled her eyes.

'Fifteen thirty-six,' someone replied. 'Rohan Rust.'

Caoimhe's heart did a double-beat in her chest. *Rohan Rust.* She had seen him, in glimpses, around town, in the newspaper, on race reports, running. An absolute Renaissance. An ode to beauty and style. Lithe. Magnificent.

'Does Rohan Rust come to training?' she asked, hopeful, before Dean could respond.

'No. All our good runners go to the Harriers.' The coach turned to look directly at Caoimhe. His eyes twinkled. 'Don't you go joining them, Caoimhe.'

Caoimhe melted. She giggled and looked down, crossing her arms over her stomach. She tried to think of something witty to say in return. Something that would validate the attention. She was with the men. Not Dean. The Men. The real men. She had to prove her place here. Demonstrate that she was equal to any one of them. She was stronger than some of them: she knew that. Head to head, fist to fist, she knew she could take a couple of the skinny ones down. What better way to illustrate her value than dominating a man in a physical fight.

'Oh,' she had said, 'I never know what I'm going to do next.'

Ella

ELLA HAD BAD breath. She had had bad breath for as long as she could remember, for as long as she knew that people had breath and it could be bad. She brushed twice a day, two minutes each time, inside her teeth, outer side of her teeth, front, back, chewing surfaces. She had a special scraper designed to clean her tongue. She flossed a minimum of twice a day, sometimes more if she was at home and feeling self-conscious. She experimented with flossing before brushing, flossing after brushing, reading forums online to see which was best and finding nothing conclusive on the matter; for each article that said one way, there was another to contradict it. She used mouthwash, making sure she bought a different brand every so often so as not to create a homeostatic environment in her mouth which would allow bacteria to breed. Once, when Ajola was away on a school residential, she booked a week off work and experimented with not brushing, flossing or mouth-washing at all, to see if it was something in the chemicals that gave her bad breath. It wasn't. She had regular check-ups with the dentist, who always sounded impressed when he examined her teeth but she was too shy to ask him about the bad-breath situation. She changed her diet for six months, cutting out meat, dairy and fish to see if that was a factor. It wasn't. She infused her diet with fresh fruit, vegetables, probiotic yoghurt, sugarless gum; she bought a tiny irrigation machine that was designed to clean out the cavities around her tonsils of any undesirable food matter. Nothing made a difference. She had bad breath. The only route left available to her was to go and see a therapist who might be able to diagnose her with some sort of personality disorder that was causing her to imagine that she had bad breath. She was reluctant to commit to this idea, though; she wasn't sure she could withstand the embarrassment of being told by a healthcare professional that she was perfectly sane, she just had terrible, terminal, hopelessly bad breath.

She was sure the bad breath was the cause for every missed opportunity, overlooked promotion and failed relationship. Why else did the women in the Internal Policy Office not invite her out to Friday tea when she got her first major job after graduation? Why did Georgia Railings get the Paris position instead of her, even though her performance was far superior? Why had Tanvik not yet texted her back after they went for drinks? It was the breath. Surely, it was the breath.

'Don't. Not Ella.'

'With the breath?'

'With the breath.'

She would just have to hope that remote working really took off and she could complete all her work hours without coming into contact with anyone.

As things stood, that wasn't possible yet. And so, she made

the commute from her and Ajola's flat to Charing Cross every morning, chewing her gum. She picked up fresh fruit between the station and the office, chewing her gum. She waved hello to everyone on her floor, making sure that she put in a new piece of gum just as she went through the door so she could begin to chew it as her breath wafted out into the self-contained atmosphere of the office.

Her first appointment that day was with someone looking for advice regarding a claim for negligence. The details her trainee had collated were brief and she read through them with a furrowed brow.

'Can I send him through?' her trainee asked a few minutes before the scheduled appointment time.

Ella put her fruit in her drawer and put another piece of gum in her mouth. She had practised the art of chewing and talking without making it apparent that she was using gum. She nodded.

The man who came in appeared to be very tall when standing in the doorway and Ella drew herself up in her chair out of instinct. As he approached her desk, however, she noticed his rounded shoulders, uncut hair and considerable girth and judged that his apparent above-average height was probably some sort of optical illusion.

'Good morning,' she said, shaking his hand. 'My name is Ella Ramsey.'

He extended a pale hand which had a few sparse hairs scattered across the knuckles. The sleeves of his suit jacket were an inch or so too short, revealing his wrist bones.

'I'm Eric Martins,' he said and pushed himself into the chair opposite Ella's desk. He had shaved recently and angry red spots were blossoming on the flesh of his neck and chin. 'Are you a lawyer?' he asked.

'I'm a solicitor,' Ella said, sitting down. 'Lawyer is a bit of a catch-all term. I can offer you advice and help you, should a claim be appropriate. Am I right in saying you want to look at suing for negligence?'

'Yes, that's right. But I want to actually do it. I'm not looking for advice.' He sounded irritated. He clasped his hands over his worn leather belt and fixed her with an unrelenting stare. 'I'm here to start the claim. I want my money.'

'That's understandable,' Ella said. She tucked in her chair to show that she meant business. 'So, are you looking to make a claim against a company or hospital? I apologize for asking again but I'm afraid we don't have many notes.'

'Against my parents,' Eric said shortly. 'I did explain this.'

'Right.' Ella glanced down at the notes her trainee had made. 'Take me through it again so that I understand.'

'I'm suing my parents for negligence,' Eric said. 'They owe me living expenses.'

'For what time period?' Ella asked, making notes in her ledger.

'Well.' Eric looked up at the ceiling. There was a faux chandelier there that Ella never used. 'They allowed it until I was eighteen. I'm twenty-seven now, so nine years, plus all the years until I die.'

Ella nodded and rubbed her forehead with the end of the pen.

'OK, living expenses. And what's the basis for your claim?'

Eric held out his hands as though this was obvious.

'I didn't ask to be born,' he said. 'They took that decision away from me. And now I'm expected to, what? Get a fifty-hour-a-week job? Become a wage-slave? Go through the tireless motion of commute, work, commute, sleep until I die? Take any money I earn to pay rent to live on this planet? What right do they have to subject me to this lifelong servitude?'

Ella underlined something on her ledger. She moved the gum imperceptibly around her mouth, then scratched the inner corner of her eye. Her brother would laugh her out of the building if she presented him with this. But she couldn't say that to this man's face in case he threw something at her. She made a non-committal noise.

'You might have a case,' she said. 'Let me talk to a senior solicitor.'

Safa

SAFA MARRIED HAARIS when she was nineteen years old and he was twenty. They had played in the same street as children, gone to the same sixth form and applied for the same university. They had life experiences in common, a shared culture, their families were in and out of each other's flats all the time. This man was educated, successful, kind and she knew him.

They negotiated and decided that Safa could graduate and get her master's degree before they had children. Haaris himself dropped out of university and started working in the grocery store that her father owned. Safa had always imagined being married to an extremely successful, wealthy man who drove a BMW and wore silver Rolex watches. They would live in a giant mansion in Hampstead that her husband would be able to afford with a pay packet laden with numbers. He would work long hours but come home and shower her and their children with love and gifts. She would repay his hard work and dedication to their family with a spotless home, well-behaved children and delicious meals. She had never imagined that she would be the main breadwinner, that the BMW would be in her name and the mortgage for her dream house calculated on her sole income. She worked long hours and came home to shower her husband and children with love and gifts. It was sometimes difficult to keep the home spotless, the children well behaved and the meals delicious whilst also working a sixty-hour week. Their groceries came delivered to the door and the most annoying thing was that Haaris would leave them out on the side for her to put away when she came in.

'Why can't you just put them away?' she said, seeing the cans and cereal boxes stacked on the table for the fourth week in a row.

'Why would I bother putting them away when you're just going to take them all out to cook dinner?' he called back from the lounge. He had recently bought a PlayStation 5 and his endless gaming on it proved a welcome distraction from his encroaching on her own free time.

'Because it goes off,' she called back, rummaging through the bags.

'Not in less than a day.'

'Milk will.' She tutted. 'You've just left the milk here.'

'Listen, you don't understand.' She heard an explosion from the game. 'I work more intense hours than you. I'm on my feet from eight until two. I don't get any respite. You don't even get into work until nine thirty.'

'Yeah, because I have to do the nursery run!'

'That's easy. Listen – you're not listening. Yeah, two seconds, just talking to the wifey.' He leant back so his head appeared through the doorway into the kitchen. 'I work six hours of intense labour every day. Every day,' he repeated. 'I don't get

Sundays off. I don't get Saturdays off. You swan into the office at nine thirty, you sit at your desk, you go for coffee, you chat to Pam from accounting. I'm face to face with customers.' He made a chopping motion with his hand on his palm. 'Six hours straight. You don't understand. When I come in, I need to put my feet up. I need to relax. Putting the groceries away isn't my responsibility. It's yours, yeah? You get me?'

She glared at him.

'You get me,' he said and retracted his head. 'Yeah, I'm back, bruv,' he said into his mic. 'Just getting my munch sorted.'

Once, she had left all the non-perishables out on the kitchen table, to see if he would ever put them away. He didn't. He just left the coffee tub and bottles of squash there for days. She also tested him to see if he would ever fill up the dishwasher. He didn't. He just left all his crockery on top. It took just as much effort to open the door and drop the dish in as it did to drop it on the counter. She ran the dishwasher with all her crockery and left his stuff there, waiting for him to notice or say something. He didn't. He just kept piling it up.

'Put your dishes away!' she shouted at him when he stacked the fifth plate on top of the others.

'All right.' He scowled at her. 'Calm down. You can just say it nicely, you know.'

She knew that Sophia had similar problems with her husband but she resolutely went round tidying up after him. Clothes not in the laundry basket: Sophia picked them up. Things not put away in the kitchen: Sophia cleared them away. Crockery in the sink instead of the dishwasher: Sophia put them in. Safa had considered doing this but she thought the silent acceptance of these menial tasks was humiliating and would wear her away until she was nothing more than a grey husk. She much preferred to test Haaris, to observe him like a scientist, refusing to get involved in the delicate ecosystem, following the prime directive, before suddenly shouting at him when she could no longer stand his absolute lack of awareness. Who was going to put those dirty dishes in the dishwasher? Who? Who? Why should it be down to her? How would this man live without her to snip and snap at him and keep him in line? In every school history lesson she, Sophia, Caoimhe, Ajola and Ella had ever sat in they had been saturated with tales of the titans of innovation and victory: Winston Churchill, Isambard Kingdom Brunel, Charles Darwin and a host of Henries and Edwards and Williams. It's no wonder these men achieved greatness when they never had to consider making their own lunch or washing their own bed sheets. They didn't have to spare a thought for such daily trivialities; their minds were free to wander at leisure. To achieve such standards of greatness that could only be mythologized. And there, in the shadows, her story untaught to children but present if you searched hard enough, was some grey, washed-out woman, haggard from childbirth, pinching her cheeks to make them rosy, sucking in her internal organs to appear attractive, staring in astonishment as the husband she tended to and catered for and moulded her whole life around found her dull or hysterical.

Safa tried to get her own back in small ways. Often, she would stay up late to finish her work, sitting in the darkness of the kitchen with her laptop screen illuminating her face in a blue-white transcendent glow. She would listen to Haaris making his loud way from the living room, up the stairs, to the bathroom, where he would proceed to spend about forty-five minutes. In the early days of their marriage, she couldn't understand how someone could spend forty-five minutes in the toilet, two to three times a day. He was in there so long, he made it a habit to take in his phone and headphones as well. She had offered to make him an appointment with the GP to see if he had IBS but he angrily refused.

'We have to do something about it,' she said. 'I sometimes can't leave the house on time because you're in the bathroom. I can't go down to the shops without the kids because you're in the bathroom.'

Haaris was always blissfully unbothered by the predicament. For a good long while, especially when the children were under the age of three, Safa had presumed he was spending so long in the toilet to avoid household duties. He could not be expected to attend to a crying child if he was in the toilet. He could not be expected to warm a bottle if he was in the toilet. But as the children got older and the immediacy of parental roles diminished, he still continued to spend long periods of time in the toilet. Then, one day, out of nowhere, a spark of divine intuition, a message whispered through a thousand channels of collective unconscious, told her what he was doing in there for forty-five minutes at a time, always with his phone, always with his headphones. Part of her was relieved because it meant that when he came out, he wouldn't pester her to touch him. It was already hard enough to be intimate with a man who was gaining weight from inactivity, had greasy hair and needed to be reminded to shower and change his underpants. Suddenly, she didn't begrudge him the time in the toilet. It put distance between them. She sat downstairs with her children when he started a session and pretended that she was a single mum and this was her idyllic life without a husband. She played loud games with them that he wouldn't normally tolerate if he wasn't sitting on the toilet with his pants around his ankles and his headphones in his ears. And at night, sitting downstairs at her laptop, when she heard the toilet flush and the lock click open, she would always rush upstairs to initiate sex, knowing he wouldn't be able to get it up. Her enthusiasm and his impotence at once freed her from any accusation of failure in her wifely duties, and the joy she felt from her calculated, savage vindictiveness and his desperate hopelessness gave her such a glorious sense of liberation and power. It was a cruelty and she loved to do it.

'That's what a psychopath does,' Caoimhe once told her over breakfast in her flat in Surrey.

'So a man is allowed to take his pleasure when and how he sees fit, but I'm not?' Safa reached across for the orange juice and caught Caoimhe's disapproving eye. 'It's fucking hilarious,' she said.

Ajola

THE SKY HAD been threatening since lunchtime. Heavy rolls of grey-purple cloud covered the sky, a perpetual yawning, a gaping maw, turning the air dark. Just as the school gates opened and the parents came flocking in, the torrent was released. It came suddenly, with no pre-empting drizzle or gentle shower. The heavens opened. Ajola stood in the doorway to her classroom and contemplated. The heavens opened.

The rain droplets were thick and heavy. They cracked on to the dry pavement and spattered against the tree leaves. They hammered against the window and clattered on the tin roof of the PE shed. There was no wind present and the rain fell straight down, water at terminal velocity, with no buffer between the moment it slipped from the cracks in the cloud and its ultimate end on the baked tarmac of the playground. Children shrieked as they left their classroom doors. Parents bounded through the puddles with coats pulled over their heads. Scooter wheels flashed through the sudden rush of water gushing down the pavement, sending waves before them. Some parents waited under the canopy of trees, their children poking their heads out, upturned, to gaze at the falling rain. Others walked, resolute, in the downpour, soaked shirts clinging to flabby stomachs and naked arms, strands of hair plastered to make-up-smeared faces, their children dancing along excitedly behind them. A few parents tried to duck inside the classroom to escape the relentless deluge but the teachers had to object, ushering them back into the storm.

Ajola stood in the doorway to her classroom and contemplated. She was secure here. All her children had been dismissed. She could stand and watch, unhindered. The rain fell centimetres from her nose. She was on the very boundary between storm and calm. She could choose, at any moment, to commit herself to one or the other. She watched the parents panic as they were left stranded under the tree without an umbrella. She listened to the excited screams and exclamations of others trying to brave the rain. You can't outrun raindrops. You can't dodge the falling water.

Meg came out of the neighbouring classroom door, flinching as the rain hammered down on her. Her mother danced to her side and together the two of them dashed through the burgeoning puddles. Meg looked at her mum as they flew by, smiling in wonder at the storm, the rain, her mother's astonished face. Her mother laughed and grabbed her hand and then the two of them were away, flitting through the rain and the crowds towards the road. Ajola watched them go, her being not worth a glance when the rain was thundering down like this, when the drains were bubbling over, when the threat of the black clouds, the storm, the torrent triggered adrenaline into a flood, sharpened your ears and your eyes, electrified your muscles, compelled by hundreds of thousands of years of evolution to seek the safe, warm security of your dry home.

Ajola turned and shut the door. She walked to her desk and sat down on the wheelie chair. When she had been a girl, probably less than ten, her great-grandma had taught her a spell for composure.

'A sprig of lavender, fresh, running water and the ancient words.'

These were some inflections of a tongue Ajola still didn't understand. As a girl, she had thought it was Albanian but now, a more proficient speaker as an adult, she still didn't recognize it. Ancient words, seeping from a time before modern language had begun to take form.

Ajola didn't have any lavender but she had a lavender-scented candle that a student had given her the summer before. She held it to her nose, closed her eyes and inhaled. The scent was cheap and tacky. Not real lavender at all. Perhaps it was designed to smell better when lit, but she knew better than to light a candle during a spell.

'Flame is the symbol of destruction and purge,' her great-grandma had told her. 'Not necessary for spells. Spells draw from a deep, flowing river. A channel of peace and life, of overflowing spirit. There's no fire down there. Fire is a tool of man. This magik is woman.'

Ajola ran the water at the sink by her desk and shut her eyes, candle by her nose, whispering the ancient words to herself. She wasn't surprised that the spell didn't work. This was a flat rendition of something, barely a reflection.

She opened her eyes. Outside, the rainstorm had ceased as suddenly as it had begun. Weak, yellow sunlight was blinking through the branches of the trees. The last few parents and children who had huddled together for safety were walking past, laughing and talking loudly, glad to be heading home together. She turned off the tap.

She had never felt so lonely as she did at that moment. There was an anguish in her soul, loss, regret, guilt, a heavy, damp material wrapped around her heart. She knew it would pass. Time heals all things. Grief. Anger. Loneliness. Leaving nothing but scars that draw the skin tight at odd moments, ghosts, a reminder. She was thankful for Sophia and Safa, Caoimhe and Ella. Without them, she really would be desolate.

She had started reading *Wolf Hall* by Hilary Mantel. She had never been bothered by it before because she generally avoided things that came highly recommended. Now that several years had passed since its publication and it had fallen largely out of the public consciousness, she felt compelled to read it. Much to her surprise, in her stricken state, in her abject loneliness, she found herself becoming infatuated with the character of Thomas Cromwell, an infatuation that kindled suddenly, literally from one page to the next, and then leapt into full flame when she found a picture of his Holbein portrait from 1532, a picture that was now saved to her camera roll, where she could glance at it whenever her resolve began to tremble, whenever she needed reminding of the joy life could bring. What could it be about this figure, this entity that existed no further than the synapses between her neurons, that was so far removed from her life as to be quite intangible? The calculated gaze? The thick bowl cut? The sallow jowls just starting to round with age. In reality, she knew she must be transposing all her desires into this empty template served up by history, but it didn't stop her lying in bed at night, dreaming of him.

She stood up and began the task of switching off her computer, the projector monitor, the speakers and the class iPad. There were hundreds of photos on this from the class, colourful snapshots of gleaming eyes and wide smiles leaping off the screen. Moments captured in time, unthinking, on the presupposition that these times would be infinite. She couldn't bring herself to delete them.

Perhaps it was Cromwell's intelligence that she was so enamoured with, she thought as she walked down the deserted corridor towards the main door. His cunning, his anticipation, his ability to artfully remove the men who stood in his way. She wondered if Meg would grow up to fantasize about fictional characters, or even historical ones. Would she transpose all her heart's desires on to blank templates as she, Ajola, was doing, or would she reach the age of twenty-seven with enough self-esteem, purpose and security to find happiness by more tangible means? She hoped it would be the latter, but in her dark heart, in the well of cynicism that she knew was actually a periscope to reality, she doubted it. Meg was already set on her course and unless someone could conjure the power to move heaven and earth to help her, she would reach twenty-seven as unsure and lost as Ajola herself. Abject loneliness. Misplaced grief. An empty heart, sucking in whatever strange characters passed by like air into a vacuum. Ajola put a hand over her eyes. She was meeting up with Safa, Sophia, Caoimhe and Ella for lunch the next day. She would feel less gloomy when she was with them. For the last fifteen years, she always had.

She got into her car and started the engine. It was surprisingly hot inside, despite the dark afternoon clouds and the recent downpour. She pulled on to the main road and checked her rear-view mirror. Ultimately, she had to believe there was some help for Meg. She just didn't know where it was. Can't help, can't be helped. An absolute waif. A waste. She turned on the Audible recording of *Wolf Hall* and drove home listening to Thomas Cromwell trying to secure Henry VIII's marriage to Anne Boleyn.

Witchcraft

THE FIVE WOMEN stood together in the doorway and stared at the dead body. Not a breath was taken among them. Their eyes, transfixed, could have been from the same, unblinking creature.

'Call an ambulance,' Caoimhe finally said. She stepped free of the group, towards the body. 'I think . . .' She glanced back at Sophia. 'I think he's gone, though.'

'Call the police,' Ella said. Her jaw was clenched, the edge of the gum protruding from between her teeth. 'Someone check the back door.'

Caoimhe stepped lightly over the body and into the kitchen. They heard the rattle of the door.

'Locked,' she said, coming back in. She looked around the living room. 'Whoever did this must have come and gone from the front.'

'Or still be in the house,' Safa suggested, glancing up at the stairs.

'Shut your noise,' Caoimhe replied fiercely. 'Sophia.' She put her trembling hands on her shoulders. 'Are you OK?'

Sophia blinked. She was so pale, her blue-green veins were visible in her jaw.

'Yes. I'm fine.' Her voice was little more than a rasp. She cleared her throat. 'Fine. What's happened?'

Caoimhe knelt down beside the body. Her hands were still shaking. She clenched them into fists, once, twice, trying to get a hold of herself.

'Don't come too close,' she said, holding out an arm. 'He's got – it's a big – on the back of his head.'

'Where's Isla?' Safa asked.

'At my parents'.' Sophia hadn't moved. The door was still open behind her, her key hanging from the lock. A tumbler turn from one life. 'Chris isn't home tonight,' she said. 'He's at his brother's.'

'I'm going to call the police,' Ella said, getting her phone out. 'Sophia, they're going to search the place. Top to bottom, so grab anything important now.'

'There's a notepad under the bed that details all the ways I want to kill Chris,' Sophia whispered.

The vixen cried out again. The night was warm. The moon, bright. There seemed to be no substantial boundary between the inside and outside. The women looked at one another, reading each other's faces.

'Definitely go grab that first.' Caoimhe sat up on her heels. 'Stick it in my bag.'

Sophia still didn't move. Time seemed to be running very slowly. How long had she been standing here? Why was nothing changing?

'Chris isn't home tonight,' she said, blankly. 'His brother lives in Farnham.'

'There's his phone.' Safa nodded to the mantelpiece where Chris's phone was indeed propped up against a vintage twin-bell alarm clock. 'Maybe check that.'

'We really shouldn't touch anything,' Ella said sharply as Caoimhe got up. 'This is a crime scene.'

'It's worth just double-checking,' Caoimhe said, picking it up. 'Maybe Sophia is in danger. Pin code?'

Sophia recited it, and Caoimhe unlocked the phone and walked over to the doorway, flicking through the home screen, her eyes searching the apps for anything that might help them.

'Messages?'

'He always uses WhatsApp.'

'OK, let's check WhatsApp.' Caoimhe sucked air through her teeth. 'Last message was from you, about four hours ago.'

Sophia's expression finally changed. She frowned and looked up at Caoimhe.

'I never messaged him four hours ago.'

Caoimhe took a deep breath and held the phone closer to her.

'It says: Can't wait to see you. Give me ten.' She lowered the phone and looked across at Sophia.

'I was with you guys four hours ago.' A thin, pink blush was spreading along the base of Sophia's pale neck. 'I met Safa at exactly six thirty.'

Safa looked at her.

Caoimhe scrolled rapidly through the phone.

'Are you sure you didn't text him by mistake?'

'That's not me. There's no message chain there.' Sophia leant over to glance at the phone. Her chest cavity felt hollow. 'Look.'

'It's your name and profile picture,' Safa pointed out.

'It's not me. Click on info. See, not my number.' Sophia got her own phone out and handed it to Caoimhe, who unlocked it. 'It's not me. Those messages aren't on my phone.'

Sophia tried vainly to inject some vehemence into her voice. Her whole body felt as if it was in low-power mode.

'This is weird,' Ella said. She was chewing more frantically than ever now, making up for the last few minutes. 'It feels like a set-up.' Her phone was still in her hand. 'I'm calling the police.'

'No!' Caoimhe barked. 'Hold on. Let's just get our heads on straight.' She was holding both phones limply by her side, breathing sharply, eyes darting. 'Sophia, go and get that note-pad first of all.'

'The police are going to question everyone.' Ella took a deep breath. 'They're going to go through all of this with a fine-tooth comb. What we did, when and why.'

'Get the bloody book,' Caoimhe snapped at Sophia, who hadn't moved.

'I'll get it,' Ajola said and darted for the stairs. 'Where is it, Sophia?'

'Under our mattress.' Sophia took a step back and sank on to the doormat. 'There's loads – I have – There's lots of jour-nals and notepads there.' She looked up. 'It's the green one.'

'Oh shit,' Caoimhe said. She still had Chris's phone in her hand. 'I'm looking at his emails, Sophia. He sent an email to some work guy at three o'clock today saying he was having a special evening at home with you.'

'That's not true.' Sophia looked green now as Safa crouched down next to her and stared into her eyes like an optometrist. 'I was always going out with you tonight. He's at his brother's. Ask his brother. Who's the work guy?'

'It just says Jake@EhringhausenMortgages,' Caoimhe read. Sophia looked perplexed.

'He's never mentioned a Jake. He doesn't know a Jake. Why would he be emailing some guy named Jake about me?'

Safa stood up, pulled the keys from the door and shut it, closing them all in. Ajola came down the stairs, the tattered notebook in her hands.

'Something is going on here,' Caoimhe said. She was searching through Sophia's phone now, the glare illuminating her face. 'Someone has planned this.'

'He sorted a lot of money out for some dodgy people in the past.' Sophia looked up at them. 'I mean, he never actually said, but, you know, I knew.'

'Ella' – Caoimhe didn't look up – 'don't call the police until we get our stories sorted.'

'There's nothing to sort,' Sophia said. She watched Ajola put the notebook in Caoimhe's bag. 'I've been with you guys since six thirty.' She looked at Safa, who nodded slowly. 'He can't . . . It won't—'

'They're going to want to know all your movements,' Ella said. She realized she was sweating, the skin under her top suddenly hot and clammy. 'What time did you leave here?'

Sophia frowned. 'Six. Around six. I dropped Isla off at five at Mum's for tea. And came back here to get ready.'

'And Chris definitely wasn't here?' Ella plucked her shirt material away from her neck. 'No one was hanging about?'

'No, no. He's in Farnham tonight.'

'I'm going to be straight with all of you.' Ella moved her gum around her mouth. 'I've studied cases like this before, at work. These texts and emails don't look good. And there's ninety minutes between you leaving your mum's and meeting us that no one can account for.'

'You can't be serious?' Safa said. It felt like a story one of them might have told when they were fourteen and sleeping on the trampoline. It wasn't real.

'It's not me,' Ella replied. 'Like, we need to burn that notepad as well. If they find that, this is done.'

'That isn't the main concern,' Caoimhe said. 'The main concern is, Sophia didn't send the text. Chris probably didn't email this random Jake guy. Somebody else did.'

Safa bit the end of her knuckle, hoping the pain would anchor her into reality. No one moved.

'Somebody else did,' Ajola echoed. 'Somebody else is trying to make it look like Sophia was here tonight. Those money launderers?'

'We are each other's alibis,' Safa said, taking her knuckle from her mouth. 'We're safe, together.'

'That only works if we can prove we had nothing to do with it.' Ajola looked around at all of them. 'We might find ourselves being investigated. How long has it been since we opened the door? Who can vouch for the time we pulled up?' Each of her sentences was like a puncture in Ella's chest. 'The car that was behind us back there? What's it going to look like – we get in and wait nearly ten minutes, staring at a dead body, before doing anything?'

'You told me not to call!' Ella cried and her gum fell from her mouth.

'If we had called, who knows what might have been triggered, what other traps these people might have put in place to frame Sophia,' Ajola said. Her words sent a shiver through all of them. 'It's only luck we know about those two messages because we checked his phone.' Ajola drew a shuddering breath. '*We* have to take control of this, now.'

'You're mad.' Ella flicked her gum into the bin and put a new piece into her mouth. 'You want us to, what . . .' She held out her arms and turned around, appealing to an invisible audience. 'Cover this up?' Her voice rose in pitch. 'That's the one thing that will make us look most guilty.'

'We already look guilty,' Ajola cried. 'Look at us! Look at that!' She pointed to Chris's body. Like a black hole, it drew everything inwards, light, focus, air, an object with gravity so intense none of them had the strength to escape it.

'Chris is already dead.' Ajola lowered her voice. She exhaled loudly through her nostrils. Her heart was thumping in her chest, trying to leap free. 'Sorry, Sophia. I can't begin to understand how you must feel. But there are two options here. Number one, we call the police' – Ella made a sound, which Ajola chose to ignore – 'and we trigger whatever the people really responsible for this want us to trigger – what we, ourselves' – she touched her chest, trying to slow her voice down – 'have already started, simply by being here tonight. Number two, we save Sophia and cover this up, and no one need think anything.' She held out her hands. 'What would Thomas Cromwell do?'

'Ajola!' Ella cried. She snatched Sophia's phone from Caoimhe and began swiping through it. 'For God's sake. This is real! Thomas Cromwell should have no bearing on what we do next!'

Sophia pinched her chin. 'How could we even go about covering this up?' she whispered.

'I'm not covering up a murder,' Ella said, still searching frantically through Sophia's phone. 'Sorry. I won't be able to sleep ever again. I'd prefer to call the police, get investigated, face the UK justice system and hope that it serves me well.'

'Yeah, tell me about that.' Caoimhe nervously adjusted her watch strap. 'How fair the UK justice system is.'

Ella said nothing. Her body was cold now, the sweat freezing against her skin. She put Sophia's phone down on the arm of the sofa and then put another piece of gum in her mouth.

'What if I could guarantee that no one would ever find out?' Ajola said in a hushed voice. 'About Chris, his body, his murder. That it would have been as if he had simply vanished off the face of the earth?'

'What are you talking about?' Safa said.

'We do a spell,' Ajola whispered. 'A powerful one. My great-grandma taught me how to conceal. It won't let us down.'

'This isn't the time for your witchy Wicca Hogwarts shit!' Caoimhe clapped her hands together. 'This is real, Ajola. There's a dead body right here. We're going to have to talk to the police. This is real!'

Suddenly, blue and red lights illuminated the room, turning the pool of Chris's blood a deep purple, like the clouds of an approaching storm. They all turned to look out of the window. Under the brilliance of the moon, they could clearly see a police patrol car pulling up outside the house, between the hedge and the road. It stopped. The two front doors opened and two police officers stepped out. One set a hat on her head; the other hitched up his trousers. They surveyed the road and then turned towards Sophia's house.

'I'm going to faint,' Ella said as Ajola sat down heavily in

41

the middle of the floor and shut her eyes. 'I think I'm going to be sick.'

The doorbell rang. Caoimhe looked at Sophia and then reached across to the door handle.

'Let's just go for honesty,' she said. She looked at Ella. 'And hope the UK justice system serves us well.'

Caoimhe opened the door. The faces of two police officers loomed large and radiant under the bright, night sky.

'Hello.' Caoimhe gave a shuddering breath. The air outside suddenly seemed very cold compared to the house. Were they about to spend the night in a police cell? What did handcuffs feel like when they were clamped around your wrists?

'We had a call about a disturbance?' the male officer said, peering around the door. He looked at Ella propped up against the mantelpiece, Ajola sitting in the middle of the floor, eyes still closed, Safa and Sophia kneeling on the doormat, hands clasped together. 'Who's the homeowner here?'

'Me,' Sophia squeaked, raising her hand. She didn't have the strength to stand.

'And you all are . . .?' the woman said, glancing around at the others filling the room.

'Friends.' Caoimhe was frowning now. 'We just came back from a night out. Not five minutes ago. This was all here when we got here.'

'No worries,' the male officer replied. He seemed bored. He cast Chris's body not so much as a glance. 'No loud music playing? No one shouting outside?'

'Not at all,' Caoimhe said, still frowning. She looked over her shoulder at the prone figure in the pool of blood. 'This is just how it was.'

'Anyone else here?' the male officer asked. 'Anyone upstairs? Kids? Partners?'

'Just us for the night,' Caoimhe replied. 'Girls' night.'

'OK. Try and keep the noise down,' the woman said. She took her hat off and smoothed back her hair. 'Maybe stay out of the garden. Keep it to the living room.'

She glanced around the small lounge. The male officer held his hand up in farewell and then they both turned away and headed back to the car. Caoimhe watched them go. When their patrol car had skidded off down the road, she turned to the others.

'What the hell just happened?' she breathed.

Ajola opened her eyes.

'Witchcraft,' she said. 'Wicca. Hogwarts shit.' Ajola looked around at them. 'And that was just me for two minutes. If we all pulled together, this body would be concealed for an eternity.'

'You're insane,' Caoimhe said and Ella put a hand over her eyes.

'We're in it now.' Safa stood up, dusting off her hands. 'They were right here and we didn't say anything.'

'They couldn't have seen it, even if we had.' Ajola leapt to her feet. 'It was concealed.'

'Don't talk such rubbish,' Caoimhe said. 'Safa, you've got dirt on your chin.' She put her hands on her hips and looked around the room. Her gaze settled on Ella, who was still holding on to the mantelpiece. 'What do we do? We can't call the police now and say, oh wait, there's actually a dead body here.'

Ella pressed her lips together and shook her head. 'We should have said something,' she hissed. 'We should have just said.'

'They would never have been able to see him,' Ajola said loudly. 'Because of the spell.'

'Shut up! They couldn't see him because of the' – Caoimhe gestured – 'table. The table was in the way.'

'We should have said something,' Ella repeated, slightly louder.

'But we didn't,' Ajola said. 'And Caoimhe's right: we don't have that option now. We can't get the police involved without raising some serious questions as to what we were just doing.'

'So . . .' Safa looked at Sophia. 'What do we do now?'

Sophia pressed her lips tightly together. She thought about the notebook detailing all the ways she could kill Chris. She thought about his smug, serene expression when he was pretending to be asleep instead of looking after Isla. She thought about her four friends, and how they had each given her a page of research on the Victorians in Year 10 when she had forgotten her homework folder.

She held out her hand and Safa pulled her to her feet.

'Let's hide the body.' Sophia let out a breath. 'Let's cover it up.' She looked at Safa and dusted off her hands as well. 'I can deal with the grief of having no grave for him. I – I've thought for a long time about living without Chris. It was all fantasy to stop me from suffocating. But I can deal with the reality. Isla will miss him. His parents. His brother. But—'

'But the other side of that is us potentially going to prison,' Safa said.

'Are we being serious?' Ella let go of the mantelpiece. 'We aren't being serious?'

'Trust me,' Ajola said. 'This will work. We didn't say anything. And that was to our advantage. We'll act instead. Magik runs through our veins. It's part of what makes us who we are. That's why we've been persecuted for hundreds of years. Men fear our power. They make us demons. Anne Boleyn used witchcraft to protect herself and Thomas Cromwell recognized that. He admired her for it.'

'Will you stop going on about Thomas Cromwell!' Caoimhe cried, throwing her hands up. 'Look, we can't call the police back, can we? It's too strange that we didn't mention it just then. It's not an option now. So.' Before a race, Caoimhe tried to sink into a state of mind that existed beyond her normal consciousness. It was hard to find, hidden between the seams of her everyday thinking, but when she got there, all the background sound, the crush, the noise, the heat of other people's bodies, faded away. She felt each second, complete and eternal, and gave no thought to anything beyond that. The sensation helped her focus, each stride, each breath, each beat of her heart. She found that space now, and lowered her arms. 'That means we're covering this up, right? We're hiding this body, right?' She looked around at them, nodding slowly, encouraging them to nod also. 'Right. So.' She swallowed. 'Let's start doing this, then.' Stride, stride. 'I think we should do a preliminary clean of this place.' She gestured at the pool of blood. Breathe. Breathe. 'Remove the body. Then come back and do a proper clean.' Beat. Beat. 'I'll do the blood.' She nodded at Ella. 'Maybe you and Safa can put the body in the car. I don't think Sophia should do that.'

'Sophia can come with me,' Ajola said. 'We need camomile, basil, sage and dill.'

'Do not waste your time on that, please!' Caoimhe said. 'Go research a place we can put the body instead.'

'I already know where to put the body!' Ajola snapped. 'I already know,' she said, more gently. 'But I need the herbs to bind the spell.'

'I'm not doing a spell!' Caoimhe cried. 'This isn't Year Seven, Ajola! This isn't those witchy books you bought from WHSmiths.'

'How can you explain them not seeing?' Ajola nodded her head at the body. 'They looked right in here.'

'The light! The table!'

'Listen!' Safa said, holding out both her hands. 'We're hiding the body, anyway, right? So, let Ajola do the spell. It can't hurt.'

'No!' Ajola snapped. 'No! This will only work if we all do it. And this will only work if we all believe in it.'

'Well, I don't,' Caoimhe said. 'Spells are nonsense.'

'You do spells all the time!' Ajola replied. 'When you throw a penny in a fountain, or when you blow out the candles at your birthday. Teeth under the pillow, lucky shoes, decorating a Christmas tree, singing the national anthem before a football match. Going to worship, saying a prayer. They're all ghosts of ancient spells, Caoimhe. And they all have one thing in common: the people doing them believe in them.'

'I can believe in it,' Safa said. 'I thought that policeman looked straight at the body. I thought we were done.'

'I can believe in it.' Sophia looked at Ajola. 'I remember the WHSmith books.'

Ajola looked at Ella.

'Ella?' she said. 'Will you shut your eyes and make the wish?'

'Well, yeah.' Ella shrugged. There was no going back. Her failure to point the body out to the officers at the door had placed her in this spot. Now it was all about damage control.

Get ahead of the utter and complete chaos that this all might descend into. Small steps. Logical steps. She put an extra piece of gum in her mouth. 'If that's it, I can do that.'

'Caoimhe, it's just you,' Ajola said. 'We need five links in this chain.'

'Let's just get rid of this first.' Caoimhe pointed at the body. 'Me, Ella, Safa. Ajola, fine, you can get your potions with Sophia. Keep her away from this.'

'I know you believe,' Ajola said. 'You can't not. Magik flows in all of us. It courses through our veins. Our blood, our moon.'

'Let's just get going.' Safa patted her on the shoulder. 'Save it for the burial, Ajola.'

Ajola took Sophia into the small kitchen. Through the window, lined with various potted herbs, they could see the garden light was on, casting a bright white spotlight into the middle of the dark grass.

'That's on a sensor,' Sophia said as Ajola opened her cupboards. 'Someone must have been the garden recently.'

'Camomile tea,' Ajola said, taking a box off the shelf. 'It's dried.' She breathed out slowly. 'But it will do. Have you got a bag?' Sophia passed her a Lidl Bag for Life. Ajola dropped the entire box of camomile into it. 'Fresh basil,' Ajola said. She reached over to the windowsill. 'Parsley. Coriander.' She passed a hand through the leaves. 'No sage or dill?'

Sophia shook her head. 'Who called the police?' she murmured. 'We weren't making any noise.'

Ajola paused, her hands half in and half out of the cutlery drawer. 'I don't know,' she said and drew out a long knife. She slammed the drawer shut. 'Someone who wanted the body to be found, maybe. I'm taking the coriander plant as well. I think

I read somewhere that you can hang it above your doorway to ward off negativity.' She put the knife and the pots in the Lidl bag. 'Where are your dried herbs and spices?'

Sophia pointed to another cupboard. Behind them, Ella and Safa had wrapped a towel around Chris's head and were now securing it with Sellotape. The noise of tape ripping from the roll reminded Sophia of Christmas Eve. Wrapping presents. The secrecy. The dark outside.

'Dried sage.' Ajola held up a small, plastic tumbler. 'It'll do.' She moved the other jars aside. 'No dill. Oh well. I think I can make this work.'

Ella and Safa hoisted the body between them and began to move to the front door, which Caoimhe was holding open.

'It's clear,' she said. 'But move quickly. I've opened the boot.'

Ella and Safa staggered crossing the threshold and Caoimhe stepped in to support the sagging midriff.

'It'll be OK,' Ajola said, watching Sophia. 'Trust me.' She found herself calm. Focused. As though this was all premediated and she had visualized each step a thousand times before acting it out. It would be OK. Later, she would lie in bed and think about Thomas Cromwell. She was sure he would have been as focused and clinical as her had he suddenly had to conceal a death for the King. He might even be proud of what she was doing now.

'I know,' Sophia said. She could see the innards of Safa's BMW boot. The little white light was on inside. Such a little light. So normal. So innocuous. 'I do.'

Caoimhe came back in, slightly breathless. She smelt of the outside air.

'I've got a spade. Bin bag,' she said to Ajola.

Using another bath towel, they mopped up the pool of blood and thrust it into the bin bag. Then, they all washed their hands, dried them using kitchen towel and stuffed that in the bin bag as well.

'One body, one bag to conceal,' Ajola said, watching as Ella tied the top of the bag in a tight knot. She gestured to the Lidl bag. 'We can do this.'

'This place look good?' Caoimhe glanced about at the living room. 'No blood traces? Nothing obviously out of place? Sophia? Say someone came round now. Would they notice anything?'

Sophia, pale lips pressed together, looked about her.

'No,' she said. 'I don't think so. Oh. His phone.' She pointed to the arm of the sofa where Caoimhe had left it. 'Maybe we should get rid of that.'

Ella untied the bag and Safa dropped it inside.

'Wait, shouldn't we switch the phone off?' Safa said. 'Can't they track it?'

'Not here,' Caoimhe said. 'Then they'll know it got switched off here at this time. We'll do it in some random location en route to the burial site. We should also stop somewhere else, completely different, and bin that notebook.'

'How do you know this stuff?' Safa asked. She felt extremely passive, watching the others fly into action, moving where they moved, doing what they did. Where was her own urgency? She didn't feel she had processed anything yet. She was a passenger in the scene, accepting everything. She was still waiting for her brain to catch up. Yes, that was it. She was just assimilating the information. She would drive the car. That's how she would contribute. Let the others sort out the finer details.

'Netflix. That gives me an idea,' Caoimhe said. 'Let's chuck in some of his clothes as well. His wallet. Has he got a laptop?'

'His laptop is over there.' Sophia nodded to the coffee table. 'His wallet?' She shrugged. 'I haven't seen that.'

'I'll check his pockets,' Caoimhe said. 'Sophia, go upstairs and get a few changes of clothes for him. As if he was planning to run away.'

Sophia nodded. She slowly climbed the stairs. How many times had she made this journey, with Chris sitting on the sofa below her, laughing loudly at some inane show and she biting the inside of her mouth with suppressed loathing and contempt? The landing was dark. She flicked the light on. Another movement a thousand times completed but now utterly different, and never to be the same again.

Inside their bedroom, she opened his drawers and took out one of his three pairs of underwear, a spare change of socks and his tracksuit bottoms. She could smell him on the clothes. She held them to her, waiting for some expression of grief. Waiting for an emotional catharsis. Nothing came. There was no lament. She just felt sick. It was so like Chris to die and not deal with any of the tidying up.

She came back downstairs and dropped the clothes in the bin bag.

'You OK?' Safa asked her. 'You ready?'

Sophia nodded. 'I'm sure the shock will catch up with me later,' she said. 'Right now, I just want to get it over with and go to bed.'

'I've put our location in the satnav,' Ajola said, coming in through the door. 'Two hours away, so if you're hungry or thirsty or need the toilet, sort that out now.'

The Copse

THE SATNAV INSTRUCTIONS ended in the middle of a dual carriageway.

'Keep going,' Ajola said to Safa, glancing at the dim-blue phone screen mounted to the dashboard. 'We just need to find somewhere to park.'

'Across two lanes of traffic?' Caoimhe said but Safa hushed her.

After about two miles, a roundabout came up.

'Take the second exit,' Ajola said. She had unmounted her phone and was navigating around the map with two pinched fingers. 'Keep going, about half a mile.'

'How do you know this place?' Ella asked from the back seat. 'It's completely random.'

'My great-grandma used to bring us here,' Ajola said. 'She lived in Avebury. This part of the country is very old. Ancient. The soil. The trees. Pull over here, over here.'

'Won't it be suspicious?' Ella asked as Safa indicated and they pulled up in a small dirt layby. 'I mean, if anything is discovered. A witness might see this car and track us.'

'Have faith that it won't be discovered,' Ajola said.

Safa turned off the engine. In the darkness, the car clanked beneath them.

'I just feel' – Ella moved her gum around her mouth – 'concealing a body rule 101 is: don't park your car in an obvious place and then drag the body in full view of everyone passing on the road.'

Ajola took a deep breath and shut her eyes.

'Stop thinking with your minds,' she said. 'Trust the process.'

She got out of the car. She felt very light. Serene. The moon was bright overhead, clear and orbital. A great cavern of ice. There was not a breath of wind to be found anywhere.

Sophia carried the spade and the bin bag of bloody towels, and the other four heaved the body out of the boot and lifted it up the steep bank that ran alongside the road. At the top, they saw the great, undulating visage of the North Downs stretching away in front of them. Shadows of trees and rock formations, fence posts and outcrops were cast across the plain, stretched and dotted, brilliant and clear under the moon.

'This way,' Ajola said, heading down the far side of the bank, the head wrapped in Sellotape held firmly in her hands. 'Not far. Towards that wood there.'

The wood was a shadowy presence atop a steep rise. The trees on its crown hung in a circle, their trunks bent and gnarled, their branches twisting like petrified bones. Amongst their roots was a ring of small, ancient stones. The light of the moon dashed between the wood, and the shadows were stark.

In the centre of the circle, they dropped the body. Sophia dumped the bag on top. Ella took the spade and stuck it firmly in the ground. It shuddered in the cold earth, remaining completely upright. They looked around at one another.

'What now?' Safa asked.

'Surely we're not going to bury him right in the middle of this circle?' Caoimhe said. 'It's going to be so obvious. We should find a thick bit of wood.'

'No,' Ajola said. 'Circles have power. They're complete. They're infinite. They can bind spells.'

Caoimhe tilted her head back with an exasperated groan.

'Are we going to have to speak Latin or Greek?' Safa asked, trying to catch Caoimhe's eye.

'No,' Ajola said, turning to look at her. 'We're using a magik that is hundreds of thousands of years old. It comes from the very earth itself and flows through all that we are. Why would we use such a young language to speak to it? Christians, Satanists, Latin. The old world doesn't speak this language.'

'Let's just dig a hole.' Caoimhe pulled out the spade. 'I reckon that should be the first step.'

They dug. Taking it in turns to lengthen, widen, deepen. Ajola sat on one of the stones near the edge of the copse and began to arrange the herbs that she had brought. The moon hung behind her like a spotlight.

'How deep does it need to be?' Ella asked, resting on the spade.

'About two more feet,' Caoimhe said as Ajola replied:

'That's fine.'

'Let's just dig two more feet.' Caoimhe took the spade from Ella and began digging again.

'Either this body will be found here or it won't,' Ajola said. 'Two more feet won't change that.'

'Ajola's right,' Safa said. 'If anyone decides to dig here, they'll find it. No matter how deep it is.'

Caoimhe silently dug the spade into the soil and shifted one more sod of earth. Then she stepped back and sat down on the edge of the grave.

'I keep remembering,' she said, looking up. The moon glistened in her eyes. 'This is real life.'

'Put the body in the grave,' Sophia said, taking hold of the legs. 'Come on.'

They slung the body in the ground and tossed in the bag. Then, using the spade, their shoes, their knuckles and the backs of their hands, they pushed back the upturned mud. It slowly covered legs, shoes, clothes, each clod of heavy peat obscuring the body from the light. Sophia didn't feel anything. She didn't even feel joy. She wasn't here. She was in the moon, watching from far away.

'This is insane,' Caoimhe said when the dirt was level. 'What are we doing?'

'Make a circle around the site,' Ajola said. 'Join hands.' Ajola took Caoimhe's dirt-stained hand solidly in her own. 'You are woman. You are intuition,' she said. 'You are more than this flesh assigned to you on earth.'

They held hands. Silence spun around the copse. Ajola shut her eyes and looked down at the soft ground that held all their feet.

'I'm going to ask for the magik to bind the spell,' she said.

Caoimhe exhaled loudly and shook her head. Safa smiled at her.

Ajola continued: 'Keep your eyes shut. You'll feel it.'

She began to talk. The branches above them rustled. The

ground beneath their feet tumbled and fell. Nothing moved. The earth ached. It bore them down, deep into the grave, into the soil, past the layers of rock. They were completely limitless. They were stretching across the sky. They were the circumference of the moon.

Ajola stepped forward, breaking the circle, and pressed the herbs into the earth above Chris's grave.

'Protection. Luck. Purity. Salvation,' she said in English as she retook Caoimhe's hand. Then all was silent, all was peace. Above them, beyond the outstretched fingers of the trees, the moon shone, luminous and watchful.

SEVEN YEARS LATER

Caoimhe

THE FLOODLIGHTS ABOVE the Astroturf illuminated the beads of sweat gathered on the hairs of Mateus's arms. There was sweat on his temples. On his upper lip. Pooling, no doubt, in the hollows of his clavicle. His shirt, stretched between his broad shoulder blades, was dark with patches of sweat.

'Good session tonight,' Aidan said, jogging up behind them. He too was drenched with sweat. Sodden. Saturated. He leant forward on his knees and thumped Mateus on the back. 'Never knew you could run so fast, mate.'

'Me? It's her you want to worry about,' Mateus replied. He winked at Caoimhe.

Caoimhe swelled with pride. She folded her arms across herself and lifted her chin. Something witty to reply. Something modest. Humble. But funny. Something that would impress them.

'Well—'

'You see Rohan Rust's new five-K PB?' Aidan elbowed Mateus. 'Fifteen thirty.'

Around them, the rest of their training group began to con-
gregate, puffy red faces, dark patches, heaving chests. Caoimhe
was still the only female in the top runners' group. The only
one who could keep up with the men's standard. Here was her
status. One of the men. They were frozen, their temporal state
halted. She could cut through the scene, like ice.

'Would that have been a club record?'

'No. Dean Weaver's is fifteen twenty-eight.'

Caoimhe rolled her eyes to herself. She hated when Dean
Weaver broke another record. There was only so much speed
in the world. Only so much progression. It was finite.

'Ah, Dean.' Mateus put one hand on Aidan's shoulder and
the other on Caoimhe's. She automatically straightened her
back. She loved the weight of his hand. Just the thin barrier
of her T-shirt all that was separating bare skin from bare skin.
Mateus sighed. 'Our local legend.'

'Rohan Rust's ten, half and marathon times are all way faster
than Dean's,' Caoimhe said breathlessly.

'Not by much, girl,' Mateus said and squeezed her shoulder
with his heavy hand. 'Not by much.'

Caoimhe laughed and allowed the point to be conceded.
They moved to a row of benches between the Astroturf and
the leisure centre. There was a terrifying, earthy scent men
gave off after exhilarating exercise and her nose stung with
it. It was rich in the air. Women just didn't produce the same
smell.

'I didn't get the message about the shirts,' Mateus said loudly,
leaning forward on his leg so that his quadriceps bulged. He
never spoke directly to one person. He addressed the group at
large and people gathered to listen. When, once or twice during

the countless training sessions over last seven years, he did turn his full attention to Caoimhe, to ask her a personal question, to make a personal comment, she always felt heady with the interest. He turned his head, alternating legs, and looked up at Caoimhe now, smiling.

'What?' she said, glancing down at her shirt.

'Red and yellow shirts. You and Porter. You must have conferred before the session, eh?'

Caoimhe glanced at her shirt and then at Porter, who was wearing a similar colour. He just rolled his eyes but Caoimhe bent over and pretended it was hysterical.

'No one ever invites me to things,' Mateus lamented, pulling his leg behind him. 'Always left out.'

'Excuse me.'

They all turned. A woman was standing behind them. Slim, elfin, with her long hair piled on the top of her head in a floppy knot. Caoimhe frowned at her. She was wearing jeans and a grey sweatshirt.

'Is this the running club?'

'We are the running club,' Mateus said. He held out his hand. Caoimhe stared at it. It felt like betrayal. 'I'm Mateus. Nice to meet you.'

'Evie. I was just coming to chat,' the woman said. 'I'm thinking of joining and I, well' – she looked at Caoimhe, whose face remained impassive – 'wanted to see what you're all about.'

'What sort of times do you do?' Aidan asked. 'We've got different groups based on your PBs.'

'Well, I'm not always PB best.'

Caoimhe looked at her shoes and crossed her eyes.

'No shame in that,' Aidan said. 'None of us are.'

'Under twenty minutes for a five K?' Mateus asked, leaning forward and speaking delicately as if he were asking if she was on her period.

'Oh yes,' the woman said. 'Yes, I'd say so.'

'You're with us then,' Aidan said. Caoimhe rolled her eyes. Did this woman really think she could run with them? 'We meet here Tuesdays and Thursdays, sometimes Fridays. Do a mix of efforts. Azaiyah is our coach. He's the guy over there in the high-vis.'

'OK, cool, cool. I'll talk to him.' Evie looked between them and her eyes settled on Caoimhe, who suddenly felt unnerved, and looked away. 'Thanks.'

'The club needs more women,' Aidan said as Evie made her way over to where Azaiyah was helping someone stretch out their hamstring. 'Feminine touch. Always nice to look at as well, right, Caoimhe?'

Caoimhe made a non-committal noise.

'I'm out of here,' Porter said. He raised a hand to Azaiyah. 'Thank you.'

'Me too,' Caoimhe said. 'Thanks, Azaiyah!'

He raised a solitary hand in farewell. Caoimhe tugged her car keys out of the too-small pocket where she had wedged them for the very purpose of jangling them right now. She always carried a little Darth Vader keychain, a gift from Safa when they were sixteen, and she brandished it flamboyantly now, trying to get the men to see the figure.

'Do you like Star Wars?'

'My friend gave it to me. She said I remind her of Anakin Skywalker. You know, powerful, the dark side.'

Laugh, laugh, laugh, innocent bumping of shoulders.
'You're so funny! I love it when girls love Star Wars!'

But they didn't see the keychain and, if they did, they didn't care to ask.

As she slid into the car seat and picked up her phone, she saw she had a missed call from Sophia. Her heart skipped a beat. This terrifying spectre. This luminous ghost, gazing up at her. She thought she had cut Sophia from her life.

Someone hammered on her window and she jumped. It was Mateus. He raised a hand and she quickly waved back.

Caoimhe put the phone on the seat and drove slowly home. Over the last seven years, there had been a fear poised around her beating heart, ready to suffocate it at any moment. Sometimes, she felt watched, and the fear would tighten in her chest, dark figures around each corner, whispering just beyond her reach. She had distanced herself from the others, living abroad for several years to be sure of it. At first, it was an unconscious distance. But, as the years wore on, it became self-preservation. If anyone ever found that body, she didn't want them to come looking for her.

Outside her house, she picked up her phone again and held it against her ear, bracing herself, before dialling Sophia's number. In the field behind her house, the swollen head of a hot air balloon was slowly inflating into the dark, pin-pricked sky.

'Hi!' She tried to sound upbeat. 'Sophia? It's Caoimhe!'

'Mum!' a voice at the other end called. 'Mum! Your phone!'

She waited. She heard thudding in the background. The phone shifted. She looked at the hot air balloon. The skin was becoming taut.

'Hello?'

'It's Caoimhe. Is everything OK?'

'Caoimhe.' Sophia breathed out heavily. 'Someone knows about the body.'

Ajola

YASHICA WAS SEVEN years old and she was a bitch.

Her hair was always immaculately coiffed, ringlets curled around her ears and cascading down her neck. She was in the top group for every subject, always won first place in sports day and was on the U11 side for the football team. She never put a foot wrong, never spoke out of turn, never needed to be told to do anything twice. But she was a bitch, and Ajola knew it.

The other girls in the class paled in comparison to her. Sometimes, literally. Next to Yashica, Lucy's blonde hair appeared almost translucent. She stood, shivering, at Yashica's elbow at break time, a colourless ghost that you wouldn't believe even existed on the same plane as Yashica.

'Miss Pugh, you're my favourite teacher, *ever*,' Yashica would always say at the end of every day, smiling at Ajola with a close-lipped, tight-cheeked smirk. 'Thank you for teaching us, Miss Pugh!'

And then she would perform a perfect tuck jump, arms

elongated, hair flowing, a cheerleader at an All-American football game.

It didn't fool Ajola. Once, during lunch, a student had stuck
a Post-it to the back of Ajola's chair that said 'Give me rubbers,
please'. There was something about the use of punctuation
and the handwriting that made Ajola suspect Yashica. When
she slowly peeled it off her chair and dropped it into the bin,
crumpled into a tiny fragment, without so much as a word of
acknowledgement, she could see that same close-lipped, tight-
cheeked smirk on Yashica's face. *Bitch.*

Yashica could do nothing to endear herself to Ajola. She
imagined Thomas Cromwell would never have trusted her
either. She would have been a snake in King Henry's court,
whispering in people's ears. Ajola, like Cromwell, was naturally
interested in the quieter, more reserved students. Perhaps not
quite as vapid as Lucy. Someone like Daisy. Daisy, who had
wide, glistening eyes and thick hair scraped up into a messy
ponytail that lay curled between her shoulders like a comma.
Daisy, who always scurried after Yashica. Daisy, whom Yashica
deigned to pick for partner work. Daisy, who wasn't just clever
but *greater depth*. Yashica told Daisy how to sit, how to organize her pencil case, how to eat her lunch. Sometimes, Ajola
found Daisy sitting by herself in the cloakroom, face in hands,
on the very edge of being upset. But she would never talk to
Ajola. She would just skitter off.

'I'm worried about her,' Daisy's mother had told Ajola at
their first parents' evening in September, the leaves of the sunflower clock ticking behind them. 'I know she's good at school,
I know she excels at maths, but, at home, she has such temper
tantrums.'

Ajola had sat up straighter. Someone had left a strange wicker man on her desk that evening and she turned it over nervously in her hands. It was the sort of crap Lucy gave her.

'She gets so *anxious*,' her mother said, lowering her voice on the final word as though it was blasphemous. 'And I just think, maybe, the teachers don't understand because she gets such good marks.'

'I understand.' Ajola's voice sounded empty. She cleared her throat, trying to sound more emphatic, clutching the wicker man tighter. 'I do.'

'We've tried going out for walks or meditation but' – her mother spread her hands, demonstrating to Ajola that she had nothing concealed in her palms – 'she gets so worked up.'

'I understand,' Ajola said again. They sat in silence. Ajola tried to conjure up a way to articulate everything that was broiling inside her. 'I do.'

'She's only seven.' Daisy's mother looked down at her fingers. The sleeves of her woolly jumper were pulled far over her wrists. 'She doesn't need to be this anxious all the time. She can do all that when she's grown up.'

Daisy's mother looked up and gave Ajola a smile. Ajola tried to smile back. It was conversations like this that stifled Ajola. They sucked the noise out of her head, leaving nothing but a vacuous space, perhaps a memory of home, Tesco checkouts, the emptiness of a Friday evening.

That lunchtime, the lunchtime it all started again, she went into her classroom to eat her sandwich in silence, in the dark. There was such a weight upon her heart, she was sure she would burst into tears at any moment. Yashica and Daisy were by the drawers, and when she came in Yashica stood up with such a sharp, controlled motion, Ajola knew she was doing something she oughtn't.

'Miss Pugh, you're my favourite teacher' – skipping past her and out of the classroom. She stuck her head back in through the door – '*ever*,' she said with that charming little smile.

Daisy followed in short, sharp steps, head bowed.

'All right, Daisy?' Ajola asked, giving her a thumbs-up. Daisy made a noise but shied away like a nervous deer.

Ajola sat heavily on her chair and looked at the new wicker man that Lucy had left on her desk. It had mismatched eyes. She pulled her phone out of her bag. She never usually checked her phone during the day. She usually sat in the staff room with everyone else and acted like a normal person. But the day had been so strange, so off-kilter. She felt she had to look at her phone just to reassure herself that no other tragedy had occurred.

And there was the text from Sophia. How long had it been since she had texted her? For the last seven years, she had been at this school, in this beige classroom, a period of abject stasis devoid of agency, with very little word from the others. And now, today, of all days, here it was.

Call me ASAP.

Her great-grandma always told her, in elaborate Albanian, that bad things came in threes. Earlier, Ajola had already discovered the first bad thing that day. Sophia getting back in touch out of the blue could mean nothing good. It was surely the second.

She stood up and went out of the fire exit, down the alley to where the bins were kept. Seven years ago, she had wanted to stay in touch with the others. Wanted it with all her heart. She truly believed in the magik. It would protect them, always. But the others clearly hadn't felt the same way. After giving statements to the police confirming Sophia's uneventful movements that night, they had fallen away from her, one by one. She didn't even have a number for Ella any more.

Ajola wedged herself in a damp corner, untouched by the sun, and called Sophia.

She answered on the first ring.

'I knew you'd call me back,' Sophia said breathlessly.

'Is everything OK?' Ajola asked. The brickwork scraped her back. It would probably leave a red smudge on her shirt. 'Is everything – is everything all right?'

She already knew it wasn't. Her heart started a drumroll in her chest. She knew what the words would be before Sophia spoke them.

'Someone knows what we did with Chris. They named all five of us as being there. They want something from us.'

Ajola sucked on her lips.

'Let's give it to them,' she said. 'Talk to the others. Let's meet up.'

When Sophia had hung up, she went back inside the classroom. The little wicker man was now on the floor, winking up at her.

Ella

IT HAD TAKEN almost seven years, but Ella had finally confirmed a date for a hearing for Eric. She had dossiers of evidence, reports, studies and expert testimony to help bolster his claim that his parents owed him compensation for the event of his birth. When he had first laid out the claim before her, she had thought it semi-ridiculous and tried to politely deter his emphatic persistence. If she hadn't become a parent, she would have let Eric float away, bobbing on the tumultuous waves of the sea, drifting farther out of sight until he was completely forgotten. Now, she understood. The audacity. The entitlement. How dare people rip a soul from the void and encase it in ten pounds of flabby flesh, to grow and wilt and suffer. It was an absolute outrage that this was happening. And Eric was a relative success story. A loved son. A supported child. What about the others? How could birth not be an infringement on human rights.

When Ella's son was six months old, she had held his head tightly between her hands and screamed in his face. He wouldn't be quiet. The noise was incessant. Her outburst didn't stop the noise, but it had made him cry in a different way. More bewildered than incandescent. She had promised herself never to do anything like that again. But it was so easy to do it. And it came from nowhere. The decision bypassed her critical thinking faculties, a hand jerking away from a hot saucepan. It was already done. Seeing his shock, feeling the reach, the expanse of her anger, was refreshing. It wasn't about power, or fear, or anything so base. It was the catharsis of released anger. It was a relief. She knew anger needed to be flexed. A sudden, sharp release and the tension was done. It was rejuvenating.

Sometimes, the guilt came seeping up afterwards. Seeing his shocked expression, his fear. It was unsustainable. All just too cruel. How could she be a mother. She didn't talk to anyone about it. She hadn't spoken to Safa or Caoimhe or Sophia or Ajola in years. After what they had done, after she'd had to endure verifying Sophia's alibi in a statement to police, she wanted to erase all traces of them from her life. She had moved house and not told them her new address. Their absence, and the fear she felt from their actions, manifested inside of her like a parasite, sucking the colour from her life, the verve, the wonder, the magic. No wonder she was not a fit mother.

She had watched a video in a work seminar about how important facial expressions are to children. In one exercise, a mother smiles at her baby, counting, talking, repeating the baby's babbles back to her. The baby smiles and waves. The bond between mother and baby is palpable. Then, for the next exercise, the mother turns away. When she turns back, her face is blank. Her smile is gone. Her eyes are lidded and dark. The absence of feeling is more horrific than any ghoul or grisly phantom. A mother utterly devoid of soul. Ella had never seen anything so chilling. The baby is shocked. It stares. It tries to coo and babble. It tries to point. The mother shows no reaction. The baby contorts in its seat, balled fists, red-faced, making a strange bleating noise. The mother doesn't even blink. The baby cries. After ninety seconds of this cosmic horror, the exercise is over and the mother gratefully smiles and rushes to embrace her baby. At this point in the video, when faced with the reunited embrace, Ella, in a humiliating loss of control, burst into tears and had to be led by a clerk from the seminar. She couldn't articulate her sadness. It was too deep to be known to her. She just cried whilst the clerk, a junior who had barely been at the company a month, awkwardly handed her tissues and asked her if she wanted a drink.

She would fight for a baby's right to compensation for birth without consent. People needed to be made accountable. Benjamin hadn't been born when Eric had first walked into her office. He was four now. He slept in her bed, in little spaceman pyjamas, his body radiating a warm heaviness that soothed her and made her fearful, all at once.

When the unknown number came up on her phone, she presumed it was from Eric and called for her secretary to answer it.

'Tell him I'll talk to him at our appointment tomorrow!' she shouted into the adjoining office.

The ringing fell silent. She heard Maduka responding.

'Hold on,' she heard him say and rolled her eyes.

'It's all down for tomorrow!' she called loudly.

Maduka appeared in the doorway, the mouthpiece of the phone smothered in his palm.

'It's someone called Sophia.'

Ella's heart stopped in her chest. She couldn't draw breath.

'She says you know her and will want to speak to her.'

Ella was sure he would be able to see it in her eyes. The blood. The body. The copse on the hill. Her face was flushing. How guilty she must seem!

She managed to jerk her head at him and he retreated, closing the door between them. Ella sat, frozen, watching the light flash on the desk phone. She didn't want to answer. To cultivate a connection. This was stupid of Sophia, calling here. Ella couldn't risk it. Even now. God forbid Sophia was ever arrested. If that happened, Ella needed to be as far away from her as possible.

'Sophia.' She pressed the phone into her ear. 'Hello.'

'Hello.' Sophia sounded breathless.

'I've got a big case on,' Ella said quickly, trying to ensure the silence didn't expand. 'That one from seven years ago, actually. So I need to be quick.'

'How strange,' Sophia said. 'That's the second thing from seven years ago to come back round this week.'

Ella went cold. She felt the blood drain from her skull, down her cheeks, away from the very fingers that held the phone containing Sophia's voice to her ear.

'Oh my God,' she breathed. 'When? How?'

'Someone texted me,' Sophia whispered. So quiet. 'They saw us.'

Ella sucked her gum into her windpipe.

'Shit!' She coughed it back out. 'Who?'

'I don't know. Ajola says we should meet up Thursday and discuss it.'

'I can't meet up,' Ella snapped. 'No one can see us together.

I've got this big case on. If my brother gets a sniff of this, he'll kick me out the door.'

'I know. I know.'

Ella waited for her to say something else, but the line was silent.

'I can't.' She pleaded. 'I've been paranoid enough as it is.'

'I understand,' Sophia said. 'Do you want me to keep you in the loop?'

'No.' Ella felt tearful, then angry. 'Sorry, Sophia. I can't do any of it. Delete my number.'

'OK.'

The silence expanded. Ella waited for Sophia to hang up but nothing happened. They both sat, hushed, phones pressed, hard, to each ear. A breath away and yet separated by so much space. When Maduka appeared in the doorway with a quizzical hand, Ella broke it off.

'Goodbye, Sophia,' she said.

'Goodbye, Ella.'

'Everything OK?' Maduka asked as Ella set the receiver in the cradle.

'No. Yes. She's a friend from school.'

'Nice. Reminiscing?'

Ella spun around in her chair to look out of the window. Her heart was thundering. Surely Maduka knew.

'Something like that.'

Safa

SAFA'S HUSBAND HAD alternated between sending her desperate, begging texts and ones that threatened her life.

You fucking bitch.

You'll be so fucking sorry.

She had blocked him before she left him. Taking the immense step to leave required huge amounts of energy and she had read that it was possible to relapse if there was open communication. It would be easy to reconcile but not so easy to wake up one morning in a year's time and find herself right back where she started. So she blocked him. Being blocked hadn't perturbed him, however, and he had started texting and calling from random numbers or emailing from throwaway accounts. She couldn't for the life of her believe the time and effort he was putting in to harass her, given putting groceries away had been so beyond him. She had changed her number a few times but he kept rooting the information out, like a boar searching for truffles, almost certainly from family members who felt that she should just give him another chance.

'Yes, Safa, he's inconsiderate. Yes, he doesn't appreciate you. Yes, he's lazy. Yes, he's sent some extremely offensive texts. But he's your husband. You need to stop being so stubborn and forgive him.'

She had given him the house and the car. She didn't need to. The mortgage was in her name, the monthly repayments came out of her account, the insurance was registered to her and she was the primary caregiver to the children. But the alternative would have left him homeless, and if he was homeless, she would endure a much harder time shaking him loose. She could imagine him staying with a procession of sympathetic relatives, all rubbing his back and commiserating with him, whispering about what kind of woman would make her own husband, the father to her children, homeless.

She wanted a clean break and she was prepared to front any expense to get it. She rented a small flat near the school, paid the childcare, bought a used Fiat 500, Hello Fresh meals, Tesco Delivery, a weekly cleaner, a quality divorce solicitor. She had the least amount of savings of her adult life but the rewards were totally worth it. She never felt any resentment dragging the bins out at 6 p.m. on a cold, rainy Thursday when it was only her and her children using them. That piece of mind was priceless.

It had taken her almost seven years to reach this point. Burying Chris's body had been the catalyst she needed to leave. If she could bury a dead body in the woods, she could do anything. She was no longer a passenger. Leaving was never as easy as walking down the front path with each child under her arm, though. It was extricating their lives, their families, her courage, the insidious tentacles that were wrapped around her, drawing her closer to him and his greasy hair and his unwashed underpants, bunched around his ankles as he sat on the toilet with his headphones in.

On the night that Sophia called, Safa would have loved to have been able to say that it was the worst news she had received that day. But it wasn't. Her cousin's wife, Emaan, who had always been an ally in the fight for her own agency, sent her a text about an hour before Sophia's call came in.

Don't worry. I know what's happening and I'll put a stop to it. Don't open any attachments.

Safa frowned at the screen. Both children were asleep in their cramped bedroom, shadowed visages of Princess Jasmine and Prince Eric grinning at them from the walls. She was in the small lounge, using her laptop to watch *Seinfeld* on her brother's Netflix account. There was a pot of L'Oréal Paris Pure Clay Detox Face Mask open on the arm of the sofa beside a small evil eye pendant, four blue concentric circles, that a homeless woman had handed her at Baker's Arms as though Safa had dropped it.

What do you mean?

I think Haaris has made some sort of deepfake of you.

Safa's heart rate exploded. She thought she might crumple the phone in her hands like a sheaf of paper.

What do you mean? How do you know?

Sufiyan saw it on his phone today. He tried to get him to delete it but Haaris got all moody. Just don't open/look at anything on your phone or emails.

What if he sends it to the office?

Three little dots appeared. Then they vanished. Then they appeared again.

Don't you have some sort of company filter?

Safa felt acid bubbling under her diaphragm. She suddenly had the worst indigestion of her life. The smell of the detox face mask made her feel sick. Her fingers trembled as she typed her response.

Yeah, but there's still IT guys who will have to report it. How bad is it?

Don't the office know about the harassment though?

I let HR know a while back. But they'll think it's real.

The three little dots appeared again. They seemed to be there an age.

I would email them tonight. Say your ex-husband, who you've reported as having harassed you, might send in some pornographic deepfake material. Tell them you've reported it to the police.

I haven't reported it to the police though.

You need to. Sufiyan said it wasn't good. Trust me on this. Let's meet tomorrow. Email HR now.

Safa started typing, then paused. Her own three dots must be bobbing up on the sister screen. Then she minimized the app and opened her email with shaking thumbs.

Safa paused again. She gazed around her living room. The little photo of her, Javeria and Aleena on the cupboard. The sofa cushions that Haaris had always hated. The copy of *Pride and Prejudice* from GCSE English Lit that she was trying to get through as an adult. Safa had thought she would be safe here. The evil eye pendant was useless. She put a thumb and a forefinger over her eyelids. Emaan was right. She had to get in front of this. But she wouldn't use the word *pornographic*. It was too loaded. There was no point alarming anyone unnecessarily. She put the phone down and dipped two trembling fingers in the face mask cream. She smeared a streak across her forehead and then down the bridge of her nose. The website said it would act like a magnet to draw out impurities. It would cleanse deep.

She rubbed her fingers into her palm and then picked up her phone. She tried to draw a steadying breath.

At the end of the email, Safa paused. Her whole body was thrumming with electricity. She felt frantic. Parts of her were shaking that she wasn't even aware had muscles to tremble. She took another deep breath. Keep it professional. Be measured and composed. She reread the email.

I will be making a police report in the morning and will keep you updated with the progress of the case, she finally typed, reining in her desperate fingers, refusing to allow them to skitter across the keypad. She was a D6. She had several teams working for her. She couldn't fire off an agitated email at ten o'clock at night. People would think she was berserk.

Kind regards, Safa Asaad, she typed. Thank God she had kept her last name.

She hit send, went to open WhatsApp and tell Emaan, when her screen went blank. For a second, she was sure the email to HR had triggered something. A close-down clause. She was going to be fired for gross misconduct. For bringing the company into disrepute. Then, a huge, unknown number blared out across the top of the screen. The slider flashed indignantly at her, demanding to be answered. The fear in her chest cavity was replaced with anger in one, huge, rushing wave.

She snapped the call open.

'Leave me the fuck alone!' she shouted.

There was silence from the other end.

'Hello?' a woman's voice said. 'Sorry? Safa?'

Safa bit her knuckle. Shit.

'Sorry, who's this?' she said quickly.

'It's Sophia.'

Safa let out a long breath. The smell of the face mask was suddenly too much. Sophia. Of all people. She hadn't spoken to Sophia, to any of them, in years. It was for the best. She had wiped her phone of their numbers and messages. If she tried to divorce Haaris and then it came out she'd been involved in a murder cover-up, that she'd lied in a statement to police, she'd lose any chance of getting visitation rights, let alone custody.

'Sophia. Sorry. I'm sorry. I thought it was Haaris.'

'Is everything OK?'

'Yes. It's fine.' Safa's heart was thumping in her chest. It didn't seem to have a rhythm at all. It was just thundering against her ribs, beating against her breastbone. 'Why are you calling me?'

'Somebody knows what we did.'

Safa had no air in her lungs to give strength to her voice. She felt herself collapsing inwards. This was exactly why she had tried to keep Sophia at arm's length.

'Safa? Will you meet with me and the others?'

Safa looked at the photo of the girls.

'I never wanted you to call me,' she whispered.

'I know.'

'Text me the details,' Safa said. 'I'll think about it.'

She had received a gif during the call from an unknown number. She very nearly lost herself and opened it. She clamped her forefinger to her palm at the last second, the sound of alarm bells cutting through her fear and singing clearly in her ears.

Sophia

IN APRIL, BEFORE the five of them were summoned back together once more, Sophia had finally seen Jill Caister. For real. In the flesh. A mum from school was turning thirty and had invited out basically every woman who had ever dropped off at the school gates. Sophia had gone knowing everyone without knowing anyone, and resigned herself to standing awkwardly in the corner all night. She gave the birthday girl a cheek press *mwah mwah*, handed over her card and lamented her own thirtieth birthday party.

'A long time ago now.'

'Not that long, Sophia! Don't do that to yourself!'

'Soon I'll be inviting you to my fortieth!'

She had turned from this exchange to address the barman and there was Jill Caister. Sitting on a bar stool, gesticulating effortlessly with a glass of red wine in hand, chic honey hair pinned back from her head. Around her were three or four mums from the school gate. They were all contorted into some stage of hysterics, eyes fixed on Jill as she entertained. She had always been funny at school. Full of stories and hilarious jokes.

Sophia felt her face blush and quickly turned away. She patted her own hair. She smoothed down her clothes. In Year 6 Jill had once asked her why she always had jack-ups. Everyone had laughed. Now, trousers with jack-ups were the fashion. In fact, Sophia was wearing jack-ups right then: beige chinos that finished at her ankle, revealing a slice of skin before the tongue of her shoe. Would Jill notice? Would she point out the jack-ups and make a withering comment.

'Twenty- three years and you haven't changed your trousers, Sophia?'

'Are they the same pair from 2000, Sophia?'

'You never did understand fashion, eh, Sophia?'

Sophia slid down the bar, trying to get as far away from Jill as possible. Her face was flushing worse than ever. Under the intense scrutiny of Jill's gaze, her adult-self would crumble. The entire image she had managed to craft at the school gates of a respectable mother, a working woman who could talk and socialize and was assimilated into mainstream society, would shatter. Jill would draw from within her all those little traits and habits that denied her her womanhood. She was still just eight years old. Flat, pale, naive. Writing her endless, pointless stories in the ICT suite.

The birthday girl danced away to greet another mum, who handed her a bottle of champagne. Sophia took that as her cue and, head down, left the pub altogether. She went home and drew the curtains, afraid that Jill's face might pop up outside the window.

'Oh my God! You left so early. What are you? Twelve?'

Sophia had spent seven years floating through a half-existence. It had taken her a while to come out of the shock of Chris's death. It had made her so anxious for so long. There was such violence there. For many months, she had to learn to bear the weight of scrutiny from police, family, friends, as they combed through her and Chris's life. Upon discovering nothing untoward, the weight had eased, but never completely. Chris, declared long-term missing now, would always be a question mark, for everyone. She had kept her job at the doctor's surgery, mainly, she felt, through pity. Now, Isla was growing up into a stable human being and Sophia was writing, regularly, beautifully, incessantly. She hadn't had anything published yet but she knew that without the pervasive presence of Chris, her time would come. She would continue to grow. She couldn't believe Jill had chosen this time to come into her life once more.

Sophia had often found herself wondering, in still, deep moments, like the centre of a lake, what Jill would think of the events surrounding her husband's demise. Caoimhe wiping the blood with a kitchen towel, the body in the boot, the Wicca circle of trees, Ajola chanting as the stars winked down at them. It was all very Jill. Very eerie, very *gothic*. Imbued with the elements that Jill sought out whilst they were at school. Was she better than Jill for having done it? Wiser, sage, heavy with secrets. Or would Jill see through it all and just recognize the pathetic little eight-year-old who couldn't stand up for herself. The luminous spectre of Jill had dogged her for over twenty years, popping up, sometimes ethereally, sometimes more tangibly. One of her biggest fears, a gut-wrenching stomach-surge that caught her in the early mornings and prevented her from getting back to sleep, was that Jill would become a famous author, whose books would be turned into multi-million-pound franchises and whose face would grace the cover of magazines. She would wrinkle her nose at the camera. She would look straight at Sophia and feel Sophia looking back.

After the birthday party, Sophia braced herself to meet Jill at the school gates. She didn't know why fate, the great cosmic turning of wheels and spheres, had conspired to bring her back into the orbit of Jill Caister, but it had. She stopped writing and, for several weeks, spent her free time every morning putting on make-up, styling her hair and selecting a co-ordinated outfit, activities she hadn't done in seven years since Chris had been alive.

'Why are you trying so hard all of a sudden?' Isla asked her one morning as she put on her school shoes by the front door. 'You don't fancy someone, do you?'

Sophia had snorted.

'Like who? Mrs Musgrove?'

'No, like some rich dad from the doctor's surgery who's going to end up moving in with us.'

The idea was so repulsive to Sophia, she made a vomit sound.

'No way,' she said and slipped her own shoes on. She opened the front door. 'I just want to feel good about myself.'

Isla had slowly walked past her, frowning directly into her face.

Then, after weeks of nothing, one Friday, on her day off from the doctor's surgery, when she had allowed herself to wear simply a pair of Sainsbury's small men's tracksuit bottoms and a T-shirt that didn't cover her disgustingly pale upper arms, there was Jill. At the school gate. As if in a dream.

Sophia walked up the path, Isla having already gone through

the main doors. It was Jill. No doubt. Trust Jill to turn up on the one day she dressed like a seven-year-old. Surrounded in a halo of golden morning sunlight, beaming at the other women who had gathered at her elbows. Had she always been so tall? Did she whiten those perfect teeth? How was her hair so luscious?

Time normalized. Sophia was staring at Jill, and Jill was now staring right back at her. She wanted to quickly look away, to hide her shame. The tracksuit bottoms! The T-shirt! The Nike flip-flops that had belonged to her dead husband! It was as if every horror that had been etched into her soul over the years was being regurgitated before her. How long had she been staring, unsmiling – a second? Half a second? Maybe a quarter?

She decided to hurry home. But as she stepped on to the top path, fully committed to smiling politely and then skulking off, she suddenly changed her mind. It had been twenty-three years. Twenty-three! And Jill had always been smart and funny. She had been good fun. It might be nice to have a new friend. After the burial, she had deliberately lost touch with Caoimhe, Safa, Ajola and Ella so they could all have plausible deniability if she ever got arrested. Jill could offer a substantial friendship. They could go to clubs together. Perhaps Krav Maga or Creative Writing. Jill was no longer an immature eleven-year-old. She was a woman now. Reasonable. Responsible. It would be good to have a friend.

'Jill,' she said and stopped at the gate. There was no need to be ashamed of her clothes! She was a woman. She had periods, she'd given birth, she went for regular smear tests. She wore the medals of womanhood regardless of her choice in trousers. 'Oh my God, how are you?'

Jill looked out of the side of her eye and turned her head slightly away. For one horrifying moment, Sophia thought she was going to ignore her. Then she let out a little laugh and said, 'Fine.'

'Let me guess,' Sophia said, trying to draw up from within her some of her fun personality. 'You're married to Joseph Burton.'

Jill laughed again but, this time, it seemed more genuine. She made eye contact with Sophia and there was a twinkle there. A little gleam. Sophia smiled back. She was suddenly compelled to embrace Jill.

'How do you two know each other?' another mum at the gate asked.

Sophia and Jill continued to smile at one another.

'We went to school together,' Jill said. She was wearing beige chinos that finished at her ankle, revealing a slice of skin above the tongue of her shoe.

'Primary school,' Sophia added. 'Nineteen ninety-seven. *Titanic* and *Harry Potter*. Kathleen Henny's mum always came in to help at lunchtimes.'

'The one who looked like Justin from the Darkness.'

Sophia laughed, much louder than she had wanted to, but she was nervous. There was something so comforting about seeing Jill's face. So familiar, so warm and centring. She forced herself to look away because she was mooning at her as if she was in love. 'What are you doing here, Jill?'

'I live here,' she said as though it was the most obvious thing in the world.

'Yes. But how? Why here?'

Jill raised a shoulder in a one-sided shrug.

'I could ask you the same thing,' she said.

Jill was being deliberately obtuse, but Sophia just laughed. Inexplicably, she was desperately excited to explain to Jill how her husband had vanished one night seven years ago. Maybe Jill would be intrigued. She would think, ah, Sophia isn't like everyone else after all.

'Did I tell you we're going back to Arizona in July?' Julie, a parent from Isla's class, suddenly announced. 'The Grand Canyon,' she added in a terrible impression of an American accent. 'I mean' – Julie put a hand to her chest – 'the majesty of the place, it just, it just reminds us how trivial we all are.'

The other mums all murmured in agreement. Jill caught Sophia's eye. She raised her eyebrows in mock-shock and mouthed *not me*. Sophia grinned back.

The text sprang up on her phone in June, soon after that smile at the school gates. The sight of it momentarily took Sophia's breath away. She heard the great wrenching of the gears of her life as a spanner was hurled into them. The text blared up at her, loud and imposing, deafening. Isla was in the kitchen getting a juice but she might as well have been on the moon. Sophia rubbed her thumb across the screen and stared at it.

I know where you buried your husband.

Hey bitch. Another message flashed up, almost instantly. Jill Caister. What you up to?

FINSBURY PARK

Caoimhe

'WELL, BEFORE THE pandemic, Screenworks used to own that unit' – Aidan pointed ahead – 'that unit' – he pointed over his shoulder – 'and . . .' – he looked around at the buildings towering above them and then inclined his head at a huge, hulking warehouse, grey, like the hull of a ship – 'that unit there.'

'Rent must have been astronomical for all that space,' Mateus said and Aidan gave an enthusiastic 'hmm'. Caoimhe tried to think of something clever and interesting to interject into the conversation here, but she couldn't think straight. She kept glancing about her, wondering who might be watching.

'Next rep.' Azaiyah held up his stopwatch. 'On my whistle in three, two . . .'

They exploded forward. Mateus to the front straight away, Porter and Aidan on his heels, Caoimhe on theirs, and then the interchangeable mass of James, Ian and Chris behind. There was a good turnout that night, although Caoimhe was pleased to see the new woman, Evie, wasn't there. She had been hanging around since last Thursday, hair piled on top of her head, oversized Garmin on her skinny wrist, having the audacity to finish before Caoimhe on every rep. Caoimhe almost hadn't come out to training that night, either. After Sophia's call, she had postponed her work projects and just sat at home looking out of the window for any suspicious figures. It would be safer to stay at home. But she couldn't do it. She felt compelled to turn up. To show the new woman she was a force to be reckoned with.

'They do logos,' Aidan said after they'd finished the 500-metre rep around the industrial estate's lorry park. 'Logos on hats. Jumpers. Business cards. Not generic ones,' he added. 'Personal ones.'

Porter nodded and wiped the sweat off his moustache with a thumb and forefinger. Mateus was breathing hard, hands on hips, pelvis thrust forward, his thinning hair sodden, saturated, with sweat. Caoimhe looked at his broad shoulders. She couldn't work out if she fancied him a little bit. Just a lil bit. There was something about physical prowess that was so attractive.

'Always money in logos,' Mateus said.

Caoimhe racked her brain for an addition to the conversation. Pandemic, rent, storage, floor space.

'Advertising.' Porter nodded. 'Old as time.'

'That's wild,' Caoimhe settled for.

'Next rep.' Azaiyah put the whistle in his mouth. 'Three,' he said, voice muffled around the metal. 'Two . . .'

They leapt off again. For this rep, Caoimhe drew level with Aidan. He'd gone too fast on the first set. She deigned to run beside him for 450 metres and then, for the final fifty, she cruised ahead, an untameable power, feeding off his fatigue, his fading gait.

'You do sweat,' Mateus said, looking at her as she finished right behind him. 'You are mortal, eh?'

'Logos on cars,' Aidan said, coming to a stop beside them. 'Vans, lorries.'

'That's wild,' Caoimhe said again.

'Bet they lost money during the pandemic,' Porter added.

'I know someone' – Mateus pointed at Caoimhe and she felt herself blush – 'business *expanded* during the pandemic.'

'On my whistle,' Azaiyah said.

Caoimhe took advantage of Porter's hesitation and shot in front of him, tucking in close behind Mateus. Every time he lifted his trainer, she made sure she put hers right on his footprint. She could see the sweat patch on his back. She wanted to reach out and put her palm between his shoulder blades.

'I always asked him,' Mateus said when they'd finished the rep, '"Mate, what do you do?"' He turned to smile at Caoimhe. 'He would tell me "nothing". Must do something. They don't pay you to do nothing. And he still said, "Nothing." So I said, "Can I have a job?"'

Caoimhe laughed extra loudly.

'That's wild,' she said.

'Last rep!' Azaiyah announced as the rest of the group came tearing in around them. 'Last one. Bring it together for this last one. Three, two . . .'

Caoimhe tore off beside Mateus. She kept pace with him, to the top of the park, around the street lamp, across the gated entrance, down, down towards Azaiyah, standing near the back in his fluorescent jacket, staring at his stopwatch. She could feel Mateus slowing. How much was he ahead? A second? Half a second? Maybe a quarter? She had never been this close to him before. Not in seven years. She knew it was worth her coming out tonight, despite Sophia's call. She thought about surging ahead and beating him in the final metres but chose against it. She wanted him to like her.

He let out a loud groan as they finished and promptly collapsed on the floor, laying back to stare at the sky.

'That rep wasn't *that* fast,' Azaiyah said, glancing up from the watch.

'It's this one here.' Mateus sat up and nodded at Caoimhe. 'On me, every step.'

'It's not steep, but hard,' Porter said as the rest of the group finished. Caoimhe liked the way they formed a circle, unspeaking, and she stood in their ranks, shoulder to shoulder with the men. An untameable power. One of the boys. God, she was glad that new woman wasn't here.

'Like my lovemaking,' Aidan said and everyone laughed loudly, heads tilted back, Adam's apples bobbing, broad chests heaving with cavernous laughter. Caoimhe gave a laugh, too, but made sure it was the antithesis of the men, tinkling, light, demure, rubbing her earlobe as she looked down with a smirk, a smile, knowing. Hmm, hmm, a sex joke, how scintillating.

'I just knew you'd say that,' Mateus said.

'I don't like to disappoint.'

'Unlike your lovemaking,' Porter chipped in and everyone laughed again. Big, solid, sounds. *Ha. Ha. Ha.* Caoimhe tinkled in her throat again, rubbing her earlobe. Had to make them like her.

She glanced over her shoulder and saw someone leaning by a lorry trailer up the road, watching the group. Their face was hidden behind a large pair of sunglasses. They sipped from a Costa Coffee cup.

'Let's go,' Caoimhe said, turning away. She clapped her hands and pointed towards the canal cut-through that led to the leisure centre.

'I like a woman in charge,' Aidan said.

'You coming Thursday?' Mateus asked her as they walked.

'What's Thursday?'

'AGM.'

'No.' Caoimhe nearly scoffed; why would she ever go to an AGM? But she didn't want to offend Mateus, so she just shook her head. 'I'm in London.'

'What do you want to go to London for? It's full of immigrants.' Caoimhe laughed. 'It's true,' Mateus insisted.

She didn't know what he meant by that, but she wanted him to fancy her a little bit, just a lil bit, so she nodded and said, 'That's wild. I'm meeting my friends.'

Now Mateus did scoff.

She ran back home after the training session, having been too afraid to take her car in case someone got into the back seat. The sun was just beginning to set, turning the cerulean blue a mystic pink. Caoimhe had read that when Krakatoa erupted in 1883, the explosion had been so large and the fallout so devastating, sunsets around the world had become vivid crimson for months afterwards. It must have been like this. Something tangible in the air. A feeling. A threat.

Crossing the pedestrian bridge over the main road, she saw him. It was a moment on which she felt etched, the incident looming so large it created an impression on the fabric of time. He was running down the shadowy road, directly beneath her.

Slim, strong, sinuous. Arms and legs, elbows and knees and thick, dark hair. His black beard was cut to a point, offset above by sharp, angular eyebrows. A red and orange skull cap, mystic, like the sky, covered his hair. His gait was solid, fluid, like the meander of a river, and he was travelling so fast.

She gazed down at him and he, sensing her, looked up. They stared at one another. It was a second, maybe half, maybe a quarter, but it stretched, eternal, he approaching the bridge, she running over it. Her mouth gaped. He looked as if he was scowling, so defiant were his eyebrows.

And then he passed under the bridge exactly where she was, so that, for a heartbeat, their bodies were aligned. She stopped running and turned to watch him canter down the road, both of her hands resting on the top of the railings. It was worth risking coming out just for this. He glanced back over his shoulder and saw her standing there, beneath the glowing pink sky. She had never met Rohan Rust. She had read about him in the local paper. She had seen his name published at the top of race reports. She had heard everyone at her running club praise him. But actually seeing him was like seeing a celebrity. It felt predetermined. Etched in the stars. She was destined to see him like this. To know him.

He turned back to face the way he was running and disappeared out of sight on the bend. Caoimhe let out her breath.

Ella

ELLA HAD MET Felix just days after they had bound Chris's body to the earth. Back then, she felt that the two events were symbiotic. One breathing against the other. He was tall and slim, smartly dressed, with clipped, clean, light brown hair and sharp blue eyes. When she first saw him, she wondered how anyone could be so handsome. By the time she told him she wanted to separate with a view to divorce, she thought he looked like a homeless man asking for spare change outside the Londis. He worked as an engineer for a company which, in 2016, had just landed a government contract. They met at a dinner in Whitehall and then again, a week later, at a fundraising event in Islington. He was a decade older than her but, in the early days, he didn't look it. At that Whitehall dinner, their eyes had met across the room. Ella had felt as though something had struck her. For a moment, she was paralysed. Her eyes fixed to his. She could not blink. It was as if this man was known to her. Something about him familiar, a face she knew. He was staring back, mouth shut firm, long arms and slender hands frozen in the act of pulling out his chair from the table, bright eyes sharp and focused. She wanted to cross to him. She wanted him to cross to her.

Time suddenly caught up with them both and she was introduced to a barrister who worked at the Doughty Street Chambers, whilst someone pulled out the chair for him and gestured for him to sit. She spent the rest of the night craning over everyone's heads, trying to see him, as he was craning his head back to look at her.

'I feel I know you,' he said later at the fundraiser in Islington. They had finally come to close proximity at the bar. She had recognized him at once and, when he saw her, he turned from the people he was talking to and offered his hand to shake. She felt the contact in the recesses of her heart.

'I feel I know you,' she replied and put a piece of gum in her mouth.

The blank void that had been created by her distancing herself from the others, from distancing herself from what they had done in the copse, Felix filled like rushing air. It was a relief to have him. He made her feel as if she had shed her old life. The body. The ground. That hadn't been her. That had been someone else.

They got married in 2017, a small ceremony, just the two of them in a register office, and had Benjamin in 2019. Felix's job was very stressful. It aged him. He became gaunt; his light brown hair became thin and grey. The angular wrists that had seemed so lithe and masterful in 2016 suddenly appeared emaciated. The frequency of his working from home increased, as did the phone conversations where he raged, shouting and gesticulating as he strode around their front room, his eyes flashing. His family was from Germany originally and when he was in one of these moods, a few choice phrases crept into his language that she couldn't translate into English.

She felt she had made it very clear she was considering ending things. She raised her grievances with him in a logical narrative several times over the years. She explained how she was feeling. She communicated explicitly. But he would shake his head, sure that nothing would ever change for them. The night she told him she was leaving, the horror of it made him put his hand to his mouth. She had seen people do it on TV but never like this, in real life. It was an instinctive gesture. He covered his mouth. He was repulsed. Revulsed. Horrified. That day, he was gaunter than ever, dark shadows under those sharp, bright eyes, his thinning hair longer than usual and unkempt. His smart attire had slowly faded from his wardrobe over the years and he stood before her in a pair of tapered tracksuit bottoms and a sweatshirt whose sleeves were too short for his long arms. She had felt sorry for him. It would be so easy to decide not to leave. To sit down and embrace him, to calm him and undo the horror she had created. She didn't, though. Her breaking heart spurred her on and she left. Six weeks later, when she actually presented him with divorce papers, he cried. She had never seen him cry before. He pinched the corners of his eyes with a thumb and a forefinger, bowed his head and cried. During those six weeks, he had taken to wearing a baseball cap to cover up his terrible hairline. Seeing him hunched over, forcing back tears, unshaven and with that baseball cap on, Ella had very nearly retracted the papers.

'You need to see someone,' she said instead. 'A doctor or a therapist or something.'

She wondered how someone could change so much in seven years. His looks, his presence. He was just someone different now, as she was, too.

Upon reflection, the timing of Sophia's call wasn't unusual; Felix and the burial were symbiotic. It made sense that as Felix left, Chris's body was going to rise from the earth.

Her appointment with Eric that Thursday was meant to be brief. She had instructed Cynthia Colum, the barrister who usually worked with her firm, to take on Eric's case and represent him in the civil court proceedings. Ella now just wanted to pass this information on but Eric tended to get side-tracked and would often pontificate for long periods of time on the merits of anti-natalism.

'We can add that in,' he told her after reading from a *True Detective* meme.

'I'll see what Cynthia thinks,' Ella said, making a note to never bring up *True Detective*. She raised her hand at him and half got up from her chair. He didn't move. He was scrolling through his phone. He had put on a little more weight in the last seven years and had a scraggly beard that seemed thicker at his neck and thinner on his face. His sunglasses were perched on top of his curly hair and as he jerked his head up to look at her, the sunglasses slipped off the back of his head. Ella imperceptibly moved her gum to the other side of her mouth. The waistband of his trousers wasn't high enough and, as he bent to get the glasses, she could see about a third of his completely smooth and hairless arse crack. He sat up and Ella pretended she had been looking at her phone.

'Still,' he said, jerking down his T-shirt and putting his glasses back on his head. He nearly dropped his phone, juggling it against his belly with his flabby, hairless hands. 'It shows this case has merit.'

Ella walked around the desk and opened the door for him. Maduka jumped out of his chair and held up his hands in an apologetic way. For a heart-stopping second, Ella thought the police were here. They knew. After seven years, it was all over. Her brother would sack her. She would go to prison. Then she saw Felix sitting on the leather settee by the window. He still had the baseball cap on. Even worse: tapered tracksuit bottoms that emphasized his skinny legs and a dark sweatshirt under a puffy sports gilet. She froze when she saw him, paralysed, as she had been seven years before, but with a distinctly different feeling in her chest. He rose gently to his feet and raised his eyebrows at her, adjusting the peak of his cap. It cast a dark shadow over his already haggard face.

'I just think we should show this feeling is universal.' Eric's voice floated from inside her office.

Felix glanced behind her and then back to her face.

'I just want one moment.' His accent seemed particularly strong. Was it because she had become desensitized to it whilst they were together? He held up a skeletal finger. It infuriated her to see he was still wearing his wedding ring.

Maduka had the sense to get up from behind his desk and pretend to file some papers at the cabinet.

'Felix. You can't just turn up here. I have appointments. This is my work. My brother would hate it, especially with . . .' She gestured at him. 'There's a' – she held out her hands – 'perception I need to uphold.'

She turned around and looked at the back of Eric's head. He was still in his chair, chin tucked on to his chest, scrolling through his phone.

'Eric,' she said, trying to find control. 'I have another client. I'll see you tomorrow when we meet with Cynthia.' Eric turned, resting one arm on the back of the chair. He looked past Ella to Felix. 'Maduka will send you the information.'

Eric heaved himself up, adjusted the waistband of his trousers and moved out of the office. He had a funny smell about him. Not quite sweat, not quite cologne. She tried not to inhale as he passed. Maybe this was how people felt when they smelt her breath.

'Why are you here?' Ella said when he had gone.

'I was working nearby,' Felix said, 'and just thought I would come in and see you.'

Maduka stood up and left the room, closing the door behind him. Ella breathed a sharp sigh.

'Felix. We're not married any more. It's inappropriate for you to turn up here.'

'Not inappropriate.' He held his splayed fingers against his chest. 'How inappropriate? We were married six years. We're raising a child together. It is very appropriate.' Felix drew up one side of his mouth and glanced into some faraway corner of the room. For one second, Ella thought he might start crying again. 'I want us to talk tonight.'

'No, Felix.'

'Just about logistics.'

'I can't, Felix. I'm going out tonight, anyway.'

His head jerked up. She wasn't sure where that lie had come from.

'Going out where? Who has Benjamin?'

'Seline.' The lie continued. 'I'm seeing Sophia and the girls.'

'Sophia? After all these years? Why?'

That was a good question. Felix's appearance seemed prescient, on that day of all days, as though he knew before she did. The two events had always been symbiotic.

'I just am.'

'Why Seline? You're paying someone to look after him?' He put a hand on his chest again. 'I will look after him.' His other hand curled into a fist, the same fist he used to beat the steering wheel when people didn't indicate. 'You must ask me.'

'Felix, I'm not ringing you up to get Benjamin all out of routine.'

'I'll keep his routine. Dinner, bath, bed.'

'Felix. No. It's not appropriate.'

'This word again.' He shook his head and folded his arms. 'What could be more appropriate?'

'I divorced you so we could stop having these conversations,' she said. 'Please go, Felix. It's going to be really awkward if my brother needs to have you removed.'

He stood, long and lean, shoulders curled like a question mark. She really wished he wouldn't wear the hat. It would be better to take it off and just shave his thinning hair. Go bald.

When he had gone, she texted Sophia.

I'm coming. I'll have Benjamin with me.

When she had filed for divorce, she had wanted Felix to contest the custody arrangement. He was a better parent, always steady with Benjamin, calm. Loving. She, on the other hand, tormented Benjamin. She screamed in his face; she pushed him away when he was upset. But she couldn't tell anyone, and her solicitor had organized for her to get sole physical custody. She had wished so badly for Felix to fight this. She would have let him have it. Let Benjamin grow up with someone who didn't torture him. But Felix hadn't said anything. He must think she was the better parent. God, she was evil. How could Benjamin possibly assimilate into society with a mother like her.

Maduka came back in the room and raised his eyebrows at her. Ella just shook her head. This was why she needed Eric to win the suit.

Safa

SAFA HAD LEFT some steaks out on the side to defrost while she went to pick the girls up from school. She used a pair of scissors from the kitchen drawer to shear a hole in the plastic and let the air circulate. When they returned, Javeria and Aleena clattered into the family room, shouting at one another and shedding their school clothes behind them like layers off a chrysalis.

'No television yet!' Safa said. 'I need to see spellings and times tables.'

The school always set an inordinate amount of unnecessary homework. Make a rainforest in a jar. Draw a poster to persuade people to go green. Research Roman numbers. Ajola said it was all crap to tick an Ofsted box. But spellings and times tables were important.

'I didn't get spellings!' a voice wheedled down the hall behind her.

'Get them online!' Safa called back. 'Your teacher posts them online!'

She picked up her phone. She had a notification from Emaan.

She had only just said goodbye to Emaan an hour or so before. The two of them had gone to the local police station to make a report about harassment, but the haggard-looking desk attendant had told them it would be more effective to do it online.

'It's quite serious,' Emaan said. She leant across Safa to talk through the plastic grille. 'It's traumatizing and is threatening her job.'

'I understand. It is just faster to do it online.'

'Come,' Safa said and tugged Emaan's hand. The phone call with Sophia had spooked her. Uneven shivers cascaded down her spine. She didn't want to be anywhere near the police right now. 'Let's just do it at home.'

'It's easier to do it alone at home than here with an officer?' Emaan's voice was indignant.

The attendant spread their hands.

'It's up to you.'

Emaan looked at Safa.

'Let's go home,' Safa pleaded. She felt as if there was a 'suspicious' label flashing over her head. She couldn't lose custody of the girls.

'Just to let you know,' Emaan said, raising a long finger at the desk attendant. 'If anything happens to her, any type of verbal assault or physical altercation or if she faces some sort of disciplinary at work, I'm coming back here to raise it with' – she waved her finger – 'whoever is in charge.'

'The online support is really good,' the attendant replied.

So they sat in Safa's tiny living room instead and typed the details into the online form.

'I got a message and a gif,' Safa said as Emaan pulled the

laptop on to her knees. 'But I didn't open it. It could have been anything.'

'We'll put it down,' Emaan said and her fingers clacked frantically over the keyboard. 'It's all harassment if you're afraid to look at your phone. Where did you get that from?'

She nodded at the evil eye pendant Safa had taped to the edge of her laptop.

'Some homeless woman. Fat lot of good it's doing me, though.'

A pit opened up in her stomach each time a message from Emaan came in now. She was so grateful to have her in her life, but it did seem that their only topic of conversation was Haaris and how he was a plague upon her soul. How nice it might be to open a message from Emaan asking if she wanted to go to the cinema.

Safa picked up her phone and walked to the side to get the steaks. When she got to the counter, she saw a dark black smudge under the plastic, smeared against the pink flesh of the meat. She poked the smudge, finding it hard, like a mole on someone's skin. The edges bristled.

She reached for the scissors and sliced open the packaging to get a better look. It was a great fat fly, lying completely still on the meat. Safa had never seen a fly stay so still for so long. Its wings weren't moving and it wasn't rubbing its hands together. She wondered if it had become frozen on the meat and perhaps gone into a cryogenic state. She peered closer. Beneath the fly were three or four oblong specks of white. Frost? Fragments of string from some stage of the butchering process? As she watched, another white speck was squeezed from the fly's round body and added to the pile. She had never seen anything so horrifying in her life as this, a housefly laying its eggs on her dinner. But she could not look away. Part of her wanted to squash the fly immediately, but another, stranger part wanted to lift the meat to her eye and examine the birthing process more closely. How long had the meat been out? An hour? What if flies did this in her kitchen all the time? How many fly eggs had she consumed in her life?

Her phone pinged again in her hand and she jumped. Another message from Emaan.

Tell me you aren't upset! Now you're free!

She opened the messages and scrolled up to see the pictures that Emaan had sent. The first was a screenshot taken from Instagram of Haaris with his arm around the shoulders of a young white woman. She was very beautiful, leaning into Haaris and staring at the camera with dark, soulful eyes. Safa lifted the screen to her eyes and examined the picture more closely. It was definitely Haaris. She swiped right to the next picture. It was a screenshot of Haaris's bio, several love heart emojis *@hellomissdaniellebloom* and then an emoji with hearts for eyes.

She lowered the phone. How strange. Inside her, there was an absence of feeling. Almost as if the pit that had opened at the sight of Emaan's message was now sucking all her emotion into it. And what unusual timing. Right after Sophia got in touch. She swiped up and examined the photo of the smiling white woman carefully. She was too beautiful for Haaris. Was something else at play here. Was this a threat?

Definitely not upset, Safa typed back. Perhaps confused would be a better assessment.

Man, tell me about it. What in the actual freck?

Safa set her phone down on the side and picked up the packet of meat. She felt curiously dizzy. Is this what people meant when they said news sent their head spinning? Her stomach wasn't nauseous, not at all, it just felt heavy, as though she had stepped off a ride and her brain didn't realize she was now standing still.

'Forget the spellings,' she said, walking past the living-room door. Both girls were kneeling at the coffee table, pencils in hand, bent over their sheets of paper. She felt a strange electricity in her cheeks. 'Let's go and get a KFC.'

Javeria and Aleena cheered and jumped up. Safa collected her keys and they all clattered out of the flat. On the way down the front path, Safa dropped the packet of meat – fly, eggs and all – into the dustbin.

Ajola

WHEN AJOLA FIRST started teaching, before she buried a body, she had had a pupil called Meg. Meg was extremely bright. Not just bright, but *greater depth*. She was only seven years old, but she had read novels far beyond her years: *Great Expectations*, *The Hound of the Baskervilles*, even *The Great Gatsby*. She was a real-life little Matilda. She didn't have many friends and found it hard to verbalize in class, always averting her eyes and pulling her sleeves down over her hands. There was a spark there, though, a glimmer of something that Ajola felt her soul respond to. She sometimes caught Meg looking at her and she would smile and there would be an understanding.

'She's such a handful at home,' her mother told Ajola one night after school. She had booked a special appointment to talk to her while Meg waited nervously outside the door, chewing her nails, her big eyes shining with tears. 'I can't control her. You won't believe me, but she screams. She bangs her head against the walls.'

'I believe you,' Ajola said without blinking.

'I see the worst of her. She, she . . .' Her mother looked up at the sunflower clock above the board; the leaves were ticking closer to four o'clock. Her neck had flushed red. 'She is very bright. We know that. But she pushes herself too hard. I feel she gets no downtime.' Ajola was nodding. 'Then she's tearing her hair out or throwing things. She'd be mortified if she knew I was telling you this, by the way.'

'I won't say anything.'

Meg's mother looked at her fingers as they each picked the nail of another.

'But I also think she isn't being challenged. Stimulated?' Ajola nodded. 'I just wish Meg had a close friend who . . . I don't know.' Meg's mother lifted her shoulders up and then dropped them. 'I don't expect you to be able to do anything,' she quickly added, placing a hand on the table. 'Maybe she needs therapy.'

'I can put her on the list to see the school counsellor,' Ajola suggested. 'Maybe you can take her to after-school clubs?'

Meg's mother just lifted her shoulders again and gave a pained smile. She picked up her little bag and swung the thin strap over her shoulder. When she opened the door, Meg rushed to take her hand. Ajola felt a little left out.

For the rest of that school year, she tried to forge a bond with Meg. They could discuss stories together: Shakespeare, Virginia Woolf, Ernest Hemingway. They could just sit and chat. She wanted to provide the downtime. She wanted to provide the stimulation. She wanted Meg to know she would never, ever be alone. Sometimes, in fleeting moments, she thought she was building something. A smile, maybe, that knowing look. Then Meg moved up into Year 4 and it all evaporated.

After Ajola had buried a body, Meg left the school in Year 6 no different to how she had been in Year 3. Gifted, brilliant, but alone. Over the years, Ajola had sometimes accidentally said Meg's name in the place of another pupil's. She didn't know why. It was just always there. On the tip of her tongue. Many times, Ajola had tried to find her. Typing her name into Google and Facebook, or scouring lists of prize-winners from the local secondary school. Her name never came up. She only existed now with Ajola, in her classroom. In the faces of the students she scanned every day, looking for that spark of recognition.

Then, that morning, just before Sophia called, Ajola found her. She was still staring at her phone, trying to put all the pieces together, when Yashica and Daisy came into the classroom. The room was dark.

'Can we stay in and finish our homework?' Yashica said. 'Please, please, please, pretty please with a cherry on top?'

Ajola stared at her, unblinking. What child said things like that? Had Yashica heard that somewhere and genuinely thought it would sway her? Or was she using it ironically? Yashica's big brown eyes blinked up at her. Her smirk seemed teasing, taunting. *Bitch.*

'Maybe,' Ajola said and Yashica jumped in the air (a perfect tuck jump, arms extended above her head like an Olympic gymnast) and screamed. 'But I have to go and talk to Mrs Greene about break duty.'

'Ohhhh, boo!' Yashica cried.

Daisy hadn't moved at all in the exchange. It was hard to tell if she was even smiling behind her jumper sleeve.

Yashica pouted and stuck her hip out, then turned and strode out of the door.

'Are you OK, Daisy?' Ajola asked.

Daisy looked up at her with her huge eyes. There was that spark. Ajola wanted to say something. To breach the gap. She could almost see the connect between them: she just needed to grasp it.

Daisy nodded and then turned away as well. Ajola leant forward and put her face in her hands. She had received an email that morning from an address she didn't recognize. It contained a link to a BBC News website, one of the forgotten fluff pieces, with the headline 'The Unanswered Questions'. The thumbnail for the link was a picture of Meg's mother.

Ajola had clicked the link immediately and been presented with a huge image of several people, all standing grimly like Meg's mother, the aesthetics grey.

How can we go on with so many unanswered questions? I spoke with several parents whose children all died by suicide, in order to try to understand how they came to terms with such a horrendous event.

Meg was just fourteen when she took her own life. She was a bright, gifted pupil who had so many hopes and ambitions for her future.

'I often wonder if it came from nowhere,' her mother said, 'or if I should have known.'

That meant Meg had been dead for four years. All this time, and she was already dead. Meg was dead. Who had sent her the email? Ajola could remember playing iSpy with her class and Meg had said 'W' when it was her turn and no one in the class could work out what the 'W' might be. And then Meg had pointed to a crumpled piece of paper by the bin. Of

113

course! A wrapper. And now, whenever Ajola played iSpy, W for Wrapper was always her go-to one. And it came from Meg. And now, she was dead. The horror of it made Ajola grasp her mouth. She couldn't help it. She was repulsed, revulsed, horrified. She thought of Meg so often. So often. She had haunted her thoughts. And now, she was dead. It was her ghost that haunted her. Unbidden. Why? She was already dead. All this time, and she was already dead. Mirrors. Layers. Her soul calling to hers. She is dead now. Time is not linear. Time is not singular. Time revolves and repeats. Did Meg know Ajola's heart now? How her teaching was shaped around her. How her presence was in every class she stood in. How she saw her in the face of Daisy. Ajola was the silhouette left by Meg. And she had been dead all this time. Who had sent the email?

'We took Meg's ashes and scattered them in some of her favourite places to walk,' Meg's mother told us. 'She loved being outside and now she will remain there forever.'

So visceral. Meg was ash. She had seen Meg run the 100-metre sprint on sports day, looking up and smiling at her all the way to the finish line. And now she was ash. Outside in the corridor, the reception teacher was banging through the art cupboard, complaining that there was no red acrylic paint. No red. No red paint. What sort of school was this. Can you mix orange and white to make red? Does anyone know if you can mix orange and white to make red? Didn't she know Meg was dead?

Ajola put her face back in her hands. Bad things came in threes. Everything is layers and mirrors. And Meg was dead.

Sophia

BEFORE SOPHIA HAD gone to secondary school and met the others, she had attended a small, leafy primary school. SATs results were exemplary, the sports team won all the trophies, the parents were heavily engaged in the PTA and the head-teacher had links with Cambridge University so that trainee students from their PGCE course would be placed there. It was after joining this school, aged eight, that Sophia had first met Jill Caister.

Jill had the same skinny wrists as Sophia. She had the same way of scrunching her hair into a knot behind her head. She had the same reading level, and the pair were also the only girls in the top group for maths. Jill played with Sophia at break time. She sat next to her in class. She invited Sophia round to her house for sleepovers where she told the most amazing ghost stories that Sophia had ever heard. Jill, obviously, had all the best toys and gadgets, CDs and devices shipped over from America. She had a vintage Mickey Mouse twin-bell alarm clock, which would speak in Mickey's voice on the hour. Sophia had never seen such technology before and Jill just let her play with it, over and over, listening to Mickey crow as she manipulated the dials on the back. Sophia loved the clock so much, she bought one off eBay when she was twenty-three, just after her wedding to Chris. Sophia had never had a close friend before. She had been grateful that Jill, who was pretty, funny and popular, allowed an interest in her.

Sophia signed up for the gymnastics club in Year 4 and when she told Jill, Jill had wrinkled her nose in distaste.

'Oh yeah, I'm doing that too,' she said. 'I love gymnastics.'

This comment introduced to Sophia the first glimmer of something other than love and joy and warm compassion for Jill. She didn't know what it was. It was a darker, more slippery feeling and it was curling its way around the top of her stomach, just under her ribs.

After a few sessions at the club, Sophia was picked to be on the school team for the annual schools' competition. She had always expected this. Why wouldn't she be? She had been practising. Jill was third pick, and that slippery, slimy feeling in Sophia's stomach intensified.

'We're going to be competing against each other!' Jill said to her after the team was announced, pointedly ignoring second pick, an excruciatingly shy girl called Bethany. They were standing out of the rain in an old PE shed. 'Who will get the most points?'

Sophia was silent.

Not long after, Sophia had found a copy of *Prince Caspian* in the school library.

'It's an Aslan book,' she told Jill, showing her the front cover. 'Look, *Narnia*.'

'What's Narnia?'

'You know. *The Lion, the Witch and the Wardrobe*.'

Jill wrinkled her nose in distaste and brushed rubber crumbs off her work. The next day, she showed Sophia her copy of *Prince Caspian*.

'I got it from Smiths,' she said, opening the book and creasing down the first page. 'It's got illustrations. Does yours have illustrations?'

Sophia looked at her tattered copy.

'No.'

'Now we can see who reads it first,' Jill said. She blew some invisible piece of fluff off the page and then burrowed down, hand over her eyes to signal that she was reading.

Sophia had put the book back the next day.

'It got a bit boring,' she said. 'Plus, my mum is going to buy me a new book tonight. *Harry Potter and the Chamber of Secrets*. It's the second book about this boy who finds out he's a wizard.'

Jill wrinkled her nose.

'Sounds dumb,' she said but, lo and behold, the next day, she had *Harry Potter and the Chamber of Secrets* in her tray.

'It's so good!' she told Sophia. 'Have you read yours yet?'

'No, not yet. I only got it last night.'

'Well, I have. And it's so good. Way better than the first one. You have to read it, Sophia. You won't believe how good it is. And Harry is so funny. I think I'd definitely get in at Hogwarts, and me and Harry would be best friends. I'd write to you, though. I'd send you Owl Post, you know, and tell you how much fun it was being in Gryffindor with Harry.'

'I'd get into Hogwarts too,' Sophia said quickly.

'Nah,' Jill said and slammed her tray shut. 'You haven't even read the second book. You don't know all the spells.'

Being with Jill started to uncover a welt of unhappiness in Sophia's stomach. She tried to sit with Bethany more. It turned out, Bethany had actually read all the Narnia and Harry Potter books and had also moved up into the top group for maths. She was completely silent most of the time. Looking back as an adult, Sophia could not remember a single conversation she and Bethany had. It must have been about something, maybe about *Harry Potter* or *Titanic*, which she and Bethany watched on VHS at her house and both silently cried to, Bethany's face blooming with vibrant red blotches, when Jack drifted into the obsidian depths of the North Atlantic. It must have been something.

In Year 5, she and Bethany did a class presentation on *Titanic*. They had wanted to do it on *Harry Potter* but there wasn't enough material to show the class, just two small books and a pull-out from a newspaper which had excerpts from the unreleased third book, *The Prisoner of Azkaban*. With *Titanic*, there were posters, pictures, history books, videos and interviews with Jack and Rose. Of course, after their class presentation, Jill went to the exhibition in London and came back the next week to do an even bigger presentation, with even more material. Bethany didn't seem bothered by this total declaration of war but it made Sophia rage. How dare she?

She didn't voice any of this, of course – how could she. She just made sure she won the Year 6 district gymnastics competition. Bethany came sixth and Jill came ninth.

'I would have won,' Jill told her, chic honey hair tied up in an exquisite knot on her head. 'But my foot slipped as I went on the bar. If I hadn't slipped, I would have beaten you.'

Directly after the competition, Jill asked Joseph Burton to be her boyfriend and she knew, she *knew,* that Sophia had fancied Joseph Burton since 1997.

'Ew!' she had said back when Sophia had told her. 'He's so ugly!'

Sophia started writing with gusto after the release date for *Harry Potter and the Goblet of Fire* was announced. She wanted to be original and write a five-book series. Not about wizards. Too cliché. Maybe about dragons. A boy who goes to dragon school.

She started typing up her ideas in the ICT suite at school, Bethany sitting beside her and reading what she wrote. Jill came in, took one look at them with her wrinkled nose and then sat down on the neighbouring computer and started writing as well.

'I'm going to do a trilogy,' she said. 'And be famous, like J. K. Rowling. What's your story about, Sophia?'

'Dragons,' Sophia replied without looking at her.

The next week, Jill came in with a four-page typed story about a family of dragons that she read out during presentation time. Sophia burst into tears when she heard it. The teacher took her outside to ask her what was wrong, but she couldn't articulate her thoughts. Jill is stealing from me? Jill is copying me? It sounded ridiculous.

Jill then started sitting with Bethany and whispering behind her hands to her. Sophia asked to play hide and seek with them but when she went to hide, Jill and Bethany ran off to play with Joseph Burton.

'You're going to secondary school soon,' her mum told her as she sobbed on her bed. 'No Jill, no Bethany. A totally fresh start. Ignore them.'

Sophia did. She bought *Harry Potter and the Goblet of Fire* the day it came out and read it in two days.

'Oh my God, haven't you even finished it yet?' Jill said to her when she brought the book to the school barbecue at the end of term. She was sitting with Bethany and the boys, scrolling through her new Nokia 3210. 'I finished it in, like, two hours.'

Sophia said nothing. She read the book at the barbecue. She ignored Bethany and Jill. Let them have each other. She purposely went to a different secondary school. She managed to make real friends with Caoimhe, Ella, Safa and Ajola, and was astonished that these relationships didn't feel toxic. She went to Exeter University and once thought that she saw Jill Caister entering one of the lecture halls as she went by on a bus. It was only a split-second glimpse. It had looked just like her. But surely Jill Caister wouldn't have tracked down what university she was going to and then applied to go there as well. That would be psychotic. No, she had not seen Jill Caister again until April 2023, just as she was preparing to apply for a certificate of presumed death for Chris.

The day after speaking to Jill again that first time, Sophia found she was in a hurry to get to the school gates early, to try and intercept Jill before anyone else did. She did her hair and make-up, picked out a smart red and black chequered shirt with fitted, *casual* jeans, little black pumps and her faux Ray-Ban sunglasses.

Isla turned her nose up at her as they were putting on their jackets.

'Just tell me you're seeing some guy you met at the doctor's,' she said. 'I won't be mad.'

'I'm *not*,' Sophia said, opening the front door.

'Then why are we going so early? We've got, like, twenty minutes. They're not going to let me in.'

Sophia paused, hand on the latch. Seven years ago, she had opened this very door to the sight of Chris lying on the floor in a pool of black blood. One tumbler turn to the next. Same door. Same latch.

'Yeah, maybe we are early.' Sophia didn't want Jill to judge her on Isla. Not that there was anything wrong with Isla, but she was an accessory, an extension of herself, that she couldn't control. She wanted Jill to see her as a single-service human. 'Should we do your spellings?'

'Yuck, no, Mum. What is with you? Let's just wait here.'

Isla sat down heavily on the shoe box. Sophia, after a pause, sat down opposite her. The open door swung between them.

'Can I get a phone?' Isla asked, fiddling with the vintage alarm clock that was mounted to the wall, ready to greet people as they came in.

'In September when you go into Year Seven.'

'Aminah has one now.'

'That's great. I'm really happy for Aminah. What an achievement. Well done.'

Isla laughed and put a hand over her face.

'Don't,' she said.

'Believe me, phones aren't all that great,' Sophia replied, and Isla tutted. 'No, it's true. Apparently phones prevent superficial boredom, which is important for reaching profound boredom, which is when we can be our most creative.'

'I'm profoundly bored by this conversation, though.' Isla stood up and put her bag on her back. 'Come, let's just go.'

They reached the school gate in the early wave of parents

and pupils. There was no sign of Jill. Sophia waved Isla inside the classroom door and stood to one side at the school fence, looking up and down the road. Cars pulled up. Children staggered out. Pushchairs rattled by. Toddlers screamed. The Year 6 boys from Isla's class thundered down the front path shouting at one another. Which direction would Jill come from? Which class did her child go to? Sophia tried to find a *casual* pose to adopt. Reclining on the bench. Hands on hips. Staring into the horizon. But Jill never came. The stream of pupils dried up. The school doors slammed shut. The parents began to drift away.

As she stepped into the road, a car honked loudly. She jumped, then turned. Jill was waving from the front seat of a Range Rover Evoque, one hand covering her mouth to hide her laughter. Sophia's heart leapt and she broke into a little jog to reach the car as quickly as possible.

'Jill,' she panted, reaching the window. 'I was looking for you.'

'Oh my God, you jumped so bad.' Jill had Clubmaster sunglasses on. She checked her reflection in the rear-view mirror. There was a little wicker animal dangling there, like the sort she used to make as a child. 'Loser. I wasn't at the school gate.' She turned to smile at Sophia. 'I don't have kids.'

For anyone else, Sophia would have questioned this. But not Jill. It was so Jill to make friends with a bunch of mums and do mum things without actually being a mum. In that instance, Sophia felt a little bit jealous of Jill. How free it would be to have no kids. To spend all her money on sophisticated cars and sunglasses. She had always thought the opposite, that having kids was the greatest bragging right. It was one of the reasons she'd had Isla so young. She was a mum. What could top that? But looking up at Jill's elevated position, her sleek hair untouched by pregnancy hormones, the leather interior of her car untarnished by children's hands, she felt like a medieval peasant.

'Get in,' Jill said. 'Let's go and have some fun. Life's for fun!'

Sophia gleefully raced around the car and pulled open the passenger door. She had to hop up to get into the Range Rover and, as she did, she caught a glimpse of Jill's footwear: Nike flip-flops.

'It just, you know,' Jill said in an American accent as Sophia shut her door, 'reminds me of my place in the universe. How trivial we all are.'

Sophia grinned.

'Julie is like that,' she said and did up her seatbelt.

'I don't want to be harsh to her,' Jill said. She looked at Sophia. 'I don't want to judge her. I want to be kind. But that is totally something a loser would say.' Sophia laughed, uninhibited. The Range Rover roared away from the kerb. 'I mean' – Jill sneered and took her own sunglasses off – 'come on. Something that massive makes her feel worthless? Sounds like she has esteem issues.'

'Julie has massive esteem issues,' Sophia said. She reviewed that in her head. Was she being mean? Was that too bitchy?

'Ow, Sophia,' Jill said. She reached across and took Sophia's sunglasses off her head and put them over her own eyes. The intimacy of the gesture made Sophia's heart flutter. 'Seeing the Grand Canyon would make me feel more important, you know?' Jill looked at Sophia through her own glasses' lenses. 'Ya know?' she repeated in an American accent.

'Oh, I know.'

Jill pretended to pout and pose, scrunching up her golden hair in her hands like a model and glancing at herself in the rear-view mirror.

'That the Grand Canyon exists as a great feat of nature just reinforces that I too exist as a great feat of nature.'

'I never get why people say stuff like that,' Sophia said. She was trying to work out what someone fun and exciting would respond with. 'Like, dwarfed by nature. I never got it.'

Jill pouted at her reflection, then whipped the sunglasses off her face and pointed them at Sophia.

'That's why I like you, Sophia,' she said. She threw the sunglasses so Sophia had to snatch them out of the air. 'You get it. Hey, you'll love this.'

Jill's iPhone X was mounted on the dashboard. She scrolled through to her Audible app and the next second, *Harry Potter and the Prisoner of Azkaban* was booming out through the speakers.

'Got the whole set,' Jill said, as the Range Rover stopped at a junction. 'It's like three solid days of *Harry Potter*.' Sophia let out a laugh. 'We could binge the whole series.'

'Audiobooks?' Sophia asked.

'Movies.' Jill nodded at her. 'The real deal.'

'Yeah, maybe,' Sophia said. She had never watched the films. It seemed like cheating to her. Devoid of magic. Still, it might be fun to watch them with Jill. 'So, how come you're not at work or anything?'

'Work from home, bitch,' Jill said and Sophia was surprised into a laugh. 'WFH.' Jill hit the horn on the steering wheel. 'I got nothing but time. You want to go to the cinema?'

'Yeah, sure. What do you do?'

'I should ask you what you do, Miss Sophia Shepherd. Or are you someone else now?' She raised her eyebrow over her sunglasses. 'Mrs Sophia Burton?'

The joke wasn't as funny the second time round but Sophia laughed anyway. She glanced out of the window. She could see the driver of the neighbouring car, her arm resting on the open window. They were so close, the eczema on the driver's wrist was visible. As she watched, the driver reached over with her other hand and scratched the dry patch of skin; Sophia could see the blood well up in the cracks.

'Do you keep in touch with anyone from school?' she asked. 'Bethany?'

Jill scoffed.

'Not that loser.' She tooted the horn again. 'So, tell me. How is Joseph?'

Sophia gave a more restrained laugh.

'I haven't seen him since the Year Six end-of-term barbecue in 2000,' she said.

'So, you aren't Mrs Sophia Burton?'

Sophia didn't deign to laugh this time.

'I married a guy I met at Exeter University,' she said. 'Chris Johnson.'

'Mrs Sophia Johnson. Isn't Johnson a euphemism for dick? You're Sophia Dick? Sophia Cock. Sophia Penis.'

It wasn't funny, but no one had ever said this before. Sophia was shocked into laughing again.

'I'm happy with Johnson,' she said.

'I bet you are.'

Into the following silence, punctuated only by Stephen Fry

explaining how Harry felt about his aunt's impending visit, Sophia said:

'I once thought I saw you at Exeter. Outside a university lecture hall.'

'Weird,' Jill said, indicating on to the dual carriageway. 'You've been fantasizing about me all these years. What does Chris do?'

'He was in finance.' Sophia stroked her nose. She suddenly didn't know how to bring up his disappearance. It felt like showing her hand too quickly.

'And now?' Jill prompted.

'And now, he's dead. We buried him on the moors.'

'And now, he's vanished, he ran away from home.'

'And now, I don't know. He walked out and left me one day seven years ago.'

'And now, he's not,' Sophia said. 'But what do you do?'

'Copy-editing,' Jill said quickly. She glanced at Sophia. 'It's really cool. Like, I read all the manuscripts before they hit the stores, suggest rewrites, do edits, everything.'

'Books?' Sophia said. 'You work in publishing?'

'Technically, I'm freelance.'

Sophia turned to look out of the window. She felt insanely jealous.

'That's . . . so cool,' she said. She very nearly reached forward to direct the air conditioning away from Jill and then realized what a bitch move that was. 'So cool.'

'Yeah.' Jill shrugged. 'Just lucky, I guess. Ha, remember when you wanted to be a writer when you were eight?'

At that moment, Sophia had two choices. She could either reject her companionship with Jill, as she did in primary school, and spend the next twenty years sick with bitterness and envy, or she could embrace it. Jill was cooler and more talented than her. So what? It must say something about Sophia if such a person wanted to spend the day with her.

'Yeah.' Sophia laughed. 'I still do, really.'

'Really?'

'Yeah. I write, a bit. A lot.' A good deal more, now Chris was dead. 'Uh, so whereabouts do you actually live?'

'Are you going to sit outside my house and stalk me?'

'No-o.' Sophia gave a nervous titter. 'Just—'

'I've got a penthouse by the river,' Jill said. She nodded her head once or twice. 'So cool,' she added. 'Great views.'

'Wow. Sounds amazing,' Sophia said. She tried to conjure up the emotion of being genuinely happy for a friend. Imagine this was Caoimhe talking. 'Well done.'

'Yeah, I know. My boyfriend actually bought it for me. It's not rented.' She looked sharply at Sophia. 'We don't pay a mortgage on it.'

'Lucky,' she said. 'What's his name?'

'Jared,' Jill replied.

'Cool name.'

'Yeah, he's *American*.' She put a faux-American accent on. She was always so good at accents. '*Stateside. Jared Winchester.*'

'What does he do?'

'I can't really tell you that,' Jill said in her normal voice. Sophia laughed as though this was a joke but Jill looked at her sternly. 'No. Seriously. I can't.'

'Oh. No problem.' Sophia turned to watch the trees speed past the window. On the Year 6 bowling trip, she had asked Jill if she wanted a Polo, and Jill had laughed and laughed for weeks. Sophia had patiently waited until Jill had relented and let Bethany tell Sophia that POLO actually meant Pants Off Legs Open, so Sophia was basically asking Jill to have sex with her. She could patiently wait again.

Jill looked at her.

'Don't be mad.'

'I'm not mad.'

'I can send you a picture of him. I'll do it tonight when I get home. I'll try and choose a good one.'

Caoimhe

WHEN CAOIMHE LEFT her house to go to Finsbury Park, she saw four drakes chasing a female duck. The five of them had come through the broken hedge that bordered a man-made lake and were now waddling down the pavement, the female duck at the front, quacking indignantly, and her four pursuers in a smart line behind. The female duck was moving at a terrific pace and, finally, frustrated, the drakes broke out of their line and cornered her by the wheel of a Toyota Prius. The lead duck jumped on her back, beak clipping her neck to hold her in place. The other drakes quacked eagerly, trying to dislodge both parties. Caoimhe felt violated by the whole thing. She made a loud squawking noise and ran at the circle of ducks. The female duck managed to slip free in the commotion and hurried towards the reeds and rushes that had been planted around the lake. The four drakes came squawking after her, desperate to clip her into place again.

Caoimhe darted after them. She would save this duck. This duck would not be raped. They were all so fast. Caoimhe had

129

no idea a duck could be so fast. Another drake made an attempt to mount the female again and Caoimhe hissed and waved her hands over her head. The ducks didn't care. Maybe this was a mating dance in the duck world. The female quacked and ran around in circles while as many drakes as possible chased her. A flirty game. Plus, what was she going to do? Follow this duck around for the rest of the season to make sure no drake penetrated her? Ducks were probably raping each other left, right and centre all over the world, right now. Drakes probably had to rape the female ducks to ensure there was actual duck progeny. The sexual drive of the drake to pin down the reluctant female and impregnate her might be all that stood between ducks and absolute extinction.

Caoimhe turned away from the ducks. Leave them to it.

She took a convoluted route in, constantly checking she wasn't being followed. The District Line from Richmond and then the Piccadilly to Holloway Road. Here, she walked the mile or so back on her journey to Highbury and Islington, back to the streets she, Ajola, Ella, Safa and Sophia had roamed whilst at school. She missed them. She wished they hadn't done what they did; she wished they had remained friends. Directly after burying Chris, once she'd spoken to the police and confirmed that she had seen nothing that night, Caoimhe had moved to Copenhagen for a few years, hoping the police wouldn't bother extraditing her if they arrested Sophia. Caoimhe kept up with the developments online. There were local news articles here and there about a loving husband gone missing, pictures of Sophia looking downcast in the living room where they had mopped up Chris's blood. Caoimhe combed through every search result, reading and rereading the information, looking for any hints over suspects or leads. There was nothing. After several months, the articles faded away, pushed to the bottom of Google, hidden under pages and pages of other stories. The police never got back in touch. Caoimhe dared to believe they might have got away with it. But she didn't dare contact the others.

Caoimhe moved back home and focused on becoming Run Britain's number-one female runner in the postcode, opposite Rohan Rust's number-one male. It became an obsession with her and, once she had made it to the top, two years ago, she religiously checked her rankings almost every day, to reassure herself that she was still Number One. And she had been, until Evie – a Pokémon name, the most basic evolution, a *normal* type – joined the club, with race times that made Caoimhe's look disgusting. It was embarrassing. Who was she if she wasn't the best runner in the postcode? She imagined her mother giving her an affronted look, hands clasped in front of her cardigan, cheeks red with indignation at her daughter's failings.

'Get your elbows out then, Caoimhe!'

'If she can do it, you can!'

The terror that had washed in upon discovering she was now second best, not on par with Rohan Rust, had been dwarfed by the abject horror of Chris's body rising from the grave. She might be about to go to prison for murder. Run Britain suddenly seemed so unimportant. How strange.

When she got off at Finsbury Park, she didn't want to be there. She should have stayed at home. Maybe gone running. Maybe stayed in Copenhagen. Why was making plans so easy but fulfilling them so hard. She stopped by the barrier and wondered if she could just go back. If she stayed, she would be fucking miserable. But if she went back, she'd be fucking miserable. There was no way to escape the misery.

Someone jostled her from behind and she moved aside to let them pass. Anyone could see her standing here. The barriers were busy with people coming in and out of the station. It was strange to think every one of these shapes was a human being. A person. A sentient life form with frustrations and failings just like her. With fucking misery, just like her.

As a bus rumbled away from the kerb, she saw Ella standing at the top of the steps. She had her phone pressed to an ear with one hand and had the other wrapped around a fat toddler. Caoimhe pushed her hair off her forehead. There was Ella. It was all going to be OK. During Year 7, Caoimhe had been friends with a small group of girls that had come up from primary school together. One day, at lunchtime, sitting under a tree by the tennis courts, Janet had been talking about a film she had seen and she oh so casually dropped the 'N' word into the conversation. No one else even blinked, but Caoimhe, whose paternal grandfather had moved to London from Lagos as a student, had felt as though someone was shining a hot light on her. She started to go red and dig around in the dirt with her thumb. Her heart rate increased and she didn't know why. When Janet said the 'N' word again, just as laissez-faire, about a minute later, Caoimhe pulled a face.

'I feel weird you saying that,' she said, examining her thumb in the dirt instead of looking up.

'Oh *no*. Oh my *gosh*!' Janet said and put one hand to her mouth and another on Caoimhe's wrist, her bare fingertips touching Caoimhe's bare skin. 'I don't mean you. At all. At. All.'

Caoimhe nodded, still transfixed with her thumb in the little dirt hole. It was a few days later that she had met Ella in textiles and started talking to her, and that was the end of Janet.

She raised a hand. The fat toddler saw her approaching before Ella did. Caoimhe tried to recall his name, which she'd heard vaguely through the grapevine of social media. Benedict. Benton. Benicio. He was staring at her with a frown on his face, a straight, severe brow. As Caoimhe approached a stride at a time, she felt her nerves peel away.

Ella turned and saw her, and her relief, her pleasure, was mirrored in Caoimhe's own face. She pinned the phone to her ear with her shoulder, let go of the toddler's hand and embraced Caoimhe. Caoimhe's arms engulfed her back. What was this. This feeling. A belonging. A trust. A quiet moment of solace that sat in the centre of misery like the eye of the storm.

'Felix, I have to go,' Ella said, pulling away. 'Yes. No. Fine, fine. Right, goodbye.' She slipped her phone into her pocket and looked at Caoimhe. She smiled. 'Together again,' she said. 'Oh, can you just grab him before he takes the tube to Pimlico.'

Caoimhe reached out and grabbed the little boy's hand. She didn't know how much force was appropriate so just held him in place until Ella bent down to pick him up.

'Is his dad coming for him?' Caoimhe asked as Ella struggled with the toddler.

'Oh, no.' Ella set the boy down between her legs and sat on a bench.

Caoimhe chose to remain standing, looking down at Ella. It felt more direct, more intimate, than sitting side by side on the bench.

'No,' Ella continued. 'Felix and I broke up. Separated. Divorced.'

'Oh. Sorry.'

Ella waved her hand.

'You know.'

She let out a breath and shifted on her seat. The boy was leaning forward, straining against his clothes, trying to reach something invisible before him.

'I know,' Caoimhe said. 'How is it being single?'

'Much better,' Ella said, 'than being married.' She wrinkled her nose. 'But Felix is doing this annoying thing. It doesn't really matter.' She lifted the boy up on to her knee. He howled as if he'd been slapped and threw his head back, colliding with Ella's chin. 'Oh shit,' she gasped, leaning forward. 'Shit.' The boy was howling worse than ever now. 'That hasn't chipped a tooth, has it?'

Caoimhe bent down to investigate and Ella pulled sharply away.

'No. But your lip is bleeding.'

'Shit,' Ella said again. 'Benjamin, you're fine. It's fine. Don't make that sound.'

Benjamin. Of course. Benjamin was the boy's name.

Ella dabbed at her mouth with a tissue pulled from inside her cuff. Caoimhe could always remember her own mum having a tissue on the inside of her cuff. She sat down on the bench next to them.

'Has it been hard on him?' she asked.

Ella pulled her phone out of her bag and loaded up a YouTube video. Benjamin snatched the phone off her and held it close to his face, the colourful shapes reflected in his eyes.

'Oh no. Benjamin has no idea what's going on.' Ella put some gum in her mouth. 'If anything, his behaviour has improved because I got him an au pair on the days I work. This isn't child-of-divorced-parent behaviour. This is just general-child-dickhead behaviour.'

Caoimhe laughed. Ella offered her the packet of gum but Caoimhe declined.

'What annoying thing does Felix do?'

'What?'

'You said he's started doing an annoying thing?'

'What? Oh. Yes. He is still wearing his wedding ring. Pisses me off. He comes into the office with it on and I know it pisses my brother off as well.' She looked at Caoimhe. 'You remember how my brother is. I bet Felix still ticks the *married* box when filling in forms.'

Behind them, a double-decker bus rumbled up to the kerb. The doors hissed open and a steady stream of dark-clothed passengers got off, cutting across the flow of pedestrians on the pavement, heading straight for the station entrance. A man with a pair of oversized headphones and a teenager visibly chewing gum got up from the bus shelter and moved towards the bus doors. Somebody broke their stride to sneeze into the bin next to Caoimhe. She and Ella looked at each other and burst out laughing.

Ajola

AJOLA GOT OFF the bus last. A man with oversized headphones and a young woman whose jaw was working overtime climbed on to the bus as she was climbing off. It heaved away behind her and almost immediately another one pulled up. Ajola moved towards the benches where Ella and Caoimhe were sitting.

'Hello,' Ajola said, putting an arm around Caoimhe. 'I thought I was late. Ella, your lip is bleeding.'

Ajola sat down on the other side of the bench, so that she was facing the road and not the station. Caoimhe leant back so they could look at each other face to face. Ella dabbed at her lip.

'And how are you?' Caoimhe asked. 'Me and Ella were just sharing stories. Did you know Ella is divorced?'

'No?' Ajola looked at Ella. 'No?'

'And I'm having an identity crisis,' Caoimhe said, 'because I am no longer the best runner.'

'But you've never been the best,' Ajola said. She twirled a finger in the air as if she was trying to reel in candy floss. 'Your identity crisis comes from the disconnect between your dreams and your reality.'

Caoimhe twirled a finger back.

'Doesn't make me feel any better,' she said.

'Bollocks. Oh, sorry.' Ajola put a finger over her lips and jerked her head at Benjamin. 'My First Swear Word.'

'Don't worry.' Ella smoothed down Benjamin's dark hair. 'He's heard it all before. Though not bollocks, actually.' She clicked her fingers. 'That's a new one.'

'There you go, Benjamin.' The boy glanced at Ajola. 'Didn't your mum tell you I was a teacher?'

He looked back at the phone without a word.

'God, if Felix knew I was taking him to a pub after seven p.m., he'd be livid,' Ella said.

'It's Haringey,' Caoimhe reassured her. 'Worst thing that's going to happen in a pub here after seven p.m. is they'll over-charge you for a bag of crisps. Come on.' She stood up. 'Let's get out of the open. I feel like anyone could be watching us here.'

As they passed into the shadows under the rail bridge, the road and pavement mottled with grey-white spray, Benjamin tried to dart away, jerking Ella to one side.

'What are you playing at?' Ella snapped, swinging him off the floor. He was laughing. 'Do you not understand that you could die if you run into the road?'

Overhead, a train thundered across the bridge. The few slim rays of light filtering through the rails flashed. Benjamin flung himself backwards, howling, but Ella held him firmly in place. Above them, a pigeon floated from one rafter to the next.

'I'll hold him,' Ajola said. Ella's hair was all out of place and a patch of deep red was blooming at the top of her neck.

'It's fine.' Ella tried to push her hair from her eyes and keep him steady. 'I do this all the time.'

'Yeah, so let me have a turn,' Ajola said.

She reached out and took Benjamin from her. He went stiff. She set him on the pavement and looked at him. The Year 6 teacher at her school always gave misbehaving children the Stern Look and the Sharp Word. It always seemed so contrived. So *Dead Poet's Society*. Aha: *'There's a time for daring and a time for caution, Benjamin, and a wise man understands which is called for!'*

Life wasn't a Hollywood movie. It was unlikely students would take your carefully constructed nuggets to heart. So she just smiled at Benjamin, took his hand and continued walking down the pavement, towards Safa's waving figure.

Sophia

JOSEPH BURTON HAD black hair and bright blue eyes. He had been exceptional at English and had won a prize in Year 6 for a regional writing competition. He was the most talented boy on the school football team (lithe, skinny, tenacious) and Sophia was sure they were soulmates. He even looked like Harry Potter.

'Yuck. I was best friends with him before you got to the school,' Jill told her when Sophia admitted, excitedly, that she fancied him. 'We used to go round each other's house every day, after school. I used to pick out his underwear for him. He'd say, what boxers should I wear today? The yellow boxers or the green boxers? And I'd choose.'

Sophia had flushed bright red. She had never imagined a pair of boys' boxers before, let alone Joseph Burton's. She had no idea what to do with that information. She started wondering why she had even told Jill in the first place. She should have buried that knowledge deep down. What did she expect? That by somehow giving the crush weight in the real world, instead of relegating it to the confines of her imagination, it would be returned to her in a more tangible form? Allowing it to manifest. Reality breathing life into fantasy. Well, in some way, that turned out to be true, because Jill asked to be moved in DT so she and Joseph Burton could be paired together. Sophia had ended up working not even with Bethany, but with Simon, a devilishly pale, skinny little thing, with soft, colourless hair, who cried when the bit of wood he was holding slipped off the table and scraped the end of his finger. Sophia had to console him whilst watching Jill and Joseph. Joseph was holding Jill's hand and staring intensely at her as Jill playfully put a finger on her chin. Simon howled.

'It's just meant to be,' Jill told Sophia as they walked home. 'He said he'd take me to the PE shed and kiss me if they win when he's captain. Jill and Joseph. The two Js. And Sophia and Simon. The two Ss. You suit Simon.' She nodded at her. 'You really do. And I' – she put her hand to her chest – 'suit Joseph.'

The World's End wasn't too busy and Sophia only had to move one or two dirty pint glasses to get a seat. She waited anxiously at the big table by the door, afraid someone was going to ask her to move, continuously glancing out of the window behind her for sight of the others. She chewed off a strip of her thumbnail. The door opened and she stood up before she could see who it was. It was them.

Caoimhe came in first and they embraced.

'Sophia!' Ajola cried. She led Benjamin by the hand into the booth. 'You've had your hair cut.'

Sophia touched her short hair as they all scooted on to the seats.

'Last week. I'm going for my Year Ten German Exchange look.'

'Suits you,' Ella said.

Safa nodded.

'It's nice.'

'Very nice.'

'Nice.'

'Thanks.'

The table fell silent. They all looked in different directions, except Ajola, who looked straight at Sophia.

'Uh.' Sophia clasped her hands together. Now they were all here, she had no idea how to start the conversation. Seven years ago, she would have just said it all in one gasping rush. But now, with the time, the distance, that didn't seem appropriate. 'Should we get something to drink?'

They ordered a strawberry-mint mocktail pitcher and sat around the table sucking on their straws. Benjamin was bent low over the phone screen, his head barely visible above the rim of the table, ignoring all of them.

'I've got an actual leaf of mint in mine,' Caoimhe muttered, fishing it out with her fingers.

'It adds to the flavour,' Safa said, watching as she wiped it on the table.

'Nah, I'm good.'

'Guys,' Sophia managed to say before they all settled back into an impenetrable silence. 'Well.' Her voice quivered in her throat and she drummed her fingers on the table. What if they all got up and left? 'Should I tell you?'

'Can we just pretend none of it happened?' Ella asked, swapping her straw for another piece of gum.

'I don't think so.' Sophia took a deep breath. The tremble in her voice was embarrassing. She felt as if she was eleven

141

and presenting something in school assembly. She cleared her throat. She just had to say. In a gasp. In a rush. 'Because someone knows. What we did.' Ice clanked in Ella's drink and Sophia lowered her voice as if the sound was an interjection. 'Thing is, they've tried to act anonymous. But . . .' She rocked forward slightly in her seat and whispered, 'I think I know who it is.'

'Who?'

'Can you remember Jill Caister?' Saying Jill's name out loud felt like a satanic incantation. It was dangerous. Sophia would look up and Jill would be walking in through the door, summoned before them like an underworld demon to upturn their table.

'You went to primary school with her?' Ella said, slowly. 'Wasn't she spiteful?'

'She turned up to our school's Year Eight disco.' Caoimhe remembered. 'Right? Although she didn't even go to the school. And she told everyone that her boyfriend was Tom Felton.' She laughed. 'She was *insane*.'

'Correct.' Sophia nodded emphatically and allowed her voice more volume. 'Anyway, she's just moved close to where I live.'

'Small world.' Safa raised her eyebrows.

'Tell me about it. We've been hanging out a bit' – Sophia ran her hands along the table – 'chatting, you know. I've spent my whole life thinking she was a bitch, but' – she shrugged – 'as an adult, she seemed great.'

'Hungry,' Benjamin said, loudly.

Ella rolled her eyes at Sophia and pulled a packet of crisps out of her bag. Benjamin took them and burrowed back down under the rim of the table.

'But as time went on,' Sophia continued, 'I started to get a weird feeling.'

'How so?' Ajola asked.

Sophia scratched under her eye. She wanted them to believe her, to share her outrage, but it all seemed so much smaller and more trivial when spoken out loud.

'I don't know.' Sophia grimaced. 'It's hard to articulate it and sound normal.'

'What was she doing?' Caoimhe asked.

'She turned up at school wearing similar clothes to me. Like the exact same tracksuit bottoms and flip-flops.'

The table was quiet.

'That's not that weird,' Safa said at last.

'No. No.' Sophia shook her head. 'But it's lots of things. I mean, she doesn't have kids at the school, she just goes there to hang out with the other mums. Like the Year Eight disco!'

'That's a little strange.' Ella looked at Ajola. 'Right? You can't have someone random outside the school every day.'

Ajola shrugged. 'It's unconventional, obviously,' she said. 'But if she's stopping by with a group of mums and not inter-acting with kids, it's not like the school would call the police or anything.'

'And,' Sophia continued, trying to grasp the root of her dis-quiet, 'when we go out, she only ever orders after me and always gets the exact same thing. She mirrors me when I touch my hair. That's why I cut it. At first, I thought I was just insecure because of our friendship from school. But she might actually be unhinged.'

'What makes you say unhinged?' Ella asked.

'She showed me a picture of her boyfriend. Who apparently is some super-rich guy who bought her a penthouse, blah, blah, blah.' Sophia was pulling her phone out of her pocket. The tremor in her voice had vanished but now the tips of her fingers were shaking with a desperation to be understood.

'What does he do?' Safa asked.

'She won't tell me.'

'What?' Caoimhe curled her lip. 'You what?'

'I know, right?'

'Have you met him?'

'No.'

'He's not real,' Caoimhe said, flatly. 'Guaranteed. Tom Felton all over again.'

'Right, that's what I thought. So she sent me this picture.' Sophia put her phone on the table and began swiping around with her thumbs.

'Thirsty,' Benjamin shouted.

Ella dug in her bag for a bottle of juice and unscrewed the lid for Benjamin without looking at him. Sophia turned her phone around and they all leant forward to see. Benjamin snatched the bottle from Ella, slopping juice on to the table, which all of them ignored.

'That is a terrible angle,' Safa said, squinting at the phone screen. 'Why even bother sending that?'

'I didn't think anything of it at first,' Sophia explained. 'But then I was watching *Gilmore Girls* with Isla one night.'

'I hate that show,' Caoimhe said.

'I used to, but now I'm getting into it with her. Anyway, there's this guy in it, this character from like season two, 2002, and I don't know.' Sophia turned her phone back around and searched for the man on Google. 'Don't they look similar?'

She held the phone screen up and swiped between the two pictures.

'The guy from *Gilmore Girls* and the picture Jill Caister sent you?' Ella frowned. Sophia used a finger and thumb to zoom in on the photos and emphasize her point.

'Kind of, a bit,' Ajola said, kindly.

'He is familiar,' Caoimhe said.

'I know. I know.' Sophia turned the phone back around and gazed at the screen. 'But I couldn't get it out of my head. There was something about the picture she sent me, the weird angle, and then this guy, this actor. I googled him and he's played by someone called Jared Padalecki. Jill told me her boyfriend was called Jared Winchester.'

'Winchester?' Caoimhe said.

'Perhaps it's just a coincidence?' Safa suggested.

'Coincidences might just be a sign from the great collective unconscious of the universe,' Ajola said. 'Women always have an easier time finding their way into that.'

Sophia didn't know what she meant by this. She slowly put her phone back in her pocket. Her story had fallen flat. They didn't believe in the sinisterness of Jill.

'Sam Winchester,' Caoimhe said, slowly.

'No, Jared.'

Caoimhe shook her head. Something exploded in a high-pitched shower of sparks on Benjamin's screen.

'Sam Winchester is a character from a show called *Supernatural* about two brothers who hunt monsters,' Caoimhe explained. 'Show me that picture again.'

Sophia quickly took out her phone again and pulled up the photo. Caoimhe peered forward and then nodded.

'I thought he looked familiar.' She leant back. 'That's Sam Winchester. From *Supernatural*.'

'You see!' Sophia cried, elated. She looked at the photo again. 'I knew it. She's crazy.' She nearly smashed the phone on to the tabletop in her triumph. 'It's just like in Year Five when she told me she knew Daniel Radcliffe and they were going on holiday together.' Caoimhe grunted with amusement. 'She's still doing this! And, and, and, and' – Sophia's words caught on the tip of her tongue and she had to swallow to regain composure – 'now we get contacted out of the blue after seven years.'

She rocked forward, quite involuntarily, her face flushing with exhilaration.

'Can I just say . . .' Ella put a hand on the table. 'Is it completely out of the blue?'

They glanced around at each other, passing eye contact as though it was a precious stone. Benjamin's show whirred excitedly beneath the table.

'What do you mean?' Safa asked, quietly.

Ella glanced around at the bar, seeing if anyone was looking towards them. She leant forward.

'Over the years,' she whispered, 'did anyone, ever, notice anything? Any strange events? Odd happenings?'

'I did.' Sophia nodded. 'But I was afraid, maybe, it was the people who, you know' – she lowered her voice – 'actually killed Chris: the moneylenders I told you about.' She was whispering now. 'The police never found anything. From them. Or us. I think, in the end, they just presumed Chris ran off with another woman. They stopped being interested after a couple of months and now, unless, you know, anyone discovers his body, he's just a missing person's statistic until I can get him legally declared dead. I thought the strange things, what I saw, were threats from' – she tucked her chin to her chest – 'the real murderers. To make me stay quiet.'

'What did you see?' Ella asked.

'I got weird things sent to me in the post. Newspaper cuttings about missing people.' Sophia was still whispering, making the others lean in. 'Articles about women going to prison.'

'Oh my days, I got that too,' Safa said and her normal speaking voice suddenly seemed very loud. 'I thought it was Haaris threatening me.'

They looked around at the others. Caoimhe nodded slowly.

'Same. Also, someone kept posting weird comments on my LinkedIn. I thought it was a scammer. I had to explain to a couple of clients that I'd been hacked.'

'I got a few weird texts.' Ajola folded her arms. 'It went on for about . . .' – she thought – 'six months, pretty consistently. Just listing punctuation. I thought it was a virus or something. Every time I blocked them, another number started sending them. Same with emails. So many emails thanking me for signing up for their newsletters.'

Sophia felt a reassuring tightness in her chest. After all these years, they had still been connected, experiencing the same terrors, just separately.

'It took me ages going through to unsubscribe,' Ajola went on. 'Recently, I also got an anonymous email with a link to an article about the suicide of one of my students. I had no idea who sent that.' She shook her head. 'I emailed them back, but they never replied.'

'I got the emails, too,' Ella said. 'Not about the suicide. Obviously. The newsletters. And the texts. I thought maybe it was some bitter client. There was a spell of a few weeks where someone left painted stones outside my work, as well. I thought it was a local Scout project.'

'Painted stones?' Safa frowned.

Ella nodded, chewing her gum slowly.

'Someone stole my phone,' Sophia told them. She hadn't revealed this to anyone, not her parents, not the police, and had just tried to pretend it never happened, terrified about who might have taken it and why. Telling the others now felt like a relief. They were all connected, still. 'A few years ago. Literally, swiped it from the table as I turned to check on Isla. It had everything on there. Bank details, work hours, your guys' information.'

'So, someone has been watching us for seven years?' Caoimhe said. 'And now they've reached out.'

'WhatsApp.' Sophia nodded.

'Encrypted,' Ella pointed out.

'What exactly did they say?' Ajola asked Sophia.

Sophia took out her phone again and turned it around to them.

I know where you buried your husband.

You. Caoimhe. Safa. Ella. Ajola.

I need you to do something for me.

'They know our names,' Ella hissed. 'Shit.'

Benjamin glanced up at her.

'Shit,' he repeated. Ella pointedly didn't look at him. He went back to the phone.

'This text arrived right after Jill Caister appeared on the scene.' Sophia's voice was as soft and breathless as spider gossamer. 'It's got to be her.'

She felt triumphant, linking this all back to Jill, as if she was defending her dissertation to a panel of judges. They had to understand now.

'Let's not do anything rash,' Ajola said, holding up her hands as though someone was pointing a gun at her. 'Let's remain calm.'

'Text back.' Ella pointed at Sophia. 'Now. Say, who is this?'

'New phone. Who dis?' Safa gave an awkward laugh, but no one joined in.

'This could all be a prank or a bluff.' Caoimhe shook her head. 'Just don't reply.'

'I am not going to be able to sleep at night,' Ella announced, 'with that chain of messages in existence. We have to reply. We have to find out.'

'And say what?' Caoimhe looked at her, shoulder raised in indignation.

'Pics or it didn't happen?' Safa tried again.

Ella tutted.

'It's not funny.'

'What do you suggest?' Ajola asked her.

'Let's meet them.'

'Are you crazy?' Safa's eyebrows shot into her hairline. 'They might murder us.'

'I don't know,' Sophia said. She turned the phone around and examined the message for the thousandth time. When she had first read it, a deep, resounding siren had been set off inside her skull. Now, with the others here, the siren continued to wail, but more quietly, in the distance, like a foghorn from a foreign shore. 'It doesn't seem very murdery. More blackmaily.'

'Aren't we admitting culpability if we text back, though?' Safa said. 'Someone innocent would ignore it. Or forward it to the police.'

'Someone innocent wouldn't get the text in the first place,' Caoimhe pointed out.

Ajola scratched her head.

'How about we say, if you have any information regarding my husband's disappearance, I'd like to meet with you.'

'*We'd* like to meet with you,' Ella corrected. 'Let them know we're all coming.'

'United,' Ajola agreed.

'I'm happy with that.' Sophia nodded. At the meeting, she could prove this presence was Jill. Then they would know she was right. 'Caoimhe, Safa?'

'I don't want to meet them,' Safa said. 'But I don't want them to rake it all up either.'

'Let's just send the text.' Caoimhe clapped her hands together. 'Maybe they won't reply. It could just be someone fishing and we can all put our minds at rest.'

She looked around the table. The others nodded. Sophia flashed a text across her phone with skidding thumbs.

'I'm doing it now.' She looked up. 'Typed it. Should I send?'

'Send,' Ajola said.

'Sent.' Sophia put the phone down. This would draw Jill out. Show everyone what a psycho she was. 'We haven't seen each other in so long.' She smiled. 'I know, I know why. It was too dangerous. But now we're here.'

'Let's get something to eat,' Caoimhe said.

Ajola

AJOLA'S MUM HAD been a student of her father's. Growing up, it was a romantic fairy tale they told her, a story of two soulmates meeting in the most unlikely of places. Her mother at university, away from home for the first time in her life. Her father, an intelligent and charming professor, looking for an equal. What was a more natural and comforting pairing than teacher and student?

But her mum had been eighteen and her dad nearly forty. And her mum was very narrow-boned. Skinny. Short at only five foot. Child-like, whilst her father was a foot taller and borderline overweight. He had a great sagging belly that hung over his belt, like a jolly king from the myths and legends.

As a child, Ajola hadn't worried about the belly; she just presumed all dads were older, smarter and fatter than their wives. As she grew and saw other dads, she started to worry about the belly. About the age. About her dad's loud and commanding voice beside her mother's quiet, hushed tones.

At school, Ajola was smart. Not just top of the class smart but *greater depth*. She got huge pleasure from working out maths problems from workbooks in her dad's study. Ajola had visions of being in her twenties, wearing a white lab coat and working out problems on a chalkboard in a fancy university in Paris or Geneva. She didn't have any friends until Year 7, when she sat with Ella in top set English. She'd yearned for friends when she was at primary school. She used to look at the other girls paired up, playing unicorns or colouring in sunflower clocks, and she would wish with all her heart that she could join them. But she didn't get it, couldn't get it. There was a great, deep, rich world of intimate connection that provided fulfilment and *catharsis*. She just couldn't find it.

She tried to make friends with her Year 5 teacher, who seemed smart and funny and *grown up*, hanging around the classroom at lunchtime and trying to come up with reasons why. But she was too shy. She could never say anything. She wished the teacher had initiated something. She knew she just needed to be cracked open. Then, the rich world would come flooding in and she would be at peace.

'I was just like you at school,' her mother told her after another failed after-school club. 'Quiet, not many friends, smart, anxious. It's nothing to worry about.' She smiled at her. 'It'll all work out. Just like me.'

This made Ajola cry.

She often cried at home. She raged. She had tantrums, throwing herself at doors or smacking her palm against her head. Her mother would shout back at her. Ajola didn't know what to do to stop it. She felt so angry, so frustrated, all the time. It felt as if, at school, she could keep it together, but when she got home, she looked at her parents, the great belly, the tiny frame, and something broke inside her.

Her great-grandma would remonstrate with her mother in Albanian. Ajola didn't know enough Albanian to work out what she was saying. She liked to think she was standing up for her. Maybe she, too, was harbouring some unresolved issues from the pairing between her granddaughter and grandson-in-law. It smelt unnatural. It caused uneven ripples on the surface of the water.

It was around this time, as a teenager, her great-grandma started sharing spells with Ajola. Ajola oscillated between feeling the spells were silly and childish, and being utterly convinced that she was tapping into the greater power. A sense of meaning. Fulfilment. Catharsis.

'Ancient,' her great-grandma whispered to her. 'Forgotten.'

Ajola tried to be as normal as possible whilst at school, terrified Caoimhe, Ella, Safa and Sophia wouldn't want to socialize with her if they found out she was a freak. The trouble was, there were so many hours. So much time. Endless, relentless. No fulfilment. No ultimate meaning. Ajola developed severe anxiety at around sixteen and dropped out of college. The others couldn't understand it. Neither could she.

'You're throwing your life away!' her mother said to her.

Ajola didn't have an answer to that. She screamed back at her. She stayed in her room and read books or stared at the blank ceiling. She didn't want to be alive but she didn't know how to kill herself. Ashes. Visceral. The unanswered questions. She just wanted everything to stop. The End.

'You know,' Ajola said as they came back from ordering at the bar, 'if this were Tudor times, if Thomas Cromwell was Chief Minister, this meeting would be seen as a coven of witches.'

'I haven't heard you mention Thomas Cromwell in seven years.' Caoimhe smiled across the table at her and placed her cutlery down.

Ajola held out her hands.

'You could have,' she said. 'But none of you stayed in touch.'

'Come on.' Ella looked serious. 'We couldn't. After what happened. It was safer to separate.'

'Do you feel safe now?' Ajola replied. 'With this spectre watching us? There was always going to be fear and doubt' – she leant forward on the table – 'and that is why you stay together.'

'But for protection,' Safa said, 'if the police started asking questions.'

'The spell is our protection.' Ajola grinned. 'It's protecting us right now.'

'You really believe that?' Safa asked as Caoimhe rolled her eyes.

Ajola continued to smile at her. She wasn't sure. She always told herself she believed. It made everything much easier. It affirmed her. Looking at Safa's earnest face now, she was forced to confront that belief. Was it there? Was it real? Or, once examined more closely, was it just an empty ideal designed to make herself feel better?

'I do.' She hoped she sounded convincing. They all fell silent. Ajola banged her hands on the table and the glasses jumped. 'I tell you what I hate,' she said loudly, trying to recentre herself. 'When you live with a guy' – she pointed at Safa – 'and everything you do, they somehow interpret as sexual.'

Sophia laughed.

'I've missed you, Ajola.'

'You're picking up something off the floor.' Ajola snapped her fingers. 'Sexual. You're stretching in the doorway.' She snapped again. 'Sexual. You're lying on your side watching television.' *Snap.* 'Sexual. Women in relationships can't exist without men believing it's for sex.'

'If' – Caoimhe held out her hand and rolled her eyes – 'you just existing turns your partner on, it sounds like he really values you.'

'He values you because' – Ajola pointed a fork across the table – 'of the sexual fulfilment you provide him.'

'Romantic relationships involve sex,' Caoimhe said. She looked around at the others. Safa wrinkled her nose in response, Ella was bent over the phone with Benjamin, and Sophia deliberately looked the other way. 'That's a central pillar of a romantic relationship. If there's no sex, you're room-mates, friends, whatever. Nothing wrong with that, as this coven test-ifies.' Ajola laughed and lowered the fork as Caoimhe went on: 'But married, spouses, partners, whatever, they're going to be having sex. Oh no! How awful! Cancel the patriarchy now.'

'You know, you only get so many vetoes,' Safa said. 'They keep track. They remember.'

'I don't see that as a problem.'

'But it *is* a problem,' Ajola said. 'It's always a problem. The woman comes in from work, exhausted, dishevelled, sweat-stained pits, greasy hair, trying to work out when she can see a dentist for a cavity, and the man is like, this woman exudes sex. See how she teases me, she tempts me, she drives me wild with an insatiable desire.'

They all laughed. Benjamin's show trilled.

'I hate the phrase "balls deep",' Ella said, turning away from

Benjamin. Caoimhe nodded sharply at him but Ella waved a dismissive hand. 'He doesn't know what it means.'

'What does it mean?' Safa frowned. 'What's wrong with it?'

'Balls deep?' Ajola said as Ella put another piece of gum in her mouth. 'When you love something so much, you're balls deep.'

Safa shrugged.

'So?'

'When you love something so much,' Ajola said, leaning forward, 'the only way you can possibly articulate the scope of that love is to conjure up the image of you penetrating it so utterly, deeply and completely with your penis that your dangling testicles are the only part of your sexual organ that remains outside. That your body is, literally, balls deep in the object of your desire.'

Safa laughed and held her hand to her mouth.

'I thought it was something to do with football.'

'My brother uses it so casually at work. Balls deep here, balls deep there,' Ella said as Safa leant back in the booth, laughing, and covered her face with both her hands. 'Balls deep in this hearing. Balls deep in the judgement. Balls deep in the performance evaluation.'

'Stop!' Safa said, making Benjamin glance up for an instant.

'I don't know why I hate it,' Ella said, shaking her head. 'But I do.'

'It's because, first and foremost' – Ajola pointed at her – 'it's a well-known figure of speech that excludes women. Women can't be balls deep.'

'Sure we can!' Caoimhe exclaimed. 'If I want to be balls deep, I go balls deep!' Someone at the bar glanced over his shoulder at her. 'I'm balls deep in this conversation right now.'

'But you're not. You don't have balls!'

'It's a figure of speech. It's metaphorical. It's allegorical. It's symbolical.' With each word, Caoimhe pointed down the table at Ajola while Sophia reached out and waggled the end of her finger. 'Anyone can be balls deep, Ajola. Stop gatekeeping our balls!'

'I'm saying, it's a male experience,' Ajola replied. 'The notion of being balls deep is an experience that men understand. They coined that phrase. Sure, women use it. But it, first and foremost – ah!' She made a noise over Caoimhe's protests. 'It's a male's experience.'

'You can't just talk over me.'

'*Balls deep*,' Ajola squeaked in a little voice. 'Equating absolute love with the male experience of sex. *Balls deep.*'

'Quit it!' Caoimhe threw a napkin at her. 'You're living in semantics. What would Cromwell say about your myopic view of men? Of language? About your gatekeeping of phrases that encapsulate and articulate?'

'Thomas Cromwell would be shocked, *shocked*' – Ajola exclaimed. The person at the bar picked up their drink and moved away – 'that in decent society, people were so casually using a figure of speech that revolved around genitals and sex. It would be scandalous.'

'Now that, I don't agree with,' Sophia cut in. 'Weren't they bawdy in the Tudor times?'

'We're becoming so sensitive as a society,' Caoimhe said.

'The opposite!' Ajola exploded. 'Did you know fellatio and cunnilingus used to be seen as deviant behaviour in the twentieth century? Now it's first-date material.'

'Not the first,' Caoimhe said.

'Weren't the Romans bawdy as well?' Safa asked. 'And the Greeks?'

'Yeah, didn't they find bawdy graffiti in Pompeii?' Ella said.

'Can women be bawdy?' Safa shrugged.

'No,' Ajola said. 'Else there'd be comparable female figures of speech to balls deep. Busting a nut, having a boner, getting a hard on, balls of steel, balls out, the dog's bollocks, how's it hanging, Billy big bollocks.'

'God, how do you know so many of these!'

'They're all bawdy male phrases! Where are the bawdy expressions related to the female anatomy and experience?'

'How weird does bawdy sound now?' Safa said. 'Bawdy, bawdy, bawdy. It's lost its meaning.'

'Off their tits,' Caoimhe said as the waitress brought their plates over. 'There's a bawdy expression related to female anatomy.'

Caoimhe

WHEN CAOIMHE WAS thirteen, her mother sat her down and handed her a small Marks and Spencer's carrier bag.

'What's this?' Caoimhe asked, turning the parcel over in her hands.

'Open it,' her mother said.

They were sitting opposite one another at the long dining-room table. Caoimhe was still in her school uniform, the smell of cold air clinging to her clothes. Her mother was wearing her house cardigan, hands clasped comfortably over her stomach, a small cup of tea steaming in front of her. Caoimhe slowly unwrapped the bag. She had no idea what it could possibly be, what little trinket or secret her mother had stowed away for her in there.

She pulled out the item inside (small. Delicate. Soft) and held it up to the effervescent light streaming in through the French doors.

It was a training bra.

Caoimhe tutted in disgust and dropped it as if it had burnt her.

'Why have you bought me that?' She tutted again and shook her head.

'You're developing now, Caoimhe.'

Caoimhe stood up suddenly from the table, knocking over her chair. The surface of her mother's tea wobbled.

'You are so annoying!'

'You're going to have to wear it someday. You're starting to look ridiculous in your school shirts.'

Caoimhe gave a shriek of annoyance and ran from the table. She clattered upstairs, slammed her door shut and fell on the bed. She could hear her mother calling after her. Enraged, she rolled on to her front and pummelled her pillow into the mattress.

The next day, she found the training bra along with a spare in her top drawer. She took her scissors from her school pencil case and cut the bra into tiny pieces. She tossed the (small, delicate, soft) fragments out of the window, where her mother would have to pick them up from the flower bed.

In the end, she had to start wearing the spare. When she was fourteen, the backside of the crest on her PE shirt inexplicably began to irritate her skin. After three years without a problem, it suddenly began to chafe. She kept plucking at it throughout every PE lesson, trying to draw the fabric away from her skin and prevent shiny red welts appearing. When she realized it was the indisputable evidence of her developing bosom, she had pummelled the pillow into the mattress again, hot tears stinging her face.

When she was fifteen, she noticed hair growing on her underarms. She raged about that as well. How unfair! How could life be so unfair! In the mirror in her bedroom, she examined her underarms, looking at the long, black, wispy hairs. How could she get rid of them? Buy a razor? Impossible! She tried ripping them out with pieces of Sellotape but that only irritated her skin. As the weeks went by, the hair grew longer and thicker. She was sure people could see it through her shirt. Hairy Caoimhe with her hairy underarms. A razor seemed like such an enormous decision. Such a commitment to hygiene maintenance that she had never had to consider before. How much did a razor cost? How often did you need to buy one? Could you reuse a razor? What if she accidentally cut herself and bled to death? And her mother would make such a big deal of it.

'*What do you need a razor for?*'

'*What are you hiding?*'

'*Hair on your underarms?*'

'*Hair?*'

'*Hair?*'

'*Hairy?*'

'*Let me see! Lord, let me see!*'

She decided not to tell her mum. But that meant waiting until she was sixteen to buy a razor because they were an age-restricted item. When she finally bought one and got it home, she sat on her bedroom floor and examined it. The rows of blades. The ergonomically designed handle. A weapon of femininity that was alien to her. It was actually pretty easy to use. The ugly hair on her underarms vanished in a second. The smallest whisper. Gone. She took the opportunity to start shaving her legs as well, something she had never considered before. The razor left her legs long and lean, glossy, silky, just like the adverts on television. She sat in the dark and silent privacy of her room and enjoyed stroking her new legs.

'Oh my God! Caoimhe finally shaved her legs!' Fiona Green shouted across the hall in the next PE lesson. Everyone looked. Even the boys. 'Now you just need to comb your hair!'

'Shut up,' Ajola replied and kissed her teeth. 'Why are you so obsessed with her?'

The last step on Caoimhe's journey to a proper, polished and primed woman was her period. She didn't get her period until she was seventeen. In Year 7, a girl had come up to their table in a desperate whisper and asked for a pad and Caoimhe had given her some paper. Later, in Year 9, on a school trip, another girl had been going down the row of students outside the ladies' toilet, asking each of them for a tampon. When she got to Caoimhe, she deliberately skipped her, and asked Ella on the other side. How could she have known that Caoimhe hadn't started yet? Was it some private club where the members all recognized one other?

'You're lucky,' Sophia told her when she brought it up. 'It's a right pain.'

Caoimhe didn't feel lucky. She saw the other girls with their pads and tampons stowed away in their bags. She watched them skip swimming on certain days. She heard them discussing headaches and nausea and their remedies for it, how they put up with physics whilst cramping up, how they revised whilst taking ibuprofen.

'I got my period when I was fourteen,' her mum told her, unprompted, one day.

'Mum! Don't tell me that!'

'I'm just letting you know so you can prepare. Girls often start at the same time as their mothers.'

But age fourteen came and went and Caoimhe didn't start her period. She had her first kiss, she did her GCSEs, she tried a cigarette and bought alcohol underage all before her period arrived. She started to worry that she was a freak. Some kind of half-woman, perhaps with an undiagnosed condition. Did she have an undescended scrotum? Had the doctors wrongly assigned her gender at birth?

The anxiety ate her up. She fixated on a bump in her oesophagus, running her hands up and down her neck. Was this a malformed Adam's apple? How long should she leave it before booking a doctor's appointment and saying, I've never had a period. They would probably take her for tests. Her mother would say, you should have told me years ago and we could have saved you!

So, when her period arrived at the age of seventeen, she was relieved. She was normal. A woman. It was all fine.

She often thought back to those early teenage years, her angry, red face in the mirror as she scratched at her underarm hair. Her frantically rubbing her sore breast at the end of the day, enraged that she would have to wear the bra, that her mother would win. She had never been like the other girls. It was probably why she was so outstanding at running. She was just different. Complex. Multi-dimensional. Unique. A winner.

'Don't you care that he gets his greasy hands all over your phone?' Caoimhe nodded at Benjamin. 'Or if he smashes the screen?'

'It's totally insured.' Ella put her knife and fork down. 'It's got the highest level of insurance you can imagine.'

'I'm insured out of my arse, mate,' Caoimhe said in a deep voice.

'One I always use on the kids,' Ajola said. 'Now we're *equals pequals*.'

'We are *not* equals pequals,' Safa said sternly.

'We watched those DVDs for hours.' Sophia held up her fork. 'I've gone fucking mental for olives.'

'Remember when Super Hans runs to Windsor?' Safa said. 'That's you, Caoimhe.'

Caoimhe smiled. She felt a bit deceitful accepting that role, now she had Evie to contend with. Or was that a thought only a loser would have?

'Obviously.' She lifted her chin. 'I am really good at running.' They laughed. Benjamin glanced up for a second, and then looked back at the phone screen. 'I'm going to start training with an oxygen mask,' Caoimhe continued, each word only intended to reassure herself. 'I know my worth.'

'Nothing is more deceitful than the appearance of humility,' Ajola said.

'Where's that quote from?' Sophia asked.

'*Pride and Prejudice*. Mr Darcy says it.'

'Oh my gosh, I'm reading *Pride and Prejudice* right now.' Safa opened her arms. 'Isn't that weird?'

'Weird.'

'The collective unconscious,' Ajola said and pointed a mushroom around at them.

Sophia picked up her phone. She sucked her breath through her teeth.

'Guys,' she hissed, holding it up. 'They've texted back.'

'What do they say?' Safa peered forward to see the message.

It was blazed across the middle of the screen, so loud and visible, Safa instinctively cupped her hands around the phone.

Let's meet then. Zoom?

'That's insane.' Safa sat back down. She glanced around at the others. 'We can't.'

'I think we can.' Ajola nodded. 'Last time, we bound the spell in good faith' – Caoimhe groaned and put her hands over her face – 'as a solid unit. As women of the earth. As *Wicca*. It protects us.'

'If it protects us, why is this person suddenly texting then?' Caoimhe asked, not moving her hands off her face. She wished Ajola wouldn't talk like this. It trivialized it. 'What happened? Did the guarantee run out?'

'Perhaps something happened to weaken the spell,' Ajola said. She put her knife and fork down. 'Something in each of our own lives has shaken us to our marrow and caused the bonds that hold Chris in the earth to unravel.'

'Al-ayn,' Safa said as they looked at one another. 'The evil eye.'

Ella

ONCE, ELLA WAS typing up some case notes at home. She was sitting on the sofa in the upstairs office, head down, glasses on, her fingers darting across the keyboard as her eyes flashed between her immaculate handwriting and the screen.

Without any warning, no sound, no shift in air pressure, no humming of the spheres, Benjamin collided with the side of her head, exploding her glasses off her face and knocking her laptop to the floor.

She was so enraged. The anger blossomed within her. Before Benjamin came into existence, she had no idea she had the capacity for such anger. What a well of rage and discontentment lay within her. And it sprang from nothing. No source deep in the mountains. No trickling. All at once, a torrent. She had looked online and the advice was always 'Count to ten to dispel anger'. Count to ten? Had the writers of these articles ever felt anger? It came from nothing. There was no one. There was no two or three. There was nothing but ten. And it came as quickly as a slap across the face.

She had pushed him into the sofa cushions. He looked shocked, then angry, then afraid. His sudden emotive changes did nothing to dispel her anger. It made it worse. This was all his fault. This whole situation was his fault. She wanted to pick him up and let his feet dangle off the floor, like Thanos did to his enemies. She didn't. Perhaps that was the most chilling thing.

'Don't do that!' she snapped.

She pushed her nose right up to his nose and bared her teeth like a wildcat. He bared his teeth back at her, tears slipping from his eyes. His skin had gone very red. He raised a hand and slapped the side of her face.

Ella furrowed her brow in the most contorted way she could and hissed at him from the back of her throat. He looked so shocked. She felt the taut energy leave his body.

'Don't do that,' she hissed again. 'It's really annoying.'

He was breathing heavily, his chest rising and falling, his cheeks almost purple from his anguish. She waited, trying to gauge whether her anger had dissipated yet. It had. She stood up.

'Now, go away,' she said.

He sniffed and rolled off the sofa on to the floor. She watched him climb to his feet. She felt no remorse. No guilt. No sorrow. In any other relationship in the world, friend, partner, sister, niece, nephew, cousin, if one person came out of nowhere with a flying kick designed to hurt you, you would be able to raise your hands in return. To make a formal complaint. To ask to be removed from that person. But, as a parent, you just had to accept it. Benjamin stopped at the door, turned and roared at her, baring all his teeth, his own fists clenched by his side. Ella looked back with a silent glare.

'Go away,' she said quietly.

'No! You go away!' Benjamin shouted, his language clear and articulate.

'I wish I could.' Ella picked her laptop off the floor and sat back down. Her notebook had been thrown across the room in the scuffle. 'I wish I could.'

Benjamin had stomped off down the hall. Truly stomping. His impression of an Angry Person. Ella had plunged her hands into fists and hit her own leg. It wasn't fair. That was the point. It wasn't fair.

'I say we talk to them.' Ella put her knife and fork down. 'I don't want to skulk around this for the rest of my life, looking over my shoulder and thinking every knock at my office door is the police. Let's send them a Zoom link.' Something screamed from Benjamin's screen. Ella couldn't handle any more tension. This had to end. She took a deep breath. 'I can organize it from a new email account. This weekend, maybe?'

'Text that now,' Caoimhe said and pushed her empty plate away.

Sophia's thumbs darted across the screen. They heard the text *zhwm* out and then, almost immediately, a *zhwm* back in.

'That was quick,' Safa said. 'They must be constantly on their phone.'

'Thumbs up.' Sophia showed them the screen. 'It's on.'

'Thumbs up.' Caoimhe shook her head, disgusted. 'An emoji. They used an emoji to confirm.'

'Welcome to the future,' Ella said. Benjamin started tapping his screen hard with one finger. Ella gently slid her own finger across to start the next show. 'Before I had kids,' she explained to the others, 'whenever I saw a child sitting on a phone or tablet in a restaurant or whatever, I always used to think, boo hoo, how terrible, what awful parents, what suffering kids. I tell you' – the fear about their situation, the tension, the texts all lent vehemence to her voice – 'I would not be sane if I didn't have a phone to give Benjamin whenever we're out. I don't know how previous generations did it.' Ella gingerly touched her swollen lip. 'I don't know how people without 4G do it.'

'Everything is relative,' Ajola said. 'Maybe there are tribes deep in the forests that say, I just don't know how people without hand-whittled flutes do it.'

'People in medieval times saying, I just don't know how people without spinning tops do it.'

'People in the Stone Age saying, I just don't know how people without different-sized rocks do it.'

THE PAN

Sophia

'YOU WANT TO come with me to buy a new cat?' Jill asked at the school gate the following day.

'A new cat?'

The children were just filing in through the classroom doors, their mums waving them off from the fence, buggies and scooters scattered across the pavement. Sophia had deviated from her usual fashion choices that morning, wearing a purpose-bought M&S burgundy mini dress, with a smart lace collar. She felt a little overdressed in it but, for once, she and Jill didn't look as if they had coordinated their outfits.

'Yeah.' Jill waggled her sunglasses at her. They were faux Ray-Bans, like Sophia's. 'I'm picking her up from a seller this morning. Want to see a picture?'

'Go on then.'

Jill got her phone out and turned it towards Sophia. She scrolled through some pictures of herself posing in front of the mirror. 'Sorry,' she said. 'They're for Jared. Oh . . .' She swiped past a picture of Cillian Murphy. 'That's just a guy I met on Tinder.' She put a secretive finger to her lips. 'Don't tell Jared. Here we are.' She held up a photo of a little grey kitten. 'Baby Isla, isn't she cute?'

'Isla?' Sophia said. Behind her, the school door slammed shut. 'That's my daughter's name.'

Jill shrugged and minimized the photo.

'I don't name them. They come' – she lifted her sunglasses up – 'pre-named, Sophia. Do you want me to change the name of the cat, just for you?'

'What's this?' Hannah, another mum, asked, coming to stand near them. Jill leant her forearm on her shoulder as if they were buddy cops from a movie. 'Changing the name of a cat?'

'I'm adopting a little kitten today,' Jill said. 'Sophia thinks I need to change the name the rescue centre gave her.'

'I never said change it.' Sophia held up her hands. 'I just think—'

'Boo, Sophia,' Hannah said and stuck her tongue out. 'Don't be so petty.'

'I'm not. The name is fine.'

Jill gave a self-satisfied smile and put her phone in her pocket.

'Me and the other ladies are going out for lattes,' Hannah said, singing the last word and putting her hand in the air like she was on the stage. 'You two fabulous ladies coming?'

'You know it,' Jill said. 'Sophia? Or do you need to go round the neighbourhood renaming pets?'

Hannah laughed. Sophia drew herself up.

'No,' she said. 'I'll come. The name is fine, seriously, Jill.' Timid. Meek. 'I shouldn't have said anything.'

Pathetic.

'I love this shirt,' Hannah said, plucking at Jill's red and black chequered shirt. 'Love it, Jill. Where did you get it?'

'A Tinder date bought it for me,' Jill said. She winked at Sophia and then put a finger to her lips to Hannah. 'I'll tell you more about it later.'

Sophia frowned to herself. She longed to love Jill. She yearned to just be friends with her. Jill was so funny, and so beautiful and so engaging. Her attention was worth ten times that of anyone else. So why did she feel the need to be such a psycho! Instead of nurturing a genuine friendship with her, Sophia was forced to warily navigate her suspicions about blackmail, treading softly, watching carefully, teasing out answers from Jill's strange behaviour and comments. It was just like when they were eight; a friendship offered on an open palm, but some darker, ulterior motive concealed in the other fist. She hated how familiar the feeling in her stomach was. After twenty-six years, how had she not escaped it?

At the café, Sophia tried to duck behind Jill in the queue so Jill would order first but Jill re-ducked behind her. Sophia thought about re-re-ducking but it would look too weird. She tried to order the most bizarre drink she could think of (an almond milk hot chocolate with a shot of hazelnut) but Jill tutted and flicked her arm.

'That's my signature drink.' She pouted at Sophia. 'You don't have to copy me at everything, you know?'

Sophia sat at the end of the table and watched as Jill sashayed to sit with Hannah and the other mums. They were all laughing over a Tinder story Jill was telling. She wondered how Jill would navigate the Zoom meeting at the weekend. Would she obscure her face? What angle was she working here? How did she know about Chris? Who names a cat Isla?

Safa

SAFA PAUSED THE laptop. Outside, thick blue clouds were gathering on the edge of the evening. Javeria and Aleena were asleep in the bedroom next door and Safa was logged in to Emaan's Instagram account, stalking the woman Haaris had met. Danielle Bloom.

Just living my best life. Seeking adventure wherever I go.

She posted several times an hour, seemingly chronically online. There were photos of her on the beach, rock-climbing, holding a glass at a garden party. What the hell was she doing with Haaris? The LGBT+ flag was all over her socials. Photos of her drinking. She was over a decade younger than Haaris. Was he having a midlife crisis? Was Safa? A tingling in Safa's jaw cascaded down her neck, through her shoulders and into her hands. Her brain was going round and round as her body sat still on the settee. These two simultaneous developments could not be a coincidence. Danielle Bloom and the text from beyond the veil. Were they somehow related? Was she going mad?

Make sure you are using inclusive language in everyday speech.

Underneath this was a list of words that Safa didn't recognize. Did Haaris understand these terms? How was he more progressive than she was now? How was he embracing some ultra-new liberal mindset and she was left hunched over in this little flat, being blackmailed?

She closed Instagram, making the brightly lit and over-filtered photo of Danielle Bloom in sunglasses holding a placard that said 'SEX WORK IS WORK. FIGHT FOR FEMALE EMPOWERMENT' dwindle to nothing. She sat on the sofa and stared at Kramer frozen on the laptop, a big yellow and red logo stamped by his ear, the evil eye pendant winking at her from the keyboard. She had to let Haaris go. She was meant to be moving on. She had to focus on meeting a blackmailer on Zoom.

She abruptly sat back up. No, she couldn't let this go. This would suffocate her. And, who knew, maybe it was all a set-up. This Danielle Bloom was whoever had texted Sophia. She was the one who was going to meet them on Zoom at the weekend.

Safa picked up her phone, opened Emaan's Instagram again and then scrolled to find Danielle Bloom's account. She tapped the private message icon and then paused, thumbs hovering over the keypad.

Hi, she typed, then deleted it and minimized the app. She dropped the phone on to the sofa and hit play. After a few seconds, she picked up the phone again, sat up straight and reopened Instagram.

Hi, she typed. My name is Safa, I was married to Haaris. Safa paused and looked up at the ceiling. Would you like to meet up and chat? I can buy you a coffee? She quickly backspaced that in case Danielle thought she was calling her cheap. Would you like to meet up for coffee and chat? Would be nice to get to know each other!! She backspaced one of the exclamation marks. Too eager. Maybe erase both of them? No. A full stop looked psychotic. One exclamation mark was friendly but not too zany. She tilted her head back and looked at the ceiling again. Yes, that was fine. She would talk to Danielle Bloom. There was nothing wrong with that. Safa hit send, minimized the app and then rapidly stood up before any other thought could cross her mind.

Ella

ON THE DAYS where Felix had Benjamin overnight, Ella would cycle into work. London was steadfast in the early morning. Greys and silvers, wide, empty roads, the glimmer of the sun on untouched glass. She liked being the only one waiting at a red light. She liked the way the shadows broke at vacant cross-roads and intersections, on the deserted bridges. She liked the pale blue morning sky. Cycling, the cold wind whipped at her face and tugged her hair behind her. It was a wind just for her; it had been waiting in the dark alleys and cobbled streets all night for her to come streaming past, to reach out, to stroke her face with long, pale fingers.

As she cycled, her wheels humming steadily beneath her, she saw glimpses of the other early-morning spectres. People like her, whom the wind waited to catch. A woman wearing huge head-phones on the second floor of an office block, slowly dancing, mop bucket abandoned behind her. Someone wearing a lanyard, carrying a disposable coffee cup, quick-stepping towards the Underground. A man rattling up the shutters to his newsagents, a pile of newspaper wrapped on the stoop beside him. Two window cleaners suspended from winches at the top of a tower block, swinging, side by side, as they washed the uppermost windows.

When Ella had been at university, she had done a module on the metaphysical poets. There was a notion, hundreds of years ago, of the Ptolemaic universe: a universe in which the Earth sat in the middle. And beyond the Earth were the seven spheres of the heavens, each a layer beyond our world. The higher one went up through the spheres, the more wonders were revealed, the increasingly perfect everything became, the higher the intelligence, the more beautiful the life. At the very top, the seventh sphere, *seventh heaven*, sat God. To ascend through the spheres was to be *uplifted*. The moon was the first of these celestial spheres. Anything *sublunar* was earth-bound, human, open to decay, flaws, inconsistencies, inconstants and imperfections. Through the pursuit of higher functions, art, virtuous activities, and with the rejection of senses, desire and lust, a person could move through the spheres and experience a seventh heaven through their time on earth. The spheres were beings themselves, intelligences, angels, and they made harmonious music. Sometimes, on quiet mornings like the one Ella rode through now, if you listened, you could hear the harmony of the music that the spheres made.

Somehow, in her life, Ella had fallen into a sublunar hole. At one point, she was sure she was ascending through the spheres – being admitted to the roll, quoting John Donne, analysing civil cases and arguing for the rule of law. And now, that week on her first night off for ages, how had she tried to uplift herself? To move through the celestial bodies and nourish her soul, the essence of her existence? She had sat and watched *Avengers:*

Infinity War whilst eating a pizza. And the most critical engagement she had with the movie was that she felt Thanos was right. She wanted the Avengers to lose. Thanos was trying to stop climate change, poverty, famine, global resource shortages. And this group of egotistical sociopaths felt it was their duty to prevent him. The hubris. The entitlement. What right did they have to subject people to ongoing servitude?

Growing up, no one ever told you having children would relegate you to sublunar nonsense. Girls were led to believe having a child would be the culmination of their life's purpose. That there was no joy, no love, no fulfilment akin to having a child. It was seventh heaven itself; it was to transcend through the very spheres swirling above our heads. But now Ella knew the truth. It was all a lie. Once superhuman, she was now sublunar. Temporary, base, decaying and flawed. Burying a stiffening corpse and having a child were the most basic, biological function humans could do, driven by fear, desire, sex, lust, the lower functions. Of course it was sublunar.

She got off her bike and wheeled it round the back of the office to lock it up with her Abus City Chain 1010 bike lock. Beneath the bike rack, there was a little stone, painted black with a white five-pointed star drawn unsteadily in the middle.

Ella picked it up and rubbed her thumb across it. Not a Scout project. A reminder. The Zoom meeting loomed over her, casting a huge sublunar shadow over the case she was supposed to be focused on. She glanced around. Anyone could be watching her. It wouldn't be hard for someone to come by the office without being seen. She clutched the stone tightly in her hand and then put it in her pocket. She didn't want it anywhere near her, but she couldn't risk her brother finding it.

She put her helmet in her bag and changed the gum in her mouth. A new tactic she had recently adopted was regularly changing the flavour of the gum. Not just spearmint, spearmint, spearmint, but spearmint, strawberry, cinnamon, cool mint and wintergreen. There had to be something about the enzymes in there that would break down bad odours. Some kind of science. Chewing madly, she buzzed her way in through the back door and hurried up the stairs. Cynthia would be here at nine thirty so they could go to Westminster together for some last-minute procedural changes and to give Eric a walkthrough of the court process before the hearing on Monday. Ella had suggested that Eric meet them there.

She put her bicycle bag down under her desk and pulled her court clothes out of the large wardrobe behind Maduka's desk. Her phone started to buzz from her pocket. It was Felix. She rolled her eyes. Trust him, on one of the biggest days of her career, to be calling before seven.

'What?' she said, holding up the clothes by the hanger so the hems didn't drag on the floor.

'Benjamin doesn't have a bottle for nursery.'

'Well, buy him one, then, Felix. Problem-solve.' She pushed open the door to the bathroom. Her voice echoed off the tiled walls. 'Work systematically to reach a satisfying conclusion.'

'Naturally, but where is the bottle he usually has?'

'I don't know, Felix. My house, your house, at nursery. Things go missing.'

'Is his name on it?'

Ella knew it was but she didn't want to give Felix the satisfaction of answering.

'I don't know.' She hung her clothes on the back of the toilet door.

'You don't know?'

'No, I don't. Why don't you buy him one and then write his name on it and then *you'll* know.'

'I must be at work at eight,' Felix said.

'Yes, and I'm at work now.' She kicked her trainers off. Felix was silent for a long time. Ella tried to unhook her shorts with one hand and the little black stone fell to the floor. It didn't skid or bounce. It stuck resolutely in place, as if it was magnetized, the star glaring up at Ella. 'I have to go, Felix.'

'*Ja, ja,*' Felix said, then, more quietly, '*ja.*'

Ella hung up. She picked up the stone, checked there were no feet in the other cubicles, and dropped it into the sanitary waste bin.

She returned to her office in more professional clothes and took out her dress shoes from under her desk. Cynthia and Maduka came in just as she was switching up for her third piece of gum for the day (cool mint fresh).

'So,' Cynthia said. 'Thoughts?'

Ella moved her gum around her mouth. Her first instinct was to think Cynthia was talking about the meeting at Finsbury Park. The text. The stone. The watchful eye. The Zoom meeting. As she slowly chewed, her mind, her disgusting, sublunar mind, caught up with her.

'I can't honestly see the judge granting anything.'

'It got through mediation,' Cynthia said. 'And there were some big sums there.' She smiled. 'Greedy bastard, eh?'

Ella spent a few seconds making sure her gum was hidden inside her teeth.

'I don't know,' she said finally. 'It's taken seven years to get to this point. His parents have offered him so much, inside and outside of mediation. If he really was just greedy, why keep pursuing it? I think he wants to set a precedent.'

'You think he has high-minded values?' Cynthia asked.

'I do. I wouldn't have chased this case round and round for seven years if I didn't. You must think so, too?'

'I do,' Cynthia said, slowly. 'I do.' She checked her watch. 'We should go. I'm curious, though,' she said as they left Ella's office, Maduka meeting them in the corridor. 'Why have you pursued it so vigorously all these years if you don't think the judge will grant anything?'

Maduka shut the office door behind them and they set off for the lifts.

'High-minded values?' Ella said. She couldn't articulate her answer. Because she *wanted* him to win? Her dress shoes echoed off the black and white tiled floor. She suddenly hoped they didn't run into her brother. 'I don't know. Maduka' – she turned to him – 'would you sue your parents for giving birth to you without your consent?'

'They've got nothing to sue for,' Maduka said and then laughed to show he was joking. 'No,' he said as they stepped out of the front of the office and on to the street. A black car was waiting for them. 'Life is a gift. You can't sue someone for a gift.'

'A gift that you couldn't refuse?' Cynthia said.

'A gift that I want,' Maduka replied.

'I – Oh no.' Ella stopped. 'He's here.'

Eric was hurrying up to them, phone out in one hand, hitching up his trousers with the other. Maduka, Cynthia and

Ella, paused mid-step by the open car door, watched him trot towards them. Eric had wet hair scraped back on his scalp and had shaven the beard hair from his neck, leaving little purple pin pricks against his soft flesh. His white shirt looked creased, and he was wearing jeans.

'We might have to change him,' Cynthia said.

'I thought we were meeting you there?' Ella said as Eric reached them.

'Oh.' Eric glanced at her, then climbed into the car first. 'I thought I was meeting you here.'

'It's fine,' Cynthia said as Ella looked at her. 'Maduka, can you sit in the front?'

Caoimhe

'BE PATIENT, ANAKIN. *It will not be long before the Council makes you a Jedi Master.*'

Anakin Skywalker hadn't been appreciated either.

Caoimhe leant forward and adjusted the huge bag of ice that was strapped to her foot. She had taken a nasty tumble at training and her ankle was throbbing. At the time, she had felt mortally humiliated more than anything else. She had jumped up, brushing off everyone's concerns, the pitying looks, Mateus's mischievous wink replaced by a sheen of second-hand embarrassment, Evie's tender words, and threw herself into six more 400-metre reps with more blood and vigour than she had mustered in her entire life. She wanted to catch Evie, but she was always a second ahead. Just one more second. How did she do it? The bloody Pokémon. How did you run one second faster? On the terracotta vista of another planet's sky-line, Anakin Skywalker lamented his wasted potential.

Caoimhe put her fingers in her ears, the frantic action and explosions of colour like something from a faraway dream.

She wanted to rage. She wanted to push her hands into the soft cotton wool of her soul and tear it apart. To eviscerate it. Where was her Obi-Wan Kenobi? She could excel, she knew she could, she just needed to grasp the opportunity and prove herself.

Evie had been strutting around at training in a tight pair of shorts that made all the men sidle over to talk to her. Evie. Bloody Evie. One-second-faster Evie. The worst part was Dean Weaver had come back to the club tonight. Gone was the dumpy, fat bloke from seven years ago who couldn't pace himself over 200 metres. Here was a machine. Lean, controlled, a running gait so sculpted and perfect it could stand in the Accademia Gallery beside David. He had absolutely magnificent legs. She wanted to make a plaster cast of his thigh. The bleached blond haircut, reminiscent of Paul Gascoigne from the 1996 Euros, was spectacular when it was racing away on 60-second 400-metre reps. Sixty seconds! Repetitions! The tattoo of Aristotle or Socrates or Plato, or whoever the robed and bearded figure on his forearm was, no longer stank of hubris but of divine distinction. After each rep, he and Evie had circled each other, talking, panting, sparring with questions, parrying away with answers, two masters of the craft sizing up an equal. Caoimhe had been gasping at the back, her ankle emblazoned with pain, dirt and tracks of blood smeared on her palms. She felt ashamed to even stand there, marked as she was by how ordinary her talent was. How adequate. How satisfactory. A useless nobody. She shifted her ankle on the ice and lowered her hands. The Zoom meeting was tomorrow. She should be focused on that, not running. Or should she focus on running and not that? Who even was she?

She needed someone to tell her. She put her hands over her face. Anakin Skywalker focused his anger. He used it to dominate.

Ajola

AFTER DROPPING OUT of college, Ajola ended up working in Tesco. It was no Parisian mathematics lab. But she got paid. She could take care of herself in such a way that she need never rely on her parents again. She need never look at them again. The thought was such a vindictive delight, it gave her purpose.

She was very laissez-faire about it with the others, as though it was part of the plan, as though she was Jeremy from *Peep Show* wandering through life without a care. She spent a long time each morning sorting out her hair and make-up, making sure the company-issued Tesco shirt fitted in a complementary way, checking there were no scuffs on her black pumps. Every Friday, once their shifts had ended, some of the checkout staff went to the pub across the road. Ajola had always made excuses to avoid going with them because she didn't think she could maintain the bubbly facade she so painstakingly applied all day. Instead, she went home and sat on her own, in her parents' house, and then, when she had enough money, in the studio flat she rented as far away from them as possible.

It had all seemed so exciting at the start. Looking back, it made her sick. The idea that a malevolent force had been watching her for seven years didn't surprise her. She felt she was living a life that had never been intended for her. She should have stayed at college. Gone to a proper university. Ended up in Paris in a lab coat. None of that materialized. Here she was, waiting for a Zoom meeting with a blackmailer. Alone in the abandoned universe, dogged by sinister figures with unholy intentions.

Ella

'ELLA,' SOPHIA SAID. Her Zoom background was filled with drifting clouds. 'How secure is Zoom?'

'Sophia,' Ella replied. Even alone, she was still chewing her gum, a force of habit she couldn't escape. 'Zoom calls aren't recorded and no one can hack into the conversations because of encryption.'

'Like the NSA,' Caoimhe said.

'That's America. It'd be GCHQ here. Before you speak!' – Ella said sharply as Sophia opened her mouth – 'we need to actually check encryption has been enabled. Not even developers can get to the content if encryption is enabled.'

'How do we check?' Safa asked.

'It's in Settings.'

There were a few seconds of mouse clicks. Ella's heart was drumming in her chest, not faster, just harder. She had had to do a lot of reading up on encryption in preparation for this. She hoped she'd got it right.

'I'm all good,' Caoimhe said. Her background was completely

blank, like she was a deity speaking to them from the void.

'Can I record it?' Sophia asked.

'Everyone gets a disclaimer saying the meeting is being recorded,' Ella explained. 'You can. But our visitor will know.'

'Got it.'

'There's a forty-minute limit,' Ella reminded them. 'Just so you know. I'm not paying premium on this.'

'That's insane,' Ajola said, speaking to them from a Parisian skyline. 'Insane.'

'Can you remember in Year Ten,' Safa said from inside an aquarium, 'when we used to try and fit all those different words in conversations with Dr Smith? Like eucalyptus tree?'

'And Millennium Falcon.' Sophia nodded. 'He never caught on.'

'I don't suggest we do the same today,' Ella said. 'We have to take this seriously.'

'I am.'

'Find out what they know.' Ella chopped her hand into her palm. 'What they want.' She found she wasn't nervous. She was clinically focused, as if she was presenting a brief to her brother. No emotions, no doubt, just purpose. A beating heart, not faster, just harder.

'How long should we wait?' Caoimhe said into her camera. 'What if they never show?'

'Could all be a bluff,' Safa suggested. 'That would actually make me feel better.'

'Not me.' Ella shook her head. 'Living the rest of my life thinking—'

The Zoom chimed. A sixth person had joined the waiting room.

'Oh shit,' Sophia breathed. 'This is it.'

'Let them in, Ella,' Ajola said.

Ella smoothed down her shirt and composed herself to the camera.

'All right,' she said. 'Here we go.'

Safa

THE PERSON WHO appeared in the final Zoom window was clearly a woman: narrow shoulders, honey-coloured hair tied high on her head, elfin wrists and hands. The background of her camera showed a completely blank white wall, devoid of any pictures, colour, smudges or hand marks. She was also wearing a wooden, full-face masquerade mask, shaped like the Greek God Pan, with stubby horns protruding from the head and a triangular cleft nose in the middle. Safa put her hands over her mouth and nose to stifle a nervous laugh.

'Hello,' Ella said.

The Pan held up a finger.

'This cannot be recorded.' Her voice was quiet, soft, barely loud enough to ignite the yellow border around her Zoom window.

'No. It's not.'

The Pan slowly lowered her finger. There was silence. Someone's microphone crackled. Safa thought she might burst under the tension. She wished she could mute her camera so she could unravel in peals of unrestrained, overzealous laughter. Was this Danielle Bloom? What would Haaris say if he could see her now?

'Are you wearing the mask because we know you?' Sophia asked.

'I'm wearing the mask so you can't know me,' the Pan replied.

'Let's just begin,' Ajola said. 'There's a forty-minute time limit on this.'

'You don't have premium?' the Pan asked.

'It's not totally worth it,' Ella said.

Safa pressed her lips together and put her hands over her eyes to try and control herself.

Ajola

'YOU OBVIOUSLY KNOW what happened with Sophia's husband seven years ago,' Ajola said. The Pan didn't move. 'You want to use that information to get us to do something.' The Pan nodded, slowly. Ajola opened out her hands. 'Let's first hear what you want us to do and then we'll decide whether we're prepared to do it.'

The Pan made a scoffing noise behind the mask. Her microphone crackled.

'You are going to do it,' she said. She looked at her fingers as each one picked a nail of another. Ajola tried to physically prick up her ears, to catch any intonation or vocalization which could give a clue to this person's identity. 'I already know you will.'

'What did you actually see?' Ella cut in. 'Seven years ago. Can we get that out in the open?'

'Yeah, your information might be totally useless,' Caoimhe said, flatly, 'and you're just chatting shit.'

'Let's be polite,' Ajola said, studying the image on the screen before her. 'But also' – a bird flew between her and the Eiffel

Tower – 'Caoimhe's right. Can you share with us what you saw seven years ago?'

'I was there the night your husband, Chris, died. I saw you bury the body. I know the location of the body.'

Ajola drew a sharp breath. Was there something familiar in that voice?

The Pan adjusted her mask. 'I know you misled the police in all your statements from that night. I know you were all involved. Feel free to ignore me – I will just take the police to the burial site. I'll give them your names. And then it will cease to be my problem.'

'An allegation like that will ruin my life,' Ella said. 'Just tell us what you want us to do.'

'I want you to kill someone,' the Pan replied. 'I want you to bury their body so no one will ever find it. Just like you did seven years ago.'

The following silence was so utter and absolute, their mics might all have been collectively muted. Ajola sat quite still, letting the words sink in, too afraid to even twitch a finger. This was, surely, the third bad thing.

'I'm not doing that.' Caoimhe laughed, breaking the hush. 'No way. We buried a guy once and it was not fun. It's been torture for seven years. I moved to Europe to escape it.'

'That's fine, you don't have to,' the Pan said. The yellow outline around her Zoom window now flashed like a warning light. 'But then I'll go to the police.'

Ajola took a sudden, silent gasp of air, unaware she had been holding her breath.

'Everything you said could all be circumstantial evidence,' Sophia said quickly. 'Only your witness testimony implicates us.'

The Pan slowly turned her masked face. The blankness was chilling. Ajola felt her resolve tremble under the vacant eye-holes. She wanted to slam her laptop shut. To lie down. To stare at an empty ceiling.

'How will it affect your application for the certificate of his presumed death, Sophia? It could delay it indefinitely. And without that certificate' – the Pan shrugged – 'Chris's case will always remain open.' She gestured to the camera. 'An unanswered question. For all of you.' They were silent. 'Safa, Ella' – the Pan held her two palms out – 'what about your custody arrangements?'

'What?' Safa jerked upright as though she'd been slapped.

'I'm sure a judge would be willing to reconsider if the children's mothers are under investigation for murder.' Safa's mouth went slack. Ajola could see the colour drain from her face. She felt sick. 'And you, Ajola,' the Pan said. 'One of your students committed suicide four years ago.'

'What's that got to do with anything?' Ajola said quickly. Her stomach lurched. She wasn't going to vomit, surely, not now. She shifted in her chair.

'I'm saying it doesn't look good if you are then arrested for murder. Do you think you'll ever teach again?' the Pan said and Ajola's face flushed red. 'What will your colleagues, your students, the parents think? One dead student, then done for murder. It'll leave your reputation in the gutter. And that's just if you're arrested. Imagine when you're found guilty. Your presence will be a dark blemish on the lives of those children.'

Ajola's tongue went limp.

'This is how I know you will do what I want.'

Caoimhe

'YOU CAN'T THREATEN me with anything,' Caoimhe said. She pulled her shoulders back, exposing her sternum like someone about to take a punch. She was more solid than the Pan, probably stronger, too. Head-to-head, she could take her. 'I'm not going to go and kill a man based on what you may or may not have seen.'

'Yes,' the Pan said, thoughtfully. 'But I think the other four will do what I've asked them. So your inclusion is inconsequential to me.'

Caoimhe snorted loudly.

'Nothing about me is inconsequential.'

'Yet you refuse to step beyond your comfort zone and truly prove your potential.'

Caoimhe frowned and raised the corner of her lip in a sneer, but she felt rattled.

'Is that meant to sway me?'

'Does it? I thought you weren't like the other girls. One of the men. What might a man do in this situation? What would Anakin Skywalker do?'

Caoimhe's head began to froth, all the bubbles rising to the top of her brain, her blood suddenly fizzy. She had the bends; she had risen from the ocean floor too quickly and now her veins were flooding with nitrogen. How had the Pan been inside her head? The others were motionless, jaws set, skin off-colour.

'Who is it you want us to kill?' she asked.

Sophia

'HOLD ON, HOLD on.' Sophia held up her hand. She had to slow this all down. 'We're not killers. We just turned up and Chris was dead, so we buried him because it looked like I was going to be framed for it.'

The Pan was silent for a beat.

'You never even killed him?' She snorted and put her hands over her masked face. 'Oh, my days.'

'He worked in finance,' Sophia snapped. 'He had some weird clients. People who dealt with large sums of money outside the law.' She took a deep breath. 'I always presumed it was one of them. Someone he pissed off, or someone who thought he had too much information. The police never took that seriously, though. They always thought he'd just run off.'

'And they never suspected you?' the Pan asked.

Sophia was silent.

'I had four alibis,' she finally said. Someone's microphone crackled again. 'Look,' Sophia continued. 'We're not killers.' She glanced around at the other Zoom windows. Everyone was staring back at her, like that night, seven years go. 'How about,' she said to the Pan, 'you kill the guy' – she held out a hand – 'and we'll bury the body?'

'I could kill him.' The Pan laughed loudly, the mask muffling the sound. 'I would kill him. I want Trent Davies dead. But you're going to do it. It's safer for me this way.'

'That's not fair,' Ella said. Her voice was decidedly un-Ella. It was almost a whine. Sophia had never heard such a tone from her before and it scared her.

'What a shame.' The Pan leant back. 'I'm not here to be fair. I'm here because I need someone dead, and you're easy to manipulate.'

There was silence across all six Zoom windows. The only real movement was Ella's jaw working as she chewed her gum.

'Do we have a timeline to decide?' Safa asked. 'To sort of weigh it up and get our heads straight?'

'You have a timeline to get it done,' the Pan replied. 'Either he's dead by the twenty-first of June or I take the police to the body.'

'The twenty-first of June?' Ella cried. Sophia flinched. 'That's in four days!'

The Pan shrugged.

'How much time do you need to kill a man? I'll WhatsApp you his name, his picture, his place of work, his address, his work schedule. Wednesday is the day he gets the bus home alone. Do it then. All other times, he's with someone.'

Sophia rubbed her forehead. This was moving too quickly. Why did Jill want her to kill a random person?

'Of course,' the Pan continued, 'I'll need to see his dead face when it's done. I won't just take your word for it.'

202

That was such a Jill comment to make.

'What if we accidentally kill the wrong guy?' Safa asked.

'Then I guess you're going to prison, Safa.' The Pan reached forward. 'The twenty-first of June,' she said. 'I'll send you the information.'

Her Zoom window vanished. There was silence. Sophia could hear the foghorn clearly in the distance. Then they all started talking over one another.

'This is crazy!'

'Can't we go to the police? Blackmail is illegal!'

'So is burying a body that you found in the kitchen, though.'

'We need to take time away,' Ajola said, holding up her hands. Sophia realized she hadn't spoken for a while – most unlike her. She looked very pale. 'We can all agree this is some serious—'

'Shit,' Caoimhe finished.

'Exactly. Let's take time and come back, when we've thought, you know, in context' – Ajola looked around at the other Zoom windows, her jaw set – 'what direction we want to go in.'

'We only have four days,' Ella reminded them. 'How much time can we take?'

'Let's talk again tomorrow night,' Ajola said.

'Another Zoom, or WhatsApp?' Caoimhe suggested.

'We can't WhatsApp the decision to murder a man,' Safa said. 'Zoom? I can do another Zoom, though.'

'What if things go bad for us and the police do get involved?' Ella said. 'All our devices will be confiscated and searched, our data, our messages, our history.'

'You said Zoom was secure!' Sophia cried. She was trying to keep up with the conversation, all the information flying at her. How had they lost control after seven years of being in charge?

'It is secure. But' – Ella shook her head – 'the police will be able to see we keep having Zoom calls together, after seven years of no contact.' She was gesturing frantically with both hands. 'That's the sort of unusual behaviour that will make them dig deeper.'

Sophia clapped her hands to her head and groaned.

'OK. It's OK.' Ajola's voice was calm and secure. She had composed herself. Sophia felt as if they were back in food technology when the smoked mackerel had exploded all over the inside of the microwave and Ajola had managed to salvage their kedgeree dish. Ajola held up a thumb. 'We don't Zoom.' She extended her finger. 'We Flickcall. Nothing unusual about us watching a new movie together. I'll send you the link. Easy. Tomorrow night.'

Sophia took a deep breath and let her hands slide down her face.

'Be careful,' Ella said. 'All of us. We have to accept that whoever that was can see everything we're doing.' She looked at each of them. 'She knew things about us.'

'Secret things,' Caoimhe agreed.

'She's been watching us for seven years.'

Sophia's heart had been strumming in her chest since she had closed her Zoom window. That night, she hadn't slept at all. She had gone down to stand in the garden at one point and look at the stars in case they provided some cosmic intervention, but there was nothing. So, she got her phone out and went on Jill's Instagram page. She'd already pored over it a thousand times and there was nothing to tie her to the Pan, no elaborate face masks, no hint at Greek mythology.

She minimized Instagram and went on Facebook. No one she knew posted on Facebook these days but that wasn't to say there wasn't something. She went on Jill's profile and clicked through her photos. There weren't many and it was easy to go back through the years. She paused briefly on 2016 just to check there was no photo of the five of them carrying Chris's body to the car, and then kept scrolling. When would she have graduated? Around 2010, if she hadn't had a gap year or sandwich year. By the time Sophia got to 2011, she had found what she was looking for: Jill in plain, long black robes with a mortar board perched on her perfect golden tresses, holding her rolled-up degree in the air in celebration. There were lots of graduation photos. Jill having a drink of champagne, Jill with other girls, Jill standing between two tall, handsome men. Sophia was looking for a close-up of the degree certificate. There was none. Annoyed, she scrolled down one of the group photos and scanned the comments.

Love you, girlies.

Always having fun x

Good times.

Nothing helpful at all. Then, she found it.

Jill in the mortar board and black robes, but this time, she had a graduation hood around her neck. The hood was blue-grey with a brighter blue trim, the exact colour and design that Sophia had worn on her own graduation from Exeter in 2010. Sophia used her thumb and forefinger to zoom in. There was no doubt. It was the exact same design. Jill had gone to Exeter University. She had graduated from there. They would have been there at the same time. That face outside the lecture hall all those years ago probably had been Jill.

'Mum?'

Sophia jerked around. Isla, bleary-eyed and in her pyjamas, was standing in the kitchen doorway.

'Why are you in the garden at six o'clock on a Sunday?' she asked.

'Couldn't sleep,' Sophia said, putting her phone away and moving towards the door. She tried to smile at Isla as they passed.

'Is this about the guy?' Isla asked with a sigh.

Sophia's heart lurched in her chest and she froze. She stared at Isla, her face sculpted with guilt. How did Isla know?

'The one from the doctor's surgery, right?' Isla said.

'Doctor's surgery?' Sophia frowned.

'Yeah, the guy you've been dressing up for. I don't mind. I'm happy to meet him.'

'Oh my God.' Sophia breathed a sigh of relief. 'Jesus. No, Isla, there's no guy at the doctor's surgery. I genuinely just couldn't sleep.'

Isla didn't look convinced. Sophia went out for a walk to try and clear her head. There was a thick mist lying dormant on the earth, sinuous and supple, clinging to the air, motionless in its gravitas, bisected only by two beams of blazing light.

Jill's black Range Rover Evoque was parked at the end of her street, headlights aglow. Jill wound down the window as Sophia drew level, and winked at her. Her thick honey hair had been cut to match Sophia's Year 10 German Exchange look. It looked much better on her.

'There you are,' she said. The Pokémon theme tune was

blasting out on her Bluetooth. 'Want to come and meet baby Isla?'

Hatred rushed into Sophia like air filling a void.

I wanna be the very best, like no one ever was.

Jill thought Sophia was a loser like Bethany, that she should still be sitting with Simon. Jill didn't think Sophia could kill a man.

To catch them is my real test, to train them is my cause.

'Hello!' Jill said and beeped the horn. 'Are you dumb?'

Sophia couldn't muster a response. She just stared up at Jill, feeling dirty and dusty in the gutter, devoid of thought, devoid of action. But, inside her skin, she was raging.

You teach me and I'll teach you.

'Boo to you then.' Jill stuck out her tongue. She started the engine. Sophia opened her mouth, but no sound came out. 'Text me when you're not being weird.'

Pokémon!

Safa

BEFORE 2023, SAFA had never gone to Eid Prayer. Haaris always went. Sufiyan did. Her dad, her brother. But never her. She stayed at home with Emaan and her sister and made platters of food with Ammi and her aunties. That year, for Eid al Fitr, she had wanted to go. She wanted some guidance, to feel part of something bigger.

'Thirty-three years old.' Her mother clucked in her mouth and waved a tea towel at her. 'Haaris won't have you back unless you prove to him that you are a good wife. Come in the kitchen and serve the meal for when he gets here.'

'Ammi, I'm not eating dinner here whilst he's here,' Safa had said. She was at the door, putting her bag around her shoulder. Emaan was on the sofa, trying to appear busy on her phone. The men had already gone. Javeria and Aleena were sitting on the carpet, comparing Lego houses.

Her mother raised her hands and looked heavenward.

'Give me strength!' she cried. 'Not sitting with your family on Eid. No wonder your husband divorced you.'

Safa gave Emaan the side-eye and Emaan smirked as she looked down at her phone.

'I'll come and eat when he's gone. Emaan will text me and I will come back then. Javeria and Aleena are here and he can spend Eid with them.'

'You are destroying your family,' her mother said. 'You know, I spoke to him. He wants to get a new wife. A good, Muslim wife who works hard for her family.' Safa shut her eyes, nodding. 'I said to him, I begged him: don't divorce Safa.' She waved the tea towel again. 'She can't be a divorcee at thirty-three, a single mum with two daughters.' She shut her eyes now and shook her head in a deep lament. 'He can give you another child, a son. Inshallah.' Her face lit up and she nodded at Safa. 'Yes? And then your son can take care of you when you're old, like me.'

'Ammi, that's . . .' Safa shook her head. 'Ammi, I don't want to do that at all. Why would you even suggest it?'

'You young generation,' her mother said, walking away. 'It is not Mickey Mouse.' She pointed over her shoulder at the television, where the girls were watching *Encanto*. 'Handsome prince comes and happy ever after. You need to make sacrifices.'

'It *is* Mickey Mouse!' Safa said back as her mother shut the door into the kitchen. 'That's what it *is*!'

'Just go,' Emaan said from the sofa. 'I'll text you when he's gone.'

Safa nodded and bent down to kiss each daughter.

The streets outside the mosque were packed with men and teenage boys, some in smart suits, others wearing white jubbas, all with topis on their heads. Safa felt like an utter imposter. She kept her head down and weaved in and out of the crowds until she latched on to a small group of women near the mosque doors. Inside the mosque, after taking their shoes off and placing them on the racks, the women pushed their way up a small staircase to a private space above the main prayer hall. The main prayer space was already packed, with men spilling out into the foyer and down the front steps.

'There's a guest speaker,' a woman said beside her. 'Arabic scholar. They've had to add more prayer times to accommodate everyone.'

'I've listened to his Cambridge University podcasts, ' someone replied. 'Amazing theologian.'

Safa nodded, impressed. She felt herself sink into her place in the universe. Surely this was a sign that she was on the right path. She was making the right decisions. She was meant to be here.

After they met the Pan, Safa, in a single, quiet moment, had found herself remembering Eid Prayer. Maybe she wasn't on the right path at all. Perhaps there was no path. There was no guiding hand; she was in charge of everything that happened to her. The Pan's words had chilled her to her core, ensuring such a strong grip on her innards that she doubted she would ever truly relax again. Prison. Haaris victorious over her, living with Danielle Bloom and raising Javeria and Aleena without her. She couldn't let that happen. Could she murder to avoid it, though? Such a weight, the decision between the two. And yet, she was in control of which decision to take. Was there a certain peace in that? Perhaps she could fully reclaim her life. Perhaps she could become a murderer.

Ajola

SHE LEANT ON the wall at the back of her house and began to pick at the red brickwork. It was cold. Chips splintered away, covering her fingertips in red dust. Was it pica where you were compelled to eat non-food items? Ajola always used to eat chalk as a child. She loved the dry sensation in her mouth, the earthy taste. Her mum used to snap at her about it. Her great-grandma used to tell her to eat plasterboard because she might have an iron deficiency. She touched her fingertip to her tongue and felt the roughness of the brick dust.

She hadn't been able to sleep that night. At around 4 a.m., she had gone to the toilet and been sick. It had been so banal, as though everyone woke up and vomited. She had wiped her mouth and gone back to bed. When the sun started to creep in around the edges of her curtain, she had got up again and gone to stand outside. There was a low mist, which left droplets of dew on her eyelashes. It was at times like this she wished she was addicted to alcohol or oxycontin or something. Anything that would take the edge off. Stop her thinking.

Ajola resisted the urge to eat more brick dust. Maybe her great-grandma was right. Maybe she did have an iron deficiency. A solitary wisp of cloud drifted overhead. She pictured Meg's mother and the shape her face would take if she heard that Ajola was a murderer. The sensation turned Ajola's insides to water and she had to crouch down, sure she was about to shit herself. How could the Pan know about Meg? Had the Pan been there? Some ethereal spectral form, even then? Where was Thomas Cromwell in all this?

Ajola wished she'd never become a teacher. She'd fucked her own life, fucked Meg's and was now probably going to fuck Daisy's. She wished she'd become a maths researcher in Paris, with the white coat and the chalkboard. No responsibility. No accountability. Then none of this would ever have happened. Looking back, she had no idea what was going through her mind when she suddenly took it upon herself to stop her education, when she chose to step into this, the abandoned universe. Her parents had been devastated in an angry and *accusing* way. Ajola couldn't believe either of them had the audacity to speak to her about it. Those two. Those *two*? Who were they to try and advise her? She wished there had been someone else, just as she wished for a guide now. A role model, a Thomas Cromwell. A hug. Sincere eye contact. Admiring intimacy. Genuine concern. *What should I do? Why am I feeling like this?* But there was no one. Her Thomas Cromwell was a dream and she was all alone. Murderer.

Ella

THAT SUNDAY, INSTEAD of being able to filter the information from the day before, transcend this earthly realm and achieve a higher level of thought, Ella had to watch Benjamin, who was a dinosaur.

He was adept at roleplaying, a real Daniel Day-Lewis, able to throw himself into each and every character. His most critically acclaimed role was the velociraptor. He would stalk around the living room, neck contorted, teeth bared, fingers twisted into talons, and roar like a velociraptor. The roars were endless and undulating. They stung her ears. She was sure he did it at just the right frequency and pitch to turn her brain into scrambled egg.

'Stop!' she shouted at him that morning as his roar reached such intensity, his throat crackled. 'Stop!'

On her lap was a scrap of paper where she was trying to list all the pros and cons of killing a man. She did not want to be doing this on the first weekend of Eric's trial. She did not want to be abusing the harmony of the spheres for this. Was there anything more sublunar than murder?

Anger clouds were circling around Benjamin. She could see them, watch him draw them into himself like oxygen. The audacity.

'Go away!' Benjamin shrieked. The last syllable ascended into a scream, far more inhuman than the velociraptor. It splintered her skull and pinched her cheeks.

Ella jumped out of her seat and ran at Benjamin. In that instant, she didn't know what she was going to do. She didn't know if she was a ten or a one. She didn't know if she was going to scream in his face or give him a two-footed kick to the chest. He didn't move. He just glared at her thundering approach, fists by his side, screaming, tears like crystals on his cheeks. A mouth so wide she could count all his white baby teeth. A mouth so wide she could see all the way down his crimson gullet.

At the last instant, she dodged past him and ran down the hall to the toilet, where she slammed the door and locked it. After a pause, a deep intake of breath, he started hammering on the wood and screaming. Dust tinkled off the door jamb and cascaded around her.

She sat on the toilet and put her headphones in, her chest rising and falling separate from her desires.

That afternoon, as she washed his hair in the bath, watching as the white suds dissolved under the gentle torrent from the shower, both of them pretending earlier hadn't happened, she came to the stark realization that she should never have had Benjamin. That had been the thought, the ear-worm, which had been wriggling away in her grey matter for four years. She should never have had Benjamin and her mother should never have had her. But she couldn't help any of that now. She just had to do what needed to be done to keep moving forward. Maybe there was nothing more metaphysical than murder.

Caoimhe

SHE SHOULD HAVE stayed in Copenhagen.

Caoimhe went for a recovery jog on Sunday. The morning was heavy, the sky overhead filled with ominous grey clouds. Any other time, it would be comforting. But after that Zoom call, it was a threat.

Could she really murder someone to validate herself? Obviously not. But there was more nuance to it than that.

Caoimhe ran down the hill towards the bridge from which she had once spied Rohan Rust. This time, she was him, on the lower road, her feet falling as his had done, her elbows emulating his, her form the embodiment of his. They were but a breath in time away.

She wouldn't be the one to deal the killer blow. She'd be on clean-up crew. She'd already done that and survived. And it wasn't simply validating herself. It was realizing her potential. The Pan had said it. She would go from being Anakin Skywalker, slave boy on a lost desert planet, to Darth Vader, the most powerful entity in the galactic empire.

As she approached the bridge, she looked up. She knew he would be there. It was knowledge that she had been born with. An innate knowing to her. Just as she passed through him, he passed through her.

Rohan Rust was moving slowly across the bridge, his gait more lackadaisical than usual, his head turned to the side, not dead-set ahead like normal. Caoimhe slowed and gazed up at him. Her mouth drifted open. Was there anything, ever, so perfect, as Rohan Rust. His dominance, his majesty. If she murdered a man, if she became a galactic force to be reckoned with, she could speak to Rohan Rust. She could run beside him, hold his perfect hand in her own.

As the entirety of her body beheld him, Caoimhe became aware of a figure running beside him. Laughing with him. Joking. She didn't think she'd ever seen Rohan Rust smile. Caoimhe recognized his running partner from her running style as easily as you would recognize someone's face.

It was Evie.

Absolute anguish clutched at her heart. She felt ready to burst into sobs. She could no longer feel her feet. Evie? Fucking Evie? How had Evie managed to find Rohan Rust? How were they together? Caoimhe was a thousand times prettier than Evie! And probably funnier too.

Caoimhe stared up at the two of them. Evie was laughing now. They were sharing a joke. And she was down here, in the gutter. She waited for the tears to come gushing out of her, but they didn't.

Next instant, they had crossed the bridge and were out of sight. A great gasp filled Caoimhe's lungs, almost a sob. She put her hands on her hips. She took a deep, steadying breath. She didn't belong in the gutter. She was Darth Vader, galactic evil who struck terror into hearts. She could do it. She could climb up. She could stand with Rohan Rust on the bridge. First, she just needed to kill one man.

Sophia

THAT SUNDAY MORNING, just hours after she had seen Jill outside, there came a knock at Sophia's door. On the doorstep, leaning up against her front window, were a man and a woman.

'Sophia Johnson?' the woman asked. She held out an ID card. 'I'm Detective Laura Stone; this is my colleague Josh Paulton.' The man showed his ID. 'We're from Thames Valley Police. We have a few questions regarding your husband's disappearance.'

Sophia felt air rush into her lungs. She stopped moving. Tears of fear pricked her eyes. She set her front teeth together. She had no idea how to act. Laura Stone and Josh Paulton stared back at her, their faces void of any emotion, carved from blank stone. What would an innocent wife say?

'Why?'

Her voice was thin as gauze. Thank God Isla was out.

'Maybe it's best if we go inside,' Laura Stone said and gestured behind Sophia.

Sophia didn't think her legs would work. She was stuck to the spot. An invisible but very real force field was holding her in place. She couldn't move. The police would try and move her. They would be unable to. They would call a doctor. He would be unable to move her as well. She would become a medical marvel, tourists visiting from all over the world to see the woman cemented to the ground, frozen in time. Isla would have to go and live with her grandparents. They'd need to build an awning over her so she didn't get wet in the rain.

'Sophia?'

'Yes.' Sophia stepped backwards into the hall. 'Yes.' The detective stepped inside, Laura Stone's polished shoes resting on the spot where they had cleaned up Christopher's blood with towels and bleach. 'Have a seat,' she said. 'Do you want a drink?'

'No, thank you.'

They both sat. Sophia stared at their shoes. Was there a stain on the wood? Was that a stain? How had she missed it after seven years. She rubbed her eyes. No, there was nothing there.

She wasn't sure how a woman who hadn't buried her husband would act. Would she pace? Would she cry? Would she sit down? Would she talk? Or be silent? Sophia patted her blazing cheeks with her hands. Her heart was fluttering away in her chest.

'You look nervous,' the man said. 'Don't be. Do you want to get yourself a drink? Coffee? Tea?' Sophia was shaking her head. 'Water?'

Sophia paused.

'Yes, OK.' She had read that drinking water helped prevent you from blushing too dramatically, and right then she needed to not be so red. She could feel her heartbeat in her neck and ears. Her skin must be crimson. 'Let me just get myself a drink. Do you want anything?'

She had already asked them that.

She went and stood in the kitchen and filled a pint glass with water. She glugged it, staring into the back garden. On the night of Chris's murder, the sensor light had been on.

'OK,' she said, coming back into the living room and sitting down opposite them. The water sloshed about in her stomach. She tried to breathe deeply and reduce the blush in her face. She must look guilty as hell.

'No need to be nervous,' the man said and smiled at her. 'I know this can all be very daunting but, trust me' – he put a hand on the coffee table between them – 'we're here to help.'

'I'm not daunted.' Sophia tried to relax in her seat, to erase the brusque tone that her words had been wrapped in. She held out her open palms. 'I'm ready.'

Laura Stone checked a delicate watch on her wrist. Sophia felt a bead of sweat drop on to the small of her back. It felt as if the vintage alarm clock mounted on the wall was making a sound. A high-pitched sound.

'Why now?' Sophia asked to quieten the noise. 'After seven years of nothing? Have you found him?' She very nearly said 'something'. *Have you found something?* She swallowed audibly.

'We have received an anonymous tip,' Laura Stone said slowly, 'about your husband's case. We have deemed, so far, the tip to be credible due to verifiable details left by the person who made the tip. We would like to go over the information you gave us seven years ago, corroborate it with the tip and see if it raises any actionable leads.'

Sophia swallowed again. What had the Pan done? The sound of blood rushing through the vessels of her brain was suddenly so loud. Was it always audible? Did the mind fine-tune things like that out? Was Laura Stone still speaking? She blinked several times. Was she about to pass out?

'Right,' she croaked. She looked at the vintage alarm clock. Its noise had abandoned her. Everything was silent. 'I . . .' She cleared her throat like someone scraping two bricks together. 'I, er, I really need another drink.'

She got up and stumbled to the kitchen. Why would the Pan do this? Did she really believe Sophia couldn't murder someone? If she did commit the murder, would the Pan now be able to call the police off? She had to tell the others. She had to make these two believe she had nothing to do with it.

When she went back into the living room, Laura Stone was sitting forward, resting her forearms on the edge of the table. She had very long, slender fingers. She and Sophia looked at one another. Sophia swallowed. Laura Stone didn't blink.

When she sat down, she burst into tears.

'It's just so agonizing.' She sobbed. 'To not know.'

When she had been younger, she had hated when she started to cry. She could never help it. Hot tears pricking at the corners of her eyes. Her throat closing up. Her nostrils flaring. It was infuriating. Why was her body's defence mechanism to any strong emotion – anger, fear, sadness, frustration, elation – to cry? She spent years trying to shut it down. To clear her throat loudly and scowl, to tightly fold her arms to smother the sobs. When she was pregnant, however, a clerk at the bank wouldn't let her access her account because she didn't have the right form of ID. She was hot, she was tired, she was parked on double yellow lines and wouldn't be able to get home and back before the bank shut. She had burst into tears then, unable to hold them back, and, like casting a magic spell, the clerk had relented.

'I can verify some details and open your account that way,' he said. 'Date of birth? Address?'

Since then, she used the tears when she needed something. She never manufactured them. No. She just didn't squeeze herself shut as she used to. It was manipulative as hell, wasn't it?

She let the tears flow forth on the sofa in front of the detectives. It was never uncontrolled sobbing. That wasn't her way. It was punctuated speech, shaking breaths, red eyes and a wet tissue.

'I just wish I knew what happened,' Sophia said, wiping her eyes in a clumsy and ungainly way. There was an art to crying well, to making it look like the tears were unwelcome. 'There are so many unanswered questions.'

The words hung in the air around them. Meaningless. Damp. Pathetic.

'Maybe we could book a date for you to come to the station,' the man said. 'And get what you've told us down on the record.'

'I didn't tell you anything,' Sophia said stupidly.

'It's just for the paperwork,' Laura Stone said, shaking her head in a what-can-you-do sort of way. 'Like we said, to see if this tip can be corroborated and lead anywhere.'

'I don't know,' Sophia said. 'I feel, I feel like—'

'Anything you tell us might not only help us locate Chris but save potential other victims. There's a big picture, Sophia. And, at the very least, perhaps we can confirm that Chris isn't part of it.'

When they had gone, Sophia got her phone out and angrily texted the Pan.

Why the hell did you do that?

Just a warning, she immediately texted back.

Sophia held the phone tightly in her hands, gritting her teeth together.

You fucked it, you moron! How am I going to get rid of them now? I need his death certificate!

Don't fret so. You do what I asked, came the immediate response, and I can make them go away like – and she included a gif of Neil deGrasse Tyson exploding his hands in a 'poof' gesture. I'm a woman of my word. But if you don't, if you fail at your task . . . and she sent a gif of Steve Carell from the US *Office* looking thunderous, this is just the tip (pun intended) of the iceberg. I can drip feed way more incriminating information.

The US *Office*? Not even the UK? Sophia shook her head. The Pan, Jill, really didn't know her at all. She thought Sophia could still be manipulated. That she would shy away from the task and let someone else control her. Jill genuinely believed, after all these years, that Sophia truly belonged with *Simon*. And now she was just waiting to send her to prison. Sophia would show her. She wasn't weak. She wasn't pathetic. Jill had no idea, and Sophia couldn't wait to see that realization in her eyes. The glee. The unbridled, unadulterated glee. Sophia clutched the phone so tightly the edge bit into her fingers.

'Just wait,' she whispered to herself.

'Is Flickcall secure?' she asked her laptop camera later that evening.

'I looked into it,' Ella said. 'They collect technical information but personal communication is never logged and they don't have third-party analytics. So yes, secure for us to talk.'

Four small video chat windows were lined up on the far side of Sophia's laptop screen. On the main screen, *Peep Show* was rolling, Jeremy leaning up against a Land Rover in a pub car park.

'*Yeah. This is cool. Just don't think about the dead dog. If I don't think about it, there's always a chance it didn't happen.*'

'I never get why Jez doesn't just chuck the dog in the bushes,' Caoimhe said, 'and say it ran away.'

'He's an idiot and he panicked,' Ella replied. 'Every single episode is based on that premise.'

'Let's not get too fixated on the show,' Ajola said. 'We're not actually here for a watch party. We're here to, you know, decide what to do.'

'I was thinking.' Safa's voice drifted out from her screen window. 'Can we pretend to do it? To murder him?'

'Three days isn't enough to outmanoeuvre her,' Ella said. 'And she wants to see the body.'

'So, you're saying we have to kill him?'

'Guys.' Sophia's voice was urgent. 'The police came round this morning.'

'*Stop trying to marry everyone, Mark. No need to marry people.*'

'The police?' Ella's face was stony-grey. 'Really and truly?' Sophia nodded.

'The Pan called them?' Safa confirmed in a soft whisper.

'She gave them an anonymous tip about Chris's disappearance. I don't know any more. They're going to call me into the station next week to give a statement.' Sophia took a deep breath. She was surprised at the firmness of her own resolve. 'The Pan said if we kill the guy, she'll call the police off. If we don't, she'll give them more information. I don't see we have a choice now.'

'If we do it,' Caoimhe said, scowling, 'how easily can the Pan stop the police investigation, though?'

'Yes!' Ella hissed. 'What if everything is already in motion? They're coming for us!'

'We could be fucked either way,' Caoimhe said.

'Clearly, though, the police investigation is nothing without the Pan's anonymous tip,' Ajola said. She laced her fingers together at the edge of her camera and Sophia was, once again, relieved for her composure. 'If we kill the guy and the Pan withdraws, or contradicts or discredits whatever she's said, we're free.'

'But are we *sure* the Pan will withdraw if we, you know, kill someone?' Ella asked.

'Oh.' Sophia nodded confidently at all four of them. 'I think she will. We can make sure of it. Jill is behind this. Trust me.' The image of Jill's face floated up in her mind and she scowled. 'She thinks she's set me a challenge I can't do. She'll relish me failing and her being the one to send me to prison. I mean' – she gave a shrug – 'she probably even had something to do with Chris's death.' Sophia took a deep breath, trying to soothe her clamouring mind. 'Jill cropped up at the same time as the Pan. She loves poisoning any nugget of my identity. This is very manipulative, very her. I feel, I think, I need to respond in kind.'

'It is very *Single White Female*,' Caoimhe said. 'Remember when we watched it at Ajola's sleepover? You have to confront this issue at the root, Sophia, and stab her in the back with a screwdriver.'

Sophia rolled her eyes.

'I wish.'

'What if it's not Jill, though?' Safa said, her voice still so quiet. 'Does that change your mind?'

'No,' Sophia said loudly. 'I can't go to prison for my husband's murder. Jill will read about it and think I'm some poor, domestic housewife who tried to outsmart the system and failed. She'll pity me. I couldn't live with that.'

'Surely we shouldn't do everything based on what Jill would think?' Caoimhe said.

'My whole life I've been wondering what Jill would think.'

There was silence. Sophia's mind was racing ahead of her. She was breathless. If anything, she was impatient.

'What if she keeps on asking us to murder people for her, though?' Safa said. 'What if we can't escape?'

Ajola scoffed.

'No way,' she said. 'If this is done, she'd be terrified of us.'

'If I do this' – Sophia's heart was pounding at the thought of Jill's horror-struck face – 'then Jill will know what I'm capable of. I'd be a fucking murderer.' Caoimhe laughed at her earnestness as Sophia said, 'She can't do shit to me.'

'That's fair.'

Sophia bit the edge of her thumb. She had never been Simon's partner. Pathetic. Meek.

'I'm going to do it,' she said slowly. 'I'm not asking you to help me. But that's my answer. I'm going to show her.'

'*Fuck! Ah! There's a . . . There's a dead beast in our bin, Jeremy!*'

Ajola

AJOLA SCRATCHED HER nose.

'Do you remember in Year Seven when Max Hastings said he fancied someone,' she said, 'and we were all trying to guess who it was, for ages, and then he told us it was Vaporeon from Pokémon?'

Safa snorted with laughter.

'The fish?' Ella said. There was some strange background noise coming from her FlickCall window that she was dutifully ignoring.

'Fish Pokémon.'

'The little blue one that was like a mermaid but had the face of a cat,' Caoimhe said. 'I remember that. It was the first time I really thought he was weird.'

'I can't imagine telling people that.' Safa straightened up. 'You'd have to torture me to get me to part with that kind of information. Also, didn't Dave Richardson say Nala was sexy?'

'"Can You Feel The Love Tonight".' Ella nodded. 'Year Nine music.'

'Yeah, and the bit where Nala lies down in the grass, didn't he say that was really sexy.'

Ajola forced a laugh to make herself feel less nauseous. She had to rise above the fear. She had to believe in the magik.

'Really sexy,' Sophia moaned, doing her best impression of Dave Richardson.

'No, it was "so sexy",' Ella corrected her. She ran a hand across her chin. '"Ohh, so sexy."'

'That was it. And everyone laughed at him.'

'"Ohh, so sexy."' Ajola rubbed her hand across her chin as well. 'Funny. But I'm bringing this up because kids are weird, kids admit stuff, kids hold on to things. Just because in Year Eight Jill said—'

'She's the same now.' Sophia was vehement. 'Trust me, Ajola. I thought that same thing – for sure, she's matured, she's changed.' She looked dead into her laptop camera. 'But she hasn't. She's worse.'

'I honestly think maybe the Pan is a friend of Meg who has a grudge against me,' Ajola said. It was hard to give voice to this fear. It hadn't properly solidified in her mind yet; it was buried deep, an infection festering far from the surface. Something she hadn't done for Meg. Something she had done. Either way, she was sure the article had come from the Pan.

'Because she committed suicide?'

'I've searched for Meg online loads over the years. There's nothing. Just a recent article that her mum did for the BBC. How could the Pan know the connection?'

'I think there're ways,' Ella said. 'We have to assume the Pan is constantly watching us.'

'Let's not spend ages speculating on who the Pan is or which cartoon is sexiest,' Caoimhe said.

'No cartoons are sexy,' Ajola said flatly. She rubbed her

sternum; thinking about Meg in the shadow of the Pan gave her a strange feeling, like indigestion.

'Sure they are.'

'You think a cartoon is sexually attractive?' Ajola shook her head.

'You can objectively look at a drawing of someone and say it is attractive, yes,' Caoimhe said.

'A cartoon, though.' Ajola held up a finger. 'Name me a cartoon you think is attractive. Prince Eric?'

'He has terrible hair,' Safa said.

'It's the cartoon part I'm arguing,' Ajola said. 'Realistic drawings can absolutely be attractive. Henry VIII married Anne of Cleves after Thomas Cromwell showed him a portrait of her. The portrait was so attractive, in fact, that it looked better than the real thing and that's why Henry divorced her.'

'I was getting really worried we'd have another conversation where Thomas Cromwell wasn't mentioned,' Safa said. 'Thank you, Ajola.'

Ajola waved her hand.

'You can't find cartoons sexually arousing. You shouldn't.'

'Jessica Rabbit,' Safa suggested. 'People find her sexy.'

'*Men* find her sexy,' Ajola corrected. 'And, clearly, men will find Pokémon and cartoon lions sexy.'

'Don't gatekeep sexy,' Caoimhe said. 'You're being a right turn-off for our NSA agent.'

'It's GCHQ,' Ella reminded her.

Ajola smoothed back her hair. They were getting distracted. Maybe that was a good thing. Maybe it wasn't. Meg. This had to be about Meg. And Daisy. The indigestion burned in her chest. She hoped she wasn't going to lean over and vomit again.

'Sorry,' she said. 'OK, no speculation. Whoever the Pan is, we are where we are.'

'I'm doing it, regardless,' Sophia said. 'I'm not going to prison for Chris.'

Ajola nodded.

'And I don't want . . .' She looked at Sophia's box. 'I don't want Meg's mum, any mum, to think less of me.' She kneaded her sternum with her knuckles. 'Sophia, I'm with you.' She almost instantly felt better after saying these words. 'If you actually kill the guy, I can help you cover it up. I can use a spell, like last time.' Caoimhe let out a loud groan, which Ajola ignored. 'We can perform an eternal and binding force of Wicca magik. It will be our most all-encompassing endeavour. A chance for us to wield our female power once more.' She looked into the camera. 'And remind ourselves of the bonds that will always unite us.'

Safa

'I'D DO THE spell again,' Safa said. 'That was the best part last time.'

'You'd join us?' Sophia asked and Safa was almost saddened by the surprise in her voice. 'What about your girls?'

'If we can guarantee that killing this one man makes it all go away' – Safa inclined her head slowly – 'the threats, the police, the dread: I'm in.' She suddenly felt lightheaded. 'I need to regain control of my life. Haaris took Danielle, his new, white girlfriend, round to meet his parents the other day.'

'Oof, big move.'

'I can't believe they'll approve of her,' Ella said. 'Didn't you say they're super traditional?'

'Well, in Islam, Muslim men, unlike Muslim women, can marry Christians,' Safa explained. She took a few deep breaths. She was inexplicably dizzy. There was a hot, spiky feeling in her face. She tapped the volume button on her keyboard. 'So, that's not a problem. My cousin said when Danielle visited, she wore a headscarf, covering her hair, and these nice salwar trousers. She looked the part. I think they were impressed. She tucked into all the food they set out, the kebabs and rotis and spicy curry. Emaan said she was diving in with just her hands, using the bone plate, everything.'

'Fair play to her,' Caoimhe said.

'I know, right?' Safa swallowed. 'Apparently, she's learning Punjabi as well. They have no problem letting Javeria and Aleena go out with her.'

'Terrifying,' Ella said.

'That's what I mean about the Pan.' Safa wiped her forehead. 'Danielle Bloom, Haaris's new girlfriend, feels too prescient. I'm not saying she is the Pan. More like someone, something, is putting her up to it. Or, I don't know.' She really didn't. There were too many moving elements. She needed to get a grip. To refuse the passivity that had kept her with Haaris all those years. 'It's a noose around my neck. I'll do it, the murder, just to let me breathe.'

'Danielle probably just wants to steal your cultural identity,' Ajola said. 'Give it a year and she'll be educating you. Doing all the cooking, covering up out of modesty, decorating her hands in henna.'

'Haaris would love that, though.' The feeling was returning to Safa's head but her cheeks were glowing hot. She forced herself to give a nervous laugh. 'It's probably what he's waiting for. On the plus side, all his annoying texts have stopped. The calls. Emails. Visits to my work. Everything. He just gets Javeria and Aleena on his days and that's it. Doesn't even make any remarks.'

'Perhaps Haaris just picked the one person who would wind you up the most,' Sophia said. 'Maybe this is his new way of harassing you.'

'Get a new boyfriend,' Caoimhe suggested, 'and dish it back. Find some six foot six swimming champion slash hedge-fund manager who races Formula One in his spare time.'

Safa laughed, this time with more passion.

'A new boyfriend?' she said. 'First of all' – she held up a finger to the camera – 'Ammi wouldn't let me get a new boy-friend. I'd get a new husband. And second of all, I'm done with being part of a couple. I cannot imagine anything worse than being in a relationship.'

'Unmarried women are the happiest subgroup in the UK population,' Ajola said.

'That's unmarried women who are childless,' Ella corrected her. 'I saw that study. You have to be childless to have the maximum happiness.'

'Ah, sorry, Safa, Sophia, Ella,' Caoimhe said. 'Just you and me then, Ajola.'

'It is what it is.' Ella shrugged. 'Most men lead lives of quiet desperation.'

'Yes,' Ajola said, 'but we're women.'

'Is that a quote from somewhere?' Safa asked.

'*Dead Poet's Society*,' Ajola said. 'You know women die sooner if they get married.'

'Why is everyone getting married then?' Safa said. 'You die sooner; you're not as happy.'

'*Women* die sooner and are not as happy,' Ajola explained. '*Men* who are married live longer and are happier than men who never marry.'

'Can we not start going on about men again,' Caoimhe said. 'The NSA agent watching this is going to think we're all fem-inists intent on radicalizing women.'

'Radicalizing them to do what? Centre women?'

'Such a hate group,' Sophia said.

'I run with some amazing men at my club,' Caoimhe said loudly. 'My running would be worse off without their input. The human experience is a shared experience; we can't go cutting men and women off from each other.'

'I'm so glad your Nigel is so perfect,' Ajola said. 'Women can now just stop striving for equity.'

Ella

'THAT'S THREE OF us down for a murder and a cover-up,'
Sophia said.

'And a burial spell,' Ajola pointed out.

'Right,' Sophia agreed.

Caoimhe put her head on her keyboard and made the computer beep.

'And the spell. Ella?' Sophia asked. 'What are your thoughts?'

Ella took a deep breath.

'I've been terrified for seven years of this exact thing happening,' she said. 'Now that it has, I think I'm dead inside.'

'Is that a yes or a no?'

'It's a . . .' Ella shrugged. 'Can we ever go back to just being normal? Are our lives now just going to gradually descend into chaos?' She let out a long sigh. 'I've already done it once.' The sublunar. The metaphysical. Which was she? 'Sophia, if you do the actual deed, I'm in.'

From Ella's camera, there came a crackling, buzzing sound.

'Sorry,' she said, adjusting her screen. 'Benjamin is just going wild. If I spent ten hours staring at the wall, he wouldn't bother me. But as soon as I get my computer, it's like, he suddenly becomes so clingy, needs me to get him a tissue, take off his sock, turn the TV over.' She shook her head. 'It's infuriating.'

'Ah, he loves you,' Safa said.

'It's not love.' Ella's voice was sharp. 'I know that. It's control. It's manipulation. It's *We Need to Talk About Kevin.*' Sophia laughed, but Ella said, 'I'm serious. He never does it for Felix. Just me.'

'That's just how four-year-olds show love,' Safa said.

'I would argue that four-year-olds don't understand the concept of love.' Ella quickly glanced at Benjamin and then back to her laptop. 'They just know they need a parent to reassure them, feed them, clothe them. That's not love.'

'People are too quick to call any strong feeling love,' Ajola agreed. 'Spending the day with someone: not love. Appreciating it when someone cooks you dinner: not love.'

'What would you say love is then?' Caoimhe asked, eyebrows raised mockingly.

'Mainly, love is a scam.'

Caoimhe made an annoyed sound.

'I hate this whole thing about conditional love versus unconditional love,' Ella said. From her webcam, there came a loud shrieking sound and a crash. Ella rolled her eyes. 'One minute,' she said. 'Everyone, go make a cup of tea.'

Ella took a deep breath and turned away from her laptop. Benjamin was kneeling on the end of the sofa, staring at the shattered shards of a ceramic lampshade scattered all over the floor. She briefly thought about muting the mic or blocking the camera. Then she could really go to town on Benjamin.

Scream at him. If he cut his feet, it would be all her fault. At the last second, she managed to control herself. She took a deep breath and helped him off the armrest.

'OK, good boy, Benjamin,' she crooned for the sole benefit of the camera. 'I'm just going to put you there.' She set him on the sofa cushions. 'Now, I'm going to switch on the robot hoover and he's going to suck all this mess up.' She crouched down in Benjamin's eyeline and held his hands. 'It's OK. Things break all the time.'

Benjamin kicked her in the chin so hard, her jaw snapped shut. He went cross-eyed and folded his arms. Her first instinct was to reach out and grab him, but the Flickcall was right there. She could feel sweat on her back, her trembling muscles generating enormous heat.

'That hurt,' she said instead. He looked thoughtfully at her but didn't say anything. 'Here's your show.' She turned up the television. If she went to prison, she'd never have to do this again. 'Sit and watch it whilst I work.'

'I want an ice lolly,' he said as soon as she sat back at the desk.

'Well, feel free to go downstairs and get one.'

Benjamin stared at her. Ella turned back to the computer, wondering what she would do if he became hysterical and started throwing Lego bricks at her. She'd have to leave the chat. Leave the group. Scream into a pillow about how her life was not her own. That she'd be better off in prison. But Benjamin slid off the sofa and picked his way through the shattered lamp and the little rotating hoover.

'That's why I could never be a mum,' Ajola said. 'I don't have the patience.'

'You teach primary-school kids,' Caoimhe said.

'But they go home at three o'clock. My patience with them is predicated on the knowledge that they leave me.'

'Never ever kids, Ajola?' Safa asked. 'You feel a strong bond with your children. A love.'

'But not so much that it surpasses all other possible bonds of love,' Ella pointed out, quickly. 'And not so much that it justifies all the suffering. People don't talk enough about the suffering. In sex education, teachers should be telling girls: it's not some all-consuming, life-changing, ultimate love and fulfilment. It can be hell.' She took a breath. 'It's suffering.'

'Never ever,' Ajola said. 'No one can convince me that a man who is willing to get me pregnant loves me.'

'This is why the idea of conditional and unconditional love annoys me,' Ella said. 'Love should have conditions. Love shouldn't tolerate abuse.'

'What if someone said to you,' Safa said, 'I will always love you unconditionally. Wouldn't that reassure you?'

'No. I don't want to be loved by someone who will love me even if I commit war crimes.' Safa laughed. 'Who will never leave, no matter what I do. It's like having a jailer. It's a terminal diagnosis.'

'What about romantic love?'

'Romantic love is a scam by the patriarchy to control women,' Ajola interjected. 'A man's love will change your whole life. Find *the one*, get married to *the one*, live forever with *the one*. You must be able to see how insane that sounds. It's like something out of *Harry Potter* or *The Matrix*. The One. It's a fantasy. It's Disney stories.'

'There's nothing wrong with monogamous relationships,'

Caoimhe said. 'It happens all over the animal kingdom. Swans. Penguins.'

'We're not fucking penguins, though,' Ajola said and Safa laughed so loud her mic cut her out for a split second.

Benjamin came back into the room and sat on the sofa with his ice lolly. He stared glassily at the television screen. A single tear of crimson juice dripped from the stick on to his hand. Ella hoped he hadn't disrupted the tight organization of the freezer. She hoped he had shut the drawer properly.

'Are we really doing this?' she asked. 'It feels like a dream.'

'Let's take it a step at a time,' Ajola said. 'Did she send the information through about the target, Sophia? Who is this Trent Davies?'

'She did. He's thirty-six years old. He's some duty manager at Morrisons in Guildford. I have a photo as well. I'll WhatsApp it to you.'

'Has she given a reason?' Ajola asked. 'Is he a bad guy or something?'

Sophia shook her head.

'No reason.'

'Maybe it's best if we don't know,' Safa said.

'We could make a career out of this,' Caoimhe said. 'Put *Mindhunter* on next.'

Everyone laughed except Ella. She glanced over at Benjamin. He was sitting quietly on the sofa, transfixed by the television screen. He had placed the ice lolly on the arm of the sofa and it had melted into the cushion, rivers of red and gold and purple flowing across the fabric, sinking into the fibres and dripping on to the floor.

Caoimhe

'YOU'RE IN THEN, Caoimhe?' Ella asked.

Caoimhe had accepted the toll of burying another body. For Rohan Rust. Dual number ones once more. His red and black skull cap. His thick beard. The way his eyebrows formed mini mountains above his eyes. The way he slipped through the air, finding gaps between atoms that were imperceptible to anyone else. How she was prepared to plot murder just for a chance to stand level with him. She pressed her lips together. She was coming for him.

On the screen, Jeremy took a bite out of a cooked dog's leg.

'I wouldn't have believed it,' Caoimhe said. 'I've been wishing for seven years to take back what we did and now I'm volunteering to do it again.' She drummed her fingers on the edge of her laptop. 'But, if you're all doing it, I'm not going to abandon you. We're in it together, right?'

'Spoken like a true Skywalker,' Safa said.

'What can I say?' Caoimhe felt like saying something profound then. 'Don't underestimate my power,' she finally settled on. It was a flat pronouncement. Empty. 'If you're not with me, then you're my enemy.'

'Should we organize a trip to Trent Davies's Morrisons?' Sophia suggested. 'One step at a time. Shadow him a bit? Make sure we have the right guy? Work out the logistics?'

'I can drive us,' Safa said. 'If you don't mind squeezing into my Fiat 500.'

'Where's the BMW?'

'I let Haaris have it.'

Ajola tutted.

'Let's,' Sophia said. 'Tomorrow after school and work? Maybe we can scope out a local Airbnb to actually do the deed.'

'I'll sort that.' Ella put her hand up like she was in school.

'Another adventure, like the old days,' Ajola said.

'Sounds like we're ready to stalk a guy.' Caoimhe grinned. 'I kind of hope we see him beat a dog or something, to make us feel better.'

'That would be ideal,' Ella agreed.

'Guys, are we mad?' Safa asked. 'Are we actually mentally unstable?'

'We're just going to take it one step at a time,' Ajola said. 'And see what happens.'

Ella nodded. 'All things considered, this is probably the best thing to do.'

'Will we be sectioned?' Sophia asked.

'Did you try and get me sectioned?' Caoimhe said. 'Somebody tried to get me sectioned.'

'I definitely didn't try to get you sectioned,' Ajola replied. 'I guess it was just one of those freaky urban things, like those people who go on fire for no reason.'

'They could section you for trying to section me,' Ella cried.

REBINDING

Ella

ELLA CHECKED THE time on her phone. She still had five minutes or so. The sun was getting low in the sky and dark shadows were lengthening on the ground around her. She couldn't believe she was standing here during the most important week of her career. She should be at home, going through Eric's file, checking in with Cynthia.

She got her phone out and looked through her emails.

'Are you lost?'

She turned. There was a man standing behind her. She hadn't noticed him approach. He had a loose T-shirt on and paint-stained jeans. His curly hair was held back with a black hairband.

'No,' she said. 'I'm waiting for my friend.'

'Been waiting a long time,' the man commented. His left eye was slightly off-centre. He put his hands on his hips. 'Want me to get you an Uber?'

'No.' The air felt cold suddenly. Ella wished she'd brought a jacket. 'My friend says she's on her way.'

The man nodded but didn't move away. He perched on the

wall behind her and got his own phone out. Ella wanted to walk off to stand somewhere else but didn't want to be rude. She thumbed through her phone for a few minutes, then glanced over her shoulder. The man quickly looked down at his phone.

Ella put her phone to her ear.

'Oh, OK, OK,' she said to no one. She put a new piece of gum in her mouth. 'You're down there, are you? I'll be there in two minutes.'

She pretended to hang up and then hurried down the road. At the first junction, she saw a Fiat 500 zooming towards her and held out her hand in relief.

'Nearly missed you,' Safa said as Ella hurriedly climbed into the front seat. Aloja, Caoimhe and Sophia were already in the back. 'How's the hearing going?'

'Oh, great.' Ella shut the door and did up her seatbelt. 'Not as great as getting together to potentially murder a man, but still, pretty good.'

Safa pulled away from the kerb. They passed the man with the hairband, now walking up the pavement, phone to his ear.

'Remind me where we're going first,' Safa said, indicating around a roundabout.

'Morrisons,' Sophia replied. 'The Pan said he works until eight p.m. on a Monday. Let's get a look at him.'

'Then we'll go to his address?' Safa asked.

'I don't think we should complicate it,' Caoimhe said.

'Just keep it a nice, *straightforward* murder,' Safa said. 'Nothing fancy.'

'I mean, we have no need to go to his address,' Caoimhe explained. 'She wants this to happen after work Wednesday? Then let's keep it focused on work.'

'Have you switched your phone off, Ella?' Ajola asked.

'Done it.' Ella held up her blank phone. 'We should start habitually switching our phones off for periods over the next week or so. If anything happens and the police request our phone data, it will look like a regular pattern, rather than something we only did while murdering a guy.'

'Where did you get that idea from?'

'Netflix.' Ella winked at Caoimhe. 'Thought I'd do some research.'

'Imagine back in the day,' Caoimhe said. 'It would be so easy to kill someone and get away with it. No wonder Jack the Ripper was never identified.'

'There is a fascination at the moment with seventies and eighties serial killers.' Ajola nodded. 'Like they're some rare, psychological geniuses that must be studied. But if any of those men tried it today, they'd be apprehended before they even got home after the first one. They're completely average men who just got away with murder, literally, because the crime detection wasn't advanced enough.'

'Here, here,' Ella said, pointing out of the window.

'Satnav says straight on.'

'I don't know where that's taking you. It's not Google Maps.' Ella tapped the window as they passed the entrance sign. 'Morrisons' car park is there.'

Safa indicated and turned off the main road. The car park was still quite busy even that late in the day, and she pulled up in a spot near the back, hidden beneath some low-hanging branches. The car clanked beneath them. Ella moved her hair from her eyes. Just a regular trip to Morrisons. Nothing unusual about this. She double-checked her phone was switched off.

'What if people are fascinated with us in thirty years' time?' Caoimhe asked.

'Nah,' Ajola said. 'We're women. We'll be vilified. They won't make an award-winning Netflix drama about us.'

'I hope I don't get bird mess on the car,' Safa muttered, glancing out of the window.

'What now?' Ella asked. She put her phone in the glove compartment. 'Do we go in and find him? Just like that?'

'Yeah.' Sophia unbuckled her seatbelt. 'But don't let him see us.'

Ajola

AJOLA DIDN'T WANT Daisy to end up in Morrisons, like Trent, or even Tesco, like her. She wanted her to reach the lab in Paris. To spurn the abandoned universe. Ajola did not want Daisy to be thirty-four and plotting to kill a man because everything else in her life had gone so awry. If Daisy could escape that, if Ajola could save Daisy, she could save Meg. Save herself. Then it would have all been worth it.

Just before break time that day, she had called Daisy over. Yashica stopped mid-stride and turned her head sharply like an antelope that has caught the scent of a lion.

'Yes, Miss Pugh?' she said.

Ajola wondered how to get rid of Yashica without causing a scene. This was for Daisy. Not Yashicandaisy.

'Actually, I wanted to talk to Daisy alone,' Ajola said gently.

Yashica looked at the floor under her long eyelashes. This was a fine line to tread. If she was too harsh in her exclusion of Yashica, she was sure she would Regina George it somehow. Maybe grow up to wear a Pan mask and blackmail Ajola.

'Fine,' Yashica snapped and tossed her immaculate curls. 'Daisy will tell me anyway when she gets outside, won't you, Daisy?'

Her eyes flashed at Ajola, as deadly as sabres. Ajola wondered if she should pull her up on that. She could see Yashica debating it as well, keeping her eyes averted. No. Not worth the effort. Yashica spun on her heel and marched from the room.

Ajola waited to be sure that Yashica had definitely gone, and then beckoned Daisy over to her computer.

'What's your favourite subject, Daisy?' she asked. It was dim in the classroom, ghostly, the high walls of the neighbouring buildings cutting off the early morning light. Ajola found her heart was thundering in her chest. It was that malevolent beast. The haunting phantasm. She steeled herself and dispelled the spectral figure of the Pan by imagining Thomas Cromwell at her shoulder, guiding her.

'Maths,' Daisy said in her quiet voice. Ajola could see her already scanning the email on the laptop screen. She had to do it. She had to. Save Daisy. Save Meg. Save herself.

'You're really good at maths,' Ajola said. 'There's a regional primary mathematics competition,' she said. 'Happening throughout June.'

'A competition?' Daisy said and her nostrils constricted like a scared guinea pig.

'It's easy,' Ajola said. She looked at her but felt maybe that was too intense. She turned and started tidying her desk. She picked up the copy of *Pride and Prejudice* she had taken from the school library – her eye had snared on the spine after hearing Safa mention it – and tucked it on to the shelf beside her computer. 'It's online. You can do it here with me. No one else can see you or your results. The computer works it all out.'

Daisy's nostrils were still constricted but Ajola was sure there was a glimmer of something else there, something further down, suppressed. The rising earth. One of the DT masks they had made in art stared up at her and she traced her finger around the blue concentric circles blossoming all over it. Perhaps all of humanity had aligned for this moment. Bodies had been dredged to bring Daisy to her. She would never get another chance like this. She had to have a positive impact. To show Daisy what she was worth. Save Daisy. Save Meg. Save herself. She placed the mask over her own face, looking at Daisy through the eyeholes. Daisy laughed and Ajola saw some of the tension dissipate.

'What if people cheat?' Daisy asked. 'Like, if a student gets their teacher to do it for them?'

Ajola laughed out loud and put the mask back on the pile.

'I believe that definitely happens,' she said. 'I won't lie to you. Some teachers out there definitely enjoy winning and getting prizes. But it can be fun even if we don't cheat.' Daisy laughed again. 'Even if you just take part, you get a certificate,' Ajola said, 'so you're guaranteed something.'

'Who else from the class is doing it?'

'No one,' Ajola said. 'Just you. I can go through some question formats with you, if you want, so you're ready.'

'Yes,' Daisy said. She looked at her shoes. 'Yashica will want to do it as well.'

'Ah, unfortunately, you're only allowed to enter one student per class,' Ajola lied. She scratched her eyebrow, sensing an opportunity. 'How long have you and Yashica been best friends?'

'Since Reception,' Daisy said.

Ajola nodded, trying to frame another question.

'Do you enjoy playing with other girls in the class?' she tried.

Daisy nodded.

'But Yashica is my best friend,' she said. 'We always go round each other's houses after school and make things together.'

'Hmm,' Ajola said, nodding. 'Does anyone else join you? Abigail or Zara or Shannon?'

'Sometimes.' Daisy shrugged. 'But me and Yashica are best friends.'

'Do you ever wish someone else was in your group?' Ajola persisted.

Daisy thought.

'I don't mind as long as Yashica is there.'

'Do you know who broke Layla's pencil sharpener last week?'

'Oh yeah.' Daisy's face lit up. 'Zain said it was Yashica! But it wasn't. Yashica didn't do that. She wouldn't.'

'You know she didn't do it?'

'Yes, one hundred per cent. I was with her. She would have told me.'

She sounded so earnest, so honest, Ajola believed her. Damn. She really thought it had been Yashica.

'That's good,' she said.

'She did it herself,' Daisy said.

'What do you mean?'

'Layla broke her own sharpener and then said someone else did it to make drama,' Daisy said. Ajola laughed. 'Nooria saw it and she told Shana and Shana told Yashica during homework club. And then Yashica told me.'

'Gossip,' a voice said at the door and both Ajola and Daisy

jumped. Jonah, the Year 5 teacher, came through the doorway, wagging his finger at Daisy. 'It's not good to gossip, young lady,' he said. 'Hearsay and rumour aren't substantial.'

Daisy went bright red and her eyes filled with tears. She looked down at her feet and Ajola was afraid she might burst like a cheap water balloon.

'The notion of gossip,' Ajola said, wheeling around in her chair to face Jonah, 'was invented by men to prevent women from coming together and exchanging stories because that undermined the men's power.' She raised her eyebrows. 'It's almost misogynistic, Mr Cullen, to call it gossip. Are you being misogynistic?'

Jonah looked at her. He pulled a face.

'What?' he said, searching for a retort.

'Daisy is no gossip. There's nothing wrong with the free-flow exchange of information within a community.' She smiled at Daisy and was relieved she smiled back. 'Out you go now, Daisy, and if Yashica asks anything, tell her to come to me.'

'What was that?' Jonah said, smiling at her. He perched his arse on the end of Ajola's desk, making it creak and causing the pile of masks to finally slide on to the floor. 'Girls can be so bitchy.'

The five of them walked across the car park towards Morrisons. CCTV cameras were mounted to the lampposts along the parking bays, but Ajola pointed to a narrow, red-brick alley at the far side of the store.

'Away from the cameras,' she said. She gritted her teeth together. She could practically taste the red dust. 'Remember that.'

There was a long foyer inside the store with various hot-food stands, like a high street, and people were sitting at benches around these, eating pizzas and noodles from recyclable boxes, laughing and talking loudly. What did they think, Ajola wondered, when they saw the five women striding into the store, brimming with such intent? An after-work party? An intense PTA planning group? The village fete committee?

'He works on deli,' Sophia said, stopping by the newspaper stand and looking around to orientate herself. 'This way.'

'We can't just march up to the counter and stare at him,' Ella said. 'He'll get suspicious. We need to walk past, casually. One at a time.'

'Come, then,' Ajola said, leading the way. The most focused of all the PTA. 'I'll go first.'

'I hope everyone did their homework,' Safa said, 'and studied his picture.'

Ajola strode down the first aisle and took a sharp right in front of the deli counter. The store seemed strangely empty, with most customers at the hot-food vendors by the front. Trent Davies was the only person visible on deli, white apron on over his uniform and a mesh hat on his head, cutting a block of cheddar with some cheese wire. He looked just as he did in the picture the Pan sent. Ajola kept walking and then ducked down into the bakery aisle. She pressed herself into a stack of pre-packaged pancakes and watched as Sophia walked past next.

'That's him,' Sophia said, breathless, when she joined Ajola by the pancakes. 'Right, right? That's him.'

'Hold on,' Ajola muttered, gesturing at the counter. 'Development.'

As Caoimhe was striding past the counter, a slim, blonde woman in a Morrisons uniform, with a huge, chequered tote bag held on the crook of her arm, approached. She leant on the glass and smiled up at Trent. He stopped cutting the cheese and smiled back at her.

'Girlfriend?' Caoimhe whispered, joining them at the pancakes.

'What makes you say that?'

'Look at the body language.'

Ajola nodded.

'Is she the Pan?' Caoimhe asked.

Ajola thought.

'Too tall,' she finally said. 'Wrong hair.'

'She could be the mastermind behind it, though,' Caoimhe pointed out.

'No.' Sophia shook her head. 'No way. Jill is the mastermind behind all this.'

Ajola smiled. Sophia's certainty was comforting.

Safa joined them by the pancakes. 'Girlfriend?' she asked, breathless.

The blonde woman left the counter and walked towards them. They all turned and began checking the dates on the pancakes until she swept by. She went through a pair of double swing doors that led into the Morrisons back rooms.

'Got an idea,' Ajola said as Ella joined them. 'I'll be back.'

She headed for the double doors but Ella grabbed her arm.

'Don't be crazy!' she hissed. 'We have to remain inconspicuous.'

'I will be.' Ajola brushed her off. She believed in the magik. 'I worked in Tesco, remember. They don't have CCTV where there's no stock.'

Ella reluctantly let go but showed her displeasure by sticking her gum between her front teeth. Ajola glided through the double doors as though she had done so every day of her life. Save Daisy. Save Meg. And she would save herself.

The corridor on the other side was dark and badly lit. Empty roll containers were lined up on one wall. There was a clocking-in machine opposite. She moved forward, listening for approaching footsteps. The blonde woman had vanished. She imagined Thomas Cromwell standing next to her, gathering information to use at court, guiding her. This was the sort of activity that made Thomas Cromwell. She wished his actual ghost could visit her. Something clear, and real, to guide her.

Somewhere behind her, she heard the rumble of a roll container on the move. Thomas Cromwell vanished. She took a sharp left, down another corridor, and saw the toilet door. She slipped through into a small, peach-painted room, lined with little blue lockers. There was a bench in the middle and on the bench was the blonde woman's chequered tote bag.

Without even thinking about it, Ajola opened the bag. There was a lot of unnecessary crap inside: tissues, make-up, old receipts; but she also found two iPhones. They both had the same lock-screen photo: Trent Davies and the blonde woman wearing Mickey Mouse ears at Disneyland. In the bag, there was also a set of Mercedes car keys, red nail varnish splashed in the grooves like blood, a big Burberry purse the size of Ajola's forearm, and a tattered man's wallet.

Ajola took this out and opened it. Amongst the usual fluff like Tesco Clubcard, National Insurance Number and Costa Coffee loyalty card, she found a driving licence. Trent Davies.

His picture made him look awful. He was four years older than her. And his listed address was different to the one the Pan had provided: Flat 4, St John's Street.

Through a door at the back of the room, she heard a toilet flush. She dropped the wallet back into the bag and quickly left.

Caoimhe

'OH MY GOD!' Caoimhe grabbed Ajola's wrist. 'You're crazy!'

She sounded outraged but she was actually enthralled. How daring! She wished she'd had the guts to think of that.

'Found something out,' Ajola said and ushered them away from the double doors. 'Trent's address on his driving licence isn't the one the Pan gave us.'

'Huh.' Sophia frowned at her. 'I guess that's weird. Why would the Pan give us out-of-date information?'

'Maybe up-to-date information?' Ella suggested as they walked down the pet-food aisle, past shelves blaring with depictions of the same cat's face. 'Maybe he just moved house and hasn't updated his licence yet.'

'Should we go and see the other place?' Sophia led them through the checkouts. 'To see if it gives us any clue as to who the Pan is? For leverage.'

Caoimhe shrugged at her. The adrenaline that had begun pumping through her veins when Ajola had slipped through the double doors was still flooding her system. She wanted another mission. 'Yeah.' She nodded. They left the store and began crossing the car park. 'We could. How far away was it, Ajola?'

'It had a GU postcode.'

'Let's type it in the Satnav and see,' Safa said.

'That was his girlfriend,' Ajola confirmed as they approached Safa's car. 'They have matching photos on their phones.'

'If you jeopardize this for us,' Ella said, opening the Fiat door, 'I am going to be seriously annoyed. What were you doing? Just rummaging through their stuff?'

'Pretty much.'

'I thought teachers were meant to be high-minded?' Caoimhe slid into the back seat beside her and grinned.

'I didn't intend to do it. It was just too easy not to.'

Caoimhe laughed loudly, tilting her head back and looking at the ceiling of the car.

'Fifteen minutes,' Sophia said from the front seat, peering at the satnav screen. She glanced into the back. 'You up for it?'

'I am.' Safa turned on the engine.

'This Morrisons is forty minutes from the burial site,' Ajola said, leaning forward to look at the screen. 'For the spell' – she glanced around at them – 'to conceal, like seven years ago.'

'It's not actually a thing, though – right?' Safa stopped at the exit to the car park and glanced both ways. 'It's more, like, peace of mind or something.'

'It's nonsense,' Caoimhe said loudly. Her body was strumming with excitement. She wanted to run alongside the car.

'If society had never formed into a patriarchy,' Ajola said, 'the world would be full of magik.'

Safa

DANIELLE HAD AGREED to meet Safa that Monday afternoon at a milkshake shop. At first, Safa was going to ignore the text. Move on from Haaris. Reclaim her life. Commit a murder. But could she truly say she had moved on without examining this feeling inside her? Surely a woman who was really over it all could meet Danielle Bloom and not think anything of it. Like meeting the postman.

When Safa arrived, the place was empty. Even the attendant had vanished through the kitchen door. Blinding sunlight was streaming in through the glass front and lighting up the menu board behind the counter.

Oreo Cookie Milkshake
Malteser Milkshake
Ferrero Rocher Milkshake

Safa hadn't wanted to buy anything but thought that might look unwelcoming, so she got a vanilla milkshake that was so thick, the straw could stand fully erect in the middle of the cup. She left it untouched on the table in front of her and gazed out on to the road. She hadn't really had a full meal since finding out about the Pan. Her appetite had just vanished. Strange how something that was entirely emotional had such physical consequences. A bus drove past, momentarily casting her in shadow.

When Danielle Bloom did come through the door, she smiled at Safa and held up a finger, then went to the counter and rapped on its orange surface. Safa sat up and pulled her purse from her bag, awkward. Was this even Danielle? What if she offered to pay for the drink of some random person?

'Hello,' Safa said, deciding to stand up.

'Safa, right?' The woman turned to look at her. The attendant in a black and orange apron came out of the back door. Danielle held a finger up at Safa again. 'Two seconds. Yeah, could I have a Kinder Bueno shake, large, with whipped cream and marshmallows.'

'I'll get this,' Safa said, stepping forward and holding up her purse. 'Seeing as I dragged you here.'

'I always pay for myself,' Danielle said, smiling. She produced her card with a flourish and swiped it across the card reader. 'I'm just sitting there,' she told the attendant and pointed to Safa's lonely table.

'You must be Danielle,' Safa said as they walked to the table.

'And I knew who you were right away,' Danielle replied. 'I recognized . . .' She gestured to her face. Safa was unaware if she meant she had seen a photo of her or if she had seen the headscarf.

'Nice to meet you,' Safa said and held out her hand to shake.

Danielle looked at the offered hand, confused, then gave a little laugh and extended her own hand to shake.

'I don't often shake hands,' she said, sliding into the seat opposite Safa. 'It's very formal.'

'Sorry,' Safa said. 'Old-school habit.'

Danielle waved her hands.

'No, no. It's fine. Just didn't expect it. I thought you were serving me with court papers or something.'

Safa gave a genuine laugh. Danielle looked very pretty in the afternoon sunlight. Glossy black hair, tied up loosely on her neck, a pair of mustard dungarees over a black T-shirt. Chic. Effortlessly chic.

'You work in law, right?' Daniella asked.

'I'm part of a legal team at an auditor's,' Safa said. 'It's bureaucratic. Looking at infractions, procedure, precedent, that sort of thing.'

Danielle was nodding along, looking intensely interested.

'Legalese.'

'Oh, yes, definitely. And what do you do?' Safa asked as though she hadn't looked on Instagram and then googled the name of the company.

'I'm a junior desk officer for this insurance company.' Danielle scrunched up her perfect, petite nose. 'I enjoy it, but it's not really me.'

'I don't want to keep you,' Safa said into the ensuing silence. Danielle was checking her phone. Safa hoped she wasn't putting something on Instagram about her. She gave a nervous laugh. 'I thought you might actually come with Haaris.'

Danielle put her phone away and looked up.

'Haaris wouldn't do anything like that,' she said. 'It's not in his nature to intrude.'

Safa didn't know how to respond to that one. The black and

orange attendant came over and put Danielle's napkin-wrapped cup in front of her.

'Thanks,' Danielle said and took a demure sip from the straw.

'How did you and Haaris meet?' Safa said.

'I don't want to be rude,' Danielle said, putting her cup down and dabbing her mouth with the napkin. 'But I kind of don't want to get into personal information. It's sort of private between me and Haaris. I know you and him weren't amicable when you split up but' – she held up her hands – 'it's got nothing to do with me.'

'No, no, of course,' Safa said quickly. 'I didn't mean to pry. I'm just . . . you know, I'm interested. I was married to Haaris for fourteen years and—'

Danielle held up her hands.

'This isn't appropriate,' she said. 'You can't try and get back with Haaris by making me feel guilty or anything like that.'

'Oh gosh,' Safa said. 'No, no, no. Not at all.' She held a hand to her chest. 'No, believe me. I don't want to get back with him, at all. You've got me completely wrong.'

'Have I?' Danielle raised her eyebrows. 'I think I know a lot more about this situation than you do.'

'What situation?'

Danielle pressed her lips together and folded her arms. She looked out of the window towards the High Road and Safa wondered if their meeting was over. A group of teenagers in school uniform bounded past, the lead boy walking backwards with such energy, his backpack bounced up and down on his back.

'I've seen the messages,' Danielle finally said, without looking at Safa.

'Messages? From who? Who's spoken to you?'

263

'Haaris.'

'Haaris?'

What kind of bizarre relationship was this, that Haaris would show Danielle the threatening messages he had sent and Danielle would side with him.

'From *you* to *Haaris*,' Danielle said emphatically, turning back to look at her. 'It's too weird.'

'What? What messages?' Safa said.

'Haaris said you'd do this.' Danielle shook her head. 'To be honest, I don't want anything more to do with you. He told me not to meet you because you were, frankly, insane – and now I see he's right.' She started to get out of her chair. 'And you should think about letting him see his daughters or he's going to sue for full custody and I can make sure he wins.'

'See his daughters? He sees them all the time!' Safa said. 'Look, look. I can prove it. At Eid, he spent the whole day with them. My cousin sent me pictures.' She got out her phone and held it up to show Danielle. 'See. And all these were from Saturday.'

'How do I know that's not photoshopped?' Danielle said. 'Haaris said you've photoshopped pictures before so people don't trust him.'

Safa laughed.

'Oh my gosh,' she said. 'That's literally what he does. I had to talk to my work about him sending deepfakes. I've reported him to the police for harassment.'

'I'm going,' Danielle said. 'Haaris said you'd be like this. That you would say all these lies about him.'

'Wait!' Safa said and leapt to her feet as Danielle turned for the door. The black and orange attendant behind the counter was pretending to wipe something down, glancing between the two of them under his brow. 'Don't. It's not like that. I'm not crazy or anything.'

Danielle pressed her lips together and looked out of the window. A man was lazily cycling past on a rusty old road bike, the front wheel completely deflated and his trousers sagging around the seat of his arse.

'You know me and Haaris got married young,' Safa said. 'Then, I graduated and was just starting to get on with my career but Haaris really wanted a big family.'

'So?' Danielle said. 'There's nothing wrong with that.'

'No, of course, I'm not saying there is. I'm just, I'm trying to describe to you how I was feeling, at twenty-four. I was just a little bit, only a little bit, older than you and I had this career and then he was really into having kids. I felt a lot of pressure, you know. And because he wasn't working, I knew I had to keep working, I couldn't be a stay-at-home mum because we needed the income. So, I needed to be a working mum. And all these thoughts were going round my head.'

'Right there, I can hear you talking about the pressure on yourself,' Danielle said, holding up her hand, 'but did you ever stop to think about how Haaris was feeling?'

'Uh, well, no, not really.'

'Exactly. And that's your problem.' Danielle let her hand drop on to the door handle with a *thump*. 'Haaris said you couldn't ever put yourself in his shoes.'

'Well, I thought—'

'Do you know how emasculating it is to have you say that *you're* the breadwinner, *you* have to keep working, it's *your* income. How would Haaris feel being treated like just a sperm donor?'

'Well . . .' Safa rubbed her forehead. 'I didn't think, really, he was bothered. He never lifted a finger. He never asked. He never cared.' She took a deep breath. She suddenly felt as though she was going to cry. Haaris. Danielle. Trent Davies. The Pan. Was this what was needed to reclaim her life? 'I felt guilty all the time. It was like abuse, emotional abuse.'

She pressed a knuckle to one eye, hoping she wasn't about to burst into tears. She took a deep breath and thought, for one, wild second, that Danielle was about to embrace her.

Instead, Danielle laughed.

'Not lifting a finger?' She laughed again. 'That's not abuse. That's just how men are. Believe me, I have three brothers. I know. They all do that. You can't claim abuse based on dirty socks left on the floor.'

Safa took another deep breath and moved her knuckle from her eye. She nodded to her shoes.

'I guess,' she said. 'I, I just wasn't happy. I suppose that's what I'm trying to say.'

'And that's probably why he ended things with you – no offence,' Danielle said. 'He could tell you weren't happy. I mean, you had everything: husband, children, house, a great job. And you weren't ever happy. You never treated him or spoilt him or tried to put yourself in his position and understand who he was. It sounds to me like you were raised thinking men have to do everything for you and when your husband refused, you threw your toys out of the pram.' Danielle leant forward. 'Safa, men need love too.'

Tears were flooding Safa's eyes now, spilling down her cheeks. She sat down heavily in her seat. Had she been in the wrong the whole time? Could she have misunderstood the entire situation?

She nodded, not knowing how to articulate her uncertainty, still looking at her lap so Danielle Bloom couldn't see the guilt in her eyes.

'Here, have my tissue,' Danielle said, passing over her used napkin.

'Thank you,' Safa said in a hushed voice.

'I wish you all the best,' Danielle said, pulling the door open. 'I really do. It sounds like you've got a lot to personally work through. Maybe see a therapist. I'll look after Haaris.' She turned to go and then looked back. 'Probably don't message me again. I don't think we're going to get anything productive out of another conversation.'

She went out of the door, past the window and down the street, leaving her milkshake cup and Safa sitting silently at the table. She felt so empty. Worth less than she had been before.

'Here we are,' Safa said, pulling up outside a small, two-storey building. She hitched up the handbrake and leant forward to peer at the flats through her window.

There was a well-kept lawn out the front, a single flower bed and a huge fir tree that must've blocked the sunlight from the far-left flats. The others all pushed themselves up against the windows to get a better look. The sun had set by then and the garden was plagued with shadows.

'Can't see shit,' Caoimhe said. 'Should we get out?'

'No!' Ella hissed as Safa killed the engine. 'Someone might see us!'

'We've come all this way and are none the wiser, though,' Sophia said. 'Maybe there're names listed on the front door.'

Safa stared out of her window. She wanted there to be names

listed. She wanted one name to be Danielle Bloom. What would that prove? That she was right about Haaris? That she was wrong?

'Trent just probably forgot to update his licence,' Ella said as Sophia got out. 'He might not have lived here for three years.'

Safa moved her seat forward so Caoimhe and Ajola could climb out. Ella was left sitting alone in the back seat. She looked at Safa. Safa looked at her. Safa wanted her to get out. She wanted her to join in. The others were walking up the front path now.

'Fine.' Ella undid her seatbelt. 'I'm coming.'

Sophia

'AH, LOOK!' SOPHIA said as they approached the entrance. 'There!' They all turned to see what she was pointing at. Resting up in the middle of the flower bed was a little wicker rabbit. 'Jill used to make those at school! She has one in her car.'

'No way,' Ajola said. 'A girl in my class makes them too.'

'How far is this from where I live?' Sophia looked up at the navy-blue sky. Stars winked down at her. 'An hour? Forty-five minutes. Jill could for sure be living here and driving to Isla's school every morning. And she even told me she lived in a penthouse flat.'

She felt vindicated. Here was, surely, the proof. She should take the wicker rabbit and throw it at Jill outside the school next time she saw her.

'This ain't penthouse living,' Caoimhe said, glancing up at the building. She put her hands in her coat pockets.

'Yeah, but it's the sort of exaggeration Jill makes.'

Sophia looked at the intercom next to the entrance. There were six buttons but none of them had any names listed.

'It might not be linked to the Pan at all,' Ella said again as Safa double-checked the intercom. 'People forget to update their driving licences all the time.'

'Should I ring the buzzer and see?' Sophia asked, moving her thumb towards the buzzer for flat four. She felt excited. She was ready to face Jill.

'No!' Ella said and grabbed her arm. 'I thought we were being inconspicuous.'

'If it's nothing to do with Trent, we don't need to worry,' Sophia said.

'And if it is Jill?' Ajola said. 'If she comes out and sees us?'

Sophia's thumb was still hovering over the button. The urge to press it down was almost overwhelming.

'Just to hear her voice?' she suggested, staring at the button. 'To confirm.'

'She might freak out,' Safa said. 'She said if we tried anything, she'd go to the police.'

Caoimhe nodded.

'It's a big risk for zero reward.'

'Let's just stick to the original plan,' Ajola said. She took Sophia's arm. 'In and out.'

'It's Jill, though, I'm sure of it,' Sophia said. She laughed and lowered her thumb. 'She thinks she's doing this to me?' She looked at the others. 'Just wait until she realizes what I am capable of.'

'Let's go,' Ella said and pulled her other arm. 'The wicker rabbit is terrifying.'

'Let's rehearse the drive to the Airbnb,' Safa said. 'So the first time we're doing it isn't right before we kill him.'

Ella

ELLA AND BENJAMIN walked through their front door. Ella was holding her bag, his nursery bag, her coat, his coat and his shoes, which he had kicked off on the front path. It was the night before they were set to murder Trent Davies, and she needed to bath him and get him to bed by six so she could start packing for Guildford. Everything was coming together quickly. The Pan was untethered in the universe. A true being of Chaos.

'Can I have orange juice?' Benjamin asked, watching as she hung his bag and his coat on the corresponding pegs.

'No. Too late now. Bath. Teeth. Bed. You can have water.'

'I want juice,' Benjamin said, quietly.

'No. I just said. Bath. Teeth. Bed. No juice. You can have water, though.'

Ella could sense his rage simmering. Bath, teeth, bed suddenly seemed insurmountable. She checked her phone and saw a message from an unknown number.

Don't forget about tomorrow xx I'll be thinking of you.

Benjamin headbutted her leg, tendons flaring in his neck, fists braced by his side, and screamed at her. The scream changed fluidly into a wail. The transition was almost harmonious. The noise rang in Ella's ears. Her eardrum vibrated with an intensity she had never experienced before. Unheard sounds reverberated deep within her cochlea. Ella couldn't think straight. She needed to delete that text. If their phones were seized as evidence, it would be read out in court.

Behind her, Benjamin's wail intensified. It cracked in his throat, like the surface of cooling lava. She heard his socked feet thumping down the hall.

'I want juice!' Benjamin threw himself into the back of her legs. She staggered and nearly sent a response by accident.

Benjamin headbutted her again. Ella's leg gave way and she went down on one knee, dropping the phone. Benjamin hit her in the back and then leapt up and grabbed a fistful of her hair, yanking her back down. Ella had to admit, that hurt a lot. The sting was sharp enough to take her breath away. She moved her head with him to decrease the tension on her scalp and tried to prise his fist from around her hair. The thread was still open on the phone. The message winking up at her. She needed to delete it before it got accidentally uploaded to the cloud.

Individual strands of hair snapped off in Benjamin's sweaty fingers. Ella was gritting her teeth, reaching for the phone. Benjamin was still shrieking. So loud. Her ears rang. They *rang*. Finally, she tugged her hair free and grabbed the phone. Benjamin fell on her shoulder. Teeth bared, he bit a huge chunk of her flesh, his teeth sinking into her skin. She cried out, but also a part of her relished the pain. Come on, she thought, do your absolute worst. She expected him to draw blood before he let go, but he didn't. He released her and then rained a volley of tiny punches down on her arm. Ella covered her head with one arm and deleted the message with the other.

'Stop it!' she shouted, rounding on Benjamin. 'Stop!' She clamped both her hands to the sides of his head. 'Making! That! Noise! You're not crying about anything! You're just making noise!'

Tears and snot were flooding down his face. Ella had no idea why. She wasn't even gripping him that hard. He clenched his teeth at her and she felt his whole body stiffen with rage. The audacity shocked her. How dare he act like this?

She pushed him away from her and he fell dramatically, splayed across the floor. She went up the stairs, closing the stairgate behind her. He snarled at her and leapt forward. The gate trembled beneath his hands.

'Let me up!' he shrieked.

'No,' she said, staring back at him. She felt nothing for him. No love. No compassion. No sympathy. 'Ha ha,' she said.

'Don't! Say that!' He began shaking the gate. It rattled the banister and scraped the paint off the wall. Dust drifted down from the ceiling. 'Don't! Say that!'

'Ha ha.'

Benjamin screamed. The gate collapsed forward on to the stairs, gouging out a huge chunk of plaster. He staggered. Straightened. Then took a step back and performed a running kick to the twisted heap. He bounced off like a cartoon but quickly scrabbled back to his feet to charge at her again. He was completely hysterical. It was like watching a savage animal.

'Ha ha,' she taunted again.

He roared and flew at her. He crashed headlong into the uprooted gate, the fixing support slicing into the top of his head like a knife through butter.

At first, she was sure nothing bad had happened. Everything was normal. Then he clasped both his hands over his face and she saw the blood seeping through his fingers, running across his hands and dripping down his face. Rivers. Cascading.

She cried out. It wasn't a scream. It wasn't a yell. It was a sound from deep within her.

Wordlessly, she bundled him into the kitchen. She had no idea what to do. Her whole life was unravelling. The Pan was laughing at her through the window. She would film this. Take it to the police as evidence of murderous nature.

'It's OK, it's OK.' Her voice was trembling. Her murderous nature. The thought had stirred something within her. She put Benjamin on the kitchen counter. 'Everything is fine.' If she had to look at the wound and saw his brain, she was going to faint. 'It's OK. It's fine. Nothing wrong.'

She pulled off reams and reams of kitchen roll and plastered it on to his head, pressing down as hard as she could to staunch the bleeding. Benjamin was crying. Not a dinosaur. Not a savage.

'It's OK.' How could she tell the story so that she wasn't culpable? She was in the toilet when it happened. She didn't see. She was there, but he tripped. She would be blamed, regardless. Her murderous intent. 'It's OK.'

She didn't want to look at Benjamin's face. She didn't want to see the damage. An eye hanging by a sinew. A flap of skin. The white glint of bone. He started to go quiet. His cries became sobs. Sniffs.

'Do you want some orange juice?' He nodded. 'OK. No worries. Hold the tissue on your head like that. Both hands. Well done.'

The fact that he could answer questions and follow instructions was good. Her brother couldn't have her sacked for that. Probably just some sort of mandated therapy.

She moved to the fridge, then turned back to look at him through squinted eyelids. His face looked normal. A bit pale, streaks of black blood and tears, but no stringy bits of flesh. Nothing loose. Nothing gouged.

She took out the juice and poured him some in a small plastic cup. He took it and drank it without complaint. She lifted the crimson bundle of sodden kitchen paper and quickly looked at his head. There was a black mark on the top of his scalp. It was hard to see because of his thick hair and the clotting blood. Could be five centimetres long. Could be two. Could be a superficial scratch. Could have fractured the bone. She tore the bloodied kitchen roll away, then dabbed at his bloody hair with a fresh sheaf. She had to act responsible, as though the Pan was watching her. Her murderous lust.

'Come on,' she said, dabbing again. 'Let's go and see the doctor.'

'Why?' Benjamin said.

'Because you bumped your head.'

How annoying would it be if the cut was minor but he had concussion that ended up killing him. She hoisted him off the counter, slid her keys and phone into her pocket, then went outside to the car. Five twenty. She would normally be tucking him into his spaceman pyjamas right now. How fucking annoying. All this for the sake of a cup of juice.

She strapped him into his seat. She felt as though her arms and hands should be trembling but they were steady. She glanced over her shoulder. The street was empty. It was fine. Saying 'Ha ha' wasn't child abuse.

Benjamin started to doze off in the car and she was sure it was because of a serious brain injury. She pulled up into the hospital car park, almost parking across two bays, and rushed across to A and E with Benjamin clamped to her chest. The attendant took one look at Benjamin and gave her a ticket for the minor injury unit next door. They hadn't even asked what had happened. Head wound? Clinic 9.

The waiting room was full of people of a range of ages and ailments. One old man sitting in a wheelchair had a leg that ended in a stump at his knee. Benjamin couldn't stop staring at him. Another man, about Ella's age, had his hand wrapped in bloody kitchen roll of his own and was leaning back in his chair, staring at the ceiling, so pale he was almost green. Ella searched for a slim woman with honey hair, the face behind the Pan, but there was no one. It was fine. She had done nothing wrong.

Nothing to worry about, Ella texted Felix. Benjamin is fine. And she sent a picture of Benjamin sitting on the waiting-room chair, eating a KitKat. He bumped his head and I've taken him to the hospital just to double-check. Clinic 9.

She had turned off her read receipts when she had first separated from Felix because she didn't like that he could see when she had read a message or last been online. She considered ringing him but then decided if he was too busy to check WhatsApp, he was too busy to take a call.

Ella sat back in her chair as Benjamin ate the KitKat. Music was playing softly overhead. Shoes squeaked on the rubber floors. A nurse put a tray on a rack with a rattle. She couldn't believe she was here. Was this real? Was this her body? She put her fingertips on her forehead. She had always sworn to herself she would be better than her own mother. Her own mother had been cruel in a blank way. A mother utterly devoid of soul. A face etched with cosmic horror and a smell that emanated from her mouth that reminded Ella of dark drains, empty plugholes and rotten debris. Ella was sure her brother was a sociopath because of it. The absence in a hug. The sweet smell of decay on an empty kiss. She swore she would never be her mum. But she was here, sitting in the hospital, her own son with a gaping cut across his head.

She reached into her pocket for some gum but found she didn't have any on her. She'd left it at home in the rush to leave. Instinctively, she clamped her mouth shut.

The triage nurse saw them within ten minutes and wiped the cut clean.

'Is that it?' Ella said. The wound was about the size of her little fingernail. 'All the blood from that?'

The nurse smiled and deftly wiped the cut.

'Scalp wounds tend to bleed quite freely,' she said. 'It can be frightening.'

She pulled out a phone in a heavy-duty green case and snapped a photo of the cut. Ella had never seen a nurse take a photo of an injury before. She looked clinically at her. She had short blonde hair. Not long, honey-coloured. Perhaps she knew the Pan. And was taking the photo as evidence.

As they waited for the doctor, Benjamin didn't want to sit down and instead leapt around on all fours, howling like a velociraptor, his fingers covered in KitKat chocolate. The man with the bloody hand glared and put his arm over his eyes.

'Benjamin Albrecht,' a tall man in blue scrubs called from the centre of the room. 'Benjamin.'

'That's me!' Benjamin said and the man with the stump laughed.

Ella picked Benjamin up and they followed the doctor out of the waiting room and down a long corridor. They passed several empty trolleys, an old lady in a wheelchair blocking a hand sanitizer unit and a rack of towels.

'In here,' the doctor said, smiling and gesturing into a huge, brightly lit room with Disney characters plastered all over the wall.

'Buzz!' Benjamin cried and slipped out of Ella's grip. 'Mum! Buzz and Woody!'

Ella wondered who had the time to go online and find all the pictures, print them on a high-definition printer, laminate them, cut them out and then display them around the room with the alphabet and the numbers 1 to 20. Surely not the doctors. Not the nurses? Who else? The cleaner?

'Buzz and Woody,' the doctor said. 'Now, Benjamin, you can choose any chair you want to sit in.'

There were about six chairs in the room and Benjamin took his sweet time, finger resting on his lips, turning to view each chair in turn. Ella resisted the urge to snap at him.

'There.' Benjamin pointed to the only chair with arms.

'Now, Benjamin.' As Benjamin climbed into the chair, the doctor perched on a small stool with wheels. Ella took a seat beside him. 'I am Dr James and I want to have a look at your cut today. Can I do that?'

'Yup,' Benjamin said and moved his hair on his head. He hadn't quite got the right spot, so Ella leant in and parted his hair. Dr James peered at the tiny little wound.

'A little wedge,' he said. 'What happened?'

'He caught it on the edge of the stairgate,' Ella said, leaning far away to talk so he couldn't smell her breath. 'It was lying on its side.'

'He didn't lose consciousness?'

'No.'

'No vomiting?'

'No. I just wanted to bring him in because there was a lot of blood and I was worried about sending him to bed without getting him checked out.'

She said this in a rush, trying to limit any oral cavity smells.

'No, no.' Dr James spun away on his little stool. 'You did the right thing. This is what we're here for.'

His affirmation choked Ella's throat. She thought she might cry. He wasn't the Pan, that was for sure. Dr James pulled a small metal trolley over to Benjamin's chair.

'I'm just going to bandage it.' He smiled. 'And then you can go home.'

Ella wanted him to ask more questions. She wanted to tell him what had really happened. She had lost her temper. She had said 'Ha ha'. She had grabbed his head. And she had done it too hard. She knew she had. She wanted Dr James to listen and then call a counsellor. Suddenly, in that moment, more than anything, she wanted help. It didn't matter if they knew exactly what had happened. If her brother was annoyed. Even if she lost her job. It didn't matter. None of it mattered. She didn't want to hurt Benjamin again.

They heard voices from the corridor. Felix suddenly appeared in the doorway, looking taller, gaunter, greyer than ever. His cap threw dark shadows over his eyes, making him look like a harbinger of death.

'Ach!' He gasped. 'Benjamin.'

'Daddy!' Benjamin cried, smiling.

'Do you know him?' a nurse said from the corridor as Felix rushed into the room.

'Yes. I told you. I am her husband,' Felix said. 'This is my son.'

He reached out his hands as though he was going to pick Benjamin up. Ella rolled her eyes.

'The doctor is just examining him,' she said. 'Leave him.'

'What happened?'

'He caught his head on the stairgate.'

Felix frowned, shaking his head from side to side as though that didn't make sense.

'What stairgate?' he demanded. 'How?'

This was the line of questioning Ella had been expecting.

'The bottom stairgate,' she said. Between them, Dr James was wiping Benjamin's cut. Benjamin was stroking Woody's face on the wall next to him. 'It fell over.'

'How?' Felix raised his shoulders. 'I fitted it myself.' He touched his chest. 'It doesn't just fall over.'

Ella steeled herself.

'He knocked it down,' she said. 'He was rattling the bars and it fell down.'

'Strong,' Dr James said. He looked between the two of them and held up a small opaque capsule. 'I'm just going to glue the wound shut.'

'*Ja, ja*, go ahead,' Felix said. He looked back at Ella and frowned. She took a deep breath.

'All done,' Doctor James announced. 'I'll put a piece of gauze on it,' he said to Felix and then to Ella, 'and a plaster. Keep the plaster on for a couple of days so the glue can do its job, then you can take it off and, hey presto' – he smiled at Benjamin – 'all better.'

'All better,' Felix said and put a long, skeletal hand on Benjamin's shoulder. He smiled, exaggerating his long chin, his sunken eyes. 'What a brave boy.'

Was that it, Ella thought, as Dr James packed up his tools and Felix lifted Benjamin up. Everyone was satisfied with her explanation? No follow-up. No note to child services. No quiet word in a side office. Where was the due diligence? She was being left vulnerable to people like the Pan.

Felix carried Benjamin to the car park, Ella walking silently behind them. She didn't want to go home. She wanted an intervention. She wanted a social worker to suggest that Felix take him for the night. She should just tell everyone, right here, right now, announce it to the car park, that she was overwhelmed. She had no control. Her mum shouldn't have had her and she shouldn't have had Benjamin. Benjamin's injury was her fault. The Pan was blackmailing her. She had buried a body seven years ago. She should be in prison. But Benjamin would be safe. No more screaming. No more stress. No more blood.

'There you go,' Felix said, opening up Ella's car door. 'Tucked in tight and soon, tucked in bed.'

Ella's heart was thrumming in her chest. She was so tired. She should start with telling Felix. He would understand. He always *understood*. If she told him, maybe she wouldn't even have to kill Trent. He could sort it out for her. He had always been so good at sorting things out.

Felix fastened Benjamin into the seat and bent down to kiss him, his grey, grizzled stubble grating against Benjamin's soft, round cheek. Ella felt the sensation as though it was his kiss on her cheek. Benjamin made a noise like someone with wind and pushed him away with his hands and feet.

Felix straightened up and looked at Ella. He leant his arm on the top of the car and regarded her critically.

'And you?' he said. 'You are OK?'

Ella pressed her lips together.

'Why did you tell them that we're married?' She moved away from Felix to the driver's door. Stupid thought, actually. What, realistically, could Felix do. If she opened her mouth, she'd put all five of them in prison. 'We're not married any more, Felix.'

He put his long fingers against his chest and lifted his shoulders, mouth open and eyes wide, looking around as though in appeal for support.

'Technically, we are still married,' he said as she opened her door. 'Divorce isn't final yet.'

'Stop wearing your wedding ring,' Ella said and pulled the door shut. She turned on the engine and wound down the window. 'Just stop it. We're not married any more. Stop wearing it.'

Caoimhe

THE FIRST 5K race of the summer season was being held that Tuesday evening beside a dual carriageway. On one side of the trail was the roar of lorries and the thrum of exhaust engines. On the other side, the grass hummed with grasshoppers and nesting birds flitting in the hedgerows. The trail itself was utter scree, covered in loose chips that hissed when Caoimhe's trainers rolled over them. She had contemplated staying at home and getting emotionally prepared to kill a man the following day, but it was too hard to sit and do nothing. She felt so much better out in the open. The power of her muscles. The lightness of her feet. The great lungfuls of air that she could draw in as she ran at full pace. Wielding all her raw strength today would make her feel better when she faced the task tomorrow.

Caoimhe moved past the starting pen, where some runners were already congregating, and headed towards the hedgerow. Life felt so real to her that evening. So tangible. There was a slight gap here, a seam between the gnarled branches, and she went through, ducking down so that the thorns scraped against her shoulder blades and pulled at her hair. She came out on the side of a wheatfield. The hum from the dual carriageway was non-existent here and the fields rolled away from her, opening up the entire sky. The clouds were turning mauve as the sun sank, strange tendrils of pink stretching out over the hills. Another Krakatoa evening.

She turned and there was Rohan Rust jogging along the edge of the field towards her. He was moving fast and would be upon her any moment. She took a step back, trying to take everything in. His black and red skull cap, his thick, dark beard, the Nike Running swoosh on his chest, long tracksuit bottoms, even in this heat. She wanted to pause everything. To capture a snapshot of this perfect moment.

He made eye contact with her as he drew close and, this time, followed it up with a nod of recognition. She was too starstruck to do anything. She just stared at him until he had gone past. Then she turned and watched him dart through the same gap in the hedgerow that she had fought through. Her stomach squeezed and she was suddenly afraid she needed the toilet. Rohan Rust. Here. He was no distraction. He was too real. Too perfect.

'Hey, you,' Evie said to Caoimhe when she had made her way to the starter pen. 'I was worried you weren't coming. We need a strong female team. Three to score. That's you, me and maybe Rachel.'

Caoimhe didn't know or care who Rachel was. She just nodded. She was starting to feel a little sick. She hadn't raced properly in a while because she was so focused on training. The starting pen was getting busy, four hundred disparate people suddenly condensing into one solid block. She looked around the gathering faces.

'Come up the front with me,' Evie said, touching her arm. 'We'll get a good spring towards the hedge.'

'Nah,' Caoimhe said, pulling away. 'That's not my style.'

'Sure.' Evie raised a hand. 'See you at the end.'

Bitch, Caoimhe thought as she watched her effortlessly weave her way in and out of the broad male shoulders towards the front. She pulled a stray twig from her hair and flicked it into the mass of trainers and legs around her. Right at the front of the melee, she could see Rohan Rust's red and black skull cap. Her heart pounded after him. His gravitas, his aura.

She didn't have time to finish this thought because the starting gun went. The crowd lurched around her. The entire wedge of runners moved down the scree path like a rockslide. Caoimhe had to watch her feet, careful not to trip or be tripped. They rounded the hedgerow and into the woods. The ground here was thick with twisted roots, snaking over each other, some heavy and turgid, others spindly and erupting from the earth like fissures of steam. Caoimhe darted between them, counting her steps. One, two, one, two, three, one, two, one, two, three. She was flying easily, her body unhindered. It would be so easy to throw back her head and howl. Crepuscular. The air was rich. She was running home.

She began to pick off runners in the second mile: all those who were still going strong but whose second mile pace was slower than their first. She couldn't hear the lorries any more. A single bead of sweat was running from her armpit down her upper arm.

After the woods, in the final mile, the ground rose steeply. It was like climbing a ladder. The men either side of her fell away, dead leaves being brushed aside. Caoimhe felt the burn in her quads but it was a soothing burn. She could handle it. The hill got inexplicably steeper, seeming to swell at the summit so it was almost as though she was running backwards, and then it was over, and she was soaring downhill, the finish line visible across the flat fields. She could have run with outstretched arms. Any wind might have swept her off her feet. This was it. This was easy. This was something that she was born to do.

She flew through the finish line in seventeen minutes and eight seconds. Her 5K PB. So easy, so effortless. The male finishers were dotted around, sweating, talking, wiping down bare chests with dank towels. She couldn't see Evie anywhere, which was a relief. The last thing she wanted to do was to have to talk to her.

She walked back to the tent, had a drink, then pulled on her tracksuit bottoms and jumper. She checked her phone to stop her mind racing and saw a message from an unknown number.

Well done on your race. Hope you're ready for tomorrow xx

Caoimhe frowned and looked around. The club tent was empty. By the finish line, a big-toothed leggy woman with short hair was hugging Mateus. Caoimhe hadn't even cast him a thought before the race. He was wearing a pair of jeans and a wax jacket. She leant over and grabbed Evie's red Nike bag, holding it in two hands for several seconds. Then she swiftly unzipped it and rummaged through the clothes inside until she found Evie's phone. She held it in her hand. It felt very warm. Solid. She glanced around again. Still no one. She swiped up and dialled herself from Evie's phone. The number that blared up on her screen was not the same one that the text had come from. She felt a little bit deflated. She hung up and dropped Evie's phone back in the bag.

Mateus and the short-haired woman stepped into the tent and Caoimhe quickly pushed Evie's bag behind her and stood up.

'Great work, Caoimhe!' Mateus said and raised his arms as if he was going to hug her. Caoimhe didn't move, suddenly very aware of the sweat rolling down her back and gathering at her armpits. Her shirt was sodden. Sweat was quite literally dripping off her. Mateus didn't notice and put both his large, heavy hands on her shoulders and squeezed. Caoimhe beamed.

'Not running?' Caoimhe asked him.

'Just supporting today.'

'How come?'

'Got an injury,' Mateus said, vaguely. He cleared his throat.

'A magical injury?' Caoimhe said.

'It's not magical, it's real.' He glanced at her. His eyes shifted this way and that. 'I was going easy in training. My left foot.'

'Isn't that a Daniel Day-Lewis movie?' Caoimhe smiled at him. He visibly swallowed. She liked that he felt intimidated by her. An ego too fragile to race with her. That was OK. She had a little crush on him after all. This was all social capital.

'You did well, though,' he said into the ensuing silence. 'Speedy Gonzales.' He winked. Caoimhe laughed loudly. She didn't feel it was that funny but she wanted him to like her. 'First woman,' Mateus said. 'You must have been top twenty men as well.'

Caoimhe baulked.

'Where's Evie?'

Mateus turned and gestured out to the course. The big-toothed woman shook her head.

'Poor Evie,' she said.

'She stopped at the first bend,' Mateus said. 'I offered to walk her back here. She was limping pretty badly but she said she wanted to finish.'

'She hasn't finished?'

'She twisted her ankle,' Mateus explained. 'Went right down on it after about three-quarters of a mile. Nasty fall.'

Caoimhe smirked. Guess Evie wasn't so great after all.

They left the tent to watch the dregs of the race coming in, the slow and the untrained, the people who did it to 'push' or 'challenge' themselves. The spectators valiantly clapped them and shouted praise as they limped over the line.

Caoimhe scanned the tired faces for Evie. Whereabouts had she got to? She looked up towards the hill and spotted the club shirt, limping along, almost at a walk. She put a hand over her mouth to hide a laugh. She was literally dead last.

'Oh my God,' she whispered.

'I feel so bad for her,' the big-toothed woman said beside her.

'Why did she bother finishing?' Caoimhe said. 'She should have just stopped.'

'You need three runners to make a team,' the big-toothed woman replied. 'If she finishes, we get the points. Based on how we did, our team might go second.'

Caoimhe felt a pain in the back of her throat. She wasn't sure where it had come from. She tried clearing her throat but it intensified. To hide it, she scowled at the figure limping the last fifty metres towards the finish line. The well of tears that had been encased inside her for almost twenty-four hours began to split open. She quickly rubbed the back of her hand over her eyes.

'Well done, Evie,' the big-toothed woman shouted, and clapped her hands as Evie came into the finisher's tunnel.

Caoimhe gave a half-hearted clap as well. She was afraid to be vocal in her support in case she really started bawling.

'Well done,' repeated the big-toothed woman. 'All the way.'

Evie's face was a mask of pain, teeth gritted, cheeks streaked with sweat and tears.

'Well done,' Caoimhe called, but her voice cracked and she quickly shut her mouth.

As Evie came out of the tunnel, she flung her arms around both their necks.

'It's OK,' the big-toothed woman said. 'It's OK.'

'I feel I've let everyone down,' Evie said into Caoimhe's hair.

'No,' Caoimhe said, taken aback. 'No. No way.'

'Let's just get you sat down.' The big-toothed woman grasped her waist. 'What is it, your ankle?'

'Right ankle.' Evie grimaced. She put her arms around Caoimhe's and the big-toothed woman's necks and hopped between them. Caoimhe put a hand around her back and guided her towards a flat tuft of grass. 'It feels ten times the size.'

'I'll get your bag,' the big-toothed woman said. 'Is it in the tent?'

'Thanks, Rachel.'

Aha, so the big-toothed woman was the elusive Rachel. Caoimhe sat down on the grass beside Evie as Rachel walked away. Evie grimaced again and lay flat on her back. Caoimhe pulled up a long blade of grass.

'Did you catch it on the roots?' she asked.

Evie put her wrists over her eyes and spoke up to the sky.

'No, I didn't even get that far. There was some hole in the

ground. Just turned my ankle on it, almost straight away. Agonizing.'

She moved her hands and propped herself up on her elbows to look at Caoimhe. Caoimhe quickly glanced away. Evie sat up properly and tugged off her left trainer, tossing it to one side. When it came to her right one, though, she couldn't slip it off. She groaned and then started trying to loosen the laces. Her mud-streaked fingers were trembling and she couldn't slide them under the tightly woven straps.

'I can help,' Caoimhe said.

'Yeah, go on then,' Evie said and lay back down in the grass.

Caoimhe got on her knees and began loosening the laces. Evie winced.

'Sorry,' Caoimhe said, quickly, and then the mud-wet trainer slipped off into her hand. Rachel came back at that moment with Evie's red Nike bag. Caoimhe got up and hurriedly walked away, wiping her eyes. Evie was a fucking idiot for finishing the race anyway. She should have stopped the second her ankle went. That's what Caoimhe would have done. But was that why Evie was such a good runner? Did you need to push yourself beyond what was reasonably expected?

Caoimhe looked up. Rohan Rust was in front of her. He was drinking from a plastic cup, his red and black skull cap tied around his fist, his thick black hair on end with sweat. Caoimhe felt her face flush. Rohan Rust raised his magnificent eyebrows at her, but Caoimhe was too flustered to respond and bowed her head, walking past him without acknowledgement.

Ajola

LISTENING TO HER class's music performances was excruciating. There was no rhythm. No story. Ajola sat in her wheelie chair and nodded along, trying to seem engaged. It was very hot. The classroom was stuffy. She had opened all the windows wide but there was no air flow. The glockenspiels *pinged* and *ponged*. She had to go and murder someone tomorrow and all she would be able to hear would be the bloody glockenspiels.

She and Daisy had done the maths competition that lunchtime. Ajola had deliberately chosen that lunch, because she was going to commit murder the next day, and if she could save Daisy, she could save herself. Ajola had hovered around the wheelie chair as it enthroned itself around Daisy, watching as she confidently clicked through the different questions. Ajola didn't know what to do if Daisy got stuck. Would it be more damaging to her development to help or ignore? What could be used against her if the Pan was watching?

Yashica poked her head around the door once and Ajola snapped at her.

'I told you to go outside!' she said, raising her voice so that Daisy jumped. 'If I tell you again, I'll have to give you a step!'

Yashica vanished as quickly as if she'd been vaporized.

'Would you really give her a step?' Daisy asked, reading through the next question. Ajola barely had time to absorb it before Daisy had typed in an answer.

'No,' Ajola admitted. 'But she has to stay outside.'

'Product of six and seven. Sum is adding, product is multiplying, so forty-two,' Daisy said, typing in the numbers as she said them. 'I like this,' she said and clicked submit. 'Were you good at maths at school?'

'I was,' Ajola said carefully.

'Did you do competitions like this?'

Next question. Read. Answered. Submitted.

'No,' Ajola said. She took a deep breath and leant on the wall. She folded her arms, then unfolded them and pressed her fist to her palm. She wanted to add more detail but was hyperaware of the Pan. If everything she said was recorded and played back at an inquest, what would people say? Would they say she was nurturing? Or would they say she was a murderess who had driven Daisy to suicide?

'Did you like maths, though?' Daisy said.

Next question. Read. Answered. Submitted.

'I loved it,' Ajola said. 'I wanted to be a mathematician.'

'Like, an accountant?'

'No. A mathematician. Like a professor, someone with a PhD in Maths, who spends their time researching mathematical equations.'

'How come you never did?'

Next question. Read. Answered. Submitted.

'I didn't think I was good enough,' Ajola said after a pause.
'But you said you were good.'

'I know now that I was good.' Next question. Read. Answered.
Submitted. 'But, back then, I didn't know. No one . . .' She
paused, wondering how stupid it would sound to a seven-year-
old. 'No one told me.'

Daisy nodded slowly.

'I think that,' she said.

'But it's not about just being good,' Ajola said. 'It's about
your perseverance, your curiosity, your love of it. Anyone can
be good at maths and then give up as soon as a problem is too
hard. Real mathematicians work to find solutions.'

Daisy didn't say anything. She just stared at the laptop screen,
reading and rereading the next question. Ajola went back over
the words in her head. They made sense. They were honest.
They were the words Ajola would have wanted to hear when
she was seven.

'I got full marks across all my Year Six SATs papers,' Ajola
said. 'It's not such a big deal these days. But twenty years ago,
it was unheard of.'

'Wow,' Daisy said. She was still reading the question.
Ajola narrowed her eyes to read it from her position. It was
a three-part question involving equivalent fractions. She was
going to chime in with something about quarters and eighths
but decided not to when Daisy asked, 'Did they give you a
certificate?'

'No.' Ajola laughed. 'I didn't find out until I was in my twenties. My great-grandma told me when I graduated university.'

'Why didn't they tell you when you were eleven?'

'I don't know,' Ajola said, truthfully. 'Maybe to make me

work harder? It would have been nice to know I was good, though.'

Her parents hadn't said anything to her about moving out. She thought they might be shocked, or even pleased. Their apathy had stiffened Ajola's resolve. Their betrayal of her, from the very moment her father turned his eyes on her mother, meant she could never rely on them. She would never be them. At first, she had enjoyed having her own place to live. She could watch TV, go to bed when she wanted, sit quietly without interruption. She invited the others over and felt like a proper woman.

But when she was eighteen, Ella, Safa, Sophia and Caoimhe all moved away to university. New adventures. New places. Maybe to find new, life-altering connections and meaning. Ajola was left. Every holiday, Caoimhe, Safa, Ella and Sophia came home and they seemed so much bigger and brighter for all their experiences. And where was she? Was this going to be her life, unaltered, for the next eighty years? She had always been sure there was more. She thought about the chalkboard in Paris.

She signed up to the Open University, enrolling in a BSc in Mathematics and Physics. She completed the course in three years. She was too embarrassed to tell the others about the graduation ceremony, and she would never have told her parents because she didn't want them to be there. She debated telling her great-grandma, but she knew she would have persuaded her to attend. And what sort of achievement had it been anyway? She had completed the degree with ease, with little to no impact on her daily life. It was probably some Mickey Mouse degree, something with the McDonald's logo on the back that they gave out in multistorey car parks.

She didn't know where the idea to be a teacher had come from. Maybe she had dreamed it. Imagined some mentor, some Thomas Cromwell, telling her to be a teacher, advising her, offering a hug, genuine eye contact, sincere concern. *'Be a teacher.'* She applied for several teacher-trainee positions. Because of her career in Tesco, she got on to a programme that paid her to train and which also allowed her to move even further away from her parents. It was such a release. Such a sudden lifting of weight. She felt she had unlimited purpose. Her great-grandma died at about the same time. Ajola didn't feel it was sudden. It felt like the last note of a song. She qualified as a teacher. She tore into her purpose. She was so fucking thankful for this. She had come so close to sinking into the apathy of it. To becoming her parents. This overwhelming sense of relief helped her build a facade around herself. She would never go back to how she had been. She wouldn't allow it. When the anxiety bloomed in quiet moments, when she felt it blossoming in her chest, she forced herself to be loud and confident, to take up the space she might otherwise have relinquished. It was a conscious effort, a perpetual task, because she was trying to save herself, every day.

The laptop screen flashed with a big green tick. Daisy frowned at it.

'Is that it?' she said. 'It took like five minutes?'

'Eleven,' Ajola said, glancing at her watch. 'You did good, Daisy.'

'When do I get my certificate?' Daisy asked.

'Give it a couple of weeks. You can go outside now and play with Yashica.'

Ajola watched her leave. Surely, the demons were exorcized.

She dared the Pan, from whatever nook or cranny that mask was spying out of, to find fault with that.

The glockenspiels *pinged* and *ponged* around the classroom. How long had this piece been going on for? All the notes were so disjointed. The pace was just dreadful. In fact, she was sure the performer, Lucy, was just making it up on the spot. It was so bad. Just so bad. Ajola thought she might faint. The Pan, Daisy, Meg, the heat, Meg, this terrible glockenspiel music, Meg. She couldn't let Daisy end up like Meg, or herself. She could feel herself detaching from her body. Time was obsolete. The seconds stretched to eternity. Layers and mirrors. She tried to sit up in her chair but couldn't feel her body. Some of the boys at the back were laughing. What little dickheads. Ajola thought of the girls she had taught over the years, Meg, Daisy, Lucy, even Yashica, and was full of rage. They were so honest and open and ready. And they were going to grow up and cohabit with dickheads. The glockenspiels. The glockenspiels. Did anything really matter? Daisy had done the competition. She had given her that opportunity. So why was it not over? Why was she not healed? Would Trent's death make it all better? Why was life not like a Hollywood movie?

'OK,' she finally said, more loudly than she had intended. Lucy stopped playing. The spell broke. Ajola was able to sit up. She cleared her throat. 'That was lovely. Let's give Lucy a round of applause, everyone.'

The applause was smattering but Ajola kept it going, getting louder and louder with her own handclaps until she was satisfied Lucy's piece had been given the appreciation she deserved.

At the end of the day, when all the children had gone home and the cleaner had taken the bins out and the classroom was dark and empty, Ajola sat alone in the teacher's wheelie chair. The Pan had sent her a screenshot from Reddit showing Meg's face. She looked older than when Ajola had taught her but still recognizably her. Ajola could still hear the glockenspiels. She didn't think she would ever be able to stop hearing them.

Safa

SAFA SAW THE pictures the day before they were planning to kill Trent Davies. She had felt something building up inside of her. A pain. A panic. From the stress of their task. From Danielle Bloom and the malevolent presence of the Pan watching over her, threatening to cut her life as it hung by a thread. Things were starting to unravel. This was it. She was being forced to murder. And now these pictures.

She and Emaan were sitting in the living room of her parents' house, waiting to collect the girls from after-school club. Safa's older sister, Zoha, was there too, wearing her full khimar like a crown. She had just performed the Asr prayer and was now blowing contentedly on the surface of a hot cup of tea their ammi had made only for her.

'Baji, you need to make sure you perform all your prayers,' she told Safa that afternoon. 'I'm so proud of you for going to Eid Prayer in April. It is so important to have these relationships.'

'Uh huh,' Safa said. 'I do pray.'

'All your prayers?' Zoha was insistent, watching Safa from

across the room, seated in the esteemed chair next to their mother. 'You can perform qasr salah and reduce the rakats from four to two,' she said earnestly. 'It is acceptable.'

'Not every day,' Safa said. She got her phone out and pretended to be checking something.

'There is no blame upon you for shortening the prayer,' Zoha persisted, 'if that's what you need to do.'

'Uh-huh,' Safa said, still scrolling aimlessly. A message from an unknown number flashed up on the screen.

'This is why you need a husband. A man and his wife are a team,' Zoha said. 'With a husband, you can work' – she began ticking items off on her fingers – 'pray, be a mother, be a wife.'

'Uh-huh,' Safa said again.

She opened the message. There was a single line:

Don't forget about tomorrow. Remember, if you can't do it, these two get your girls xx

Below was an Instagram screenshot of Haaris and Danielle in the living room of her house. Safa almost didn't recognize it because the photo had so many filters. And the living room looked as if it had been – painted? There was a different mirror on the wall as well. And a leopard-print art feature mounted behind the heads of Haaris and Danielle. They were standing together, her arms around him, her head on his shoulder. He, inexplicably, had sunglasses on inside and was facing the camera with a defiant jaw. With the sunglasses and washed hair, and the rest of him out of sight, he almost looked handsome. The caption was: *First week living together DONE. Our slice of paradise.*

Safa pulled the phone closer to her face, enraptured with the photo, wanting to examine every tiny detail, absorb every horror. What was Haaris wearing? Did they have their shoes on? How tidy was the floor? Danielle was *living* in the house with him? Safa's head began to spin. She felt nauseous. Her stomach tightened and, for an instant, she thought she was going to vomit. She couldn't believe he would dare. It wasn't even his house. Safa paid the mortgage.

She swiped. The Pan had sent another screenshot: the two of them sitting on the bonnet of her white BMW 3 series, lips pressed together, one of Danielle's arms extended upwards for the purpose of the selfie. The sight of the picture provoked in Safa such a visceral reaction, Safa was sure that, if she opened her mouth just a little, all the puke would come out: the quinoa she had had for lunch, the tea Emaan had made her, the breakfast porridge, all of it, all over Ammi's nice rug. Her forehead stung with sweat. She was about to lose consciousness. She wanted to see more. More of them walking hand in hand in her garden, more of them getting a Drive-Thru in her car, more of them moving Danielle's clothes into her wardrobe. It was shocking. His audacity. His dismissal of her. How insignificant she was. She clenched the phone in her fingers. She wanted to scream until her trachea was wrenched out through her gaping mouth.

'And if things get very hectic, just do the obligatory prayers. It's your connection with God, Baji.'

Zoha smiled at her over her cup of tea.

Safa dropped the phone on to the sofa. She wanted to smash it against the wall. She stood up abruptly. For a moment, she didn't know if her legs would hold her. If her stomach would eject its contents.

'I have to go,' she said.

Zoha frowned. Safa walked away from her. Straight out of the back room, down the hall and out of the house. She needed fresh air. She couldn't escape the itch that was crawling around inside of her skin.

'Are you OK?' Emaan asked, coming out of the house behind her. She handed across her phone.

'I'm fine!' Safa snapped. She put a hand on her forehead and leant back against the front window. 'I don't feel very well,' she said, quietly, honestly.

'Safa,' Emaan said and hurried down the steps to put a hand around her shoulders. 'You do too much already. Don't listen to Zoha.'

'I feel like I'm not in my body,' she said in a whisper. She was enraged Haaris still had such power over her. She was meant to be in charge of her life now. Not him.

'I'll take you home,' Emaan said.

'The girls. Javeria. Aleena.'

'I'll get them. I'll drop them off. You need to rest.'

Safa didn't say anything. She didn't want to go back to the empty flat. The small, dingy space with nothing to prevent the images of Haaris and Danielle in her house, enjoying her things, her family, blazoned into her mind. She wanted to scratch the pictures from her eyes but she couldn't. She wanted to cry but she couldn't. She wanted to rage but she couldn't. She felt so impotent. All these feelings but nothing to do with them.

'Come,' Emaan said.

Safa crouched down by the front steps and put her face in her hands. There were no tears.

Sophia

THE DAY BEFORE they were set to kill Trent Davies, Jill glided up to the school fence like the Grand High Witch, wearing a burgundy shirt dress, with a smart, collared neckline. Sophia just stared at her. The other mums surrounded her, touching the fabric of the dress and cooing in admiration. Jill did a little spin for them. Sophia wanted to march over there and confront her. *What the fuck, Jill!* Maybe too aggressive. She decided that when Jill inevitably came over to flaunt the dress to her, she would be cold with her. Turn away. Give a little shrug. *I don't care.*

Isla must have sensed a change in her because she touched her arm.

'Why're you staring, Mum?'

'I'm not.'

'Is it your secret boyfriend again?'

'What?' Sophia whipped around. 'I told you. There is no secret boyfriend.'

Isla furrowed her brow in disbelief.

'Who is then?' Isla's eyes narrowed. 'Her?' She nodded at Jill. 'Isn't she your friend?'

'No,' Sophia scoffed. She could now hear Jill talking loudly about how she couldn't go out with the others for breakfast because she was going to spend her morning writing her novel. Sophia rolled her eyes. The world was such a massive place. Why did Jill feel the need to exist so closely to Sophia in such an exact way? 'She hasn't even got kids at the school. She just turns up every day for the fun of it. If a guy did that, we'd call the police.'

She looked down at Isla. Isla looked up at her. She raised her eyebrows.

'Go tell her that.'

'Yeah, right.'

The school doors opened and Isla skipped down the front path. Sophia started picking at the fence. To her surprise, Jill swept away, sashaying elegantly in her burgundy dress, iPhone X resting casually in one graceful hand, without acknowledging Sophia at all. It felt worse than a slap across the face. How dare Jill be the one to dismiss her. How dare she seize power like that.

'Excuse me.'

Sophia jumped. It was Hannah, standing, arms folded, a few feet away.

'Hi! Hannah!' She realized it had been a while since she had spoken to any of the other mums; she had been too preoccupied with Jill. 'How're you doing?'

'Fine. I just want to say, we think it's really horrible what you're doing to Jill.'

'What?' Sophia said, so confused, the *h* came out more pronounced than the *w*.

'Spiteful.' Hannah looked genuinely upset. 'You know her husband went missing, just like yours did. The least you could do is be supportive.'

Sophia rolled her eyes.

'*Her* husband went missing too, eh?'

'Rude,' Hannah said and pointed a finger very close to Sophia's face. 'You're rude, Sophia.'

'She copies everything I do!' Sophia hissed as Hannah strode away. 'She doesn't even have a child at this school!'

Hannah didn't look back. Sophia turned away. She clenched her hands into fists. She couldn't stand it. She wasn't some grey, shapeless mass to be manipulated any more. She had power. She was worthy of a DT partnership with Joseph Burton and Jill, Jill who hadn't evolved in twenty years, could sit with Simon. She hissed through her teeth.

'I'm going to scare the shit out of her,' she muttered. 'Trent Davies is going to die.'

Ajola

AJOLA WAITED AT the corner of the Morrisons, between the red-brick wall and a tangle of brambles and clover. There was a solitary bumblebee crawling along the top of the bow-topped fence that separated the main road from the Morrisons car park. Ajola could clearly see the black fuzz of its back, watch its end shuffle from side to side, observe the long, black antennae searching out in front of it. She rubbed her sternum and winced.

Ajola looked around the corner towards the Morrisons entrance. A woman in a knee-length, off-white shirt was walking into the store, pushing her sunglasses on to her head. 'This is not an oversize T-shirt' was emblazoned in black font on the front, 'it is a dress'. No Trent.

Ajola turned back and faced the red-brick wall. She scratched away some dust with her thumbnail and then tentatively put it in her mouth. She imagined Thomas Cromwell standing beside her, two assassins in the shadows. She thought about Meg. Was her heart beating like this before it happened? Was she thinking about Virginia Woolf and Ernest Hemingway? Was she remembering something innocuous Ajola said about *Romeo and Juliet*?

She glanced around the corner again and there was Trent, metres away, head down, thumbs darting across his phone. The bumblebee flew off. Ajola quickly took her thumb out of her mouth.

Oh God, here we go. How the fuck has it come to this?

'Hi,' Ajola said and held out her hand, careful not to leave the corner and come into the range of the cameras. 'You work for Morrisons, good.'

Trent made to step around her, eyes still on his phone.

'I'm just off my shift,' he said and glanced up at her. He stopped. 'But I might be able to help. What's the problem?'

'It's not Morrisons related.' Ajola laughed. 'Thing is . . . Well.' She held up her hands. 'I've tried to park and . . . Thing is . . .' Trent was smiling. He put his phone in his pocket. Ajola relaxed. 'Basically, my car is stuck. I think I just need someone to give it a push whilst I, you know' – she mimed a steering wheel – 'drive it.'

'Yeah, sure, I can give it a push. Whereabouts is it?'

'Just down here.' Ajola pointed behind her, away from Morrisons car park. 'I've been looking for someone for about an hour. You're the first person to say yes.'

'Let's go.' Trent winked at her and Ajola turned down the alley. She pulled a face. 'You know to use the accelerator gently to get traction?' he asked as they walked.

'Oh no, nothing like that,' Ajola decided to say. 'I've just been jamming it down.'

Trent laughed.

'I might not even need to push,' he said. 'I'm pretty good with cars. I can probably drive it free.'

'I found the right guy, then.'

They went down a narrow flight of stairs and then Ajola led them to a muddy verge where Safa's Fiat was parked. Trent held out his hand for the keys without hesitation.

'I can get you out of this,' he said. 'Two seconds. Stand back there in case any mud sprays up.'

'Thank you so much. Really kind. Really nice.' Ajola tried to see his face to gauge if this was overkill. 'I'm so grateful.'

He smiled at her over the top of the car, opened the door and slid inside. He pulled the car on to the road in less than five seconds, put the handbrake on and wound down the passenger window.

'Anything else?' he said and winked again.

'I don't know what I can ever do to thank you,' she said. 'Can I tell your manager at Morrisons?' He laughed. 'Oh! You said you were just off-shift? Maybe I can buy you a drink?'

Trent looked out through the windscreen, nodding slowly.

'That sounds nice.'

'I know a nice pub, out of town a bit, but the owner knows me and we can probably get some food on the house.'

'So, your way of thanking me is blagging free food?'

Ajola laughed. She walked around the side of the car.

'You want me to drive?' he asked as she opened the door.

Ajola looked down at him, unsure how she was going to hide her contempt.

'Nah,' she said. 'You're all right.'

Trent slid over into the passenger seat. Ajola climbed into the driver's seat and they set off.

'Ah, shit,' Ajola said as she drove towards the lights. 'I've left my phone at home. Mind if I swing by my house to get it? I want to put this on Snapchat,' she added into the silence that followed.

'Oh, yeah, sure.'

'I can have my housemate standing outside to chuck it in,' Ajola said, 'if I call her from your phone.'

Trent handed his iPhone X across to her without a word.

'Thank you so much,' Ajola said. 'Really kind. Really nice.'

Ella

ELLA CHANGED HER gum for the third time whilst waiting on the gravel driveway. She enclosed the old one inside a torn-off scrap from the main pack and put it in her pocket. Chewed-up gum in the black wheelie bin was the sort of inconspicuous evidence that got people put away for their crimes. She wanted to turn and run away, jump through the thick hedgerow and make off through the waterlogged fields. Just remove herself from this. Let the others do it. They didn't need all five of them.

She heard the car coming. She remembered the message from the night before. Her heartbeat quickened. She stepped towards the road.

Ajola pulled the car into the driveway. Ella smiled and held up her hand. Trent waved back, completely oblivious. Ajola wound down the window.

'Come on then,' she said and held out her hand.

'I couldn't find it,' Ella replied. She held out both arms. Was this acting? 'It's not on the table.'

'It is.'

'I swear, it's not.'

Ajola rolled her eyes and looked at Trent.

'Can you believe this?' She switched off the engine. 'Let me grab it. You want to come in and have a Prosecco for your troubles?'

Ajola was a very good actress. The tone of her voice, the movement of her head. It was all so natural. Ella had no idea she could create such a facade.

'I love Prosecco,' Trent said and undid his seatbelt. 'Sure. Lead the way.' He got out of the car and looked up at the house. 'This is a nice house.' He glanced back at them. 'Is it just the two of you that live here?'

'Yeah. Ella makes loads of money as a pharmaceutical sales rep,' Ajola said.

Ella had to chew her gum extra attentively to stop from laughing. What a strange detail to embellish.

'Yeah,' she said, nodding, 'it's true. Coupled with Ajola's work on OnlyFans and we paid for it outright.'

Trent's eyebrows floated up his forehead.

'Wow,' he said, nodding. 'OK, yes, give me that glass of Prosecco.'

Safa

'COULD BE ANY minute now,' Safa said, glancing out of the farmhouse window. Caoimhe had the roll of duct tape and Sophia was scrunching up the carrier bag. She looked gaunt. 'You sure you're OK to do it?' Safa asked.

Sophia nodded stiffly. She had gone a pale greenish colour and the corners of her mouth were quivering.

'Don't freak her out,' Caoimhe said.

'I'm not trying to freak her out,' Safa replied. 'I'm grateful she's doing it. We need her to do it. *I* need her—'

With a crash, the heavy antique bronze spotlight bar fell from the ceiling. It landed between the three of them, half balanced on the edge of one rustic oak chair and half resting on the flagstone floor. Motes of dust swirled in the trajectory of its fall. Safa took a step back.

'That nearly hit me!' She gasped.

'Quickly, let's move it,' Caoimhe said. She put the duct tape down and hoisted the end off the tiles. 'Christ, it's heavy.'

Sophia took the other end and they shuffled into the TV room. Safa glanced up at the ceiling where two more spotlight bars were fixed.

'That nearly hit me,' she said again. She couldn't work out whether it was a good or a bad omen.

Sophia and Caoimhe laid the fallen bar on the carpet and came back into the kitchen.

'There's a whole lot of dust,' Sophia said. She picked up the carrier bag.

'No, I mean,' Safa said, as Caoimhe used her foot to disperse the sprinkles of glass and masonry which now littered the floor, 'that really nearly hit me.' She looked between the two of them. They were looking earnestly back at her. 'This,' she said, pointing to the faded paint on the ceiling where the spotlight had been fitted, 'is the evil eye. Al-ayn.'

'From the Pan?' Sophia asked.

'From whoever,' said Safa. A car crunched on the gravel outside. The engine cut out. The three of them looked at one another.

Sophia held up the carrier bag.

'This is for them, I guess,' she said.

They heard the baritone hum of Trent's deep voice, followed by Ajola's and Ella's tinkling laughs. Safa turned away. Her hands were shaking.

'Hi!' she said, overly loud, as the three of them came into the kitchen. 'Hi!'

'Friends?' Trent said, glancing at Ajola.

'Kind of,' Ajola said. 'Let me get my phone.'

'Have a seat,' Safa said and dragged a heavy chair away from the table towards Trent. Not a passenger any more.

'Prosecco, was it?' Ella asked, going to the fridge.

'This service is incredible,' Trent said and sat on the chair. 'I could get used to this.'

He stretched out his legs in front of him. Safa sat opposite Trent and smiled. This was it. She was making a choice. She was reclaiming her life. She was in control now. Caoimhe moved behind him and pulled out a length of duct tape. Trent glanced at her and then Safa clapped her hands to regain his attention.

'Sorry, what's your name?' she said, quickly. 'Ajola is terrible at introducing people.'

'I'm Trent,' he said, looking back at her. 'And you?'

'Safa.' The tips of her fingers were incredibly moist. Contribute. Control. Reclaim. She swallowed. 'What do you do, Trent?'

'I'm a manager at Morrisons.'

'I love Morrisons,' Safa gushed. She glanced at Caoimhe, who had crouched down. What else could she say about Morrisons? 'So much more variety than Tesco or Sainsbury's.'

Caoimhe

FROM HER CROUCHED position on the floor, Caoimhe knew she wouldn't be able to do it. Even if she could get one leg done, she would never be quick enough to do the other. And one leg taped to a chair wouldn't be a hindrance at all. She had seen forty-five-year-old, unfit Aidan squat with 120kg just for fun. Trent was ten years younger and the adrenaline the panic set off would be more than enough for him to run with one leg taped to a chair. She exhaled slowly. She needed to improvise. She searched through the seams of the moment, trying to sink beyond her normal consciousness. Stride. Stride. Breath. Breath.

'Can we make this interesting?' she said, standing up. Beat. Beat. Everyone looked at her. Ajola in the pretence of searching for her phone, Ella pouring the Prosecco, Safa at the table and Sophia wringing the carrier bag by the door. 'It's a game the girls always did to the boys at school.' Caoimhe showed Trent the duct tape. 'Sort of like blind taste testing.'

Trent laughed and shook his head.

'You never know where your day is going to lead you,' he said. 'I thought I had nothing to do this evening except defrost a pizza.'

'You want to give it a go?' Caoimhe said. She was there. Each second complete and eternal. 'It involves duct tape.'

'They're all sort of drunk,' Ajola explained, apologetically. 'You don't have to listen to them.'

'Nah, I want to give it a go.' Trent nodded. 'Sounds exciting. Duct-tape me up.'

'OK.' As easy as that. Probably Mateus would be the same. 'Ankles against the leg of the chair, wrists on the arm rest.'

Trent complied. Caoimhe strapped his wrists and then crouched down to wrap the roll of tape a few times around each ankle.

'You shouldn't be able to move very much,' Caoimhe said, standing up. 'Just wriggle for me.'

Trent tried to move his wrists and ankles.

'Pretty good,' he said. 'What comes next? Are you going to blindfold me?'

Ajola rolled her eyes. 'This guy is pornsick,' she whispered.

'Sure.' Caoimhe stepped back. Sophia stepped forward. 'Brace yourself.'

Sophia

SOPHIA HELD THE carrier bag up and brought it down smoothly and sweetly over Trent's head. She pulled it tight at his neck and then wrapped the handles around her fingers, trapping the air inside.

'What?' Trent said from inside the bag. Sophia saw the plastic rush inwards as he inhaled, then billow out as he exhaled. 'How am I supposed to taste-test if this is covering my mouth?'

They all looked at each other.

'It's part of the excitement,' Ajola replied loudly. 'Just wait for it.'

Trent laughed from inside the bag. The plastic rustled inwards, then outwards, inwards and then outwards. At the table, Safa put her face in her hands. Ella poured the glass of Prosecco down the sink.

'How long will this take?' Safa said, her voice muffled behind her fingers.

Inwards. Outwards.

'I think I'm going to faint,' Ella said. 'I really do. I'm going to faint.'

Sophia looked across the kitchen at her. The handles of the carrier bag were biting into her knuckles, turning her fingertips white.

'Are we really doing it?' Caoimhe said. She looked at Ella. 'I didn't think we'd really do it.'

'What?' Trent asked from inside the bag.

Inwards. Outwards.

'Yeah, I thought, I don't know, we'd have been arrested by now.'

Safa took her face out of her hands.

'We're doing it,' she said. 'We're doing this. We can't do this. I can't watch a man die.'

Inwards. Outwards.

'What was that?' Trent's voice was muffled. Through the plastic of the carrier bag, Sophia could feel the muscles in his neck, the nerves and tendons, the cartilage of his larynx. It was so dense, so strong. She tightened her grip.

'Why are we having doubts?' Ajola asked. 'I thought we decided to do it to protect ourselves? Like Thomas Cromwell would.'

'Can we stop basing our decisions on what Thomas Cromwell would do!' Caoimhe exclaimed. She held out her arms. 'He got his head cut off. He's a terrible example.'

Sophia blinked rapidly, staring down at the carrier bag. She just had to remain firm. Just remain firm.

'I can't do *this* to protect myself,' Safa murmured wearily. 'It's wrong. I'm worse than Haaris if I do this. I don't deserve my girls if I do this.'

Inwards. Outwards.

'I don't think I have it in me.' Ella pressed her fingertips to her forehead. 'It's too sublunar.'

'Do you?' Caoimhe said to Ajola.

'Do *I* have this in me?' Ajola pointed to herself. Sophia looked over her shoulder at her, the carrier bag slipping beneath her sweaty fingers. '*Me*? Of course not. This is against everything I stand for. Look at that pathetic sack of shit.' She pointed at Trent. 'We're going to ruin our souls for him?'

Inwards. Outwards.

'Can't be a murderer.' Ella shook her head, fingertips now in her hair. 'Can't do it.'

'This is exciting.' The bag rustled around Trent's mouth. The plastic vibrated with his voice. 'I don't really understand what you mean, though? Is it like Cluedo?'

'The reality of this is so much worse than the fantasy,' Caoimhe said and put a hand over her eyes.

Inwards. Outwards.

Sophia felt as if red hot fire was surging through Trent, up his neck, along the plastic and into her fingers, burning her skin. She sucked in a lungful of air through her clenched teeth, then yanked the bag off Trent's head.

He smiled around at them all, his face only slightly flushed.

'Is that designed to heighten the taste buds or something?' he asked.

'Yes, Trent,' Sophia said. She had failed. Jill would win. She put the bag on the table. 'It's designed to heighten the taste buds.'

'What now?' Ajola looked at her. 'Call the Pan up?'

'Tell her to go fuck herself,' Caoimhe said.

'Maybe we can outmanoeuvre Jill without killing this guy,' Sophia suggested.

Trent frowned at her.

'Me?'

'And without going to prison?' Ella asked.

'I mean, this is all super weird,' Trent said. He laughed. 'Fun, though.'

The rear leg of his chair gave way with a crack like a gun going off. The chair pitched backwards and Trent's head caught the edge of the oak table with a bang that resonated down the length of it. He hit the floor, still tied to the chair, with a finite motionlessness, no bounce, no skid, as if he was magnetized. As they stared, a pool of thick, black blood began to seep from around his head, a dark lake, impenetrable and abject.

Wordlessly, Caoimhe pulled on her latex gloves. She bent down and pressed her fingers to his neck.

'I think he's dead,' she said, looking around at them.

Ajola

'LET'S NOT LOSE focus,' Ajola said. 'We have this all planned out. Sophia, call the Pan. Get her here.'

'We probably shouldn't mention it was an accident,' Safa said. 'Right?'

'Right.' Ajola nodded.

'Although, it sort of makes me feel better.' Safa looked down at Trent's dead body. 'In a weird way.'

'Ella, Safa, Caoimhe' – Ajola pointed at them – 'begin the clean-up. I'll get the stuff ready for the spell.'

'Not the spell.' Caoimhe rolled her eyes. 'I thought we all just came to a collective decision to leave the fantasy behind.'

Ajola put her hands on her hips. They had to do the spell.

'Was Chris ever found?'

'No, but that—'

'Ah, ah.' Ajola held up a finger. 'Was he ever found?'

'No, but it—'

'Was he ever found?' Ajola said in a sing-song voice.

Caoimhe rolled her eyes.

'No. He wasn't.'

'I'm doing the spell then.'

Ajola put on her pair of latex gloves and picked up her ruck-sack. Behind her, Safa and Ella were already wearing their gloves, Ella unravelling bin bags from the roll, Safa on her hands and knees beginning to clean the puddle of blood.

'Did you know,' Ajola said, pulling out a sheaf of herbs from the bag, 'globally, women perform on average three times as much unpaid domestic labour as men.' She looked across at Safa scrubbing the blood and Ella opening the bin bags. 'From emptying dishwashers to collecting firewood.'

'Women are just naturally suited to being able to multi-task or whatever' – Caoimhe picked up the car keys – 'so it's easier for them.'

'That's bullshit.' Ajola splashed a bit of water from the tap on some of the herbs. It was soothing, watching them unfurl and float. 'You're telling me men can build a rocket to Mars and construct a circuit board for a super-computer, but they don't realize when the carpet needs hoovering?'

'Why are you bringing this up now?' Caoimhe said.

'We've had all that time in unpaid internships to practise for this moment,' Ajola said. 'No wonder all the male serial killers get caught.'

Ella laughed from the floor.

'Men can definitely do the housework.' Safa dropped a bundle of bloody rags into Ella's bin bag. 'I think they've just been told that in relationships, women will do it for them.'

'That's unfair,' Caoimhe said. 'Some men do loads around the house.'

'Some men ejaculate when they strangle women,' Ajola said. 'You can't trust some men.'

'I'm moving the car,' Caoimhe replied. 'You water your potions.'

Ella

ELLA WRAPPED A bin bag around Trent's head and tied it at his neck. She used the duct tape to partially mummify him, strapping his arms to his side and his ankles together. It was a very neat job. Efficient, even.

'For ease of transport,' she explained to Safa.

'We never did that seven years ago.'

'We didn't have this much duct tape seven years ago.'

Caoimhe came back inside and she, Ella and Ajola hoisted the dead body between them and moved it to the car. It was parked right by the back door, boot open, a plastic covering taped inside.

'Have we got his phone?' Ella asked. The end was very nearly in sight now. Just one or two last details, and then they would all be free.

'It's in his pocket,' Ajola said. 'I turned it off as soon as we got in the car so it won't ping or Find My iPhone or whatever.'

'Let's take out the sim card just in case,' Ella said. 'Shouldn't make a difference, but just to be sure.'

'Maybe burn it a bit,' Caoimhe suggested.

'Fire is the tool of man and the enemy of innate witchcraft,' Ajola said. 'Let's just soak it in water.'

Ella used the pin from her earring to pop the sim card out and then filled up a small pot of water from the butt at the side of the house. She dropped the sim card inside and the three of them watched as it floated around on the surface. Caoimhe scratched her nose.

'This is weird, isn't it?'

'A little water clears us of this deed,' Ella said. She looked at Ajola. 'Would Thomas Cromwell have done this?'

'Maybe.'

'Stop giving a dead man credit for your ideas,' Caoimhe said. Ajola laughed. 'I'm serious.' Caoimhe looked over the pot at her. 'You're better than Thomas Cromwell.'

'I wish I had a Thomas Cromwell in my life,' Ajola said.

'You're never going to have a Thomas Cromwell in your life.' Ella poked the sim card. 'Never, ever.' She looked at Ajola. 'But that's OK. Look at what you do every day. You're probably already someone else's Thomas Cromwell.'

'How do we know when it's done?' Caoimhe asked, nodding at the pot.

'We don't,' Ella said. She fished the sim card out and stuck it inside some of the tape on Trent's shirt. 'Make sure the phone is taped to him as well. We don't want it sliding out somewhere.'

'Did he have anything else on him?' Caoimhe asked Ajola.

She had turned away and was looking intently at the side of the house.

'Nothing.' She cleared her throat. 'Not even a jacket.'

'Let's start cleaning down the inside of the car,' Ella said.

'Hoover first, then I'll get the Oxi Action and do the front; Caoimhe, you do the back.'

'He didn't sit in the back.'

'Hairs can get everywhere. Ajola, get the UV light and go over the kitchen to see if Safa missed anything.'

Safa

AS SAFA WAS scrubbing the floor for the third time with the Vanish mix, Sophia came out of the TV room.

'She's parked just up the road,' she said. 'I'll walk down and bring her back here. Should be about five minutes.'

Safa nodded. She stood up and dusted off her hands and knees.

'Anything?' she asked Ajola.

Ajola switched the UV light on and swept the floor, the table, the walls, the chairs.

'Looks good,' she said and switched it off. 'What objects can we get her to handle?'

Safa looked around. 'There's not really a hammer, is there?'

'No, though that would be ideal. A big hammer.'

'A club would be just perfect.'

'Dear SunnySurrey23, does your Airbnb have a mace and chain?'

'Personal requirements for our stay: medieval flail.'

Ajola laughed at this.

Safa pointed to the mark on the ceiling. 'In all seriousness, what are we going to do about that spotlight bar and the broken chair?'

Ajola shrugged.

'I'll message the owners later and say, whoops, that happened whilst we were staying there. Not our fault, though.'

'Yeah, in fact we should take them to small claims court. Someone could have died.'

'Could have been tragic.'

They heard footsteps on the gravel drive.

'Is that them?' Safa asked. Her nerves were quivering inside her skin, from fear, from excitement, from pure adrenaline. 'I'm putting another pair of gloves on.'

Caoimhe

SOPHIA LED THE Pan up the drive. Her face was masked as it had been in the Zoom meeting.

'Should we take that mask off her?' Caoimhe whispered to Ella. 'Just rip it right off her face.'

'No.' Ella shook her head. 'Just stick to the plan, then we'll be free of this.'

Silently, Sophia led the Pan to the open boot. Caoimhe ripped a hole in the bin bag and exposed Trent's bloodied face. The Pan looked down at it. She was very still.

'You did it,' she whispered.

'Of course,' Sophia replied.

Ella duct-taped the hole shut and Caoimhe shut the boot.

'Come inside,' Ella said and nodded towards the house.

'I told people that if I didn't come home tonight, they were to go to the police with what I know.' The Pan turned to look at Ella. 'So don't think about doing anything to me.'

Caoimhe rolled her eyes.

'Why would we go to the effort of killing this guy if we were just going to kill you? That doesn't make any sense. Get inside the house. We want to talk and we don't want anyone to hear us.'

The Pan turned her masked face to look at Caoimhe, who stuck her tongue against her bottom lip. There was nothing inconsequential about her.

'Come.' Ella moved up the back step.

They all followed. She moved down the hallway into the kitchen, where Ajola and Safa were waiting. Safa pushed the broken chair towards her.

'Sit down.'

'On a broken chair?'

'We just killed a guy for you,' Caoimhe said. 'Sit on the chair.'

The Pan sat, holding on to the edge of the chair for balance. The five of them moved to form a circle around her.

'You can't threaten me,' the Pan said.

'We're not going to threaten you,' Caoimhe replied. 'We're just giving you a debrief. You have lots of information on us and could, potentially, hold it over our heads for the rest of our lives.'

'I'm a woman of my word.'

'We're just letting you know,' Caoimhe said, 'we have stuff on you as well.'

A laugh erupted from behind the mask.

'What? There's nothing,' she said. 'Absolutely nothing. I'm completely, totally un-blackmailable.'

'That's weird.' Caoimhe put a finger on her chin. 'Because Sophia has all this evidence that you killed two guys.'

There was nothing the mask could give away, but Caoimhe heard a sharp exhale from behind the wooden visage. The Pan adjusted her position on the fallen chair.

'What?'

'Yup.' Caoimhe nodded. 'Christopher Johnson, seven years ago, and Trent Davies, about . . .' Caoimhe looked at Ella who looked at her watch.

'Twenty-seven minutes ago.'

'Twenty-seven minutes ago,' Caoimhe confirmed.

The Pan shook her head, fingers still clasped to the edge of the upturned chair for balance.

'No. There's no evidence to say I did either.'

'There's tons. First of all' – Caoimhe held up a finger – 'you dropped your watch on one of your regular visits back to Chris's grave.'

'No.' The Pan's voice was defiant. 'I didn't.'

Caoimhe stepped forward and slipped the watch from the woman's skinny wrist.

'Now you did,' she said, putting it into her pocket.

'Isn't that something serial killers love to do?' Ella nodded. 'Revisit the burial sites of their victims? Doesn't look good for you.'

'Second,' Caoimhe continued, 'your fingerprints are all over this crime scene.' She pointed. 'That chair, the door handles. Ours aren't. In fact, there's nothing in the entire world that could connect we five with Trent Davies. Only you.'

'And third' – Sophia held up her phone – 'we have a recording saying you were there the night Chris died and you would also kill Trent Davies.'

'What recording?'

Caoimhe enjoyed the tremor of uncertainty in the Pan's voice.

'From Zoom,' Sophia explained.

'That meeting wasn't recorded.'

'I recorded the screen on my phone.' Sophia pointed at her. 'You told us at the start of this that you could make Chris's death hang over all of us, indefinitely. 'Well.' She shrugged. 'Now we can hold it over you.'

'Basically' – Caoimhe put a foot on the leg of the chair and crouched down – 'you go to the police about Sophia and you go down for two murders. It's all of us versus you, Pan, and you lose.'

The mask stared up at them. Blank. Then it leapt to its feet and darted between them, heading for the kitchen door. Caoimhe snatched out an arm, low-flying, one-handed, like the peregrine falcon from the rounders' team, and caught her shin. The Pan crashed into the floor, chin first. She cried out and rolled over. Sophia bent over her and yanked the mask off her head. The Pan's hands flew up to cover her face, and she shrieked into her palms.

'I always fucking hated you, Sophia!' she screamed as Sophia tore her fingers away from her face. Not Jill.

Her skin had strange red blotches blooming all over it.

She looked just like she did in 1998 when she cried at the end of *Titanic*.

Bethany

IN JUST ONE day in 2023, Bethany made £1,500 on Anything Worn. She had started off just selling used socks, old trainers and gym gear that she purposely bought to wear once and then sell when it was sweaty. Her rule was to never do anything sexual and it turned out there was easy money to be made on the site in the most innocuous of used clothing. She cultivated a little batch of loyal followers who regularly paid for her worn clothes, and the money she made selling to these was enough to pay her rent. Bethany had never been popular. She had always been the odd one out, never quite fitting in with any social group. She was always just there: the one member of the group who didn't share stories, or who sat on the single seat, or who walked a few steps behind on the pavement. Anything Worn gave her her first taste of admiration, of not just inclusion, but favouritism.

As time went on, her followers grew confident enough to send her direct messages with specific requests. Again, nothing sexual. She made a few hundred pounds filming herself jumping in a muddy puddle like Peppa Pig in a pair of Hunter wellies, and then got a bit extra as a tip when she sent the same Hunter wellies to the client. Another follower, an oenologist, asked her to send him a box of her poo. Specifically, he wanted to gift her a bottle of Châteauneuf-du-Pape and then have her send her very next bowel movement once she had finished the bottle. She made some polite enquiries about this request (other dietary requirements, weight in grams, delivery instructions) but ultimately declined. The £1,500 day came when she filmed a video of herself berating a man for having a face like Mr Bean. That was a fun video and she really felt herself come alive as she recorded it. The man had initially said £500 but then sent her £1,000 when he received the video, and finally offered another £500 if she sent him the shoes she had been wearing: a pair of black lace-up brogues.

All told, her online life gave her a greater sense of belonging and purpose, and this bled through into the real world. Her being carried a greater weight. Bethany had never intended to start going out with anybody because it was a real distraction from all her online activities. As well as her social life on Anything Worn, she had been stalking Sophia constantly since 2010, when she posted her graduation photos on Facebook, and the other four since 2016 when Bethany witnessed them all bury a dead body together. Following all their social media accounts, googling them, cyberstalking their employment websites and turning up to places they said they would be to watch them from afar was almost a full-time job, so relationships had never been a priority for Bethany. Still, there was something wonderful about Trent. He was funny and creative. He noticed her. And he was interested.

She told him all about her popularity and success on Anything Worn, but nothing about her obsession with Sophia. Trent was a postman and often complained about this career, especially when she was able to quit her employment as a lab technician because the money from Anything Worn was so good. He had his own YouTube channel, Instagram and TikTok, where he posted lifestyle videos that involved him wearing basketball shorts and backwards baseball hats pranking Bethany. Her favourite pranks to be involved with were the small ones where he pushed her face into cake or served her heavily spiced food or pulled the car away before she could get in. She didn't mind. She enjoyed being his plaything, was honoured that he took such an interest in her and involved her in his own hobbies.

As their relationship progressed, he became quite bitter about her making more money online than him. He wouldn't let her pay for trips away or for dinner out, or for the cinema, but refused to pay himself, so they never went anywhere. When she bought him an old car for his birthday, he said she was trying to emasculate him and refused to drive it. In the end, Bethany persuaded him to let her apply for him on the Morrisons Management Training Scheme. It paid a lot more money than being a postie and had potential for future opportunities. It also meant he could mix and interact with more people, something he was very good at. He was accepted on to the scheme and she felt it was good for him to be out of the house, away from his phone. The pranks became less frequent and he had more money, so he moved in with her and let her put his name on her car.

After the £1,500 day in 2023, Bethany used the money to go and visit her grandparents in Wales. She invited Trent but his work schedule changed at the last minute so he couldn't go. She bought a special jumper to wear during the train journey, a smart cashmere one that she intended to sell to one of her clients when she got back. At the time, she genuinely didn't realize anything was amiss, even when she FaceTimed him on the second night.

'Can you put the flea treatment on Watson? I meant to do it before I went but I totally forgot.'

'No worries, babe,' he replied. 'I'll do it right now.'

She couldn't work out where in the house he was: somewhere in front of a completely blank, blue wall.

'I'll stay on the call for moral support.'

'I didn't mean right now right now.' Trent laughed. 'I'll probably do it before bed.'

'That's cool. Show me Watson's face so I can talk to him and see if he misses me.'

'Yeah, sure. Watson!' Trent whistled. 'Watson! Ah, he's out in the garden, babe.'

'Just like him. Hold the phone up at the window so I can see him.'

The phone moved around and then settled back on Trent's face.

'He's out of sight. Sorry, babe.'

Bethany laughed.

'What? The garden's tiny. It's one square. There's nowhere for him to be out of sight.'

Trent sighed and ran a hand through his hair.

'OK, babe, promise you won't be mad.'

'When am I ever mad?'

'You are, sometimes.'

'Well, I'm not. Tell me. I promise I won't be mad.'

'I asked my sister to look after him tonight. I've been slammed at work recently, late shift, early shift, I just needed a night off, to myself.'

'I totally understand,' Bethany said. 'I can't believe you didn't just say.'

'You said you wouldn't be mad.'

'I'm not mad.' Bethany laughed to prove this point. 'See. Not mad. I get it. I'm just saying, anytime you need a night off, just say.'

'I worry you'll get mad.'

'I never get mad!' She laughed again. 'Name one time I got mad.'

Trent pursed his lips and raised his eyebrows and she made herself laugh harder.

'My train gets in tomorrow around eleven,' she told him. 'I'll text you a more definitive time closer to arrival.'

'Sure thing, babe. Can't wait to see you.'

She texted him early the next morning. Train due at 10:13, is that OK?

He never texted back. She got on the train and called him an hour before getting into the station. He didn't answer the phone. She texted him: Everything OK? Again, no response. When she got off at the station, she expected to see her car waiting there, him sitting behind the wheel and smiling at her. But there was no one. She tried ringing him again and then again, and then texted him. She genuinely thought he'd died. She called his sister.

'Do you know where Trent is?' she asked before she had even said anything.

'I thought he was with you. I thought you were having a romantic weekend away. He told me to look after Watson!'

'Oh yes, weekend away,' Bethany said quickly. 'We did. I mean now, has he come over to get Watson yet?'

'No, not yet. He said three o'clock this afternoon.'

'OK, cool, I thought he was going over there now. No problem.'

She hung up. It was eleven o'clock. She would have to walk home and see if he was dead or paralysed at the bottom of the stairs. She could feel her sweat bleeding through the cashmere, increasing its sale value.

As she reached the end of the station road, she saw her car swing around the bend. It skidded to a stop beside her and Trent dashed out.

'I'm so sorry, sorry, sorry, babe,' he said and enveloped her in a big hug. He kissed the top of her forehead. 'I missed you so much. I'm so glad you're back.'

'Is everything all right?' she asked as he took her bag and put it in the boot.

'Yes, everything is fine. I'm so sorry I missed your texts. I overslept. I said I was tired. I woke up and saw them and drove straight here.'

He held the passenger door open for her and she got in.

'Overslept?' she said. 'Did you not hear your phone ringing?'

'It was on silent,' he said and climbed into the driver's seat.

'Since when is your phone on silent?'

'I told you I was tired – I was knocked out.' He pulled away from the kerb. 'You should have seen how fast I drove to get here. I'm so sorry.' He glanced at her. 'You look amazing by the way. I bet you had a great weekend, right?'

On the dashboard, his phone *pinged* as a notification came up.

'I put it back on loud,' he quickly said as she glanced at the screen.

'It's from RingGo,' she said, taking it from its mount. 'It says your parking is due to expire in ten minutes.'

'That's station parking, I paid for it as I was driving down because I didn't want to waste time when I got there.'

'It's not for station parking,' she said, swiping the app open. 'It's for the high street.'

'OK, babe, I'll be honest. My phone was on silent but I got up and drove into town for breakfast. I wanted to go to Bill's to treat myself because of how tired I've been, working and everything. I paid for parking on RingGo and then I saw all your messages and just drove straight here instead. I didn't even park. I didn't even get to Bill's. Don't be mad.'

'Oh, that's a shame. I'm not mad,' Bethany said. She put the phone back on the mount. 'Do you want to go to Bill's now?'

'Ah, now, babe? I'm all right now, to be honest. Now I've seen you.' He smiled at her. 'Let's just get home and spend some time together. I told my sister we'd pick up Watson at three so we have a few hours just for us.' He squeezed her leg.

'You told your sister it was a romantic getaway.'

'Yeah.' He laughed. 'I couldn't very well have said I just wanted a night off. You know her. She never would have done it if I'd said that.'·

Bethany laughed.

'Yeah,' she said.

'I love you, babe,' Trent replied. 'I'm so glad you're back.'

Bethany sent the sweat-laced cashmere sweater off and made £450. The next month, she missed her period. She sold the pregnancy test to someone on Anything Worn because she didn't think urine was sexual. When she told Trent, he hugged her and kissed the top of her head.

'I'm so happy, babe,' he said. 'I'm doing well at work. You're thriving. This is going to be the most loved kid on the planet.'

'We should move out of the flat, get a bigger place,' Bethany said. 'I don't think we'd be able to get a mortgage because I can't prove a stable income, but we can rent a nice house. How about that? Nice big three-bedroomed house? Big garden? Somewhere near good schools?'

'You look into it, babe,' Trent said. 'I'll move anywhere with you.'

Bethany was so excited about becoming a mum, her stalking activities went completely away. She didn't follow Sophia to the doctor's surgery, she missed a couple of Caoimhe's races, and she didn't even go to the open day at Ajola's school, which she had been looking forward to so she could drop off another wicker man. She didn't need to any more. She didn't need to gather personal information about Sophia. She didn't need to be jealous of her. She didn't need to miss her. She had successfully assimilated into society.

Bethany wanted to announce the pregnancy to both her and Trent's families at twelve weeks, so at eight weeks, Trent booked a dinner at a smart London restaurant, one of *Time Out*'s best restaurants, for them to plan the most lavish way to do it.

'I was thinking a big party,' Bethany said as they ate. The restaurant was low-lit and the servers slid past them dressed all in black. 'Obviously invite everyone, your sister, my parents, grandparents, but kind of have a small party vibe, like back garden barbecue or something.'

'You don't want to tell your mum beforehand?' Trent asked, wiping his mouth with a napkin. He was dressed in a sports jacket with beige chinos and a blue shirt with a granddad collar. He was wearing the Rolex she'd bought him for Christmas. She didn't think she had ever seen him looking so handsome.

'Hmm, maybe. That might be nice. A bonding moment.'

The waitress came and started taking their plates away. Trent cleared his throat and leant forward. He wiped his palms on the front of his jacket. Bethany took a deep breath and smiled to herself. She leant back. She leant forward. She checked her ring finger was clean.

'Bethany,' Trent said. He cleared his throat again and put his left hand on the table. The other hand went into his inner pocket. 'I actually wanted to say something tonight.' He drew out an envelope and put it on the table between them. He took a deep breath. 'I want to break up. I don't love you. I've actually found someone else. Someone from work. She's just graduated uni, got a lot of ambition and we generally get on better. My flat keys are in there.' He tapped the envelope. 'Car keys, the front door fob.' He waved his hand. 'I'm excited about moving in with her and starting a family. I've been meaning to break up with you for some time. Now, obviously, you being pregnant sort of complicates that for me. I don't mean to make any decisions for you, but I'm having nothing to do with that baby if you choose to have it. It's going to seriously mess up the life I'm planning with this girl. She doesn't want to be a step-mum, I don't want to be dropping some kid off here, there and everywhere when we're trying to raise a family. So, if you have the baby, don't expect me to be involved or pay child support or anything like that.'

From across the restaurant, a knife slid from a plate and clattered on to the floor. A waiter darted forward from the galley, reaching down towards it.

'Is this a prank?' Bethany said, looking around. 'Is someone filming us?'

'No. I'm serious, Bethany. The fact that you would even think that shows how different we are. I mean, you make your living filming videos pretending to be Mr Bean.'

'No,' Bethany corrected him, fiercely. She felt the first stirring of anger. 'I make videos where I berate men for looking like Mr Bean.'

'Exactly.' He laughed.

Bethany inhaled slowly through her nostrils, filling her lungs as if she was about to scream.

'This girl is on the management track team at just twenty-two,' Trent said, 'and they're moving me to deli.'

Bethany blinked. She couldn't believe he had been planning all this, thinking all this, whilst they celebrated the baby.

'Delhi, India?'

'No, the delicatessen counter.' Trent drummed his fingers on the edge of the table, not looking at Bethany, glancing around for the waitress. 'It's a huge deal and I want to have someone that complements the expectations I have of myself.' Trent raised his hand in the air. The waitress, who hadn't moved very far away, came back. 'Can we have separate bills, please,' he said. 'I had the pizza and the beer. She had' – he gestured at Bethany – 'whatever else was ordered.'

He paid his share and walked out, leaving Bethany sitting there, silently staring into the low-level, ambient lighting. The hatred in her was so raw. She wiped her chin.

'I'd like to pay whatever is left,' she said to the waitress.

The waitress touched her shoulder. The contact galvanized Bethany. It had always been like this. She thought about Sophia's face. Her house, her life. Not any more.

'It's on the house,' the waitress said. 'No charge.'

Sophia

THEY ALL LOOKED at Sophia. Sophia stepped forward, eyes searching the bare face in front of her.

'Bethany?' she said. She didn't look that different to how she had looked twenty-three years ago. Maybe thinner. Maybe paler. 'What the hell?'

Bethany glared up at her.

'You're so manipulative,' she said. 'You're *always* doing this sort of stuff to me.'

Sophia frowned. She couldn't comprehend this. How had Jill got Bethany, of all people, here?

'When have I ever done anything like this before?' Sophia asked.

'All. The. Time. Ever since you joined my school!'

Now, Caoimhe frowned.

'So, it *is* someone from your school.' She looked between Bethany and Sophia. 'But not Jill?'

Safa let out a nervous laugh and clasped her chin in one hand.

'Did Jill put you up to this?' Sophia asked, leaning down so she and Bethany were at the same level.

'Jill?' Bethany looked up, sharply, scowling. 'Jill? I haven't spoken to Jill in ten years. I did this because *I* hate you.'

'What?' Sophia straightened up. She glanced around at the perplexed faces of the others and then back to Bethany. 'Why do you hate me? We haven't spoken since primary school.'

Caoimhe tutted and tilted her head back.

'I can't believe we just killed a guy over who was friends with who when they were eight.' She groaned.

Sophia held up her hands.

'I have two insane people from my childhood following me around. How is any of this my fault?'

'You know what they say,' Ajola replied. 'You meet one insane person, it's probably them. You meet two, it's probably you.'

Safa let out another laugh. Sophia didn't move. She couldn't understand. What had she ever done to Bethany?

'You always thought you were better than me.' The angry red blotches were stark on Bethany's face. 'So superior. Such a special flower. And I was nothing.' The derision and contempt in her voice, the accusation, shocked Sophia. She took a step back, feeling her breath catch in her throat. 'In maths, at gymnastics, with the boys, you never thought I was worth your time. In DT, I didn't even have a partner. I had to work on my own for that whole project.'

'I never thought that,' Sophia lied. She glared at Bethany. How was any of this her problem; how could any of this invite such violence? 'I can't remember you saying much, to be honest. You were like a background character painted on to a theatre set.'

'Ooh!' Caoimhe exclaimed and Safa held out her hand.

'That is harsh, Sophia,' she said.

'She just made us kill a guy!'

'You couldn't possibly conceive of a world where I had my own thoughts and opinions?' Bethany shook her head. Her fingers picked at the Pan mask. 'Women are so bitchy. So untrustworthy.'

No one responded. Sophia looked down at the top of Bethany's head. Her hair was parted just as it had been when they were nine. Bethany. Sophia could remember her so vividly. She had been so quiet, so unassuming, the direct antithesis to this figure before her. Had she really been that dismissive of her? The sound of Bethany's fingernails scratching across the wooden mask seemed very loud in the kitchen.

'Well, OK, to be fair,' Sophia conceded, 'you proved me wrong.' Bethany pressed her lips together as Sophia explained, 'You clearly do have thoughts and feelings and . . .' – what was a nice way to put it? – 'ambition. But, Bethany,' she said, refusing to accept that she was the real villain here, 'we hung around with each other. We watched *Titanic* together. We did the presentation. We read from the same copy of *The Prisoner of Azkaban*. We were friends!'

'We only became friends' – Bethany jerked her head up and jabbed at Sophia with an incandescent finger – '. . . you only did all that with me because Jill cut you out for being so spiteful. You ignored me until it was convenient for you. Jill told me everything at the end of Year Six. Everything you said about me. That I was a loser. That I could recreate the sinking of the *Titanic* in our presentation because I was so fat.'

Sophia recoiled in utter shock.

'I never said that!' she cried. 'That's a lie!'

Bethany shook her head, the blotches spreading down her neck now.

'Jill said you changed secondary schools because you didn't want to look at my ugly face any more.' Her voice was laced with anguish. 'I was *so* insecure after that.' She raised the mask and thrust it towards Sophia like a lance. 'You know how many proper friends I made as a teenager? Zero, Sophia. Zero! I was terrified they were all laughing at me.' She lowered her voice and looked down. 'I only had Jill. And she kept me updated on everything you were doing.' She put the Pan mask on her knee and began picking at the wood again. 'That you made a burn book like *Mean Girls* but just with pictures of my face. That you were the one texting me when I was sixteen saying I should kill myself. I was too embarrassed to leave my house for prom. You're conniving, Sophia, and you always have been.'

'I never did those things!' Sophia exploded. She grabbed her own head. 'That sounds like things Jill would do! Bethany! I went to a different secondary school to escape *Jill*. She. Is. Insane!' Sophia cried, pinching her thumb and forefinger together as if she was trying to catch a mote of dust.

'This is *insane*.' Caoimhe groaned and put her head in her hands. 'All of this for a bitchy cat-fight from the playground?'

'I'm not the bitch!' Sophia exclaimed.

'Cat-fight?' Bethany glared up at Caoimhe. 'This is my *life*, Caoimhe.' It sent a chill through Sophia to hear Bethany use her friend's name as though she knew her. 'This is my *identity*. This is who I *am*. Don't make light of me by calling it a cat-fight! By reducing all this to trivial bitchiness.'

'This all sounds awful,' Ella said, stepping forward. 'I sympathize. I do. We've all internalized negative attitudes about ourselves and others. But' – she looked down at Bethany, trying to make eye contact – 'getting back to our situation, how do you know what we did seven years ago?'

'I told you,' Bethany snapped, looking up at Ella. 'I saw. I stalked Sophia.' She glared back at Sophia. 'At first, it was just sporadic, online, as a teenager. I wanted to see you fail and be miserable and alone. But instead, I saw you at university with Jill! Laughing and having fun together. I was so fucking angry! It's so belittling to be excluded like that.'

'We never went together!' Sophia couldn't believe this. 'Jill followed me there. She's followed me to my home now. She copies everything I do. She's a parasite and she's done all this!'

She opened her arms as wide as they would go, appealing to the kitchen at large. Bethany took a shuddering breath, glowering at her from under her eyebrows.

'So belittling,' she repeated. 'Especially by someone who you once thought liked you. Who you once admired. After I saw those photos, I proper stalked you. In real life, I mean. Found out where you lived, where you worked, who your friends were.' She gestured around the circle. 'Saw you get married, get pregnant, have a little kid.'

'Jesus,' Caoimhe breathed.

'I was never going to hurt you or anything.'

Caoimhe rolled her eyes.

'No, that would be insane.'

'I hated you, Sophia. I wanted to revel in the misery of your life without me, but your entire life was so fucking perfect!'

'And that's how you saw us?' Ella asked. 'You were there, that night?'

'Yeah. I parked at the top of the road when you got back from your night out. I called the police saying there was a disturbance.'

Caoimhe gave a grimace of vexation.

'Why would you do that?'

Bethany shrugged.

'I don't know. To ruin your evening.' Such a simple answer, but one that could have undone all of them. 'I didn't know at that point there was a dead body there.' Bethany brushed her hair from her eyes. 'Then I saw you carrying it to the car. Followed you out into the middle of nowhere. Such a Sophia thing to do.' Bethany's tone was mocking. 'With her close-knit group of friends who'd put everything on the line for her. The adrenaline, the camaraderie.' She made a vomiting noise.

'And it was you who sent us all the emails?' Safa asked.

Bethany nodded. She wiped her nose on the back of her hand.

'And the stones?' Ella checked.

'Yes, yes, and Ajola's wicker man, Safa's pendant.'

'I carried that around with me!' Safa cried, indignant. 'I thought it was a force for good.'

'I knew I'd use what I'd witnessed that night.' Bethany took a steadying breath. 'To destroy you, Sophia. To upend your fucking joy. I just didn't know when. I started following all of you so I could gather airtight details from your lives. But it wasn't enough. I wanted you to know I was watching. I wanted to be a part of your lives. I stole your phone, Sophia, got everyone's contact information, names, numbers, social media.' Bethany let out a loud sigh. 'Oh my God. It actually feels like a relief to say all this. Ajola, I searched you online and found Meg talking about your lessons on Reddit, and then I cyber-stalked Meg and found out she'd committed suicide.'

Ajola took a step back, a hand on her chest.

'Meg spoke about my lessons?'

348

Bethany shrugged.

'Sure. Wouldn't stop going on about them.'

'I feel violated,' Caoimhe said.

'I had to ruin your life.' Bethany looked at Sophia. 'I had to punish you for being so sly.'

'I swear' – Sophia put a hand on her clavicle – 'I swear I never did any of those things. Jill has been lying to you for years. She pitted you against me. I mean, did I ever actually do anything to you?' Bethany stared into the mask, still picking fragments of wood from the surface. 'What indication did I, myself, give you that I was deceitful? Yes, OK, I admit I became friends with you when I needed to escape Jill, but I discovered you were a good friend. You were thoughtful, you were kind; I liked you.'

Bethany was still.

'You did like me?' she said to the mask.

'Yes!' Sophia's voice was vehement. 'It was easy to talk to you. It was fun. Remember *Titanic*? We loved Jack Dawson so much, we watched *What's Eating Gilbert Grape?*'

Bethany smiled and looked up.

'People talk about Leonardo DiCaprio's Oscar snubs,' she said.

Sophia held out her hands and nodded.

'That was his first one,' she agreed. 'Should've got an award for that.'

'Remember' – Bethany smiled – 'when the flute man's dentures fell out in the library that time? Only you and me saw it?'

'Hilarious.' Sophia let out a small laugh. 'I always think about that.'

Bethany looked back at the mask. She brushed some unseen speck of dust away from the cleft nose.

'It was all Jill?' she asked. The anguish in her voice was totally gone now. The contempt. The derision. She was just Bethany, as she always had been.

'Yes!' Sophia nodded.

Bethany tilted back her head and screamed at the faded paint strip on the ceiling. Ella clapped her hands to her ears. Caoimhe exchanged a look with Ajola. Bethany contorted her hands into talons and screamed until she had no more breath left.

When she was silent, Sophia exhaled slowly and turned to the others.

'I told you Jill had masterminded this in some way,' she said. 'She's evil.'

'Why Trent?' Ella gently asked Bethany. 'Why did you get us to kill this random Morrisons guy?'

'He's not random.' Bethany relaxed her fingers. 'He's my ex.'

'That makes a lot more sense.' Ajola nodded. 'Was he abusive?'

Bethany scratched the back of her head.

'No-o,' she said, almost unsure. 'Not abusive.' She was quiet. Outside, a thrush alighted on the patio table and cocked its head. 'I was with him a long time,' she said. 'He dumped me. I got an abortion.'

'Murder does seem like the logical next step,' Caoimhe said and crossed her eyes at Safa.

'He dismissed me,' Bethany said. 'Excluded me. I hated him. It was the perfect opportunity to use what I had seen seven years ago. To destroy both of you.' She blew out slowly through her cheeks. 'I had so thought he was the one. I so wanted to *belong* to something. Like you guys.'

'We don't belong anywhere,' Safa said.

'Of course you do. You belong together.'

The kitchen fell silent.

'We need to bury this body,' Ella said eventually.

'Bethany.' Sophia looked at her, the Pan mask clasped in her two hands. She had never been Bethany; but then Bethany had never been Bethany, at least not the version Sophia had imagined. They were both greater than how they had been perceived. 'Come with us.'

'More evidence to implicate me?' Bethany asked, glancing quickly at Sophia.

'Yes,' Caoimhe said. 'Of course.'

Yes, of course. But there was more to it than that, Sophia knew. She wanted Bethany to be there. To prove, now, that she, Sophia, was a good person, a kind person and nothing like Jill. To reassure Bethany that she, Bethany, was someone, too.

'The police are going to come and question you, you know.' Ella frowned at Bethany. 'That's guaranteed: you're the ex. When he's reported missing, they're coming for you.' She moved her gum around her mouth. 'So, you'd better have a story ready, for your own sake.'

'I know.' Bethany stood up. She glanced from Ella to Sophia. 'I've prepared for that.' She looked at the Pan mask in her hands. 'I'm five foot five and have no history of abuse or breaking the law. What are they going to think?' She looked up. 'I abducted him on my own, without anyone seeing, disposed of the body, again with no one seeing, no text chain, no communication, no messages, and left absolutely zero evidence in his home, my home or my car?'

Sophia couldn't believe this Bethany had existed for all those years.

'Well, whatever you say, make sure they stay away from us.' Caoimhe looked pointedly at her. 'That was the deal.'

Bethany gave a grimace.

'He's an independent, adult man who didn't come home,' she said. 'This won't be national news or anything. Do you know how many people disappear every year in the UK? I looked up the statistics. Someone is reported missing every ninety seconds.' She nodded at Sophia. 'You must know, from Chris. Without any evidence of foul play, there's not much they're going to do, especially if it's a grown man, with all his faculties, who has every right to move about as he wishes.'

Sophia raised her eyebrows and looked around at the others.

'Sounds about right.' She nodded. 'I mean, seven years ago, they took all our statements, but then, when nothing came up, after a certain number of months, they just labelled Chris long-term missing.'

'That's chilling,' Caoimhe said. 'Missing women are always front-page news. But no one cares if men go missing. That should be a headline.'

'The headline should be about,' Ajola corrected her, 'male-on-male violence. Because any inexplicably missing man has probably come to harm at the hands of another man.'

'I can think of a case where that's not true,' Safa said.

'What if they look at your phone data or something?' Ella asked, ignoring this and looking at Bethany. 'Can that link to us?'

'I've thought of that,' Bethany said. 'I've deleted every contact number I had for you, erased every trace of your lives from my phone. They can't find anything without doing a deep dive, and for that they'll need a warrant, which there's no grounds for.' She turned on the spot to look at each of them. 'I told you, I'm a woman of my word. If there're any developments or we need to talk, I've got a more private way to get in touch. I've been planning this for longer than you.' The blotches on her face were receding. 'There's no body. There's no blood. There's no threat or coercion. They'd have no reason to do anything but ask me cursory questions, which I can answer.' She gritted her teeth. 'Which I've been *waiting* to answer.'

Caoimhe scratched the back of her head.

'Should we,' she said and pointed at the door, 'bury this dead body?'

'Yeah.' Ajola nodded. 'Let's bury a dead body.'

'Are we OK with having Bethany in the car?' Safa asked as they moved towards the door. 'No offence, Bethany, but you sort of seem mentally unstable.'

'To be fair' – Sophia almost smiled – 'we just killed a guy.' Safa crossed her eyes now at Caoimhe as Sophia went on, 'She probably thinks we're mentally unstable.'

'We're all as mentally unstable as each other,' Ajola said in a soothing voice. 'Besides, it's a ritual. It's healing.' She nodded firmly at Bethany, and Sophia felt a wave of gratefulness towards her as she finished, 'We all need to be there.'

Witchcraft

CREPUSCULAR. STARS. SOFT, grey grass. A pointed crescent. Wandering. Remembrance. It's deep in the earth. What is this innate sense?

'Isn't an hour strange,' Safa said as they walked across the undulating grass towards the copse that Ajola had found, another childhood destination for her and her great-grandmother. It had been a forty-five-minute drive, with four of them squashed into the back seat, the Fiat 500 riding extremely low on its back wheels.

'How do you mean?' Caoimhe replied.

Their shadows were cast before them, long and slender in the dusk. The grass was tinged with red.

'It's like, what is an hour? A unit of time.' Safa puffed out her cheeks. They had left her little Fiat 500 parked in an old layby on the other side of the heath. Trent's body was held between five of them, concealed in a tent bag so it looked as though they were intrepid women off on a camping adventure, with Ella carrying the spade and Ajola's rucksack. 'Why sixty minutes? Why sixty seconds? Why twenty-four hours in a day? The whole world has so many languages as well. Currencies, measurements. But everyone uses the same measure of time.'

'Isn't it because the earth takes twenty-four hours to revolve?' Ella said. A warm breeze brushed the tips of her fingers. 'Isn't that something to do with it?'

'Why not twenty-four minutes in an hour then?' Caoimhe asked.

'Maybe because the earth is a sphere.' Ella stopped, stood on one foot and slipped her shoe off her foot. A tiny stone fell out. 'Three hundred and sixty degrees. Sixty minutes.'

'No.' Ajola shook her head. She shifted her grip on Trent's body. 'It's because there are twelve lunar cycles in one year. One rotation of the sun.'

'So?' Caoimhe asked.

'Twelve fives are sixty,' Ajola said.

'Where does five come from, though?' Safa asked.

'It must be from ancient times,' Ella said. 'The Egyptians or Babylonians. They cut up time in a certain way and we all still use that method.'

'But isn't it weird how all cultures use it?' Safa said. 'Like, you don't go to Japan and get off at the airport and see that it's thirty-one seventy-six in the JM.'

Sophia laughed.

'Perhaps because time is artificial,' Ajola said. 'It's a man-made construct. The first people rose with the sun and slept with the sun. They did the jobs that were needed to be done in the time they needed. They didn't need to break up sunlit hours into smaller portions. That's a more recent thing. A capitalist thing.'

'You can turn any discussion into a TED Talk on oppression,' Safa replied.

'Because it's so prevalent,' Ajola said. 'The only unit of time that isn't arbitrary to humans is the month. Twenty-eight days. Because since the dawn of time, women have needed to be aware of this measure.'

'Isn't it strange that a woman's cycle is twenty-eight days and the moon takes twenty-eight days to orbit the Earth?' Bethany said. 'How did those two unrelated events end up with the exact same, specific number?'

'They're probably not unrelated.' Ella shifted the spade in her grasp. 'We probably evolved using the moon as a guide for us. The women with twenty-eight-day cycles could track their periods with more specificity, using the moon, and they were the ones that passed on their genes.'

'Women are the timekeepers,' Ajola said.

'How come dogs don't do that, then?' Caoimhe said.

This comment was met with silence and then Sophia started laughing. Caoimhe joined in and their laughter rolled over the heath, curling into the cocoons and shallows of the moor, winding its way on the streams of air and the rivulets of unseen currents of the Earth. From beyond, rising above the trees and rock formations, the fence posts and outcrops, the copse was visible, the cluster of trees a-fire in the setting sun. Above it, a pale sliver of moon was climbing, bright and luminous.

'Let's swap,' Safa said. 'My arms are burning.'

Ella stepped in to take the body and Safa took the spade and the rucksack. They climbed the rise to the trees and laid the body in the centre. Safa sat down on a rock in the middle and shifted her feet on the earth. Bethany bent down next to her and pressed her hands to the soil.

'How long does it take to dig a grave?' she asked.

'If we take it in shifts, not that long at all,' Caoimhe said.

'We're seven years older now, though,' Ella pointed out.

'Don't diminish the wisdom and experience of an old woman,' Ajola said and stuck the spade into the earth. It shuddered but remained completely upright. 'The patriarchy invented the crone to scare women from their power.'

'A couple of hours,' Safa replied to Bethany.

They dug. Taking it in turns to lengthen, widen, deepen. Ajola sat on a rock near the edge of the copse and began to arrange the herbs that she had brought. The rising moon hung behind her like a spotlight.

'How deep does it need to be?' Ella asked, resting on the spade.

'About two more feet,' Caoimhe said as Ajola replied:

'That's fine.'

'Let's just dig two more feet.' Caoimhe took the spade from Ella and began digging again.

'Either this body will be found here or it won't,' Ajola said. 'Two more feet won't change that.' She was looking at her phone. 'I want to wait for exactly sunset,' she said. 'Twenty-one twenty-one.'

'On the twenty-first,' Bethany said as they rolled Trent into his grave and began covering his body with heavy sods of earth. 'That's weird, isn't it?'

'It's magik,' Ajola said.

'Magic?' Bethany repeated, straightening up and dusting her hands.

'Yes, you're about to witness true magik, a spell. We're about to join together to bind this body to the earth.'

Caoimhe put her hands on her hips and tilted her head back.

'It's literally embarrassing to hear you say that to someone,' she said. 'We sound insane.'

'Doing this is the least insane thing that's happened in the last twenty-four hours,' Ajola responded. 'This is practically normal. Bethany, just enjoy it.' She glanced at her phone again. 'Nearly time.'

'Time is naught but a man-made construct. Women are the timekeepers,' Caoimhe said. 'Remember? Maybe we should just announce when the sun sets.' Caoimhe stood on her tiptoes to look through the trees at the scarlet glimmer on the horizon. 'Not sunset yet.' She crouched down, closer to the ground. 'Oh shit, sunset was ages ago.'

'It's weird at this time of day,' Safa said. 'Don't you think? Not night-time yet. Definitely not daytime.'

'There's a different smell in the air,' Ella agreed.

'The air is different,' Sophia said.

'Crepuscular.' Caoimhe stood up. 'Of twilight, of dusk and dawn.'

'I didn't know there was a word for it,' Safa said.

'It's the time I like to run.'

'OK.' Ajola put her phone away and gave a thumbs-up. 'Sunset.'

'Twenty-one twenty-one?' Caoimhe said, patting the dirt down on top of Trent.

'No,' Ajola said. 'Not quite. But I'm the timekeeper. The sun has set. I feel it in the air.'

Safa stood up and took Caoimhe's and Ella's hands. Sophia took Bethany's. They closed the circled around the centre of the earth.

'I hope we don't do something wrong and he starts climbing out,' Safa said.

Caoimhe gave a grunt of amusement.

'Start by saying our names,' Ajola said. 'Then I'll give you the herbs to bind the spell.'

'I am not saying my name.' Caoimhe glared at her. 'Just chuck them down and let's go. It's getting cold.'

'You can't just chuck them down,' Ajola explained. 'We're not littering. It has meaning. And names have power. It's a link from up there' – she raised her hands, moving Caoimhe's and Sophia's hands with hers – 'to in here.' She pulled them in so all four hands were at her chest. 'Ajola.'

'Safa.'

'Sophia.'

'Ella.'

'Bethany.'

'Caoimhe,' Caoimhe added, begrudgingly.

Ajola, still holding Caoimhe's and Sophia's hands, opened up a leather pouch at her waist and began to pull dried leaves from it.

'Belladonna,' she said. 'Take it, Caoimhe. Adder's tongue for you, Sophia. Witch's burr, Ella.'

'These are all a lot cooler than last time,' Safa said, watching as Ella took the prickled briar, set with dark, piercing eyes around its barbs.

'Last time we only had Sophia's kitchen. This time I could really resource them. Safa, pumpkin.'

'Pumpkin? What? That's so boring.'

'It's lunar magik,' Ajola replied. 'Don't worry, I've got mustard seeds for me and Bethany.' She shared out some seeds and Bethany gratefully held out her hands. 'Already, I feel the power,' Ajola said. 'Lay them down, one at a time.'

They did, rejoining hands at the end.

'Endurance, protection, healing, power,' Ajola said. 'We all stand before—'

'Sorry to disturb you,' a deep, male voice cut in. 'Are you performing?'

The Copse

THE WOMEN LEAPT as though an electric current had passed through them and whipped around, still holding hands. Two elderly men were standing on the edge of the dark trees, blinking at the six of them, the silver light from the crescent moon encircled behind their heads. One of the men was tall and angular, huge glasses taking up half of his face and magnifying his eyes. He had a blue and black Gore-Tex jacket on, zipped up to the chin, and waterproof trousers flecked with reflective piping up the sides. They flashed in the darkness. His walking partner was shorter and strangely shaped, like a beanbag. He had a laminated map hanging on a lanyard around his neck and an orange high-vis jacket on over his own waterproof jacket.

'Just rehearsing,' Ajola managed, and they carefully let go of one another's hands.

They looked around at each other. Safa put her hand over her mouth. Ella put both hands over her eyes. Bethany had shrunk away.

'It sounded very ominous,' the short man said. He gently

lowered himself to the ground. Next to him, the moonlight glinted off the angular man's glasses, obscuring his eyes. 'Shakespeare in the park? Trouble, trouble, boil and bubble?'

'Something like that,' Caoimhe said.

'We come up walking this way, don't we, Malc?' the bean-bag said.

His tall friend didn't move. It was hard to tell where he was looking in the shadows and moonlight, with his lenses reflecting back at them. His mouth was a straight line surrounded by rough-cut stubble, a blank facade facing them.

'South Downs.' The shorter man groaned. He had lifted up his laminated map and was turning it round and round in his hands. 'We were supposed to be collected about an hour ago. Our ride never showed up.'

'Did you call them?' Safa asked.

'No signal,' he replied brusquely, without glancing up.

'Have you got 4G?' Caoimhe asked.

The shorter man held up his hand and his partner handed him a Nokia 3210. Sophia looked at Bethany and they exchanged a smile.

'No signal,' he said more loudly. He held up the phone so the black-green square was visible and then spoke slowly, looking at Safa directly. 'No. Bars. No. Signal.'

'Oh, my days,' Safa said. 'Do you want us to check your route for you?' she asked. 'On the map?' She gestured to the laminated map around his shoulders. The man put a protective hand over it and got back to his feet.

'No, thank you,' he said, shortly. He raised a hand as Malc turned on the spot and began drifting down the hill. 'Don't stay out too late, ladies!' he called. 'Your husbands will start to worry about you!' He gave a loud laugh, which barked off the empty air.

'Bye,' Caoimhe said, flatly.

They watched as the two men made their way down the hill and back to the path. After a few minutes, a white glow of a torch burst into life, sweeping across the grass between them.

'They're definitely in the wrong place,' Safa said.

They turned to look at the patch of grass in the middle of the copse. Their wilted pile of herbs and seeds was scattered across the disturbed soil.

'Do we just go back?' Bethany asked Ajola. 'Will it still work?'

'It's obviously not ideal,' Ajola said, taking Caoimhe's hand. She pictured her great-grandma. Clasped hands. Curled hair. An eye as bright and alive and as real as the moon. 'But we can still bind it. Rejoin the circle.'

They came together, uniting around the centre.

In that moment, the crescent of moon just visible to her through the gnarled and reaching branches of the trees, she thought about Benjamin. She thought about him asleep at Felix's new apartment, in his spaceman pyjamas, eyes closed, mouth still, the little wedge scar visible just under his hairline. There was so much to him. So much – what? Turmoil? What a confusing problem life was, with what it brought upon us all, the urges and feelings and desires that flood our neurons and froth in our veins, pulsating through our arteries. How could we expect four-year-olds to understand, to act, as we would wish. How could we expect thirty-year-olds to maintain harmony against the relentlessness of existence. Eric was nothing but a reflection. And in that reflection, she could see Benjamin, in his spaceman pyjamas, sleeping, eyes closed, mouth still, the little scar just visible

at the periphery of her vision, the corners of the crescent moon looked razor-sharp. Sharp as a tack. Sharp as the blade of a knife. Two unfathomably precise edges pointing into the blackness of the eternal void of space. Running at night wasn't like running at twilight. Night was too absolute. It was a definitive. Dawn and dusk were analogous. Ambiguous. It gave every step weight. Meaning. The promise of infinite possibilities. She wondered if Evie had a particular time of the day that she preferred to run in. Perhaps it was in the half-light, like her. Perhaps she had no favourable time. Maybe that's what made her elite. She would like to run with Evie. She realized this suddenly and completely. Not during efforts in training. On a long run, hours and hours, into the morning, a journey of infinite possibilities. What would it be like, to share that with someone? Every answer would be revealed to her. All of life and its intricacies and mysteries would make themselves known in that

one instant, the air in the copse was balmy, a warm summer's evening, and in the next it had turned cold. As if an unseen mist or depressurized system had descended upon the six of their bodies. She wanted to wrap her jumper more tightly to her but was afraid of breaking the circle. She tried to burrow down into herself, to allow her consciousness to retreat into the deep chasms and chambers that existed intangibly and ethereally at the centre of her body. She was always good at disassociating her mind from her physical body; it was how she had survived for fourteen years in a marriage with Haaris. It was ironic to think the photo of him and Danielle had given her such a visceral reaction, when the whole of their time together was founded on her withdrawing her physical self from his. She didn't want to be bothered by the photos. She didn't want to dwell on the new decorations. The time and labour he must have devoted to them that he wasn't devoting to Javeria and Aleena, that he hadn't devoted to her in fourteen years. She didn't want to feel the unstoppable rage that erupted from her core when she thought this. Such anger. Such anger. How did she still exist with a capacity for such anger? The injustice enraged her from the tips of her toes to the crest of her crown, beyond what she had previously thought possible. What lesson could she learn from this? Why was this useful? It did nothing but allow her to sit safe with the knowledge that he had always been a complete and abject

failure couldn't happen. She always dwelt on the possibility of disappointing the children whenever she embarked on a new trip or project and tried to mitigate that outcome, but she could not consider that for Daisy. She would excel. And when she did, everything would be OK. She could save herself and Meg if she saved Daisy. The glockenspiels echoed inside her head, so loud and terrifying as to seemingly carry themselves down the hill and across the rolling plains, over hillock and tussock, notes tumbling and cascading over one another until they crashed over the cliffs and into the sea. The bloody glockenspiels. But everything would be OK. Daisy would do well in the competition. She would be happy. She could break away from the pervasive influence of Yashica. She could flourish and grow and be successful as Meg never did, as Ajola never could. Daisy would be OK. She would be. She would. The glockenspiels. The glockenspiels. The never-ending, unabated serenity of it all. Everything else was left behind. No more hate. No more bitterness. This was how life should be. She had made the circle. Perhaps she had always been part of the circle. Trent was now gone. He was there, beneath her feet, resigned to the cold, hard earth, and she was free in the serenity of it all. She could go back and make her videos, unhindered, harmonious. She was no longer anchored to one spot through discord and envy. She could travel! Florence, Copenhagen. There was nowhere she didn't belong. The air. Had the air ever been this open. She felt no more

anxiety that she felt started to drift from her body, like the incoming tides of the sea washing away messages written in the sand. Peace. She was weightless. Floating up and up, away from the buried body of the dead, through the ring of branches above her head and into the limitless sky. Strange to think Chris was still buried, soil and mineral, worms and dark, twisting shapes, intertwining themselves with his bones. She couldn't imagine him being in the limitless sky with her, though. Chris didn't belong to anything so transcendent. He was too base. She hoped Isla lived a transcendental life. A life where her soul felt. Where she could experience. And know. And be. Where she could stand outside in the dark and lift her face up to a star-strewn sky and feel the cold air and know peace. She moved the tips of her toes inside her shoes. And know peace.

'That's it,' Ajola said into the dark.

They were frozen within their circle, their hands clasped together, stiff in the cold, fingers frosted over with the weight of the magik. Gingerly, they extracted themselves from one another, groggy and bewildered, unsure where to move to in the darkness.

'That's two bodies we've put in the earth,' Ella said. 'I don't know how my conscience will withstand it.'

'Together.' Ajola looked at her. 'All these years and we needn't have worried. Did our trust in one another waver?' She nodded at Bethany. 'We belong together.' She touched her chest. 'We bear it together, do you understand?'

'I wouldn't be here without you,' Ella said.

'None of us would.' Sophia smiled. 'And I like that.'

'We should meet up and do this every year,' Safa said. 'A fun little reunion.'

'I'm freezing,' Caoimhe said. 'Let's get out of here.'

'Tell me,' Ella said, following Caoimhe to the edge of the trees. 'Do we need to invite those two old men back every year?'

'They definitely thought they were going to see some *Midsomer*-type, Woodstock hippy' – Sophia moved her hand, searching for the words as she followed the others – 'naturist free-for-all.'

'They'd probably been standing there ages,' Ajola said, beginning her steady descent down the black grass, 'and only spoke up when they got annoyed we weren't all undressing.'

'That's rank,' Safa said, putting her hand on Ajola's shoulder in the dark.

'As a youngster,' Ajola said, 'I thought it was just horny little boys that would stare if they accidentally caught a glimpse of a naked woman in the garden or something.' She stopped at the bottom of the hill and turned to look up at the moon. 'It's sad to realize, as a grown woman, that all men would stop and stare if they caught a glimpse of a woman's bare flesh.'

'That's someone's granddad.' Caoimhe walked past her. She turned and held up her finger. 'But if there isn't room here for people who stand against everything you believe in, then' – she put her hand on her hip – 'what sort of a hippy free-for-all is this?'

'That is so rainbow rhythms,' Ajola said.

'It's *Peep Show*,' Ella explained to Bethany. 'Did you ever watch *Peep Show*?'

'There was,' Safa said, leading the way back towards the car, 'a lot of new energy in the room tonight and some of it was just so rainbow rhythms.'

'And some of it,' Bethany said, 'was just so *not* rainbow rhythms.'

'Why don't you just say who you're talking about?' Sophia said, coming off the hill last. 'You're talking about me, aren't you?'

They laughed. Their shadows leaked out on to the dark grass behind them. The crescent moon was now high in the sky, small but glinting, like an eye in the dark.

RESOLUTIONS

Sophia

IT WAS THURSDAY morning when Laura Stone finally called Sophia into the police station. It hadn't changed much in seven years. Peeling pale paint on the walls, chairs that were bolted to the floor and a plastic shield separating the front desk from everyone else. Laura Stone greeted her at reception, a blue lanyard hanging around her neck. Her little face smiled out at Sophia from her ID badge. The delicate silver watch clinked on her wrist. She led Sophia into a side room with a small window set high up in the wall. There was a wooden table surrounded by three chairs. Josh Paulton wasn't there that day. There was another man seated at the table, though, dressed in a smart police uniform with crisp epaulettes on his shoulders. As Laura Stone talked, he fiddled with his hat in his lap. Sophia had been prepared for Laura Stone's imminent call from the moment she had taken Bethany's hand at the grave site. She hadn't expected this man, though. She watched him, her heart thumping so hard she felt it in the base of her throat.

'We were able to determine,' Laura Stone said once they were all seated, 'that the tip we received . . .' – she moved her hair back from her face and Sophia sensed her trying not to look at the man on her left – 'after a thorough investigation into verifiable details the, uh, anonymous tip we received about your husband's disappearance did not result in any actionable leads, and we have decided to close that line of inquiry.'

Sophia was silent.

'No Chris,' she said.

'No. I am sorry for any undue stress and anxiety we have put you through.' Laura Stone now glanced at the man next to her. 'Please understand, we have to weigh up our duty of care to investigate potential leads with credibility, and all I can say is, we're really sorry for not getting the balance right on this occasion.'

The relief was as sudden and as strong as a wave. Sophia felt the tension dissipate from her body. Bethany had done it. She really was as good as her word. Sophia wanted to put her hands in the air and cheer but had to hold herself back. A grieving wife, a lost soul.

'I can't believe it,' she said.

'We really do offer our sincerest condolences,' the man beside Laura Stone said. 'As Chief Superintendent, all I can offer is my deepest apologies on behalf of our police force.' Sophia could smell the coffee on his breath. She tried not to wince. 'We never intended to cause any stress or anxiety. I cannot even begin to imagine how you are feeling, after looking for your husband for seven years.' He spread his hands at her, showing his empty palms. 'I know there's no way for us to undo the emotional damage that this may have caused to you and your daughter' – Sophia shut her eyes and leant backwards, trying to appear as though she was in turmoil but really trying to lean away from the stench of his breath – 'but rest assured that you have our heartfelt condolences. Also' – he leant forward towards her and Sophia resisted the urge to throw herself further backwards – 'as it has been seven years, you are legally able to apply to the High Court for a declaration of presumed death for your husband. It will mean we officially close the case. I know that's a hard reality to comprehend but we have advocates who can guide you through that process. We understand it won't alleviate your pain but maybe it can help put you on the road to recovery.'

'Thank you.' She wiped her eyes but was really covering her nostrils. 'I'll think about it.'

Sophia left the police station. She felt cleaner. Purer. Now, she just needed to extract Jill from her life. Drain her from her blood like pus from a wound.

'Why are you taking them to school?' Isla asked her the next day as she packed all the items of clothing Jill had ever copied into a bag.

'I'm giving them out.'

'God, Mum, *please*, don't do that.'

'Fine, I'll donate them to the school.'

'Please *don't*! And in a Lidl bag!'

'No one knows. They'll think it's just my shopping.'

'That's even worse!' Isla rolled her eyes. 'I get it, you don't have a secret boyfriend. But you need a hobby or something.'

Sophia thought back to the six of them standing in a circle in the copse.

'I have a hobby.'

Once at the school, Isla quick-stepped away from Sophia

and ducked into the classroom as soon as possible. Sophia nervously loitered by the fence until all the children were inside, at the farthest point from Jill, who was standing in a tight-knit group with the other mums. She felt nervous about handing the bag over in front of everyone. What if she stumbled over her words. She'd look like the insane one. Across the fence, Jill put a finger to her chin and looked into the air, just as she had done twenty-three years ago whilst Joseph Burton held her hand in DT class. Sophia wanted to rugby-tackle her to the ground and beat her around the head with a flip-flop.

Her phone buzzed. A new DM from Bethany on Anything Worn, which, they had decided, would be the safest way to communicate whilst the police searched for Trent.

Been thinking how you can get rid of Jill.

Sophia glanced around the leafy street.

You're not watching me from somewhere, are you?

Ha ha. No, just got to Copenhagen.

Sophia pressed her lips together.

The police are going to help me get a death certificate for Chris, she typed.

She couldn't ask what she really wanted to in case, in the future, the police got hold of this data. She waited, watching Bethany's bobbing ellipsis, hoping she understood, and began picking the fence.

Hmm. The reply came. The anonymous tip they received must have, at first, appeared credible but, under greater scrutiny, led nowhere. Whoever submitted it must have really known what they were doing.

Sophia smiled. She glanced up and Jill made eye contact with her. They held each other's gaze and then Jill leant forward to whisper into the ear of another mum. The mum whipped around and stared at Sophia. Jill shook her head and covered her mouth with her hand, just as she used to do in Year 6. Bent over, mouth open, eyes shut, silent mirth, as though that utterly mundane comment you had just made was the most hilarious thing ever. An inside joke. Something you didn't understand. POLO. Sophia stopped picking at the fence. The other mum started fake-laughing as well, hand over mouth, shaking her head in humorous disbelief.

Tell me how to sort Jill out, she texted back.

You buried two murder victims in Wicca rituals, Bethany replied. The message popped up and was deleted so quickly, Sophia wasn't sure it had even been there. After an agonizing wait, watching the blinking speech bubble, a more permanent reply came in: Jill should be easy.

Sophia didn't hand over the bag. She walked home, thinking. Right before she reached her turning, she heard that engine roar and looked up. The black Range Rover Evoque was accelerating down the road towards her. It looked as if it was aiming right at her. Sophia jumped backwards as the vehicle, at the last second, veered out of the way. Jill was laughing behind the steering wheel, holding her hand over her mouth.

Sophia swung the Lidl bag in the air but then the Range Rover was gone. Her heart was hammering, her face flushed. The Lidl bag suddenly seemed light, not substantial enough.

Caoimhe

THERE WAS A hill just outside the town where Caoimhe lived. It rose sharply and suddenly, about a 100-metre ascent over a 600-metre stretch. Caoimhe liked to crest this hill just as the sun was coming up. She started at the bottom in the dawn light and reached the top in full morning sunlight. It was the only place on any of her training runs that she permitted herself a moment to stop, to turn off her music, pause her watch and look about her. She could see for miles in either direction, an unadulterated vista. She could see the town and trace the fields she had come through to get to this point. It put everything in perspective. Here she was. Here she came.

That morning, the one after Sophia told them she was applying for a death certificate for Chris, that the police had no actionable leads, as she stood in the golden light, turning 360 degrees on the spot to get a full and immersive feel, another figure appeared. They were coming across the fields to her right, level with where she stood. Instinctively, Caoimhe wanted to turn and run back down the hill, to avoid any stilted morning greetings or awkward eye contact. Something about the gait of the runner made her pause, though, and then it was too late to just turn and run away.

'Hello,' Evie said, taking out her own headphones as she stepped on to the road. She raised her watch and, with a *beep*, paused her run. She was wearing a long-sleeved top despite the mild summer morning. 'Fancy meeting you here, eh?'

'Yeah, ha,' Caoimhe said and looked at her shoes.

'I saw you coming up the hill from back there.' Evie gestured somewhere over her shoulder. 'You have a really strong hill-running technique – high knees, big legs. You look formidable. I guess that's why you're so good at the cross-country races.'

Caoimhe felt her neck flush. She felt as if she was being called to the front of assembly to receive a certificate. She hoped her already sweaty face and crimson cheeks would hide her blush.

'Ha, thanks,' Caoimhe said. She looked up at Evie and smiled, unsure what to say next. 'How far have you come?'

'Just seven miles, got three more to go. You?'

'Eight. Running back home right now.'

'Are you going down Witch Tree Lane?'

'Oh yeah, that way, yeah, I am.'

'Me too. Fancy running together? Always good to have a pacer for the final third.'

Caoimhe was about to politely reject the invitation. But then, suddenly and seemingly without cause, like ripples appearing on the surface of a lake, she changed her mind. Evie winked at her.

'Yeah?' she said.

'Sure,' Caoimhe replied. 'How's your ankle?'

'All better. Just iced it. Strapped it up.' Evie wound her head-phones and put them in a zip pocket at the small of her back. 'You know what is mental? How women's running gear doesn't come with pockets. I have one top, just one top, this one' – she plucked at the front – 'that has a pocket big enough for my phone. And it's bloody long-sleeved. I'm running in the summer in a long-sleeved top, Caoimhe!'

'I was wondering why you had that on.'

'Why don't they make running shorts for women with big zip pockets? I've seen them in the men's line. But not the women's. They just do this terrible one at the back of the shorts.' She turned around and showed Caoimhe the three-inch-wide, one-inch-deep pocket at the small of her back. 'They all have that. Do yours have it too?' Caoimhe laughed and nodded. 'I mean, what are we meant to fit in there? It's barely big enough for one gel.'

'It's for your tampon,' Caoimhe said and Evie let out a loud laugh. 'Why don't you just buy the men's gear?'

'It never fits. You need a good fit to activate the wicking tech-nology. Have you got a phone on you? Where do you keep it?'

Caoimhe lifted her shirt to reveal a skin-tight bumbag strapped against her shorts.

'Good solution.'

'I'd prefer a standard pocket really,' Caoimhe said. 'It's such a faff getting the phone out and putting it away. Plus, it's so loose.' She hooked a thumb through the strap and tugged it around to demonstrate. 'Bounces up and down. Can get annoying.'

'I tell you: we could make millions marketing a line of actu-ally effective women's running clothes. How many women do we see at the races? On TV? All of these women want a zip pocket for their phone.'

'Not some little pouch for a lipstick.'

Evie laughed loudly again. Caoimhe hadn't thought it was that funny but couldn't help laughing too. She felt nervous. She wanted Evie to like her. How embarrassing.

'Should we get going?' she replied, nodding her way down the hill.

'Yeah, man, let's roll,' Evie said and started to jog. 'Steady eight or eight thirty?'

'I can do an eight.' Caoimhe started jogging beside her, tempering her stride.

'Eight for a mile. Seven. Then six?'

Caoimhe grimaced and shook her head.

'I can't do six minutes for the final mile.'

'Get out of here with that noise,' Evie said. 'I saw you at that five K. You surely can.'

Caoimhe bit the end of her tongue and wrinkled her nose. She adjusted her stride as the decline became more prominent.

'Let's do eight thirty for this one then,' she said.

Evie clapped her hands once.

'Yesss,' she said. 'That's the way.'

'I thought you elite athletes just raced everywhere at maximum pace.'

'Are you joking? Majority of my miles are eight-, nine-minute miles,' Evie replied.

'No way.'

'Yeah. Maximum pace all the time is unsustainable. I would say I do maximum pace about twenty per cent, maybe fifteen, of my overall weekly mileage. All the rest of it is just running slow.'

'Running slow?' Caoimhe repeated.

'Running slow,' Evie affirmed. 'Only way to go.'

They reached the bottom of the hill and turned on to the lane. Caoimhe pulled away a bit from Evie and glanced over her shoulder.

'Eight thirty, eight thirty,' Evie said, beckoning her fingers to bring Caoimhe back. 'Nice and easy.'

'This feels *too* slow.'

'Save it for the final mile. Running slow, only way to go.'

'How many miles do you do a week?' Caoimhe asked, trying not to sound too interested as she slowed down to remain abreast with Evie.

'It really does depend. When I ran my last marathon, I was up to eighty but that was because of lockdown. I can't do eighty now. I do well at fifty, sixty. How about you?'

'Nothing like that.' Caoimhe laughed. 'Like, forty, maybe forty-five.'

'The fact you have your times with that mileage is incredible,' Evie said. 'You should look to increase it.'

'I'd be afraid of burning out or destroying myself.'

They both stopped at a crossroad, looking first one way along the empty lane and then the other.

'I can give you some of my training plans, no worries.' They crossed the road together. 'Slowly increase mileage, take it slow, slow, slow, slow, slow.'

Caoimhe laughed.

'All right then,' she said. 'That would be cool.'

'I'm looking at doing a spring marathon next year,' Evie said. 'I'll keep you updated but you should do one too. It's good to train together. Gives you real focus and support.'

Caoimhe was silent for a few steps. Imagine training for a marathon. She could. Chris's case wasn't being taken further. Bethany had been right and, so far, the police had found no link between them and Trent. She wasn't going to prison. She wasn't going to Copenhagen.

'What other people do you train with?' she asked.

'No one here. But at my last club there were a couple of us who went out together. Or I would do ten miles with this person, ten miles with that person, you know.'

'I thought I saw you once running with someone round here,' Caoimhe said, trying to sound even more disinterested.

Evie frowned.

'Who?' she said.

'Some guy.'

'Dean Weaver?'

'Oh no, it wasn't him.'

'Dean's nice, although it's no wonder why he's the best thirty-something runner in the county.'

'Why?'

'All the other thirty-year-old men have families and commitments. Dean refuses to see his kids. He's completely focused on himself. I mean, he's nice, don't get me wrong. Great guy. But it's like, you see a guy and you think, he's cool' – Evie held out her hand, her breathing having no impact on her conversation at all – 'but it's an illusion, you know. A fantasy. The reality is that every day he wipes his arse after taking a shit.'

Caoimhe laughed out loud, the comment completely unexpected. Evie laughed as well.

'Weird,' Caoimhe said. She didn't know how to absorb that information. 'No,' she said, trying to steer the conversation back to Rohan Rust, 'it wasn't him I saw you running with. Some other guy. Had a skull cap on.'

'Oh, *him*. I don't know who that is. I see him around some-times, but . . .' She shrugged.

This made Caoimhe feel amazing. Light. Beautiful. Wondrous. She felt the endorphins flood her bloodstream and had to con-sciously take a few seconds off her pace as her body tried to propel her forward.

'That's cool,' Caoimhe said. 'Yeah, send me your running plans and I can do the marathon with you next year. Or not with you,' she quickly added, 'not like that. We can train together.'

'We can sign up for the same one,' Evie said. 'It's much more fun.' Her watch beeped. 'OK, let's move up to seven minutes a mile.' She glanced at her wrist. 'Two more miles to go. In thir-teen minutes, it's all over.'

'Let's go,' Caoimhe said.

'Let's goooo.'

Caoimhe completed the final mile in six minutes and three seconds. She and Evie ran neck and neck for the whole stretch, Caoimhe always expecting Evie to pull ahead but she never did. In the final tenth of a mile, Caoimhe thought she would pull away, but she couldn't quite make it, Evie thundering along powerfully at her shoulder. As their watches beeped the com-pleted mile, Evie grabbed Caoimhe's hand and lifted her arm into the air, and Caoimhe felt as if she had just won a race.

Safa

SAFA DIDN'T WANT to look any further into Haaris and Danielle's life. She wanted to move on. Sophia had told them the police had dismissed the anonymous tip that had been submitted, and were now helping her to obtain a certificate of presumed death for Chris. Bethany had also passed on that the police had interviewed her about Trent's disappearance. They had conducted the interview over the phone whilst she was in Denmark and found no need to invite her to the station or make a formal statement. They had done it. It was over. Safa should feel as if she owned her own life again. No one could have agency over her any more. She should be free. But she didn't feel like that. She kept picturing Haaris and Danielle in her house, watching her Netflix account. It was like having a bandaged wound. It was secure and safe under the wrapping. It would only cause anguish to take a look. And yet she couldn't help but take a peek. Just a quick peek. Just to see the damage. To indulge the grotesque, to study horror. You had to look. She waited until Javeria and Aleena were asleep,

Seinfeld playing quietly on the laptop, to check Danielle Bloom's posts.

Finger hovering over Danielle's profile, Safa paused. Maybe she really shouldn't probe the open wound. There was no way it would make her feel better. She should relish the fact that she wasn't going to prison instead.

She just wanted to know, really, to *know*. Where had he found the time to do all this? She had barely found time to kill and bury two men. Yet, between working, seeing his daughters, doing the school run, visiting his parents, going to mosque, Haaris had somehow found the time to meet someone so different from him, create a relationship with them, develop intimacy, move in, pose for photos, redecorate, plan a life together.

How could he so easily allow someone into his life so intensely? She, Javeria and Aleena had caused barely a ripple upon his existence. The interchangeable face of woman. There was no imprint of his daughters on this new life. How could he spend time and effort on anything but them? Why would he want to?

But she knew all the answers to these questions. As did all women, deep down. It was just too hard to acknowledge the truth. Feeling as though she was withstanding an enormous weight, she put her phone face down on the sofa and leant back. Max Hastings used to fancy Vaporeon.

Ella

ELLA AND CYNTHIA met in an upstairs room of Cynthia's chambers. It looked like a converted attic cupboard, with a sloping ceiling, Velux windows and panelled walls on which the individual brush strokes of the thickly applied white paint were clearly visible. There were two low-slung chairs, a round coffee table between them and a mat by the door, like a welcome mat in a house.

'No one uses this room much,' Cynthia said, dragging one of the chairs backwards so she could sit on it without her knees pressing into the coffee table.

Ella sat down opposite Cynthia and put her bag on her lap. She surreptitiously put another piece of gum in her mouth. Cynthia leant back in her chair and draped one stockinged leg over the other.

'I like you,' she said to Ella. 'You're composed. You're controlled. I can suggest we meet here and you don't bat an eye. You don't suggest the cliché of going to a coffee shop.'

'Or pub,' Ella suggested.

'Or swanky cocktail bar,' Cynthia said. 'Like ITV would have you believe all barristers visit after days in court.' She clasped her hands on her lap. 'I want to talk to you about two things,' she said, 'before they send out the copy of the draft judgement next week.'

'You think it will be that quick?'

'I do. That's my first point. Eric is going to get compensation. The judge won't use any wording related to being born without consent or' – she clicked her fingers – 'what did Eric say? Flippantly creating life with no heed to its direction. It's not a win for anti-natalism.'

'Oh?' Ella squeezed another tablet of gum into her palm. The disappointment was suffocating. It had all been for nothing.

'No. But he will get compensation for living expenses.'

'That's good.' Ella put the new piece of gum in her mouth alongside the one she was currently chewing. Professionally, a victory. Personally, a crushing blow. 'Right?'

Cynthia wrinkled her nose.

'That depends,' she said. 'And it brings me on to my second point. You are going to get inundated with requests to sue parents. This case will set a precedent. Even if you never represent a single person again, they'll keep coming to you.'

'Oh.' Ella suddenly felt tired. Seven years and this was the only sensation she was left with.

'"Oh" is right. Maybe think about how that fits in with your high-mindedness.'

'It doesn't.'

'Lots of them will be in Eric's situation. Some probably even more so.'

Ella grimaced.

'But that was just something we manipulated to win,' she said. 'That's not the reason I took the case. I do, truly, think there is a case for birth without consent.'

Cynthia just raised her eyebrows. It was finite.

'I'm just letting you know. Can I have some gum?' she asked after a brief pause.

'Sure.' Ella held out the gum packet and deposited a little tablet into Cynthia's outstretched hand. They chewed in silence for several minutes.

'Well,' Cynthia said, pushing the coffee table away with her foot. 'I'll send you the draft judgement when they release it. I can't see the parents appealing, so' – she stood up and held out her hand – 'don't contact me with anything like this ever again.'

Ella laughed and shook her hand from the chair. It was a fake laugh, too high and forced.

Outside, the sky was still light. Ella had expected it to be dark, a dark London street, buses and taxis lighting up rain-soaked roads with their halogen bulbs. Instead, it was early evening. People were walking past in sundresses, open-toed sandals, holding ice creams. She tried to orientate herself, shifting her bag up her shoulder. Trent was dead. There was nothing in the papers, as Bethany had predicted. The police didn't seem to be looking for them. He was just another missing-person statistic. And now the court case was over. She needed to go home and read to Benjamin.

'Ella!'

She turned. It was Felix. She dropped her chin on to her chest. He was hurrying up the street towards her, one hand in the air as if he was hailing a taxi.

'What is it, Felix?' she asked, turning and walking in the

opposite direction. He fell into step beside her, his long legs taking one stride for her two. 'I've just had a really busy day. Busy week, really. I need to get home.'

'I know, I know. I thought I would take you out to dinner.'

'No. I need to get back for Benjamin.'

'No, you don't. I called Seline and said you'd be home late.'

She stopped in her tracks and turned to look up at him. He smiled down at her, his blue eyes the only point of energy and exuberance in his gaunt face. A cyclist whizzed past on the road right behind him.

'You can't do things like that,' Ella said, resuming walking when she realized Felix didn't understand.

'Why not?'

'We're divorced. *I* make plans with Seline.'

'Can I not make plans with Seline also?'

'Not if they override my plans.'

'But your plans can override my plans?'

Ella stopped again. Someone on the opposite side of the street in a tailored suit and horn-rimmed glasses was running towards the bus stop, trying to clamp their shoulder satchel to their thigh with every stride. Felix was still grinning at her. She felt as though she hated him.

'This is why we're divorced,' she said.

'What have you got for dinner tonight, eh?' He moved his head, trying to stay in her line of sight as she looked away. 'Something you prepped on Sunday. I know. Busy week. Reheated food. Very stressful. I will buy you dinner.' He put his hands on his chest. 'Problem solved.'

She started walking again. If she hadn't been so hungry, she would have declined, but the thought of going home and defrosting a frozen parcel while Benjamin headbutted her legs was too distressing.

'Fine,' she said. 'Dinner. And then that's it.'

'Good. I've booked us a table.'

'No. I'm not doing that. Let's just go to the Wetherspoons. I just want to eat. And you've messed Seline about.' Ella suddenly stopped. 'Actually, I can do this myself. In fact, I disinvite you from this whole enterprise.'

He shrugged and looked down the street at nothing in particular.

'I'll just follow you,' he said flatly, 'and eat wherever you eat. At the table next to yours.'

'I'll tell the waiter that you're harassing me,' Ella said, walking again.

'I won't do anything' – Felix walked beside her – 'so you'll have no proof.'

'I'll say you're stalking me.'

'I'll suggest they call the police if they're concerned.'

'Why do you make everything so difficult?'

Felix walked in silence, his long, thin arms swinging by his side. Ella just wanted it to all be over. Where was the relief?

'I suppose I want your attention,' he said. 'If I made no ripple in your life, you wouldn't notice me. But I am making waves.'

'I hate the waves, though,' Ella said. There was a Wetherspoons on the street, called Shakespeare's Head. The sign swinging outside the front had a distorted, gaunt version of Shakespeare, holding a quill, eyes staring at her from atop pointed cheeks. Ella found it chilling.

'But yet when I made no ripple, we got divorced.'

Ella screwed up her eyes.

'No ripple?' she said. 'You made ripples every day. You were always so angry and anxious. My life was nothing but ripples.'

'This is why I wanted to have dinner,' Felix said, holding out one arm in front to direct her and another at the small of her back to guide her into the Wetherspoons. She pirouetted away from his outstretched hand.

'Don't do that,' she said.

'Do what?'

'Put your hand on my back.'

'Why? It is a perfectly platonic gesture as I ensure you go through the door first.'

'Well, you wouldn't do it to a man.' Ella jerked her chin. 'You go up the stairs first and I'll follow.'

'I am just trying to be a gentleman,' he said as he walked inside.

'I thought you were making waves.'

'Gentlemanly waves.' Felix turned to look at her over his shoulder and waved his hand like a monarch. 'Like this.'

Ella didn't smile. She wondered what he would do if she suddenly ran away. She could get a McDonald's for dinner and be home in forty minutes. He would probably chase her. His gargantuan, skinny legs would cover ten times the distance that her tiny strides could muster up.

She chose a seat by the window without signalling to him, leaving him to walk halfway across the pub, past the shelves lined with tomes of English classics – Shakespeare, naturally, *David Copperfield*, *A Study in Scarlet*, *Pride and Prejudice* – before he realized she wasn't behind him and he had to double back to sit with her.

'Good choice,' he said.

A pile of cheap, plastic Venetian masks lay on the windowsill beside them, fringed with neon pink feathers. One had red lip-stick smudges on the mouth. Another had 'Bride to Be' written in glitter nail varnish across the forehead. Felix pulled out the chair opposite her. His thigh bones were so long, their knees touched when he sat down. She shifted her seat backwards.

'It's on me,' he said, scanning the menu.

'Obviously.' Ella curled her lip. 'You invited me.'

Felix took off his hat and smoothed back his long, lanky strands of thinning hair. He smiled at her.

'You should just shave your head,' she said, emotionlessly. 'You look silly with that hair.'

'That's why I wear the hat. Plus, look how thick' – he patted around his ears – 'lovely thick hair. Not even grey. Why would I shave that?'

'Shave the top part then,' Ella said, looking at her own menu.

'If I shave the top part, would you marry me?'

The request was so ridiculous, Ella laughed. She put her hands over her face and pushed her fingers into her closed eye-lids. Felix laughed too.

'See, we always have fun like this,' he said.

'We had fun like this,' Ella said, lowering her hands. She picked up one of the non-soiled masks and held it over her eyes, looking at him through the roughly cut eyeholes. 'We don't any more. Not for about four years.'

It was meant to be a joke but even as the words came out of her mouth, they made her feel ill. Felix didn't smile. Ella thought about Eric and the draft judgement that was being prepared. She put the mask down.

'Ah. Well.' Felix raised his eyebrows at her. '*Eins kommt zum anderen.*' He looked back at the menu. 'I will get All Day

Brunch and you . . .' He looked at her. His blue eyes were sharp and clear. '. . . will get the Classic Burger.'

'I'm not impressed,' she said. 'We were married.'

He laughed and put the hat back on his head, pulling the peak low over his eyes. She watched him walk over to the bar and lean on the counter, his tight, angular body looking like someone else's doodle of stairs. She tried to imagine that there was no Seline at home. No Benjamin. That the evening was an endless space of immense possibilities, rolling onwards and onwards into the next day. She wished Felix wouldn't wear the tracksuit bottoms. Even the smooth polyester ones that tapered at the leg looked ridiculous on him. When they had met, he had worn chinos, jeans, suit trousers. When they had met, when they had, when. They were both so changed from when they had met as to be completely different people.

'Maybe I call you in fourteen years,' Felix said to her when they had finished eating their dinner in silence. They were standing under the gaunt illustration of William Shakespeare. The street was now dark, the buses and taxis were lighting up the road with halogen bulbs, the amount of sundresses and ice creams had been reduced to zero. The street lamps spilled on to the road in orange puddles. Ella put a piece of gum in her mouth and looked up at Felix. She should ask him, now. He smiled back at her.

'Always the gum,' he said. 'I told you, you don't need to incessantly chew. It's pathological. Life is fragile and chaotic. Obsessively gum-chewing won't change that.'

'I'd be afraid to stop,' Ella said, quite truthfully. Now. In this arbour of honesty.

'There's too much nuance in the world for you to be exactly like your mum,' Felix said. 'Embrace the chaos.'

It was such a direct response, Ella laughed. Felix winked at her.

'Do you want me to pretend to offer to walk you to the station?' he asked. 'Or can I just skip that bit?'

'You can skip it.' The moment had passed. She hadn't got the words out.

'Very well.' He looked down at her and then touched his long, bony forefinger to his temple. 'Keep in touch.'

He turned and strode away. She watched him go, analysing his long, loping walk, the way he flitted through the puddles and the shadows. She realized she didn't even know his route home or where he was living now. He always came to hers to pick up and drop off Benjamin. All those years and now she couldn't even picture him existing beyond her.

Ajola

WHEN THE EMAIL came in, Ajola didn't even recognize it. She was going through her inbox, deleting any junk messages. History Association newsletter, ParentMail, *TES*, Class Dojo, ClassDojo, Primary Mathematics Competition Results, Microsoft Outlook, ClassDojo, Third Space Learning. Ajola paused and then hurriedly scrolled back up, her fingers unable to go as fast as her brain wanted. She clicked on the email and discovered that her hand was trembling. In that one instance, the physical processes of her body had taken over. Trembling hands. Flushed face. Stinging ears. How strange the human body was. She hadn't felt this sick when she was scanning the Airbnb for blood.

She skim-read the email, her eyes leaping midway down, unable to read word by word, line by line. Her throat closed up. She stood up. The chair fell to the floor behind her.

'Daisy!' she shouted. 'Daisy!'

The children were at lunch. The classroom empty, the corridors deserted. Ajola fled the room. She ran to the lunch hall and scanned the long lines of tables. No Daisy.

'Meg,' she whispered above the roaring chatter.

She ran down the length of the school, along the corridor, through the dark cloakrooms, past the art tables. She could feel her hair bouncing on her head and the back of her shoulders. Trent was buried forever. There were no leads on his disappearance. The police had disregarded the tip about Chris. He would soon be legally declared dead. Her heart was going to burst in her chest. It would all be OK.

She burst out of the main door and on to the playground. The light seemed blinding.

'Daisy!'

Her voice rang out over the cacophony of children's voices. Some turned to look at her, halted in their games. A ball bounced past. The midday assistants turned, pausing their conversations. Ajola shaded her eyes from the sun, scanning the different areas of the playground: the treehouse, the garden patch, the field, the football pitch, the play equipment – there! She was coming down the steps of the treehouse, looking at her, her ears picking out Ajola's voice in all this noise.

'Daisy!' she cried again and took off across the playground. Daisy, smiling, ran towards her as well. Ajola didn't know what would happen when they met. It was only a primary school maths competition after all. It didn't really merit a powerful embrace. She stopped short of Daisy but held out her arms.

'You won!' she cried as Daisy, stopping short as well, stared up at her. Her eyes seemed huge. This was surely the moment. Meg was about to be redeemed. Ajola would feel a great, cosmic movement. A coming together. Catharsis. A Hollywood moment. 'You won, Daisy!'

'Did I?' Daisy said. 'That's good.'

A ball bounced past. The cacophony continued. Ajola lowered her arms to her side. Was that it? Was it done? Save Daisy? Save Meg? Save herself?

'You did really well, Daisy.' She tried to put herself in Daisy's shoes. What would seven-year-old Ajola have wanted? After all these years, she could finally tell her.

She sank to her knees on the asphalt. Tiny bits of stones and grit bit into her kneecaps. She had no idea what words were about to come out of her mouth. Daisy blinked at her, not turning away.

'It's nearly the end of the year,' Ajola heard herself saying. 'Next year, you've got Miss Marsh. She's nice. But if you ever need me, I'm here. Just come and see me. Or write me a note. Any time. Ever. Year Four, Year Five, Year Six. When you go to the academy, when you're doing your GCSEs or at university.'

'University?' Daisy muttered, and laughed.

'Of course,' Ajola replied. 'Definitely. If that's what you want. Or maybe you don't. It doesn't matter. But I'm always going to be here. I'll never go away. You'll never be alone.'

Ajola stood back up, her knees stinging as the grit and stones fell away. She looked up, glancing around the playground, and then felt something against her. At first, she didn't know what it was. She looked down and her brain took a second to process the image. Daisy had wrapped her arms around her middle, face turned to one side against her stomach.

'Ah,' Ajola said. She didn't know where to put her own hands. She held them in the air. 'Ah. That's nice.'

Daisy broke away, turned without a word, and skipped off across the playground. Ajola watched her. Had she done it? Had she exorcized the demons? Witchcraft was memory. You felt it in your bones. Did she feel it?

She turned and walked back into the school. In the momentary blindness that the dark corridor commanded, she heard a voice.

'Miss Pugh?'

She turned, her eyes trying to adjust to the darkness, trying to locate the voice. It was Yashica. Standing by the cloakroom door, hair perfectly coiffed, hairband perched on top like a crown, immaculate school uniform and glistening shoes. Ajola rolled her eyes.

'Yes, Yashica?' Ajola said, walking past her. 'It's lunchtime. If you're not eating, you should be outside.'

She wanted to say *Not everything is about you* but stopped herself just in time.

'I wanted to ask about the maths competition that Daisy did,' Yashica said. Her voice seemed so quiet in the corridor. Ajola realized she had never heard it like this before, only when it was issuing commands in the classroom. She sounded like a different pupil.

'What about it?' she said, without turning around.

Yashica looked at her feet. Her fingers were twisting themselves over one another. She sucked in her lips. Ajola could see all this. Through the door into the girl's bathroom and the mirror, Yashica's reflection stark, perfectly clear. She turned around slowly and Yashica immediately stopped twisting her fingers. She put her hands behind her back, she lifted her chin to look Ajola in the eyes.

'What about it, Yashica?'

Yes, what about it, Yashica? Was she not woman, too?

'Could I maybe do it next year?' Yashica asked, her voice so small, a child's voice. 'I promise I'll work really hard on my maths. I know I can do it. Maybe not like Daisy. But I would like to try. I know I'm not as good but . . .' She was searching for words. Ajola had never seen her search for words before. Where was the bitch?

Ajola shook her head slightly.

'You are as good, of course,' she said quickly. Yashica nodded. She took a deep breath. Ajola hoped she wasn't about to cry. 'I'm sorry, Yashica,' Ajola said. She felt she should get down on to her knees again, to say it to Yashica's face, but then that would diminish the gesture she had given Daisy. She made a noise in the back of her throat. What did that mean? It was as though she didn't understand, even now.

She got down on her knees in front of Yashica.

'I am sorry, Yashica,' Ajola said again. 'I should have thought of you. You do work very hard. In everything. Next time, I will give you the opportunity as well.'

Yashica smiled and hugged Ajola, her chin going neatly over Ajola's shoulder. Ajola had never had a student hug her in her whole teaching career and here she was, getting two in one day. She didn't raise her arms and waited for Yashica to pull away before standing up.

'That's why you're my favourite teacher, Miss Pugh,' Yashica said. 'You say sorry and and and . . .' She was smiling now, putting on a pretence maybe, a facade of being speechless. Before, it would have annoyed Ajola. Now, she understood. 'You make me feel good.'

'Any time,' Ajola said and held out her hand for Yashica to shake. Surely, now, it was done.

Ella

CYNTHIA SENT ELLA the draft judgement as soon as it was available. Maduka handed it over to her and Ella sat in her office with it on the desk in front of her. She didn't read it straight away. Instead, she took her phone out and scrolled through old photos of Felix. His weight loss had started about the time that Benjamin was born. Back then, Ella had presumed it was because Felix had taken a new position at work. Extra responsibility, longer work hours, more people to manage and be managed by, right at the time when he was needed most at home. They had moved into a nicer house when Benjamin was three months old, courtesy of Felix's new income, but that hadn't helped anything. It was all stuff. No one was ever given lessons on what to do when a child entered their life. The weight, the accountability, the guilt, the workload. Every decision put under the microscope years later and examined in retrospect. Ella put the phone face down on the desk and pulled the draft judgement towards her. Perhaps in a parallel universe Benjamin was never born and she and Felix were living together in their first flat.

She quickly skim-read the judgement. The report contained nothing unexpected. The judge had awarded Eric compensation for living expenses and allowances from his parents, not on the basis of lack of consent for birth, but because he had been diagnosed with anxiety and depression two years previously. Cynthia had used Eric's doctor as one expert and, as another, a therapist they had sent Eric to for a few sessions. Both agreed that the anxiety and depression could be traced back to his fraught relationship with his parents and that the diagnosis made employment difficult for Eric. The judgement didn't mention anti-natalism, forced existence or loss of bodily autonomy at all, the hubris of creating a human being out of thin air or Eric's favourite Schopenhauer quote: 'Would not a man rather have so much sympathy with the coming generation as to spare it the burden of existence?', which is exactly what Cynthia had wanted. This was a clear-cut personal-injury case that had been awarded just compensation.

Ella pushed the judgement away from her as Maduka buzzed her phone.

'Martins here to see you,' he said.

Ella rolled her eyes. She hadn't expected to see Eric so soon. He must have been awaiting the judgement on the edge of his seat, ready to burst through her door the moment he read it. She shut her eyes.

She would congratulate Eric, explain when the judgement would be officially announced, and then say something to signal to him that their professional relationship was over. Thank you for choosing me to represent you? Or, I'm glad that our journey is finally over? Or, it's been a pleasure working with you? Yes, that was it, that was the one.

'Send him in,' she said back to Maduka.

'Her,' Maduka said.

Ella frowned to herself. The office door opened and Eric's mum walked inside. Ella recognized her at once from the court. She was small, a thin-boned woman with thick-framed glasses. Today, she wore a sheepskin coat that engulfed her, making her slight frame appear even smaller, just an edge that might wink out of existence if you turned your head in a certain way.

'Good morning,' Ella said, getting to her feet. She waited, expecting some sort of hostility. The woman sat in the chair that her son had spent the last seven years sitting in, plotting her downfall. The roots of her hair were going grey. She put her handbag on her lap, not meeting Ella's eye.

'Can I get you a drink?' Ella asked.

The woman shook her head, lips pressed tightly together. She was looking at her knees and there were tears in her eyes. Ella put a hand on her chin, unsure what to say. An apology felt most apt, but then that might seem as if she was taking some legal responsibility.

'I'm sorry,' the woman said, looking up. She moved a finger under each eye, wiping the tears away. 'I don't know what I came here to say.'

'That's OK.' Ella almost didn't move. Then she came around the desk and sat in the empty chair next to her. She wanted to reach out but that wouldn't seem professional. 'I didn't get on with my mum,' she settled on. 'I thought I could be a better parent. Now I have a son. He's four. I'm not a natural mother.' Ella took a deep breath. 'I feel guilty for being so hard on my mum. I wish I could take it back.'

'Being a mother is an undefined position,' Eric's mother

replied, and now she reached out to Ella. 'No mother is a natural mother. No woman's version of motherhood is all hugging and learning. It is a concentricity of contradictions. Some things we get right, and others we don't.' She looked at Ella. 'I know I'm human. An earthly body that makes earthly mistakes. And he is too. Maybe that's his point.'

They sat still for a while, delicate hand on delicate hand, Ella imperceptibly chewing her gum, then the woman wiped her eyes again and stood up.

'Thank you,' she said. 'I don't know why I came here. I thought – I saw you in court and I thought you might understand.'

That night, as Ella was tucking Benjamin in his spaceman pyjamas into bed, he wrapped his hands around her neck and pulled her to him. She was going to snap at him but didn't. He smiled up at her.

'Mum,' he said, 'your breath is always so minty.'

When she had gone downstairs, Ella got her phone out and dialled Felix's number.

Caoimhe

CAOIMHE AND EVIE ran to training together. Caoimhe was glad
Evie didn't try and talk. They just bounded along, in sync. It
was so easy to run when you were in step with someone else.
It had never felt this easy before. And Evie had a different
smell to the men. Caoimhe had never thought the smell of
sweaty men in tight Lycra was unpleasant. She enjoyed it. Her
body responded to it. She could imagine neurons and hormones
firing off through her synapses as she inhaled it. Evie's smell was
different. It was less exhilarating. More grounding. A smell to
encapsulate realism.

In the Prezzo car park that acted as an unofficial meeting
point for the club, they saw Aidan, Mateus, Porter and Dean
Weaver standing in a loose circle, feet wide apart, arms folded,
muscular torsos thrust forward. Caoimhe faltered at the sight
of Dean. There he was. Like a contestant for *Love Island*.
Crucifix earring dangling from one ear. Bleached-blond hair.
Immaculate neon-pink and yellow Nike running vest. It would
have been easy for her to slip into the weave beside them. One

of the guys. They all started guffawing. Mateus put both his hands on Dean Weaver's shoulders and squeezed.

Beside her, Evie started performing some loosener stretches by a litter bin and Caoimhe, after a pause, joined her. The men were talking so loudly in the small car park, Caoimhe could easily hear them.

'Ah, people complained about the goody bag,' Aidan said. 'It was really poor.'

'What was in it?'

'Like, a sachet of squash, an oatcake.'

'Austerity,' Mateus said. 'You were lucky they didn't give you an energy bill.'

Everyone laughed. Caoimhe glanced across at Mateus, who was looking around to see who had heard the joke, anyone on the fringes of the group, any passers-by on the road beyond. Evie caught Caoimhe's eye and pulled a face. Caoimhe smiled back. They both started pendulum swings with their right leg.

'It is hot tonight,' Porter said, tugging at his shirt. 'I'm getting wet already.'

Caoimhe glanced over again and appreciated the tightness of his damp blue shirt. They all had sculpted torsos. Toned upper arms. Lean, muscular legs. They were good runners. There was discipline to that. The focus and dedication. The mental fortitude to keep going, mile after mile, day after day. The undeniable level of intelligence needed to plan and analyse, to prepare. It was admirable.

'That's what my wife says,' Mateus responded.

All the men roared with laughter. Caoimhe folded her arms over herself and turned back to Evie.

'We should be going soon,' Evie said, glancing at her watch. 'It's gone half past.'

'You girls all right?' Dean Weaver said, joining them at the bin. He started doing a few looseners as well. 'It's hot tonight, isn't it?' He pulled his vest over his head, revealing his tanned, perfectly defined abs. 'Might have to go without this.'

He put the vest in his pocket and then jumped up and down on the spot a few times, tucking his knees tight under himself. A tattooed pair of tiger eyes glistened on his chest.

'The wicking technology works so you're actually cooler if you wear the shirt,' Evie told him.

'He just wants to show off his tattoos to you girls,' Aidan said, walking over to the bin as well. 'Which one's your favourite, Caoimhe?'

Now, Caoimhe pulled a face. The others had joined them, Mateus standing, as he so often did, close to her shoulder. She edged away from the heat that his skin was giving off. She suddenly felt repulsed. In that moment, Caoimhe couldn't believe she had fancied him once upon a time. His receding hairline. His crooked teeth. His average running times. Compare that to herself. Her superior body. Her athleticism. Her focus. It was almost embarrassing.

'I don't know.'

Caoimhe stood, suspended in the following silence. Normally, she would feel obliged to make a follow-up comment, maybe a little giggle, but she didn't know why. Evie was silent. She looked at her watch.

'Let's start running.' Evie looked up. 'I feel like the session should have started three minutes ago.'

'She's keen!' Aidan crowed.

'She wants to do well,' Mateus said. 'Nothing wrong with that.' He winked at Evie. 'I like keen.'

Evie tossed her head and looked at Caoimhe.

'We running?' she said.

Caoimhe was unsure how to communicate in large groups when her contribution wasn't just an ambiguous laugh and a glance at her shoes. She shrugged at Evie.

Evie started jogging towards the towpath and Caoimhe followed. For a few paces, Dean Weaver jogged with her and asked basic, small-talk questions about her times and her goals. Caoimhe tried to be polite and answer him in a nice way but she really wanted to run with Evie and re-enter that bounding gait of total silence and reflection.

'Yeah, I'm doing Berlin,' Dean Weaver said, loudly. 'I qualified based on my London time.'

'Cool,' Caoimhe said. She felt no need to be Anakin Skywalker here. She waited a few seconds, then increased her stride to enter Evie's orbit. She hoped it hadn't seemed rude. She just didn't want to talk. If Dean Weaver wanted to talk, he could drop back and guffaw with Mateus and the others, whose banter was so loud, it was reverberating down the street.

Azaiyah met them on the towpath and they did 800-metre reps, with Dean Weaver and Evie leading the way. Caoimhe was further back, in the scrum with Mateus, Porter and Aidan. When Mateus made a loud observation about how Evie's keenness was making them all look bad, Evie put her hands in her pockets and said, 'It's because I don't spend all my energy talking between reps,' and everyone had gone 'Oooh!' which made Caoimhe laugh.

As the session ended and they all turned to run back to the

car park, Caoimhe spotted a familiar figure standing by the trees on the opposite side of the canal. Beneath the amber light of the setting sun, the figure was hidden in the dark, dense foliage, like some sort of magical creature from a fairy tale. Caoimhe's heart leapt. She suddenly felt as though there was a spotlight on her. Everyone was staring. Everyone was whispering in the darkness beyond the illuminated pool.

'I'm going this way,' she quickly said to Evie.

Evie frowned.

'Not back to Prezzo?'

'I have to see someone.'

Evie shrugged and turned away. Caoimhe watched their retreating figures, then doubled back down the canal and over the bridge. There was a road sign by the bridge which read 'End of Valley Path'. Someone had scrawled 'Bell' before 'End' in black marker.

'Mum,' she said, approaching the wistful figure beneath the tree branches. Long shadows overlaid her face. 'Why are you in the bushes?'

'I came to watch you – Ouch.' She tried to step out of the undergrowth but got her foot caught. Caoimhe stretched out a hand and grabbed her wrist before she fell. 'I saw you with all your friends so I stayed out of sight. I was never going to say anything,' she added quickly, raising her hands. 'I was never going to talk to you. I just wanted to watch.'

'You look weird standing in the bushes,' Caoimhe said, guiding her mum back on to the towpath.

'Let me look weird. I don't care.'

'Yes, but then I look weird because you're my mum.'

'They don't know that.'

Caoimhe rolled her eyes.

'They might. We might give off some kind of aura.'

Her mum laughed and rolled her own eyes. They stood, facing one another on the towpath. The amber twilight had turned a deep orange above their heads. The canal beside them was inky black.

'That other girl is a lot faster than you,' her mum observed.

'That's Evie. She's really good, nationally ranked.'

'Well, ask her for tips!' her mum exclaimed. 'If she can be nationally ranked, so can you.'

'I know,' Caoimhe said. She looked up into the coral sky. 'She's nice. I enjoy running with her. She helps me with my sessions.'

Her mum clasped her hands across her stomach and pressed her chin to her chest, looking at Caoimhe with an 'I told you so' expression.

'What does that even mean?' Caoimhe said. 'Why are you pulling that face?'

They were in darkness now. The overhanging trees cast a canopy of shadow that blocked out the receding orange glow from the sky. Caoimhe could barely see the outline of her mum's features.

'You never used to like asking for help,' she said.

'*Mum*,' Caoimhe said, rolling her eyes. 'Don't.'

'I'm saying it's good you feel you can ask now. It's inspiring that you're still improving. I always loved watching you compete.'

'Really? I thought you hated it.'

'Don't be so ridiculous. It's thrilling. I always said, when I heard I was having a little girl, I expected it to be all dresses and bows and hair, and instead I got you: the mud, the excitement, the cheering. I loved every moment of it.'

They stood in the silence and the dark until Caoimhe held her hand up in a high five gesture and her mum, giggling, patted it with her own palm in a timid response. 'Come, let me walk you back,' Caoimhe said.

Safa

SAFA DIDN'T HEAR about it until a week after everyone else.

'I can't believe you didn't mention it!' she cried at Emaan in her ammi's living room. 'A bloody mum from school told me.'

'I didn't think you'd want to know.'

'Of course I'd want to know!' Safa scrunched up her nose.

'Why?' Emaan frowned.

Safa couldn't answer. They sat, staring at each other over the coffee table. Safa's ammi came in and put some sweets on the table between them, chuntering to herself.

'Now you must take him back,' she said, waving a stumpy finger at Safa. 'This is your only chance.'

Safa rolled her eyes.

'How long have you known?' she asked Emaan.

'A couple of days.'

'A couple of days!'

'Yeah, I saw an update on his Instagram or something.'

'And you never told me?'

'Why do you care?' Emaan replied. She reached forward and

took one of the sweets. Behind her, Safa's ammi lowered herself into an armchair. 'I thought you wanted rid.'

'I want vindication,' Safa explained emphatically.

'About what?'

'About what that Danielle said to me!' Safa said. 'In the milk-shake place. I kept thinking, are we talking about the same guy?' Emaan nodded, nibbling on the corner of the sweet. 'I thought I was going mad. I want to know that she broke up with him because he is a nightmare!' Her ammi picked up the remote and began turning up the volume on Geo TV. 'Because he is selfish, he's inconsiderate. He's too emotionally stunted to be in a rela-tionship with another human being – Mum!' Safa cried, looking towards her ammi, who was defiantly pointing the control at the television screen. 'We're trying to have a conversation!'

'A wife should not bad-mouth her husband,' her ammi said in Punjabi.

'Well, I'm not his wife,' Safa said.

Her ammi muttered something under her breath, but lowered the volume on the television.

'I want to know what he posted,' Safa said, looking at Emaan. She beckoned with her fingers. 'Show me.'

Emaan rolled her eyes but pulled her phone out of her pocket.

'There,' she said, holding it up. 'He took the link out to her profile and removed some post about them being in a relation-ship.' She turned the phone back to herself and scrolled. 'He also posted this.'

Safa grabbed the phone. There was a photo of a 64-inch tele-vision screen mounted on the living-room wall of Safa's house.

Decided to treat myself done with being nice to people and all they do is disrespect me women just don't care any more.

'Eurgh,' Safa said, handing the phone back. 'Why can't he use punctuation? That's the most disgusting thing about all of this.'

Emaan laughed.

'You want to see her Instagram?'

'Yes!'

'Too bad. She blocked me.' Emaan put the phone in her pocket. 'So, that's that. They're over.'

'I want the details,' Safa said. 'I want to know how he refused a reasonable request. I want to hear how he tried to make her out to be crazy.'

'You'll have to text him for that.'

'Yeah, right.' Safa got her own phone out. 'Maybe I'll try and meet up with Danielle again. Might be therapeutic for her.'

Emaan made a sound.

Safa frowned at her.

'What?'

'Don't bother, Safa.' Emaan put the sweet back on the plate. 'It's a waste of your time. You got vindication when you divorced him. Move on.'

Safa stared at her lock-screen photo of Javeria and Aleena (how could she go for one moment without thinking of them. They were etched on her soul. Each movement of their bodies an echo of her own. Their hearts beat with hers, their fingers grasping for what she reached for) in the garden looking at the butterflies on the buddleia bush. She had planted that bush. She had enticed those butterflies. She had taken the picture. And now she wasn't even allowed in the house.

'Eurgh!' she exclaimed, throwing her phone on to the sofa next to her. 'Why is all of this so hard?'

Sophia

A POLICE ADVOCATE had helped Sophia with the paperwork for Chris's certificate of presumed death. The unassuming forms. The mundane announcement in the local paper. A typed letter on headed paper inviting her to a High Court hearing. He was gone. They had done it.

A few days after the hearing, Bethany sent Sophia a link to Isla's school website. There was a PTA sign-up rota to clean out disused areas of the school. Jill's name was right at the top. Sophia rolled her eyes.

Hard to give up the stalking habits, Bethany texted. This is your opportunity to show Jill you're not ten years old any more.

Sophia signed herself up. Same date, same time.

'I thought this was a parents' rota,' she said to Jill when she saw her inside the PE shed. From beyond the open door, Sophia could see the grey-streaked playground and the corner of the Year 6 classroom. Isla was sitting somewhere in there. Her Isla.

Jill sneered at her. She had her short hair swept back from her forehead with a red hairband that mirrored Sophia's own.

413

She picked up a bucket of tennis balls. The wind blew the shed door back on itself with a bang. It was the only sound in the world. It might just have been the two of them in existence.

'It's actually a volunteers' rota,' Jill said, 'for people in the local community who want to support the school. And, for your information, I'm looking at making a move into primary education.' Jill raised her eyebrows at her. The movement seemed so threatening. 'So, it makes sense that I get experience in a school setting. Uh.' She turned away. 'It's just like you to copy me, Sophia.'

Sophia smiled.

'Have a seat,' she said, nodding to a pile of cricket bats. 'There's something I want to say.'

Jill scoffed. She leant outside the shed and put the bucket of balls on the edge of the trodden-down grass.

'I'm here to work, Sophia.' She straightened up and looked down her nose at her. 'Not just mess around like we're back in primary school.'

Sophia laughed.

'Not like back in primary school at all,' she said. 'I hear you've been telling people your husband disappeared.' Jill didn't turn to look at her. She offloaded another bucket of balls outside the shed. 'What happened to Jared Winchester? Or was it Sam?' Sophia tried to crane her head to meet Jill's eye, but Jill was too busy kneeling down, sorting through the tennis balls. 'Yeah, I clocked him straight away, Jill, *straight away*. It's just like that time you showed me a picture of Elijah Wood and said he was your babysitter.'

'I don't want to talk about my personal life,' Jill said. She made a dramatic motion of wiping her eyes. 'It's too painful.'

414

'Aha, I'm sure it is,' Sophia said. 'Poor you, husband went missing. How did you find out about Chris?'

'The fact that both our husbands went missing was actually why I tried to reconnect with you,' Jill said. Her eyes were watery now, red-rimmed. 'I needed someone to share my grief with. But all you want to do is mock me.'

'Uh-huh, sure.' Sophia nodded. 'But the thing is, my husband never went missing, Jill.' Jill wiped her eyes again. Sophia picked up a red foam rounders bat from a tub by the door. 'Everyone said he went missing. But that's not the truth at all. Far from it. I *know* the truth and I wanted to talk to you about the *truth*. Just me and you, Jill. Me and you, like the old days. Do you want to know what really happened to Chris?' She put the edge of the bat against the inside hinges of the door, making it swing closed and then swing open again. 'Because I'll tell you. I guess I've wanted to tell you for some time.' Jill looked at the end of the rounders bat and then at Sophia's face. From outside the shed, the wind whistled around the edge of the school. 'It'll be good to get it off my chest.' The door banged shut again. 'I killed him, Jill. I planned to kill him. I worked myself up to it. And I did it. It wasn't easy. I used a vintage metal alarm clock, like the Mickey Mouse one you used to have, remember? Solid metal with lots of little spikes and bolts. Perfect for cracking a skull. I killed him with it. I washed the alarm clock. Put it away. Left him as he was and went out to get an alibi. There were other details.' She waved the bat. 'I was trying to make it look like I did it so people would think I *didn't* do it. You understand? What's that?' She leant forward. 'Did you ask where the body is? Well, me and my friends, we took it up on to the heath and buried it. We used witchcraft, if you can believe that. To conceal the body and the crime. True witchcraft, Jill, Wicca, magik, Hogwarts, the real fucking deal. I saw it with my own eyes. And they never fucking found him. And none of us ever fucking said. The police investigated me and came up with nothing. And now the High Court have just given me a declaration of his presumed death. Case officially closed.' Sophia let out a long breath. 'Feels better,' she said. 'Much better.'

What is a friend? Ajola thought as she watched Yashica and Daisy sit side by side. What is a friendship from the inside? What is a friendship from the outside? Why do human beings search out friends? What is it about human consciousness that permits a friendship? Do other animals have friends? Surely there is nothing more rare and curious in the natural world than a friend. Someone with whom you share no genetic links, have nothing invested, no stake or obligation, and yet someone, nevertheless, whom you are compelled to endure great pain and suffering for. She began dealing the cards.

'This is called Palace,' she said. 'First three cards are face down, you can't touch them yet.' The night they found Chris's body, when she had gone upstairs to retrieve Sophia's note-book, she had seen the plan written in a small, neat script in the middle pages. A detailed itinerary of how Chris could be killed without anyone suspecting Sophia. A plan to secure Sophia an alibi. The four of them all present after a night out. 'The next layer is also cards you can't touch yet, but you can look at.' Ajola dealt out three cards each for Yashica, Lucy, Daisy and herself. Such a comprehensive plot, requiring all five of them. Why had she never said anything then, or in the intervening seven years? Not a whisper. Not to anyone. Such a rare and curious thing. 'And these three you can touch, look at and play,' she said, dealing out the last hand. 'Seven starts. Always has to be a higher card. Ten burns the pack, Ace resets. You'll pick it up as we go.'

Safa heard the door open and saw Javeria and Aleena tumbling down the hall, bags and coats clinging to their shoulders and arms.

'You're here!' she cried and stood up. 'I've missed you!'

They threw themselves at her. They had never quite embraced like this before. To an outsider, this might look like a usual greeting, but it wasn't. Compelled by something deep within all three of them, they clung together in that one instance. Javeria's and Aleena's hair was wet, strands plastered to their scalps, other curls and loose ends floating up from their heads. Safa could smell the rain on their skin. The night of the murder, Sophia had said she would pick Safa up from the station at six thirty and they would drive to get her BMW before meeting the others. Safa had stood in the rain outside the station, waiting and waiting. Her hair must have been plastered to her head in the same way it was plastered to Javeria's and Aleena's heads now.

'I've missed you!' her youngest parroted back, speaking into her elder sister's arm. They held on to each other for five, ten, fifteen seconds, a solid unit. When Sophia's car finally did round the end of the road, it was six forty-five. She had leant across and opened the door for Safa to get in. Her own hair was also wet, the smell of her wet skin flustered because she was late, harassed.

'Sorry I'm late,' she said. 'Just lost track.'

'No worries,' Safa said and got into the passenger seat. She glanced at Sophia's trembling hands. 'Are you OK?'

'Fine.' Sophia took a deep breath, turned to her and smiled. 'Let's find the others.'

Javeria and Aleena let go of her and darted away to see their grandmother. Safa looked at Emaan across the lounge. When Safa and Sophia had met up with Caoimhe, Ella and Ajola that night, Sophia had blamed their being late on bad traffic, of which there had been none. Safa hadn't said anything, not at the time, not when they found Chris's body and not since.

'Let it be,' Emaan said to Safa. 'You have everything right here.' She bent down to clear their cups away, a trio of ducks patterned on to the side of each one. She straightened up and looked in Safa's eye. 'I'd take the house back, though. It's not fair to the girls that you're living in that tiny flat.'

The canal was now pitch black, the water a fathomless streak beside them. Caoimhe led the way off the path and through the houses on to the main road. Her mother kept skip-walking to keep up with her, no matter how slow Caoimhe went.

'Hold on a sec,' she said as Caoimhe looked both ways at the crossing. The road was dark either side of them. A hundred metres away, a street lamp was beaming a jet of white-hot light on to the road, like a tractor beam from an alien craft. Caoimhe's mum had her phone out. 'I just want to text your sisters.'

'Why now?'

'I want to tell them that we're going for an evening walk together.'

'Mum.' Caoimhe rolled her eyes. A solitary car rushed past. 'This isn't an evening walk. We just met up.'

'In the evening and are now walking. Oh, Caoimhe, help me, which emoji should I use?' She held up her phone. 'I want a really, really happy one. What about this one with the eyes shut and the hands? Caoimhe, Caoimhe, look. Or this one with all the hearts.'

'I can't choose my own emoji.'

'It's not your emoji. It's mine.'

'Yeah, but it's about me. That's pretty cringey to select the emoji that I think represents how you feel about me.'

'Why do you have to make everything so difficult?' Her mum huffed. 'I'm going to use this one now. With the rolling eyes. Caoimhe' – she held her phone up – 'look, look. The rolling-eyes one, Caoimhe.'

Caoimhe looked at the phone. In the dark, the luminescent screen wavered, a tiny, silver glimmer. The stark glare grazed her eyes. The Jake Ehringhausen account had been active on Sophia's phone. The night they had found Chris's body, and Caoimhe had checked Sophia's phone for the other half of the conversation, she couldn't help but glance through the other apps. She wasn't sure what she was looking for because, at that moment, she truly didn't believe Sophia had had anything to do with it.

'The rolling eyes one, Caoimhe. Do you see it?'

Caoimhe had been compelled to look: WhatsApp messages, iMessages, the emails. Her thumbs had frantically flicked through all of it, in seconds. And there it was. An email account open. Registered to someone called Jake Ehringhausen.

'I'm only joking,' her mum said, turning the screen back to

herself. 'I wouldn't use that for you.' She put an arm around Caoimhe's shoulders. 'You're my best girl.'

Caoimhe had quickly closed all the apps down on Sophia's phone and never alluded to it again.

'Come, Mum, let's cross,' she said, stepping out into the dark road.

'Oh, wait!' her mum squawked, putting her phone in the pocket of her cardigan and hurrying out into the road behind Caoimhe. 'Caoimhe! Caoimhe! There's a car!'

'That's miles away. Come on, Mum, walk.'

Ella held the phone to her ear, listening to the dial tone purr out. She was surprised when, after four or five rings, Felix didn't answer. She stopped the call and stared down at her phone. Then she started ringing again, the abject endlessness of the phone pressed against her ear, already hot, already frustrated. Such a small thing, a phone. A tiny, inconsequential square of nothing, in which so many indiscretions, so many secrets and habits can be contained. On the night of the murder, when she had looked at Sophia's phone, trying to verify that she hadn't texted Chris, she had seen a Virtual Phone App. As a solicitor, one of her first cases, a harassment case, involved one of these. A husband was texting his ex-wife from random numbers, all procured from a Virtual Phone App. You could text, call, WhatsApp, all from one phone but using a host of different numbers, profile pictures and names. It was such an odd thing for Sophia to have. At first, Ella thought it must be for an affair partner. Weeks later, when they had met up, Ella had checked under the guise of looking at Sophia's photos. The app had been deleted. She'd never mentioned it.

Ella's phone hummed in her ear. She hung up again. What was Felix doing? Not answering was most unlike him. She looked at her phone. She had known it on the night, she just didn't want to acknowledge it. Indiscretions, secrets and habits. She started calling Felix again.

When they had been in Year 8, during one grey, drizzly day on the playground, they had buttoned all their blazer buttons into the others' button loops, creating a chain, buttons within buttons, loops within loops, one great circle. Sophia had started spinning and, like the force acting on the side of a roundabout, all the rest had spun as well, going round and round, holding on to each others' hands for support. Buttons in buttons, loops within loops. Shrieking and laughing.

'I don't believe you,' Jill said. She had taken a step back. Her hair was suddenly, inexplicably, tousled, her eyes were wide and white and reminded Sophia of the little Petri dishes of agar they used to squidge with spatulas in Year 11 biology. The sight of Jill's horror was liquid ecstasy in Sophia's veins. Her heart sang. She wanted to reach out and squidge Jill's face with her hand.

'I don't care,' Sophia said. 'I wanted to raise this with you, Jill, because you're still fucking copying me. I don't know who you think I am but you still think I am something that can be imitated. I'm not, Jill. I'm not. And unless you've killed your husband and used magik to bury him on the heath, you are never even going to come close to me. You shouldn't want to.' She threw the rounders bat back into the barrel. Jill flinched. 'So, stop trying.'

EPILOGUE

Ajola

'SEVEN OR HIGHER, Lucy,' Ajola said.

'Can I do this card?' she said, holding up a Jack.

'You can, that's like an eleven. But if you have anything like an eight or a nine, use that instead. Save the Jacks for when you need them.'

'A ten?' Lucy said.

'That burns the pack,' Yashica said. 'Ooh, that's really good for me. Burn the pack, burn the pack.'

'I think you should play the Jack,' Daisy said to Lucy. 'Then Yashica has to pick up all the cards.'

'Hey!' Yashica said and bumped Daisy's shoulder.

Daisy looked at her, then leant over and whispered in Lucy's ear. Lucy smiled, then put down an ace.

'Aw!' Yashica said. 'Oh, wait, that's good for me. That's, like, a one, right? Now I can play my five.' She put a five down and bumped Daisy's shoulder again. 'Thank you, Daisy.'

'Now you're on your final three cards,' Ajola said to Daisy. 'You can't look at them. You have to leave them face down and just choose one at random. A leap of faith. Is it going to be higher than a five? In which case, that's fine.'

'Or lower,' Daisy said, 'then I have to pick up all the cards.'

'This is tense!' Lucy said.

'Leap of faith,' Ajola said as Daisy's hand fluttered above the three face-down cards. 'Leap of faith, leap of faith.'

Lucy and Yashica joined in the chant. Daisy laughed, shut her eyes, flipped a card and placed it on the pile.

'It's a six!' Yashica shouted.

'Leap of faith!' Daisy said.

Ajola laughed. She began shuffling her cards and then looked up, across the classroom. There was Meg. By the whiteboard. As clear as day. As bright and as alive and as real as the moon. She smiled. Ajola smiled back. It was done.

Safa

SAFA'S PHONE BUZZED. She glanced down at it. Another anonymous number.

you go out with no mahram u go to the pub your haram you are just a whore i tried being nice no will see whose nice

She took a screenshot of the text and then deleted it.

Safa had started eviction proceedings. At first, she had decided to wait until the summer holidays, so as not to needlessly upset Haaris. Then she remembered he would never thank her for that. And, knowing him, he would drag it out until term started in September anyway. He had been livid when she sold the BMW from under him, taking the spare set of keys she still had and driving it to We Buy Any Car one Tuesday morning whilst he was still in bed and the girls were at school.

Now that she had decided to move out, her poky little flat had suddenly become endearing. The narrow landing, the gangway kitchen, the way she had to mute *Seinfeld* in the evenings so that Jerry's one-liners wouldn't wake Javeria and Aleena. She was going to sell the house once Haaris was out and buy somewhere smaller for her and the girls. It had taken this whole endeavour for her to realize she liked small. Big mansions in Hampstead no longer interested her. She had already begun to pack their belongings, dragging out the odd bits she had put in storage at her mother's house. Winter clothes, lampshades, a retro twin-bell alarm clock that needed winding up at the back. These objects now sat in boxes around her, ready to move to their new home.

Safa's phone buzzed again. This time, Haaris had sent a deep-fake porn video using Safa's face. Safa only saw the first split second before closing the app. She took a deep breath, then forwarded it to Emaan, for her solicitor.

whore

She shook her head and deleted the message. She would never be a passenger in her own life again. The alarm clock ticked loudly in the box beside her. She looked down at its wide, open face.

Ella

ELLA HAD INTENDED to meet Felix, talk to him, make the grand declaration. Finally be honest. It would be better for everyone. She felt so raw. Was this what it was to be vulnerable? Should she be making decisions in this condition? After Benjamin had been born, she had been in a similar state. Exhausted, stomach muscles not yet back in place, hips forever widened, hair falling out, disgusted by all food, dehydrated. She couldn't remember ever going back to normal. Why did no one talk about how traumatic birth was? Motherhood plunges you further into the sublunar. A visceral triumph. All her anxieties heightened. Raw. Exacerbated and consumed by it. Control versus the uncontrollable.

Yes, she had decided she would ask him. She would tell him. She didn't want sole custody of Benjamin. Felix needed to do it. She didn't care what her brother would say. He could sack her if he wanted. She could be so much better a mother if there was a distance between them. Everything would be better. She would be able to exist again. Felix had to do it.

In any event, it wasn't to be. She had received a call from a hospital the morning after the judge released the draft judgement.

'Is this Ella Albrecht?'

'Yes.'

'You are listed as Felix Albrecht's next of kin.'

'Felix? Why? What happened?'

'He's been involved in an accident. Are you able to come in?'

Ella called off work and hurried across London. She initially thought he had tried to kill himself, which must have been the narcissist in her. When she arrived at the hospital, she discovered he had been knocked down crossing the road in Wood Green. Wood Green. What had he been doing there? She would never have pictured Felix living in Wood Green.

'He passed away this morning,' the doctor told her in a sterile blue and white room. She had been given a few personal items that Felix had been carrying when he was struck: his phone, his wallet, an ID card from work, but no wedding ring. A nurses' station was behind them, people typing into computers, marking charts, things beeping, whirring, talking. Death. How mundane. 'We felt it best you come in.'

Ella sat down because she felt it was the right thing to do. The doctor sat next to her. It wasn't Dr James. It was someone else. He had introduced himself but Ella hadn't heard. Felix in the road. The blue and white lights flashing off his face. An earthly body meeting an earthly end.

'We can have a bereavement counsellor come and talk to you,' the doctor said. 'They can help with any questions you have, the forms to fill in.'

'Forms?'

She felt herself triumphantly unravelled. What would she tell Benjamin? How was he to process this?

'Yes, Felix is an organ donor, according to his paperwork. We're actually really interested in him donating his eyes, if that is something you would allow.'

'His eyes?'

'His corneas,' the doctor clarified. 'It doesn't need to take place immediately,' he quickly added. 'You can donate corneas up to twenty-four hours after death and the donation can take place here or at the funeral home. Just something to think about.'

'His eyes?'

'I'll get the bereavement counsellor,' the doctor said and stood up, 'with the forms.'

Ella spat the gum out of her mouth.

Caoimhe

CAOIMHE WENT OUT early, when it was still dark. She ran towards the faint blue-white glimmer that was staining the edge of the horizon. When she turned on to the bottom of the hill, the trees overhead created a canopy through which no light permeated. A pitch-black tunnel. A darkness so absolute, it pressed on Caoimhe's eyes. She urged her legs on, up the hill, through the darkness, faster, faster, faster, further, further, further, something deep and lost and wild locked inside of her, something that she wanted to break free, to release, to set loose, howling and galloping across an Arctic tundra.

She crested the hill, bursting free of the trees as the first golden tendrils of dawn light touched the shorn crops and hollow stems of the harvested fields. She sprinted, unbound, for a hundred metres, then stopped. She switched off her music. She turned in the ethereal light. The solace. The rousing air. The power. Her chest was heaving with her breaths. A bead of sweat swam down the side of her cheek. To surge. To sweat. To respire deeply on each breath. Was there anything purer than this?

She turned, looking at the vista around her. The dark town in its dark hollow, the rolling golden hills, and a figure, a smudge, with a rolling gait, gliding seamlessly along the field boundary towards her.

She made no attempt to leave this time. She took her earphones out of her ears and watched as Rohan Rust skimmed across the uneven ground, like a pebble kissing the surface of a lake, loose, free, unbound, just like her. He hopped the ditch and landed on the road without changing his stride, coming towards her as though he had found a stitch in the air and could seamlessly slip through the threads that made up the fabric of existence.

She watched him approach. He watched her. Their eye contact was intense and unbroken. He stopped, a metre from her. He took his headphones off. His skull cap. His eyebrows. His thick beard. As handsome as the eternal dawn. A complete piece to her puzzle.

'Hey,' he said. 'I know you.'

'Hey,' she replied. 'I know you, too.'

She could see specks of spittle in the beard hair around his mouth.

'You running back to town?' he asked, pointing down the hill. 'Want to go together?'

'Nah,' Caoimhe said and put her earphones back in. 'I'm going this way.' She nodded up the lane. 'See you, though,' she added and, before he could say anything else, she ran past him and along the road.

Sophia

MONTHS AFTER SHE had last spoken to Jill Caister, long after Chris had been officially declared dead, Sophia had been walking through Stratford Westfield, at the far end, near the John Lewis, when she had seen her. It was such a gut-punch moment, Sophia actually thought she might be sick. She had no idea emotions could be so physically overpowering. It truly felt as if someone had punched her in the stomach. Then, whilst she was struggling to breathe, they had clenched her stomach in their fist and pulled it out, inverting it in on itself, up, through the oesophagus, past the epiglottis, scraping through her teeth, forcing her to open her mouth, to gag and retch. Now, she had no stomach. She was empty. Hollow.

She walked over to the window of Foyles bookshop and put the tips of all her fingers against the glass. She pressed her nose against her reflection so hard, it bent. She wanted to spit. She didn't care what she looked like, who saw her. This felt as though her life was ending.

In the bookshop window, there was a huge picture of Jill's

face, a black and white picture, Jill smiling, looking mysteriously at the camera.

'*New York Times* Bestseller' was printed in decadent font underneath. 'Runaway smash hit. Debut novel. Man Booker Longlist.' Sophia couldn't absorb all the accolades. She couldn't process them. What in the hell was this?

Littered around the foot of the picture were dozens and dozens of copies of a black and red hardbound book. Sophia tore into the shop, leaving grease marks against the glass. She was too frantic to locate the book on the shelves, so she just reached around the cardboard photo, knocking it off its stand, disrupting a pile of *Pride and Prejudice*s, to take one from the display. The book was hefty. It had weight. Similar accolades were stamped across the cover, along with quotes from Richard and Judy, Oprah Winfrey, Stephen King, J. K. Rowling.

'An absolute feast for the imagination.'

'Undeniably the greatest debut novel I have ever read.'

'It will make you think, make you cry, make you unable to put it down.'

'Sure to be one of the greatest novelists of this generation.'

'No, no, no, no,' Sophia said, unable to monitor the level of her voice. She put a hand over her mouth to try and stifle herself. She began tearing the book open, creasing the crisp pages, dog-earing the parchment corners. 'No. What the fuck is this?'

Someone leaving the shop glanced at her. She didn't care. She turned to the inside of the book jacket. Another fucking photo of Jill, this time perched on a stool, head thrown back, short fucking pixie haircut looking luscious and chic. The smile. The smile. So fucking smug. The same smile that she had given Joseph Burton in Year 6. The same smile at the school barbecue in 2000 when she was reading *Harry Potter and the Goblet of Fire*.

'Meet Isla,' the front inside cover said:

> *. . . unhappily married and at a loss what to do about it. Meet her friends and their unwavering support for Isla's marital hardship. Now Isla has committed the ultimate crime: murder. She knows she can trust her friends to help her conceal the body of her husband but what she hasn't counted on is the deep witchcraft that the act will invoke.*

'Fuck!' Sophia screamed, scrunching the book jacket beneath her fists. 'Fuuuck!'

THEY STOOD IN a circle. Do they all know? Or are all five of them thinking they're the only ones? Holding hands, looking at each other, eyes to eyes, fingers to palms, buttons within buttons, loops within loops, who knows what about women.

Acknowledgements

THANK YOU TO Claire Wilson, my agent, for picking up the sample chapters for this novel and understanding straight away what I was trying to say. Since I was six, I've dreamt of having a book published. Now it's happened, and none of it would have been possible without you.

Thank you to Thorne Ryan, my editor, for being so totally enthusiastic about this story from day one. I didn't know what to expect from finally getting published, but working with you has been fantastically reassuring and I always love your vibe. Your passion definitely put me at ease and made me trust the process.

Big shout out to Anna Carvanova for all the emails and documents keeping everything on track and as sharp as it could be. I owe an enormous thank you to everyone at Transworld who has picked up this book and helped turn it into a final product that I couldn't be more proud of; it was definitely worth the wait, and I am grateful to all of you for your hard work.

Thanks to Safae and everyone at RCW for all your support and validation; you've all made me feel so welcome.

Thank you as well to all my wonderful and inspiring school colleagues, who have no idea I'm doing this. Nelli, Nat, Abi, Lucy, Chloe, Laura, Christine: surprise – I told you I was busy on Mondays and Tuesdays.

Obviously, a big thanks to my family for making me the way I am: Saqib, Isa, Paul, Tom, Jack, Joe, Sam, Mia, Claire, Esme, Mum and Dad.

Lastly, a massive thanks to Amar. Dave pointed out in Glasgow that I might have given up on my writing journey if it weren't for you, and he was absolutely correct. You have always been so enthusiastic about my writing and held me accountable to my own ambitions for over a decade. I am so glad I nudged you awake during that Foreign Office SharePoint training.

About the Author

MARIE O'HARE works as a primary school teacher. Before she became a teacher, she worked at the Foreign and Commonwealth office on EU Policy and then taught at a high school in rural Thailand. She holds a master's in Novel Writing from Middlesex University and regularly competes around the UK as a cross-country runner. She currently lives in Essex with her partner and son.